About the Author

Joseph Jack Holt was born in 1982 in the UK. He attended Exeter University studying cognitive science. He now lives in Kenya working as a business consultant. From a young age he always waved his geek flag high, with an avid enthusiasm for sci-fi, fantasy and anything off the wall. Because of his dyslexia his mother taught him how to touch type and this began his passion for writing.

Holy Empire

Book One: The Twins

J. J. Holt

Holy Empire

Book One: The Twins

Vanguard Press

A CIP catalogue record for this title is
available from the British Library.

ISBN 978 1 83794 000 4

This is a work of fiction. Names, characters, businesses, places, events and incidents are either
the product of the author's imagination or used in a fictitious manner. Any resemblance to
actual persons, living or dead, or actual events is purely coincidental.

Vanguard Press is an imprint of
Pegasus Elliot Mackenzie Publishers Ltd.
www.pegasuspublishers.com

First Published in 2024

Vanguard Press
Sheraton House Castle Park
Cambridge England

Printed & Bound in Great Britain

For Marcus, miss you brother.

Thank you to Emma who read the early drafts a dozen times and gave me some great ideas. Thank you also to Steve and Aimee for providing me with feedback. Also, a huge thank you to my mother and the horrific hours of touch-typing lessons.

Contents

Chapter 1

The Birth

Screams filled the air surrounding the tranquil fishing village of Havendale. The agonising cries bounced off the ice-encrusted surrounding cliffs, throwing the pain howls out into the frozen bay. Sheets upon sheets of snow had been falling relentlessly throughout the past two years. The desperate denizens prayed for the long winter to end cloistered around their warm fireplaces. The anguished screams that pierced the perfect stillness came from a little wooden cottage a quarter of a league from Havendale's town centre.

This cottage was typical of the dwellings around the village. The walls were made of rough cobblestone and thick logs with a heavy thatched roof to preserve the precious heat. Smoke was pumped into the icy air by a stone chimney. A small amount of the cottage's light seeped through rough-hewn glass windows onto the darker snow, generating a yellow flickering glow that gave the area a foreboding hue. Outside the door on the veranda, a small pile of firewood was heaped for the winter. Raouf had spent most of the past month taking care of his pregnant wife, so the firewood was hardly enough for the week, let alone the winter, but it would have to suffice. The young father was deeply affected by the excruciating cries of his labouring wife.

Erin and Raouf had been attempting to conceive before the long winter; finally, the time of birth had arrived. The pregnancy had not been easy for Erin, but little was here in the frigid north. She was struggling to contain the sobs of pain raging through her body as she prayed for her unborn children's lives.

"Breathe, my dear," came a scratchy, aged voice from beneath a shawl. The neighbourhood apothecary, doctor, and midwife stooped over the struggling woman and dabbed her forehead. Despite the village's lack of faith in the old hag and the widespread suspicion that she was a witch, they always sought her when someone was ill or hurt. She had warts liberally dotting her nose, cheeks, and chin, giving her face an aged, withered appearance. Her eyes, meanwhile, were a crystal-clear blue filled with a zest of life that belied her years. Her skin, however, was thin and crinkled, resembling old paper, with a greenish-yellow sickening hew.

"Is she going to be OK?" Raouf watched the situation from the other side of the room; he was tall and self-assured, but hadn't dared approach the bed after the hag had abruptly relegated him to the corner.

The elderly woman yelled, scarcely glancing over her shoulder, "Time will tell, so shut up." She turned to face her patient again and stroked a withered hand over Erin's light brown hair. To avoid worrying the father she dared not inform him that is wife wasn't faring well. The hag understood that saving either the mother or the infant would be a miracle; protecting both would be beyond her power. Nevertheless, she adjusted Erin's nightgown to assess the situation. She found something unexpected – another, much smaller bulge – when she rested one claw on the mother's abdomen to feel where the baby lay. "*That's not right*", she pondered to herself.

""What?" "Panting with anxiety, Erin clenched the sheets between her teeth as another contraction tore through her body. Yet, despite the anguish, she was just about sustaining consciousness.

As she raised an eyebrow at Erin, the hag stated, "It would seem that you are carrying twins."

Raouf's pacing was becoming an annoyance as he stomped around the tiny home, stamping his feet on the hardwood floor and making every board squeak. Finally, the hag snapped, "Will you shut up, sit down, and let me work." Once suitably reprimanded, the towering, haughty hunter sat down.

Erin was pale, perspiration dripped from her skin from the exertion, and she may have been bleeding internally, but the hag had no way of knowing that until the infants arrived. She applied a damp towel to Erin's forehead.

She said to the mother, "I'll be right back"." She rose from the bedside and approached the father.

Raouf was almost as tall as the old hag, slouched in an overstuffed chair. "You have to decide," she whispered. "Mother or the children?"

The hag's statement stunned Raouf. The fire and the tiny cabin felt too confined and tight, and he could not speak as he gaped at the diminutive woman. "What are you saying?" he stammered.

"She could have survived giving birth to one of them, but the second child will kill her. This has been a difficult birth." The hag continued, "Even if there were just one child, it would endanger the mother, but with two, she will perish. So, we could lose them all if we don't choose immediately." She let out a ragged rasp of a snarl. "I have a potion that will kill the children, giving the mother a better chance."

Raouf's thoughts were racing as he felt the encircling walls close around him. He was in the midst of a nightmare with no idea what to do. He was aware that he wasn't the wisest man. Raouf knew what he knew if it was about the woods, hunting, or how to survive an avalanche, but not this! He was regretting putting his confidence in this hag. He stood almost twice as tall as the older woman as he got out of the chair. "You'll keep them alive," he spoke sternly, yet his voice trembled as he did so.

"I cannot, not both, the mother or the children," she disagreed, indicating that she wasn't in the least bit intimidated despite the enormous, well-built man looming over her. She wrapped the shawl she wore snugly about her small, weak figure. She gave the man a warts-and-all gaze as she stared at him with piercing-blue eyes.

Raouf maintained eye contact with the decrepit woman for brief seconds before looking away. His throat tightened, and he kept repeating, "I don't know, I don't know." He pushed past her and out into the bitter outdoors without saying a word. A gust of frigid air hit the room as soon as he opened the door, causing the fire and candles to flicker and some of them to extinguish, unable to withstand the wind. A flurry of snow blew into the cottage, but Raouf was already gone.

The ageing woman trundled to the door and pulled it shut. "Pah, imbecile," she spat on the ground.

The moment the door slammed shut, the cottage's warmth soon returned. She went to the bedside after turning away from the door.

She noticed Erin's rapid decline and pulled some ginger from a little pouch hidden under her musty old cloak, saying, "Here, chew on this."

It could help, she reasoned, and it surely wouldn't hurt. The sound of Raouf's feet stamped on the porch and rocked the house. She hoped he only needed a short break; otherwise, she would have to decide the fate of Erin and her children.

Raouf regretted his hasty choice to leave the warmth of the home outside in the snowfall as the freezing air sucked the breath from his lungs and the glacial wind ripped at his skin. He had only a plain leather jerkin to keep himself warm against the chilly night air; in his haste, he had forgotten to bring his winter cloak. Nevertheless, the strain was too great for him to stay inside for even a second.

On his exposed forearms, Raouf could already feel the ice biting. In an effort to keep his fingers warm, he tucked his hands beneath his armpits. He looked into the blanket of snow falling and tried to calm himself. He could hardly make out the lights of the town just a quarter of a league away. Raouf's thoughts were racing as he walked the shaky porch boards. He had loved Erin since they were young, and she had also loved him. He was a few years older than her when they had met; her family had been travelling along the northern route through the mountains near the Everlong Sea in search of trade for furs and hammerhead trout when an avalanche had trapped their caravan. Because Havendale didn't have a vast population, it was inevitable that they would have met. She was the sole survivor, and the temple priests dedicated to The one true God took her in. Raouf fell in love the instant he saw this young girl pacing frightenedly hand in hand with a priest. Raouf frequently got them in trouble, going out of his way to see her and spend time with her.

Raouf couldn't help but reminisce on all their shared memories from their formative years. Smuggling her out of the temple to go fishing, capsizing the boat, nearly dying, returning to his father and the priest drenched, almost chilled to death, and both looking extremely embarrassed. She had kept the punishment the priests had meted out to her a secret, but he had received a good whipping. The first time they made love, their marriage, and their first kiss all sprang to mind.

He was pulled back to the present by a new gust of icy wind. A few snowflakes started to fall down the back of his neck, and he couldn't help but quiver. He shook his shirt in an attempt to dislodge them.

His thoughts were interrupted by his beloved's screams coming from inside the home. He let out a frustrated groan as he ran his fingers over his thinning blond hair. Raouf yearned for children, but he adored his wife and couldn't see life without her. The gravity of this choice tore at his soul and seized his heart like a vice. The gentle warmth pouring from the windows was luring him out of the cold, but he knew he would have to make this devil's choice. He was preparing himself to return and deliver his decision. In his irritation, he kicked the woodpile, which caused a log to fall and roll off the porch into the foot-deep snow. He let forth a wretchedly irate scream. He looked over the snow-covered terrain, taking a long breath to feel the frigid air filling his lungs. He clutched his hands and gritted his teeth, hoping Erin would forgive him.

The wind and snow died just as he was ready to return to the cabin. There was a deafening stillness in the absence of the raging gale. At the threshold, he took a moment to halt and turn to face the village, which was now visible through the snow, the lights shining at the foot of the magnificent church. A dark, mysterious figure moved briskly in the direction of his house over the snowy field in the evening light. At first, he was sure it was a wolf since there had been an increase in wolf attacks as prey in the frozen environment became rarer and rarer. He lingered at the doorway, staring at this formless creature. He drew his wood axe and held it ready. Going up against Erin and the Hag was less attractive than going up against a violent famished wolf. If it was a wolf that he could confront and fight. Then, the dark figure drew nearer, and he clutched his axe firmly; it wasn't a wolf, but a person dressed in a large, thick wolf pelt cloak as it glided through the untarnished snow. The cloaked figure was shrouded, its head hidden by the wolf's head cloak. As he approached the cabin, the wind and snow withdrew in front of him, and the area around him shimmered with a gloomy mist. Raouf guessed it was a man since the individual was at least his height, but they handled themselves differently than most people around here. They were walking bolt upright with their arms crossed in front of them, and they made no traces as they moved quickly through the heavy snow.

Raouf realised he couldn't turn away as the shadowy figure got closer and closer; he became mesmerised by the man floating through the snow towards their little abode, seemingly unaffected by the severe weather. Then, as the man came to a stop three yards from the porch, he felt his grasp on the axe loosen.

"Good evening, I've heard of your blight; would you let me enter that I might help?" he said in the common tongue, but Raouf couldn't place the stranger's thick accent.

Raouf paused, feeling as though he were awakening from a dream. Raouf shook his mind and concentrated on the man. The heavy hood still hid the man's face, but he could make out a pale, pointed chin with flecks of a neatly kept beard.

Raouf questioned, "Who are you?"

17

"My name is not important, but if you must address me, I am the Baron Von Rikton; you may call me sire. What is important is that you are about to make a grave mistake. You have been offered a hopeless decision by a charlatan that calls herself a doctor. I am here to provide an… alternative," the gentleman spoke, rolling the word 'grave' in his tongue and sending a chill down Raouf's back and into his already cold bones.

"You have my full attention, sir… sire," Raouf said after correcting himself. He leaned his axe on the railing of the deck. "What can you do, sir?"

"I have a wide range of knowledge. Furthermore, I'm happy to provide the services so that you may spend more time with your wife and both of your sons. So, I will allow you to enjoy this time if you welcome me in."

Raouf might have questioned how this stranger, this Baron, knew he was expecting twins or even that his wife was having difficulty giving birth if he had been less worried or more astute. Likewise, he would have questioned how this Baron knew that his unborn sons would be boys if he had been of a better intellect. Sure, he may have heard the cries coming from the hamlet, but Havendale hadn't had any guests in a very long time, and not even the midwife was sure of the gender of the babies yet. The straightforward woodcutter, however, didn't notice any of it; instead, his heart gleefully delighted at being assured that he could keep his wife and children.

"Yes, enter," he murmured without hesitation.

Raouf and the stranger were inside the cottage in the blink of an eye. Raouf was so engrossed in what he saw that he had no memory of entering; inside, the old hag was preparing a little vial, and foul, pungent smoke was seeping from the top. She was hovering over Erin, about to pour the concoction in the bottle down his wife's throat. After several hours of suffering, Erin finally passed out from the pain.

"Stop!" Raouf yelled as he rushed the older woman, grabbing her hand and forcing her to drop the vial on the ground. It crashed to the old oak floor, hissing and scattering its contents. Raouf leaned over the hag and gripped her wrist so firmly that her delicate hand became scarlet. Her hooked nose and piercing eyes peered up at him in a furious manner as she turned to face him. As she did, she also caught sight of an additional figure in the room. The hag saw lurking in the fire's shadows the mysterious Baron Von Rikton. The ancient woman's eyes widened with shock and fear.

"You! You cannot be here." She let out a venomous spit, easily breaking free of Raouf's hold, and grabbed her frayed robe. But the baron lifted his palm forward and stopped her in her tracks.

He whispered clearly, "Dloh." And the elderly woman froze. He lowered his hood and revealed his face for the first time. His face was angular and narrow, with high cheekbones and an aristocratic nose, and Baron Von Rikton had a pale, almost blue complexion. His jet-black hair was pulled back into a widow's peak that hung down his neck and nearly reached his shoulders. His eyes were a wonderfully relaxing and welcoming warm scarlet glow. His neatly trimmed black goatee gave him a more angular, predatory look. His ruby eyes showed no emotion as he studied the sight before him. Instead, his blazing eyes fixated on the geriatric woman.

"How did you get here at all?" Through gritted teeth that were still locked in place, the hag inquired.

The baron interrupted, "Maganwyth, you may return to your hovel now that you've done all you can." Ignoring her question. "Timbus," the baron spoke a single word in the ancient tongue, his voice taking on a hollow quality.

The hag was restrained for a brief moment until she sagged forward, freed by an unseen force. She spun around, gathered her bag and enormous travelling coat, and marched out of the cabin into the frigid night. The door shut with a sense of finality behind her.

The only sounds coming from the cottage were the crackling of the fire and Erin's laboured breathing. Then, Raouf's anxiousness overcame him, and he gazed at the baron, pleading with him to tell him what to do next.

"What now, sir?" The baron abruptly raised his hand, stopping him mid-question, and a foreboding resounding knock at the door filled the cabin. "Answer that, would you?" the baron inquired while remaining still.

Havendale was not an unfriendly town; it wasn't unusual to drop by a neighbour's house for a glass of mead, juice, or just a chat when the weather was more clement. However, this two-year winter had been brutal, and now it was common for months to pass without a house guest, and Raouf was about to receive his third call in as many days. A lump of a figure stomped in, shrugging the snow from its shoulders after Raouf unfastened the door. The man limped on unsteady legs; thick, frost-crusted pelts wrapped his warped body, protecting him from the cold. Moreover, this man was significantly malformed. His face appeared to have been drawn on by a little child; one eye hung much lower than the other; his big, bloated, red nose was smeared halfway across his face, and his jaw fell limp in one corner. He gave the baron a quick glance to get his blessing before stumbling awkwardly sideways to Erin's bed.

"Now, hold on." Raouf attempted to pursue the individual to stop him, but the baron interrupted him by clearing his throat.

"Ivan is a talented… surgeon, and your wife is in good hands, but first, we must discuss payment." The baron caught Raouf's attention, whose fiery gaze enthralled the hunter. Raouf found it impossible to look away from this towering, intimidating, pale noble.

"I'll preserve your sons and wife for a trade, do you agree?"

"I'm not a wealthy man," Raouf blustered, attempting to come up with whatever he could offer this man claiming to be a baron. The woodcutter and hunter had been suffering for the past few years, barely making enough money to support his family. He had to travel further and higher up the mountains to bring down the wood or game to trade in the town since the trees were scarce and the game even more so.

"What would you ask of me?"

"I just ask for service; I do not require 'money'," Baron responded. "Do you concur?"

"Service? I'm sure capable of providing that," Raouf replied, ready for this man to leave, but he couldn't take his eyes off the baron, who appeared to fill the room and have his complete focus.

"Excellent, I won't need your services till the end of the summer, I promise." The baron smiled, revealing teeth that were razor-sharp and predatory. "After all, I did promise you time to spend with your family. Beyond Raouf's shoulder, the baron peered.

"I see it is done," he declared.

Raouf turned around, astounded to discover his twin boys in Ivan's grotesque arms. The cries of Erin's new born babies' screams roused her from sleep. Raouf's view of the world dimmed, and all he could focus on were his two sons—both boys, as the baron had predicted. The new born infant in the right arm was much larger—pink and was already yelling at the top of his incredibly healthy lungs. Raouf felt scrutinised by the tiny black orbs that examined his every move and had a touch of terror from the youngster on the left, who was pallid and only about half the size. This boy did not cry but instead stared at Raouf. The baron's heavily accented voice drew Raouf's attention away from the kids and his wife.

"When the summer is through, I'll see you again," the baron affirmed while nodding in the direction of Ivan, who passed Raouf the two infants. A sharp shiver suddenly swept through Raouf's body as he gazed at his sons again. Baron Von Rikton and the malformed Ivan vanished. The only evidence that Ivan had ever existed was in the form of crooked, murky snow prints on the cabin floor. There was no evidence that the baron had been present.

Still drained, but the pain had subsided, Erin pushed herself up. Raouf moved to sit on the nightstand next to her. She was overjoyed as he presented the children to her.

"What should we call them?" he asked his wife as he tenderly handed the larger of the two boys to her. He cradled the diminutive child which was pale and shivering despite the warmth of the cabin. It turned its dark, piercing gaze up at him. Erin held the large child tightly as Raouf wrapped the smallest in a sheet he had taken from the bed. Erin looked down with only the love a mother could express to the bulkier new born. "We should call him Robin, after your father," she smiled as she spoke, her face glowing with pride.

She glanced at the smaller infant in Raouf's arms, and the warmth in her eyes briefly waned. For some reason, she felt a gap in her heart; a vacuum in her love; for this tiny infant, who was also her child but had pale skin and black eyes. Hatred is not the opponent of love; instead, it is another aspect of the same thing. Indifference is the complete opposite of love. It's something that never stirs up emotion on its own. She felt chilly and empty when she glanced at this child and couldn't understand why she felt such indifference towards it.

"Jacob is the best name for him." It was the name of her father, a man she hardly remembered and a man who, many years prior, had driven her and her whole family to their deaths on the ice route to Havendale.

***

Maganwyth left the cottage and trudged through the snow to return to her hut perched high on Havendale's cliff slopes. *How did he get here?* she thought to herself. *That person – no, that devil – was he ought not to be able to leave his lands.* She spat on the snow, her hot saliva steaming in the chilly air, as bitter muck formed in her throat as she complained. The snow had begun to fall again, although it was only a dusting this time.

As she climbed the cliff, she grumbled to herself. Then, in the distance, she heard a wolf howl. Even though most wolves avoided the bay of Havendale, and it was still quite a distance away, this long winter, one could never be too careful considering how hard it had been for everyone. In any case, she had dealt with many worse challenges than a lone wolf.

"Fucking imbecile," she said to herself. Raouf was a fool, even though she wouldn't have expected anything different from him. He was like his father and the father before him—the entire damned family from that side were simple fools. She had seen them all, those dumb woodsmen and hunters who cut down trees that were thicker than they were. She had hoped that Erin, the young wife, would have overcome prudence to confront her fool of a husband because they were decent people but not sophisticated minds. Maganwyth had never believed that the priests of the one true God taught such idiots, despite the fact that she disagreed with practically everything they taught.

She bemoaned, "If he is lucky, it will merely cost him his life. The baron will have asked for a bargain, which will have cost Raouf much more than he would realise." She climbed to her rude squat hovel. It wasn't much of a home; it had been constructed before most of Havendale when the first settlers had arrived. Since then, she has continued to reside there; however, before she and her two sisters shared the home, it is now just hers, alone, shunned by the community. She could see the two figures at her doorway as she marched up the narrow path to the shack.

"If you think I'll invite you in, you're more of a fool than the woodsman you hoodwinked," she yelled furiously.

In front of her residence, Ivan and the baron stood watching as she struggled up the path. The servant followed the tall, towering lord and lurched in his shadow. "I had believed you had expired," the baron remarked, rolling his r's in his thick accent. "Maganwyth Puzzlecrow," he mocked her using her full name.

"I'm not yet dead," she responded, biting back.

"More's the pity." She was slogging up the hill, her legs aching from exertion, and she was older than anybody would have believed. The baron grinned as he looked down at her.

"What to do with you?" the baron said as he pinched his fingers together and lowered his gaze to the old crone.

"Go sling your hook," she spat, walking past the baron.

"I might have you killed." As she passed him, the baron uttered a threat. Maganwyth ignored him because she knew the threat was hollow. "I would want to make one request of you." As she got closer to her door, he continued to speak.

Maganwyth took a breath. "What do you want from me, exactly?" Then, for just a brief second, her frown relaxed, and momentary perplexity appeared on her face.

"Ivan claims that the little child has the gift." After pausing, Baron Von Rikton said, "You are to instruct him."

"I haven't taught anybody for decades. No one in this hick town has the intelligence to learn even the fundamentals, much less be worth my time. None would be endowed with the gift by the gods," she scowled and hissed.

"However, you will instruct him, he possesses both the talent and the will," the baron decreed.

"Pah!" Maganwyth spat into the snow. She gave his minion, Ivan, a sneer before directing her derision on the baron, adding, "If anybody had the aptitude and temperament, I might accept teaching again. Vlad Sven von Rikton," she said slowly, giving his full name. "Who and if I teach, it will be on my terms, not yours, so get your bloodsucking visage back where it belongs." She slammed the door shut behind her while growling.

The baron hesitated for a moment. He detested rudeness, and Maganwyth had always been one of the more obnoxious sisters. He imagined that perhaps the climate of the frigid north made her rudeness worse. Then, finally, he turned his attention to Ivan, staring unobservantly at the snow with his slack-jawed deformation.

"Ivan, back to Rwelvencrest," he commanded, and as a wolf howled in the night, the baron dissolved and evaporated, leaving nothing behind but a vanishing black mist. Ivan shook his head and began to shuffle through the snow.

An owl shrieked over the freezing waters of the harbour of Havendale, reverberating off the cliffs, and then quietly descended again. The snow started to fall with renewed vigour as the hush descended.

Chapter 2

The Arrivals

Havendale, the frozen settlement nestled in the valleys of the Spine Mountains, was sealed off from the rest of the world by perilous rivers and even more treacherous mountain passes, and it had been that way for the last two years, ever since this long winter had inexplicably arrived. As its only link to the outside world, the now permanently frozen Everlong sea and the glacial streams fed into it. The little settlement carved out its meagre existence through fishing and whaling in the dangerous waters. Even the once-common foresters and hunters had been forced into fishing since the wildlife and lumber had become scarce. Few other trades could endure in this bleak landscape.

Originally a tiny fishing outpost for the princedom of Gont, Havendale was established many years ago as one of the twelve towns in the Spine Mountains. Still standing tall and majestic in the middle of the town, surrounding the main fishing hall, was several other buildings erected from that time. But the town hall proudly dominated the village's centre, the community's most prominent structure and centre. The following most extensive structure was the one true God's church, where the priest performed daily services, and the locals prayed to the one true God to end this never-ending winter. But their prayers had gone unanswered for the previous ten years.

Numerous modest stone and log homes and a few more significant structures, such as stores, bars, and storage facilities, were gathered around the town's centre to support its thousand or so residents. The clusters of little homes became progressively sparser the farther you get from the parish centre. The old lady who served as the local midwife lived in the furthest hamlet; a little rickety cabin perched high up on the surrounding cliffs about half a league from the town.

Since the twins' birth eight years earlier, the winter had stretched, and the summer had never dawned. The north's despair had developed into a terrifying struggle for existence. The settlements encircling the inlets of the Everlong Sea had only just survived, clinging on to the whaling expeditions and the trade in hammerhead trout. Trindon, the capital of Gont, received many requests for food, resources, and somebody who might stop this perpetual winter. Very few messengers returned alive; their pleas having fallen on deaf ears. The electoral prince of Gont had his own challenges. Of the thirteen princedoms that ruled the empire, Gont was among the poorest, and while it still maintained influence in the imperial court, its closest rival, Taros, had been financing raids along Gont's southern border, along with unending threats that came from the shadowy, mysterious realm of Rwelvencrest, which bordered Gont's eastern frontier. As a result, the burden of defence had caused Gont to divert much of its limited resources towards fortification and military capabilities.

A big cast iron kettle resting in a makeshift fireplace in the dark, inconspicuous shack on top of the towering, snow-covered cliff that towered over the tiny hamlet of Havendale was spewing heavy smoke. A raven's skull momentarily floated to the top of the thick green soup before falling to its depths while Maganwyth Puzzlecrow busied herself around her small hut. Maganwyth, or 'Hag', or 'Crone', as she was popularly called in the community, giggled, and murmured to herself.

"Bugger where is it, Mags?" she cursed angrily. "I'm willing to wager that boy stole it." Small trinkets and other ornaments that had accumulated on a rough-hewn wooden table were shoved to one side by the woman, who grumbled as they clattered to the ground. Her gaze finally settled on a book that had eluded her erratic motions.

When she cracked open the black leather-bound book in her paw, she exclaimed, "Mag's you fool, *salt!*" She traced her crooked finger over the page. She scowled as she tossed the book off the table and joined the throng of items lying on the ground. She quickly whirled around and hurried back to her pot. The smoke pouring from the container appeared to change colour from green to bluish as Maganwyth plucked a tiny bag from the top of the fireplace and sprinkled a liberal amount into the crock. She then gave it another whirl. She dipped her ladle into the stew and brought it to her lips as the hag's face broke into a smile. Before tasting it, she gave it a little whiff.

Finally, she murmured, "Almost."

Her wrinkled, withered lips covering her toothless gums as they repeatedly smacked together. She turned to look around her hut for something when she noticed something by her door. Peeking through a tiny knothole, she spied a little black eyeball. Her brilliant-blue eyes focused on the little peeping tom while she scowled at it. Maganwyth Puzzlecrow seldom came across a creature with a stare equal to hers, but this eye didn't flinch or turn away. There didn't appear to be any fear, simply curiosity. She knew the owner. It was the young, sickly frail child, Jacob.

"You might as well enter! You know you can't stay out in the cold for too long," she snapped. She returned her attention to her stew. *Oh, how much better it would taste,* she pondered as she briefly considered putting the little child in the braise. She momentarily licked her lips while reminiscing how much she loved the flavour of youngsters, but she hadn't grown old by behaving recklessly. Then, as she added a few more herbs to her stew, she heard the door squeak open and shut and felt a chill enter her home.

She spun and scowled at the eight-year-old child, who was small, thin, and nearly starving, wrapped in thick snow rabbit furs. *Probably trapped by his brother,* she reasoned, *he still looks like he needs a hearty meal.* "What do you want, boy?" she demanded.

With his hands clasped calmly in front of him and his gaze fixed on Maganwyth without batting an eye, the boy stood as tall as he could. His fine, delicate features remained passive. He remained silent and only cocked his head to one side.

Under the young boys' gaze, Maganwyth couldn't help but feel a little uneasy; she felt an itch in the back of her mind. Even though she was many, many times this child's age, she thought he was passing judgement on her as he fixed his stare.

"What do you want?" she repeated her demand.

He spoke in a quiet, gentle voice, just above a whisper, "I want to learn."

"You what?" She cackled as she gobbed onto the ground. "Did You come to me so you could adorn the neighbourhood peasants with chicken blood?"

"Please don't think that I wish to become a charlatan. Everyone out there already mistakes you for that. I trust in the actual power of nature and science," the little boy added, maintaining his voice. "I want to learn. You have probably saved the lives of every man, woman, and infant in the village at least once. I have been unwell for much of my life, so I would like to learn how to use your medical understanding to accomplish the same. Everyone says you possess secret knowledge lost to time."

Maganwyth stared at the child in disbelief; she couldn't believe such a little boy could speak with such maturity. The tiny youngster was still glaring at her with those dreadful dark eyes. She hesitated briefly before stumbling over to an old, dusty couch and slumping down.

"Do you understand why I reside here, far from the village, on the cliff?" she asked while grabbing a long, hand-carved smoking pipe from near the couch. She reached under the table for a little black purse, took out a pinch, and dusted something into the pipe. She sucked on it while whispering something under her breath as she touched the end with her thumb. She took a long inhale before releasing her thumb, the tobacco embers briefly glowing as she did so. She then let out a big blue smoke that filled the hovel.

The small Jacob tried to hold back a cough as the pungent fume hit at his lungs, but as he covered his mouth, a coughing fit tore through his tiny frame. He nonchalantly wiped a blood-speckled palm on his coat once his slender body stopped shivering from the convulsions.

The young boy's voice croaked as he continued. "You exist here because the village fears, hates, and mistrusts you," he responded in a quiet, raspy voice.

Maganwyth was astounded by the tiny child's insight. But she thought to herself, *I should stop being surprised by him,* as she took another suck from the pipe. "If you learn what I know, they will fear and despise you too," she warned, taking care not to blow the smoke in the young man's direction when she exhaled. Jacob of Havendale, what have you to exchange for my knowledge?"

"They despise me already," the youngster explained. "My mother and father don't care about me, and the other kids are afraid of me." He shrugged and said, "I don't care. I need to learn to survive. I've studied everything I can from the priests in the village, much of which I feel is incorrect. Regarding trade? I am here to serve and assist you."

"Your father made that mistake; therefore, you ought to be careful to whom you offer your service. You might lose your brother's affection; he cares for you in his way," she retorted.

"My brother," young Jacob's shoulders rose and sank as he spoke "My brother is everything my parents expected, but his love is… challenging," the boy concluded.

"He stayed by your bedside for over a week when you were last ill, never leaving. His love is there, and you should treasure it."

"Love won't keep me alive; I need to study your wisdom, elixirs, and cures," Jacob argued. "I'm not interested in superstition, becoming a con man who defrauds others with snake oil or reading entrails. Instead, I'm eager to learn. Will you teach me?"

Maganwyth pondered how this little boy, who had the mind and presumably the talent to be much more than an elementary apothecary, might make an exciting apprentice. The Baron Von Rikton had told her to educate Jacob, but she couldn't bring herself to carry out his orders. She detested serving him.

"Why should I teach you?" she asked finally, after a protracted pregnant pause.

"You have been the healer of Havendale for many years, many more than people think. My father remembers you from childhood, and Father Yusef of the temple remembers you. Father Yusef is one of the oldest men in the village." Jacob thought for a moment; he didn't often speak much and found that this back and forth with the witch was taking his breath. "Considering how long you've been living alone, why have you never felt the urge to share your knowledge? To improve the world? There is fear that stems from a lack of knowledge. If the village residents understand how the actual world works, they won't have to live in such fear."

"I wasn't always by myself." Maganwyth sighed and thought momentarily of her two sisters, who had departed many generations ago. Then, she fixed her gaze on the young child. "I believe I may like you. Tomorrow, check back and ask once again." Finally, she dismissed the boy with a hand wave. "Your brother is searching for you in the town."

Jacob swivelled and turned to face the door. He momentarily pondered how she had known his brother was looking for him, but he knew he would one day possess all the knowledge of the hag. He would convince her to teach him. The fresh, clear morning air surrounded him as he turned and walked through the door, swiftly closing it behind him.

Maganwyth exhaled a deep suck from her pipe as the young boy left. She then tapped it out, struggled to her feet, and limped over to the stove, where her stew was now boiling over. It was overcooked, but it would have to do. The little brat had distracted her from her cooking.

"Drat," she muttered as she removed it from the fire. She tore a peek at the now-blackened pot holding the once-blue stew that was now a deep purple. She drank it, wincing as she did so.

Finally, she murmured to herself, "It'll do." She considered educating young Jacob, even if doing so might be perilous for both.

The youngster was correct in one respect—learning the art would be the only way he could live to maturity, but it also had the potential to kill him. She also considered the baron's demand. However, this was her choice.

***

It was mid-morning, but the sun gave only a twilight glow that set off an eerie orange light dancing across the snow as Jacob laboriously descended the slope that led to Havendale. The past month had been mild for the seemingly unending winter that the Spine Mountains were experiencing. Only a few springtime plants had managed to emerge through the persistent snow. Many people were left with the illusionary hope that perhaps winter was over. Father Yusef of the one true God's church had tried to convince the villagers to pray and claimed that these spouts were a manifestation of the one true God's love. The winter has been here for the past ten years, waxing and waning but never-ending.

Jacob could hear the echoes of children playing in the hamlet, even from his perch atop the cliffs. As long as the pleasant weather persisted, Havendale was bustling with activity as their loud voices reverberated off the rock walls, along with the noises of fishers returning from their morning excursions from the village docks. Jacob trudged across the snowy walk while wrapping his coat over his feeble frame. Among the cacophony of children's voices, he thought he could hear his brother's voice.

Robin, his brother, couldn't have been more different from Jacob; whereas Jacob was skinny, small, and feeble, Robin had already reached four and a half feet tall, with thick, long, black hair, and a coppery healthy complexion, revealing muscles on his physique. Amid a snowball battle,

Robin was in charge of a small group of young boys. Naturally, Robin was winning. He rolled, dove, and launched a snowball, smashing it into the face of an older child. The air was dense with snowballs so compressed that they drew blood when they hit someone, and the compacted flakes broke open on impact, scattering a freezing spray that glistened in the pale morning light.

A group of girls admired the action from a close but safe distance beneath the awnings of the cottages. The audience giggled as they observed the boys. Robin was the subject of a sidelong gaze from Celina and Falia, two young beauties of the village. The young, attractive child was already catching his peers' attention.

The bustle of activity was visible to Jacob when he arrived at the town's outskirts, and he could see his brother having fun with the other children rolling around in the snow. For a brief moment, Jacob felt a pang of jealousy. For the tiniest fraction of a second, Jacob wondered what it would be like to participate in the 'fun', but he was out of breath just from going down the cliffside and couldn't risk catching a cold, he felt like the next one could kill him.

When Robin spotted his brother, he grinned broadly and waved. "Jacob!"

A bigger boy took advantage of Robin's diversion and tackled the younger boy into a deep snow drift.

"No Fair!" Robin exclaimed, laughing as he rose and brushed the snow off his clothes. The bigger boy smiled at Robin and gave him a friendly punch.

The youngster waved and said, "I'll see you later, Rob," before walking away.

"See you, Sean," Robin grinned and dashed across the snow to where Jacob was standing. "Jacob! Where have you been all morning? I was looking for you!" After giving his younger brother a bear embrace, Robin shovelled snow down the back of his hood and chuckled to himself.

As Robin embraced him, Jacob grimaced as the icy snow dripped down his spine. Jacob didn't return his brother's embrace. Instead, as quickly as he could, he pulled away from the hug.

"I've been up the hill to see Maganwyth," Jacob answered. He brushed the snow from his hood. Jacob found it challenging to put up with his brother's obnoxious, overbearing affection.

"You shouldn't go up there, Jacob," Robin warned. "She is dangerous and will transform you into a toad," Robin cautioned.

Jacob dismissed his brother's worries, "She has saved my life." Adding, "Several times, her medicine has helped me. Someone mentioned you were looking for me."

"Oh, yea! You'll never guess what, there is a knight in town," Robin exclaimed excitedly.

Looking at his brother with narrowed brows, Jacob questioned sceptically, "A knight?"

"Oh, yeah, and horses and armour and everything! Also, a whole troop of others," Robin continued to be ecstatic.

"How do you know he is a knight, exactly? You've never seen one before," Jacob inquired after pausing for thought.

"Well, he's got armour and banners. Let's go to the inn and see them," Robin continued excitedly.

Jacob groaned; his brother's passion for everything irked him. Additionally, Robin was always a touch too harsh with his frailer brother. Because of his brother's 'love', Jacob often received bumps and bruises. Since they had been born, Havendale had seldom received outsiders. For a long time, Havendale served as a haven for those rejected by the empire. Because of its isolation, there was limited enforcement of church law in this area. Although this had happened long ago, Telegos and Woodvale to the south had been its sole rivals as a thriving commerce centre for the bay.

Fewer and fewer visitors have arrived since the prolonged winter started. The closest thing the Spine Mountains had to a city was Telegos, a much bigger settlement that was far more likely to draw travellers these days. There have been reports of quests to end the never-ending winter, but most of such stories faded into oblivion, and nothing further was heard about such exploits. Jacob rightly assumed that these folks would be part of another group of intrepid adventurers. He had erroneously assumed that they would be ordinary, everyday would-be heroes.

Jacob recognised his error as they neared the inn. Outside the modest in, eight horses were loosely tethered, stamping in the snow next to four Gont banners planted in the ground. The banners showed a dragons head that denoted the aristocracy of Gont. The horses were beautiful creatures covered in heavy winter blankets. The Spine Mountains lacked horses since they weren't suitable for winter weather. Winter hounds were used to pull sledges, but even those animals became scarcer as fewer people had the resources to care for and maintain them.

Robin stood entranced next to the largest animal and stroked its head. Although the horse enjoyed the child's attention, it nonetheless neighed and raised its head, forcing Robin to fall backwards into the snow.

Robin heeded Jacob's order to 'Leave them alone' and rose, backing away from the horses.

Robin started to giggle.

"What?" snapped Jacob.

Robin laughed. "The horse is pooing." Jacob looked blankly at his brother, then at the horse. Sure, enough, it was, although he failed to see the humour. Jacob looked at his brother dumbfounded, who was still giggling.

"Should we go in?" Robin asked while enthusiastically bouncing from one foot to the other.

The littlest twin moved toward the inn's door without saying anything.

The Traveller's Rest was the town's only inn. A short, rotund man, Gregor, owned with his wife, Eyia. Gregor was a jovial person who enjoyed joking and interacting with the fisherman after their shifts. He was a prominent town council member and considered himself the town's morale booster. Everyone in Havendale loved and respected him. Usually, his wife, Eyia, kept herself out of sight. Rumour had it she descended from Haulfin stock. However, no one would repeat such rumours in Gregor's presence. More than a thousand years ago, before the holy church and the Inquisition had been founded, many other species coexisted with humans, and then the Great Purge swept the empire. The so-called 'Haulfin' had been mainly exiled outside the empire's boundaries. The derogatory term 'Haulfin' merely meant 'not human'. Small communities of 'Haulfin' were rumoured to have migrated into regions like the Spine Mountains and other remote parts of the empire, outside the purview of the Inquisition. Some Haulfin were retained as indentured servants inside the empire, enslaved for their capabilities and as forced labour.

Gregor's large posterior met Jacob as he cracked open the tavern door. Gregor was enthusiastically addressing his visitors with his back to the entrance. A rich, alluring aroma of roasted meats and other sweet flavours tempted Jacob's nose as the fire warmed his face. He was forced inside the inn by Robin, who trampled over him. Jacob's stumbled into Gregor's backside.

"Oi!" Gregor yelled as he turned around to face the two young interlopers. "Children are not allowed here, as you are well aware," he yelled, flailing a big, hamlike hand in the general direction of Robin and Jacob.

Robin winced; he was frequently caught stealing delectable pastries that Eyia had baked. Every now and again, Gregor would give him a clip on the thighs when he apprehended the young thief. Jacob gazed up at the fat innkeeper slyly, remembering how he had persuaded his brother to take the sweets but had never been implicated.

"We simply wanted to meet the travellers," explained Jacob.

Gregor spoke once more, but this time his voice lacked confidence. "You know we don't allow children."

From behind the innkeeper, a well-educated, soft-spoken voice proclaimed, "Oh, Let them through."

Although the intonation was youthful, it exuded power and implied disobedience was never an issue. Jacob and Robin could see the travellers as Gregor shifted to one side.

A young gentleman who appeared to be in his late teens was seated in the centre of the group. He was still tall, with bright blue eyes, a clean-shaven face, and long, groomed blond hair that was undoubtedly popular in the lowlands. He was outfitted in a gold-inlaid, chain-link breastplate and chain-linked armour with a thick heavy fur cloak over his shoulders. He motioned the children toward him with a smirking grin on his face.

There were four additional travellers. The first person who stuck out was the man standing next to the table. His complexion was as pitch-black as midnight towering seven feet like an ebony statue. But, unlike the young man, he wore exotic attire, comprising wraps made of animal skins that Jacob had only heard about, including what appeared to be tigers, zebras, and other species jumbled together in one ensemble. His face was also heavily embellished with metal studs and chains, and he wore a hood crafted of a single enormous bird head. The man's deep gaze fixed on the two children. He was holding a long spear and carrying several more slung across his back.

"Step aside, Abrias!" The young man commanded, "You'll scare the young boys."

"I am William Nadrog, Heir Prince of Gont," the aristocrat invited the two youngsters towards the table while the enormous guy, Abrias, moved to one side.

"This is my tutor in arms, Heineroth, and his son Tryrial," he smiled as he presented themselves to the young boys.

The man introduced as Heineroth was an older gentleman with a grizzled face and a meshwork of scars that interrupted his thick beard. Both wore heavy armour and thick wolf fur cloaks like the youngest man. His nose was swollen and covered in tiny black and red spots, and he had red bloodshot, rheumy eyes. He drank from a large metal tankard while grinning warmly. He was a big man with broad shoulders and an equally wide chest. *This man must be part bear,* Robin thought.

Heineroth's son, Tryrial stood out in a sharp contrast; he was clean-eyed yet possessed a faint resemblance to his father from perhaps twenty years ago, whereas his beard was neatly trimmed into a vandyke, and his eyes were free of the redness that marked his father. He was a lean man, but he still had the robust build of someone who cared for himself.

The final figure was little and barely taller than Robin. A long, light-grey cloak concealed its face with a deep hood. It revealed what looked to be a young woman, practically childlike, as it turned to face the minors. She sat a little bit away from the rest of the group with her eyes concealed by the hood. William hadn't introduce her. Robin's eyes widened in awe as he observed the towering, dark-skinned man and the three armoured knights. Something inside of Jacob was calling him to this cloaked entity, a kind of kinship, and Jacob felt attracted to it.

Upon catching Jacob's eye, William explained, "Ah, this. This creature is our guide, of sorts." He smiled warmly at the woman before turning to face the boys and grinning again. "So, when will you join the Knights of Gont?"

"Pah. The large one, maybe, but the young one seems like he could hardly raise a sword, much less swing it," Heineroth spat out his drink, laughing heartily. Tryrial joined in.

The young woman whispered beneath her hood, "Don't rule him out." She raised her head and turned to face Jacob. Their eyes briefly connected, and she said, "He has strength other than that of the body." As they continued to stare at one other, seemingly unable to turn their gaze elsewhere. Her tiny, enticing features gave off the appearance of a child's face. Finally removing her hood, she showed off her stunningly elongated pointy ears and long, black hair. Her large almond-shaped eyes glowed with a soft green glow.

A Haulfin! Although he had heard the stories, Jacob had never seen one and was astonished. As soon as Robin noticed her, he hurriedly made the sign of the one true God and stepped backwards, putting distance between himself and this creature. They were deemed abominations by the church of the one true God, so how could a prince of the realm journey with one?

"Relax, fellas, she's sanctioned by the church," Heineroth explained, seeming to find the entire exchange humorous. The large man yanked at the Haulfin's robe, revealing a substantial iron ring encircling the woman's neck. As soon as the man touched the Haulfin, she retreated and covered her neck. The Inquisition meant for the iron bands to represent a symbol of the Haulfin's 'tameness' and a master's ownership.

"I thought the Haulfin was gone," Robin dumbly added.

"Not gone, there are still quite a few in the Empire, and they have their purposes." William continued, "Right, fellas, you've had your time. Now leave us to our meal. We have a perilous journey tomorrow, and if all goes well, you will have an end to your winter."

Dismissed, Gregor corralled Jacob and Robin towards the direction of the exit. The two boys were quickly shoved out the door by the hefty barkeep, although Jacob continued to try stare around him at the Haulfin. Jacob couldn't understand why this entity had such a hold over him. Gregor shoved them outside, slamming the door in their wake.

Chapter 3

The Haulfin

Robin and Jacob staggered out of the inn and landed in the snow. Jacob could not stop thinking about the Haulfin woman. He thought she was so exquisite and that he felt a strong affinity with her that he had never experienced before.

Robin's face lit up with anticipation. "Did you see those actual Knights there? And that Black man." He bounced enthusiastically.

"He is from Arbay," Jacob informed, recalling what he had read in a book. "They dwell in the territories towards the south of the empire, and there it is reported to be summer all year, a scorching desert," Jacob added.

"Lands where it's always summer!" Robin said, looking at his brother bewildered. His perplexed expression quickly turned into a smile as he poked his brother in the arm and said, "You kidding?"

"It's not all snow, brother. There are many other places on our earth." Jacob massaged his arm.

"'If all goes well, you will have an end to the winter,' the prince said. What do you think he meant by that?" Robin mimicked the prince's aristocratic voice.

"I don't know, brother; I think they have some mission in mind to end this cursed winter. However, you should return home immediately since our father will require assistance with his load," Jacob added.

"Aren't you coming?" Robin enquired.

Jacob excused himself, explaining, "I have to go do something."

"What?" Robin insisted, giving his brother a hard shove.

"No concern of yours." Jacob frowned at his brother as his face became dejected. "I'm sorry, I need to do this. Go, assist father. I'll be home later. We'll try teaching you to read again," Jacob said in a more sympathetic tone.

Robin's face sank again, but it wasn't out of sadness but desperation this time.

Robin countered, "No, Jacob, I don't need to learn to read; I'm going to be a Knight."

Jacob grinned, "Then you will be the most foolish knight in Gont. We will get you reading." The two little boys halted as Jacob briefly turned to face his sibling. Jacob repeated, "I'll see you later." And walked away.

Robin watched his brother leave; he did love him; thought he was brilliant and had made such an effort to encourage Robin in his studies. Robin detested endeavouring to read, trying to figure out what all the chicken scratches on the paper even meant. He wondered why his brother wanted him to learn so badly. Robin exhaled. With Jacob watching out for him in various ways, Robin understood he had to take care of his little brother, especially when he was ill. *But in other respects, Jacob was useless,* he thought to himself. Robin started the arduous journey home, his feet sinking into the pristine snow. Robin was hungry – he was hungry all the time these days – so hopefully, his dad had been able to catch something to eat today. On his journey home, Robin stopped by the blacksmith. He waited at the rear of the house waiting for Falia. Finally, the young lady appeared.

"Pst," Robin called, hurling a snowball at the young woman.

The ball shattered against the young lady's dress. Her face flushed with anger until she saw the culprit. Then her face flushed for another reason. She gave a gentle wave at the young man.

"Hi." She waved. The pretty girl blushed.

Robin froze for a moment like a rabbit before he bolted away.

***

Jacob traversed the streets across the town to the imposing temple edifice. He stifled a shudder as he glanced up at the massive stone structure; it was a gloomy gothic establishment erected by Havendale's first residents many centuries earlier. The majority of old god temples in the empire were reclaimed as houses of worship for the one true God during the first Inquisition and those that weren't were demolished. The original purpose of this temple's construction was to honour Aurialla, an ancient winter goddess from the old religion.

Even the most isolated regions of the empire, such as the Spine Mountains, had not entirely escaped the Inquisition. The Haulfin had been expelled, slaughtered, or forced into slavery. A thousand years or so have passed since this occurred. Over time, humankind's recollections of the deities of the old faith faded. Leaving only a few traces that a pantheon of gods once existed, one of which was the magnificent temple in Havendale.

When Jacob arrived at the enormous wooden temple doors crafted from thick oak transported from the lowlands across the sea, substantial, heavy iron spikes jutted from the entrance. Little murder holes to the sides of each doorway and above in the enormous archway gave away the temple's proper function, at least in its early years. This bastion served as the town's final line of defence against the untamed tribes of the frozen north. Although there were still legends of the barbaric Haulfin races and creatures lurking in the Spine Mountains, they were just terrifying stories meant to terrorise children these days. The preponderance of the books in the temple – the only genuinely substantial collection of literature in Havendale – had been authored by priests of the one true God; consequently, they had a skewed perspective on the truth, Jacob had observed, and he had come to realise that not everything he read constituted the entire truth.

He struggled to open the enormous door by pressing all his weight on it, allowing him to pass through and enter the temple's vast, cavernous main entrance. His footsteps reverberated throughout the enormous stone structure, which appeared to be vacant at the moment. The stones were still a chilling reminder of their former benefactor, making it feel somewhat colder inside than outside. The main altar, which had the one true God's emblem hanging above the podium, with rows and rows of pews, pointed towards it. To close the door, Jacob turned and pressed against it using all of his weight. It clanged shut with a loud bang that echoed throughout the quiet sanctuary. The sacristy, a tiny annexe where the clergy would conduct lessons for the village's young children, was located at the back of the basilica. Jacob moved down the aisle between the rows of benches towards this classroom. The majority of the teachings focused on the one true God's wonder and grandeur, but there were also some about basic math and other subjects, enough to assure that the pupils would be capable of surviving in the real world. Robin had always hated such classes since they took time away from his day, and Jacob detested them for other reasons.

"Who is that?" A crooked, decrepit man hobbled into the main hall; his rasping, frail voice echoed out from the rear room.

"Only me, father Yusef," Jacob replied.

"Why are you here? We don't have service today," the elderly blind priest tilted his head to the side and asked. The older adult shuffled over to the first pew and slumped down. Father Yusef was the priest who had adopted his mother, Erin, when she became an orphan. "Are you going to pilfer our books once more?"

"I have to check up on something," Jacob explained as he approached the clergyman. "About the one true God," he said after pausing. "You cannot blame a young man for wanting to understand more about his splendour," he lied.

Though the twins weren't his actual grandsons, the priest grinned warmly and acknowledged that he usually felt a strong bond with them. "You're well aware that having too much knowledge might be harmful." The priest offered as a warning, but he could already hear Jacob's footsteps vanishing into the vestibule of the temple. The youngster wasn't right, Yusef lamented to himself; he was too intelligent and advanced for his age.

Most of the temple's back rooms served as the priest's living quarters and dining areas. Spiral stone stairs led below the temple; Jacob had once dared Robin to sneak down, but even his adventurous twin brother had lost his courage halfway. A raging fire heated the modest alcove that was furnished with fur rugs in the vestibule of learning, rendering it warmer. Jacob perused the books that towered above him arranged on various shelves. There were only a few dozen; Jacob had read most of them and endeavoured to comprehend them though he struggled with some.

The book Jacob was looking for was visible; it rested, perched on the top shelf, well beyond his reach. The blue leather book, titled *History of the Empire: Volume One,* was the target of Jacob's fascination, and he stepped back to get a better view.

Jacob swore to himself since it was presumably put there by an inconsiderate adult. He looked around for anything to pull it down. He could ask Yusef or one of the priests for assistance, that would raise questions.

Jacob hauled himself up by grabbing the first shelf. The book was still more than a foot over his head when he attempted to grab it. Pulling himself up and holding the next frame, Jacob struggled up another. He stood on his tiptoes to reach the book and brushed the top shelf with his fingertips. Jacob was little more than a foot off the ground. Even at this height, his stomach was already churning knots as the ground loomed below. He always had a fear of heights. By gritting his teeth, he managed to climb another shelf. His thin arms strained from supporting his weight as he reached up to grab the book but only managed to touch the cover. He tugged the volume toward the edge of the shelf, and it plummeted, striking him square in the head and knocking him off the shelves. Jacob fell with a loud snap against the rough stone flooring. A sharp pain sliced through Jacob's arm and up his torso, and his gut quaked with dread. He managed to whimper instead of screaming as he held back the agony. After a brief rest on the ground, he attempted to move onto his back while clutching his arm. The dull throbbing pain was still coursing through his body. He tried to contain the sounds of suffering, but he felt like crying as he could feel his eyes watering. In a panic, Jacob looked about because he didn't want anybody to discover him in this condition after the acute stinging subsided to a dull throbbing ache after he rested for a short while. He cautiously peeled up his sleeve to reveal a black bruise spreading across his arm and swelling. He hoisted himself into a sitting position. The bound blue book had fallen open next to him. Despite the tumble, this was his reward. He hoped it had been worthwhile. With his injured arm cradled against his body, Jacob dragged the book with his one uninjured arm. As he browsed a few pages, he thought how he would have no trouble hiding his arm from his parents, but Robin would be more problematic. Flicking through the pages, Jacob quickly found his desired passage. In an effort to concentrate, he drove pain from his mind. He started to read.

The lesser creatures and people coexisted peacefully in the early days of the empire.

The first city of Altran was founded with assistance from the lesser races.

Until the wonderful one true God appeared, they even assisted in the establishment of the political order and helped man subdue the earth and the oceans.

By choosing to cling to the shadows of a superstitious past, they were unable to perceive his majesty or glory.

The awe of the one true God drove these monsters from the empire while their devils gave them strength, and thus the first Inquisition of the church was founded.

Despite the terror of the Haulfin gripping the empire for many years, it was only through the strength of our trust in our God and the tenacious efforts of his emissaries that the empire was ultimately able to experience peace.

However, in order to be prepared for the future, we must comprehend the Haulfin threat.

They represent a perilous and seditious existence from an era that should be forgotten.

Haulfins come in a variety of breeds.

Haulfin derives from the full name Haulfin agurs gane beann ag dia and meaning, 'not man'. It is a word used to describe all of them or 'Not a divinely favoured person'.

To understand and defend against the Haulfin, we must know them.

There are a few breeds of note:

Compared to humans, the Aldar are smaller.

They are typically shorter than men – about five feet tall – and physically weaker.

Their prominent, bright eyes and erect, pointed ears make them instantly recognisable.

They boast unsurpassed longevity and ageless cunning.

These people started the initial insurrection against the empire.

They are considered to be the most destructive of the Haulfin.

However, their extended lifespans provide them access to abilities few humans have achieved.

They are an arrogant species driven by conceit.

The Dewar are short and thick, with an average height of only four feet, a muscular frame, and long beards that cover most of their faces on both sexes. The majority of the Dewar live underground in the northern highlands.

They are a covetous race that is driven by greed.

The hobby resembles a human the most closely of all the Haulfin.

Although they are about half as big, they have a typical human appearance.

Some even claim that we have a common relative.

The church regards this as being erroneous and is considered heresy.

They continue to reside on the eastern glade's slopes in the wastelands.

This race of Haulfin is gluttonous and addicted to excess.

The Gnomus is the smallest Haulfin subspecies.

They typically stand slightly over a foot tall, are small, hunched animals, and are highly skilled with complex equipment. Their name even means, 'with wisdom'.

Many of their species have fled to uncharted areas, and most of their locations remain unknown.

Their diminutive size gives them a particular place in the empire.

The Gnomus suffer the sin of Inquisitiveness, questioning the word of the one true God.

There are several other species of Haulfin, and there were numerous others now gone.

Some people reading this might believe that it was cruel to expel these species from the empire and that it would have been better for them to experience the love of the one true God.

Every effort was made to bring these beings into the one true God's presence, but the preponderance of these attempts failed.

However, there are always exceptions, and the Inquisition and the church have installed a few of these animals within the empire.

However, none will ever experience the one true God's love.

We were created in the image of the one true God, and the Haulfin are simply perverted versions of that.

As Jacob read, he noticed that the agony in his arm had diminished to a dull ache. He clutched the book to his chest and kept reading. He found out that some of the Haulfin were permitted to reside in the empire in little communes where they could be monitored, governed, and controlled. Jacob could see how the empire felt, preserving a small number for their abilities but never enough to pose a danger to the empire once more. The hours passed as he read on. The fire in the alcove faded and withered away. Jacob was ultimately forced to give up since the little twilight shining into the room made it difficult to discern the words on the page. His body ached from his fall and the awkward sitting posture, so he forced himself to get up from where he had been sitting. Testing his arm, it was still aching and stinging. The sun had set low, and an intense frost pierced the air as he left the temple and headed home.

Heineroth, the ageing knight, cared for the horses with his son Tryrial as he passed the tavern. In order to catch a glimpse of the Haulfin that he suspected to be an Aldari as he snuck by, continuously casting sidelong glances toward the inn, but other than the illumination within, he was unable to make anything out. The little child winced in agony when he accidentally jolted his arm while pulling his winter coat firmly around his fragile frame. He stopped abruptly after slipping around the back of the tavern. A petite, slender figure in a long, grey-white robe was waiting near the back entrance of the bar. Jacob recognised the figure as the Haulfin woman immediately. She maintained her position in the dim light from the tavern's rear door. She appeared to be deep in concentration as she regarded the bay. Jacob looked around to see if any other travellers were around before approaching to speak with her. She was all alone. He was uneasy for the first time in his life, yet he collected himself and went up to her. He experienced that need and kinship yet again as he drew closer.

Her form appeared to emit a gentle, warm green glow, "You are injured." she stated without turning around. "You may come close, young man; I won't hurt you."

Jacob summoned his courage; something about this woman intrigued and terrified the eight-year-old. Jacob drew nearer to the enigmatic woman, who turned to face him with a tranquil expression.

"Your arm?" she asked as she examined the little child in front of her as though reading his soul. Then, beneath her robe, she extended her long, delicate hand to Jacob.

Jacob hesitated before extending his hand to hers and grimaced as he did so. "What is your name? The prince never said," he questioned as he looked up at the Haulfin maiden.

"Don't judge him too harshly. He's a lot kinder when we're not among others," she explained. She took his hand and slowly pulled Jacob's sleeve up by running her fingers up his arm. "It wouldn't be appropriate for William to display any intimacy to me in public, and his father wouldn't dare have permitted me to come up here if he believed we were more than servant and master. You have a fracture," the woman remarked, looking down at the tiny boy with a loving smile.

She peeled up his shirt to reveal the deep, black bruise while Jacob listened. Eventually, using the old-fashioned proper term for her race Jacob asked "Are there many Aldari in the capital Trindon?"

"Aldari?" She smiled and delicately touched the wound, raising an eyebrow. "No, not many any longer; I'm aware of a few hundred in the lower quarter and a small number serving in the castle, including me. There are more in Altran, where I was born." She remembered, referring to the Empire's capital. "But none I've met yet possesses this gift."

The pain subsided as she ran her fingers over the bruise, and a gentle green light appeared to come from her hands. Jacob felt refreshed more than he had in any time he could recall, and he could even feel his breathing becoming more manageable.

"You have a similar gift," the Aldari woman noted returning her hands to the recesses of her robes.

Jacob watched in admiration as the bruising on his arm disappeared. He then rolled down his sleeve and glanced up in confusion at the Aldari.

"A gift?" He was aware that he was brighter than most kids his age and even some adults he knew, but was it a gift? "What is a gift?" he asked.

"Some people have divine gifts. You probably wouldn't be familiar with the gods of the ancient religion, although many were revered in the empire prior to the Inquisition and the church," the woman explained as she turned to face the young child and tucked her hands inside her robe. "While it was prevalent in my people, the Inquisition used to refer to these abilities as being possessed by devils; thus, you must be exceptional because it is unusual in a human like you. You shouldn't divulge your gift to anyone," she added.

"What is my gift?" Jacob questioned.

"I'm not sure." She gave the youngster a sweet grin as she shrugged, put her hand on his shoulder, knelt, and gave him a quick kiss on the forehead.

She advised, "You will find out, just don't let others know. They won't understand." And then she departed, returning to the comfort of the tavern. For a minute, Jacob stood still in the snow before realising that she had never given him her name.

She called out, "It's Ailwhyn." As she entered the tavern door.

Chapter 4

The Ambush

In the northern regions, a snowstorm was raging. Heineroth was dragging the horses as they struggled through the flurry. Tryrial stood in front of the group, bracing himself to battle against the swirling wind and snow while carrying a loaded crossbow under one arm. Abrias kept close to William shivering uncontrollably. The black giant was from Arbay, a country in the far south with vast stretches of desert where water didn't freeze even on the coldest nights.

"How do you white men tolerate this weather," he turned to face William, yelling, his deep voice resonating above the storm.

"You learn and adapt. This is a lot worse than usual," sighed William, tying his scarf tightly around his neck. Then, looking up at the peak ahead, he called, "Ailwhyn! Are you sure it's up ahead?" The short, thin Aldari fought through the dense drift.

Above the howling winds, her soft voice carried on the wind, "It's ahead. According to the legends, it will be at the foot of the next mountain, maybe an hour or more."

The snow had been battering them hard for days, getting more challenging as they neared their destination. The comfort of the Travellers Rest was now a distant memory. They would have had to turn back if Heineroth's knowledge of the mountains had not allowed them to keep pushing forward, searching for caves and other safe coves where they could recuperate. They had lost a horse two days prior when a cliff they were climbing on gave way. Underneath its hooves, the ice ledge collapsed into a deep, unfathomable chasm. Without Heineroth's prompt actions, the other horses would have died. He quickly cut the horse's reins tying them to the others, and witnessed as the beast fell away, braying in panic. Abrias was not doing well in this icy environment; he was too obstinate to complain, but William could see the Arbay-man was having trouble. He couldn't stop shaking, and one of his fingers had turned black from frostbite. Abrias had vehemently rejected Ailwhyn's healing touch. Abrias' people were fervent, fanatical devotees of the one true God, and he would never allow himself to become corrupted by contact with a Haulfin 'witch', he was prepared to perish rather than betray his god.

Sir William Nadrog, the princedom of Gont's heir prince, had access to generally forbidden information and had received the teachings of the country's top scholars. He knew how and why the church and the empire had demonised the Haulfin to maintain their control. The Haulfin were mortals like humankind; they weren't demons. Ailwhyn had a link to some ancient force of the long-forgotten old religion. She received gifts from her deity, which many people saw as unnatural, beneficial, and deviant. While serving as a handmaiden in the palace for years, she had prudently kept her gift a secret.

Her decision to expose her power to the heir prince was motivated by Ailwhyn's deed of kindness. William had been a small boy playing around the castle when he stumbled and fell down a steep flight of steps. He fractured his neck when he fell. If the young girl had not made a stand for morality, he would have died. She had utilised her supernatural abilities to heal the young teenager at great personal peril. The young slave girl and he had made a life-long agreement that he would never reveal her secret. They had developed a friendship in hiding. The slave girl and the little prince, who was one of the only kids in the palace, slowly formed an unbreakable bond.

"We cannot keep going for another hour without rest," William warned, calling to Heineroth. "Would there be any place to rest?"

The enormous man pulling the horses at the back of the group straightened up straight and swore to himself. The aged soldier strained to look into the snowstorm's blinding whiteness. Shadows of rocky outcroppings danced in his eyes as the snow swirled through the air, and a blank sheet of white covered everything in every direction. At the front of the procession, Heineroth could barely see his son's shimmering figure.

He shook his head and said, "We have to keep going; when we get to the foot of the mountain, we ought to be able to find a cave. Tell Tryrial to quicken his stride!"

When William relayed the order, the young soldier nodded and pushed forward. Even moving more swiftly, it still took them almost three hours to get to the mountain's base. The moment they reached its base, the wind shifted, the snow stopped, and the skies became clear. A colossal, gleaming white and blue stone tower rose from the mountain far above them and protruded toward the sky like a predator's fang. The snowstorm raged around the range, but it was serene here and for a league around the tower. They came to a stop, caught their breath, and Ailwhyn looked over the area surrounding them. A few patches had little plants sprouting through the thin snow. A chill raced down her back as she stared at the white tower.

"As we expected, the storm isn't natural as we suspected." She continued, "Some old magic, whose strength I can feel here, is responsible for this region's everlasting winter."

"What causes it, witch? Do you know?" questioned Abrias, who was rubbing his hands together in an attempt to regain sensation in his fingers. She could see the charred stub of his little finger and yearned to heal him with all of her heart. Her compassion and empathy boiled deep inside her, but she knew he would murder her before he would allow it.

"I don't know, but I believe it is the work of the old gods." The tall man scowled and massaged his blackened fingers as he stomped away in reaction to her response.

Heineroth groused as he circled the horses. "In any case, we're here to put a stop to it. Tryrial, get lighting a fire. Before we begin the ascent, we're going to need some food and warmth." The blue tower was encircled by cliffs, which he pointed out. He yanked a bundle of firewood off one of the horses and threw it at his child, who grunted as he caught it in the chest.

Sir William continued to admire the tower, which was an architectural masterpiece. Even though it wasn't as elaborate, it was taller than the emperor's palace, and the building's construction in the midst of nowhere was astonishing. Ailwhyn had heard ancient Aldari legends about these towers. Many of these wonders once existed and served as educational institutions for any who studied heretical magic. There was something up there, he couldn't tell if it was malevolent, but it was destroying the land and his people, and William stroked his fingers over the pommel of his sword. He got the uneasy sensation of being watched as he peered at the tower.

The Spine Mountains was a vast, inhospitable region of Gont, he nor his father had ever visited before this. Aside from pelts, furs, and ambergris, they had made little contribution to the princedom's economy. Even though the area had access to the Everlong Sea and certain mines, his father could not understand the importance of this venture to save the north.

For several months, William had to plead for permission to embark on this expedition to the north. To ultimately secure his consent, it had needed Heineroth, one of his father's dependable soldiers and guards. The bearlike man was now unloading the horses and preparing the camp. Heineroth had been his weapons instructor since he was a little boy, but more significantly, Heineroth had been his friend. Heineroth was not of aristocratic birth but had gained an officer's rank in the military, a story he would frequently recount. Even though he now held a title, he felt unsuited to a noble life. The only other youngster in the castle in Trindon, the Gont nation's capital, was Tryrial, who was a few years older than William. The life of the heir prince was not frivolous one; it was full of tutors, lessons, and functions to attend. Tryrial and Ailwhyn had provided a brief respite from this formality.

William knew how privileged he was; he only had to compare himself to Ailwhyn. Although Ailwhyn, the poor Aldari, appeared to be barely fourteen years old, she was actually older than Heineroth by a decade. While many Haulfin races were long-lived, the Aldari were among the longest-lived, with many surviving for thousands of years, but it wasn't a long life worth living underneath the empire. The Haulfin were kept as indentured servants in the workhouses, field labourers on the larger farms, and slaves in the homes of the wealthy or powerful.

He frowned at the tower. Ever since he had learnt of this location from Ailwhyn, he had been confident that this ancient magical hub was to blame for his people's endless winter woes. The other members of his group concurred, some more willingly than others. Talos Tarsus, the weasellike Inquisitor general of Gont, whose approval was required for the expedition, ultimately yielded after much debate. He needed further persuasion before he agreed to let William take possession of Ailwhyn. While Ailwhyn belonged to William's father, the Inquisition was in charge of regulating the migration of the Haulfin people. Talos made no secret of his views on the Haulfin, and he didn't want any of them alive in the empire, whatever harm this would bring to the economy. William believed Talos secretly hoped Ailwhyn would perish on the expedition.

William struggled through the snow back towards the camp. After successfully starting the fire, Tryrial desperately fanned it, encouraging it to grow. Then the snow erupted around them. There was a ferocious flurry of fangs, fur, and claws. Tryrial shouted and rolled aside as a massive claw the size of a table swiped towards him. Two of the horses were less fortunate, snared by the screaming beasts, who promptly tore out their throats, unleashing a shower of blood staining the snow. William saw the assault taking place from a distance and counted six beasts.

The creatures were eight feet tall, with huge hands framed with dark, vicious, razor-sharp claws. These animals had sought to ambush the group, their tusked features growling. Heineroth was the first to respond. He brought his sword to bear with the lightning speed of years of practised reflexes, appearing to tear his bastard blade from his back and strike the first beast in a single motion. The sword impaled the creature's head, and Heineroth brought it back to a guard position before the creature hit the ground. Although Tryrial was younger, he took longer to respond as a massive, white-furred humanoid beast descended upon him. Then, as the beast pounded the snow beside him, ripping huge chunks out of the ground, he rolled out of danger.

As the beast drew near, Tryrial rolled once more, this time holding his crossbow in his hands. He slouched back on his rump and released the bolt, which sank true and deep into the beast's chest. The robust bolt pushed the beast back, plunging deep, but the creature didn't collapse. Tryrial stumbled backwards as the beast approached and lifted its claws in preparation for the slaughter. Heineroth sprang at the beast with his sword, slicing through its tusk and eye to render it helpless.

"On your feet, lad!" Heineroth ordered. William hurried to aid his allies. He had drawn his sword, but as he toiled through the deep snow, he felt as though he was stuck in quicksand and could do anything except watch. Ailwhyn proved considerably more agile than her contemporaries and could dodge and roll away while a powerful beast attempted to ensnare her. A beast had taken Abrias by surprise, leaving him with severe bleeding on one side. Using his uninjured arm to wield his spear, the Arbay scout kept the beast at bay. He was in excruciating pain as he battled to maintain his footing.

Another beast was feasting on the flesh of the slaughtered the horses. An immense beast, the sixth and final animal, remained behind, holding back, and pacing around the melee, looking for an opening.

While his son stood up, Heineroth continued to repel the attack of the maimed beast that had been trying to eat Tryrial. William had now entered the fray, but the immense beast sprang, soaring an unimaginable distance into the air, launched by muscular rear legs before he could reach his weapon master. The beast lunged at William as it crashed into the snow next to him, bringing up a shower of snow and a terrifying roar. William could see the enormous beast's move coming long before the swipe landed and ducked beneath its arm, striking the creature in the abdomen, although his strike did little more than enrage the beast. As the enormous mountain of a beast rounded on him, he struck it in the side, leaving a jagged bleeding scar, and then he backpedalled to keep distance between himself and this giant.

Over the snow, an agonising wail could be heard. Without ever having to look, William knew that his bodyguard Abrias was the source of the scream; however, he needed to concentrate and think back to his combat training with Heineroth as he faced the beast in front of him.

'Lad, at your age, most opponents you face will be bigger than you, don't match them with strength'. The words rang in William's head, 'You are smaller, weaker, but you are faster and more agile, one day you might be able to be big and strong like me, but until then you dodge and find your chance'.

As William concentrated, the enormous beast ruthlessly swung its colossal claws at his head. *I'm not quicker, but I'm wiser,* William reflected. He drew his sword up to meet one of the swipes, and when the beast's claw met it, he felt a jolt in his arm. Most other blades would have shattered under the stress, but this one was made of Gontish steel, the best in the empire; it did bend but sprang back swiftly. William twisted around and savaged the creature's other arm, which produced a shower of blood to strike his face and briefly rendered him blind.

Utilising all of the instincts his old trainer had given him, William retreated and attempted to wipe the blood away with the inside of his elbow. Through the red haze, he could see the beast coming toward him. When it was close by and towered above him, it was ready to attack with its fangs and claws. He rotated his body, allowing the talon to impact his backplate and knock him to the ground face-first. As he struck the ground, his sword scattered out of his hands. He had time to roll over and watch the beast lunging down at him as its enormous head snapped at his throat as he put his feet up against the creature's chest, holding it at bay. He could feel his legs giving way under the creature's tremendous weight as it crushed down. The beast was trying to press itself down as William attempted to kick it away, and as it did, its bloodied claws smeared the snow on either side. The jaws snapped, and he could smell the rank breath of the beast inches from his face. The beast drew nearer and nearer, its little black eyes fixed on its prey. William felt his legs about to give way and had to use all of his willpower to fight the scorching agony in his thighs, no longer capable of repelling the beast. As soon as the young prince sensed his legs give way, the beast's head erupted in a bloody explosion. The enormous, white-haired beast sank to the ground, crushing the young prince beneath its dead weight. The prince was grabbed by Tryrial's powerful arm, dragging him free and to his feet.

"You've got to keep on your toes, Will!" The young soldier grinned.

"Weren't you on your back earlier?" William asked, panting for breath.

"No one's perfect." Tryrial grinned. "Not even me!"

There were now just two of the animals left. Heineroth had slain the one he had injured earlier and was dealing with the beast that had killed the horses. The beast following Ailwhyn appeared to be whimpering on the ground in pain, despite the fact that it had no marks, and the final beast standing was stooped over Abrias.

"Let him be," William shouted as he dashed forward to retrieve his sword. The beast pivoted; its bloodied jaws exposed. The thing screamed and withdrew, dropping to all fours, its knuckles scraping through the snow, leaving a trails of blood. It circled the group. William slashed hard and quickly with his sword, ripping the creature's eye and face. The beast withdrew when William feinted in its direction. The beast's jaw fell slack as a thick quarrel suddenly sprang from its neck, allowing William to attack. William charged forward and struck hard and squarely, driving his sword deep into the creature's cranium. The beast then sank into the snow with its lifeblood soaking the earth. William collapsed on his knees, panting with exhaustion.

Ailwhyn was standing over the monster that had been pursuing her, one hand lifted above the predator, fingers spread, and muttering under her breath. Heineroth approached and, with scarcely a pause, swung his massive bastard sword, severing the creature's scalp in half with a single motion. As the beast expired, Ailwhyn sagged onto the snow.

William was the first to speak, "What the hell were those things?" he demanded as he forced himself to stand.

"Their real name is Kubra, but the locals would refer to them as Yetis, savage monsters, extremely uncommon. I suppose they are even rarer now. In

51

the marketplaces of Trindon, their furs would sell for a fortune." Heineroth cleaned his long sword on the ground.

"Abrias?" he queried as he turned to face his son.

"He's alive," Tryrial reported. "But not for long." The young man shook his head.

Heineroth and William approached the Arbay scout. It was a stretch to describe Abrias as alive; his throat had been slashed in half, and massive gashes gushed blood with each beat of his heart.

"Ailwhyn!" shouted William.

The Haulfin stood up dragging herself over to the fallen man. Even before she reached his body, she knew it was too late.

"He is gone, my lord. I'm not sure he would appreciate it even if I did heal him," she pleaded to the young heir prince.

"Try," he commanded.

Blood splattered on Ailwhyn's grey cloak as she kneeled over the dying man. Then, she closed her eyes with her hands clasped over the bleeding body.

"*Gyia,*" she silently begged her deity to hear her prayer. Tears started to gather in her eyes as she attempted to inject Abrias with vitality. She could feel his life slowly ebbing away.

The voice of her inner goddess spoke. *He rejects you.*

"Overcome it!" she demanded, weeping, attempting to coax the magic into the dying man's body.

She and the Arbay bodyguard had never seen eye to eye, but she didn't want him to die.

"Please help me, goddess!" she pleaded, but even as she begged, she could feel the life fading away, his spirit moving on.

"No!" she screamed in her head tears fell freely from her cheeks as the last gasping breath left Abrias. She finally looked up at William with tear-stained eyes and shook her head.

In anger, William kicked the body of one of the Yetis.

"He died a soldier. Now, let's look to you," Heineroth insisted.

William looked up. Heineroth pointed to his forehead. William reached up, touching his forehead; his fingers returned with blood. He felt a sizable gash. He hadn't sensed the injury, but clearly, one of the Yetis' tusks had grazed him.

"Ailwhyn, see to the prince; you should be able to fix that," he grimaced.

When William's facial blood began to stream down the side of his head, Ailwhyn gazed at him in horror and rushed to his side. He attempted to push her away, but despite her petite stature, she persisted. It only took a brief touch before the gash healed, leaving a patch of clear white skin.

"We have to get up to the tower and finish this," William declared with resolve.

"Not before we eat and rest," Heineroth countermanded. "Now sit-down boy, we've only got one bloody horse left, and its lame. From now on, we carry our own packs."

"What does Yeti meat taste like, Dad?" Tryrial asked, eyeing the fallen animals around them, their blood steaming in the cool winter air.

Heineroth gave a short grin, "Pretty goddamn awful, I would imagine, we are best off eating the dead horses, but at least we can get some meat, get some bits on the fire we will eat before we attempt the climb. Pack a fair share though it's at least four days back to that village probably longer now we don't have anything to ride."

Chapter 5

The Tower

Heineroth and William dug a shallow grave for Abrias and gave him a battlefield funeral. William felt the grip of grief clawing at his heart. Abrias had been a true and faithful servant. The small pile of rocks would be all that would mark this man's passing.

After they ate the horses, except for Ailwhyn, very few Aldari could tolerate eating meat, and Ailwhyn was no exception. Even the smell of the cooking animals was repugnant to her.

"It kind of tastes like beef," muttered Tryrial between chewing. "If beef was tough unseasoned and tasted like leather." He spat a mouthful of gristle into the fireplace.

"Don't complain, lad!" Heineroth chewed through a chunk, ripping it apart with his teeth. "It's good enough for a prince," he joked, nodding his head to William, who idly chewed and stared into the fire.

William's hand trembled as he ate; he had almost died and had seen his bodyguard die in front of him. He was having issues with the thought of mortality. Although William had never been shielded from the harsh realities of life, this was the first time he had experienced the death of someone close to him. He had been taken to see executions by Heineroth in the town square, but those were criminals. On this quest they had fought, and he had killed bandits. This was someone he knew and cared for. Heineroth was a veteran of many campaigns against Taros and Rwelvencrest and had seen many people die. Tryrial had been away last year serving on the Taros border towers, the raids had been heavy in the previous year, and he was in no doubt that his old childhood companion had seen compatriots fall. However, this was a first for William. He chewed idly on a bit of sinew.

Ailwhyn looked over and him with concern, "Milord," she asked as she slid from her makeshift seat and sat by her prince. She touched his shoulder, causing him to jump out of his musings. "Let me help," she offered.

He nodded; she touched the side of his head. "*Trofmoc,*" she spoke in the arcane language.

William felt the pain of loss slowly fading from his mind. While he would still miss his bodyguard, he didn't feel the bottomless pit that had been sinking into the depths of his stomach.

He looked at Ailwhyn and gave a grateful smile, "Thank you, Ailwhyn." She turned to return to her seat and was stopped by his hand resting on her shoulder. "I'm sorry about this." His finger touched the iron collar around her neck. "When I'm the electoral prince, things will change," he spoke.

"You know they cannot," Ailwhyn replied. "But I thank you for your kindness," she added with a sombre expression.

"I'm serious. I think the Inquisition has too much control of the empire," he insisted.

"True, but I doubt one prince of the thirteen will make much difference, maybe if more were like you," she mumbled. "I'm sorry for the loss of Abrias." She cast her glance beyond the camp to the small pile of stones that would be the grave of the Arbay bodyguard.

His face hardened. "OK, everyone, we break camp before dusk."

"No bloody dusk in this land," growled Heineroth. "No bloody dawn, no bloody noon; it's always just this grey light."

"Cheer up, Dad," chirped in Tryrial. "Could be worse, you've been on the Rwelvencrest front."

Heineroth shrugged and nodded. "True lad, and pray you never end up there. I wouldn't wish that on my worst enemy... well, maybe the Taros."

Tryrial laughed, "Aha, the difference between Taros and the creatures from Rwelvencrest is Taros soldiers only look dead. The Rwelvencrest creatures are dead."

"Only some of them, lad," Heineroth warned. "Some are very much alive."

William listened to his childhood friend and weapon master talking. "One day, I need to lead troops on those fronts," he thought out loud.

"Still your mouth, boy," snapped Heineroth. "Your father worked fucking hard to keep you away from those places, especially Rwelvencrest. It is a land of nightmares."

"How can I lead my people if I don't know their plight?" William asked earnestly.

"You lead like your father, keep us supplied and ready, and ensure we have allies on our other front." Heineroth stated, "Leadership isn't all about war and fighting, boy, I've taught you how to fight, but Steinhardt should be teaching you how to think." He referred to the court vizier and William's scholarly tutor.

"Steinhardt advised against this expedition," William reminded Heineroth.

Tryrial looked at his prince and his father with mild amusement. "Well, let's face it, we are in the arse end of Gont, eating horse before approaching a magical tower with little more than an old fart, a naïve prince, an Aldari witch and the best shot in the land." He spat another bit of gristle into the fire. "In all honesty, all you needed was me," he boasted.

Heineroth laughed heartedly. "If you had the same skill at arms as you have with your flashing your ego, we wouldn't need the knights."

William allowed himself a smile. Ailwhyn remained silent, nibbling on a bit of bread.

An hour later, before dusk, they broke camp. They travelled light, leaving behind the lame horse and most supplies. It was a tough climb up to the tower, even with footholds carved into the stone, but it was still a long and strenuous climb. Nevertheless, after the yeti ambush, they were cautious and kept their eyes open.

Finally, they reached a broad ledge where the tower's base rested. A light dusting of snow covered the wide shelf, and carved tiles surrounded the entrance. It was much more impressive standing directly below it. It shot up with a smooth, unblemished surface, almost like a stalagmite of pure alabaster marble; at the tower's summit, a mystical blue haze floated in the air. The cloudless sky was marked with waves of this blueish hue. There was no door or seam, no mortared stone as if it had been carved from a single piece of rock. Heineroth was alone in being unimpressed.

"Well, we are here now…" Heineroth mused. "How the fuck do we get in?"

William ignored his arms master's crude language and gestured towards Ailwhyn. She nodded. The young Aldari approached the side of the smooth tower. She raised her hand, palm forward, against the stone.

She began to mumble in the magical language, "*Leasnu.*" Her pale skin deepened red and purple with an invisible internal struggle. Finally, she gasped and slumped to her knees, exhausted, but as she fell, a faint outline of a door appeared, slowly creaking open, leaving a gaping entrance.

Ailwhyn tried to stand but fell to her knees. A blast of icy air burst from within, enveloping the young Aldari. She let out a cry of pain and slumped forward face down. "I'm done, milord," she gasped.

Her glowing green eyes rolled back, and the glow dimmed as consciousness faded. Tryrial was the first to her, propping her head back.

"She's alive, sir," he muttered. "Just unconscious, fuck, she's cold." He pulled his cloak around the small woman.

The gaping entrance displayed the insides of the mysterious tower. This place wasn't safe for them to linger.

"Heineroth, carry her," William ordered.

"Fine," the old man grumbled. He lifted her tiny frame onto one shoulder effortlessly.

Finally, they entered the White Tower of Spine Mountains, the end goal of their long journey. The inside of the tower gave off an ominous white glow. The very walls were emanating light, there was no obvious source, and the apparent conclusion was magic. The breaths of the adventurers crystalised and steamed in the frigid air inside the tower. Their boots were clanking loudly on the hard white stone floors, sending echoes throughout the building. In the centre of the lower floor, a spiral staircase dominated the room. It seemed to go up forever, bisecting it every hundred steps were landings and far, far above them, a blue glow pulsed.

"Nasty," mumbled Heineroth, pulling his bastard sword free with his spare hand, he shifted the young woman he had slung unceremoniously over one shoulder.

"Dad?" asked Tryrial.

"The only way up is those stairs; every landing could be an ambush," he grunted, nodding for his son to prepare.

"Only if they know we are coming," Tryrial spoke.

"Yea, they know." Heineroth stamped his foot on the floor, sending a thunderous echo up the tower's core. William remained silent as the echo faded. He could feel his heart pumping beneath his breastplate, it wasn't fear but excitement, anticipation, and anxiety he didn't know.

"We should ascend to the top." William spoke, "If this is indeed the cause of this eternal winter, then the cause will be at the top where that light is."

Tryrial led the way up the stairs, his crossbow at the ready. Stepping carefully up the spiral stairs, he scanned each landing, looking for any danger.

"Clear," he puffed as they scaled the tenth landing.

"Can we take a breath?" Tryrial asked, looking down and wishing he hadn't as the plunging height caused his head to swim.

Heineroth was a healthy man of some years but struggled with the stairs. Carrying the young Aldari, as light as she was, was taxing his old bones.

"Yea, it looks like we are about halfway." Heineroth looked up and down. The blue glow from above them was brighter now and much closer.

The old soldier laid the Haulfin down and slumped his back against a pillar. He gasped for breath. "Tryrial, keep a watch." He waved his hand, pulling his flask out he took a long draw.

"Easy with that old man." His son chuckled. "You'll be no used to us drunk."

"It will take more than a few sups to affect me."

They rested for several minutes. They could hear the wind swirling around the tower outside, but riding in the wind, a soft, echoing voice was dancing on the edge of hearing. The words weren't eligible. William looked up, wondering what was going on up there.

"It's the old language of my people." Ailwhyn sat up, stirring from her rest.

"You're awake." William was startled. "What are they saying?" he asked.

Ailwhyn paused, listening to the wind. "I cannot make it out clearly. It sounds like a prayer to an old god," she mumbled as she pulled herself up, and William passed her his flask. She accepted it, drinking the cool water, soothing her throat. "I cannot go on." She gasped after she had sated her thirst.

"We can wait a few moments longer," William cautioned, taking his flask back.

"You don't have the time," she warned, looking up. "I can feel the energy of the tower building. Something is happening."

"Heineroth, you stay with Ailwhyn, Tryrial with me," William ordered, pulling himself to his feet, his armour clanking as he readied himself. The old warrior wheezed, nodding to his son and gave them a half salute. He listened keenly as they ascended, their heavy footsteps clanging higher and higher.

It was another ten flights, and the two came to the tower's summit. The stairs ended at a large blue-white door. The air was awash with a strange blue

58

light. The two warriors pushed open the door and entered a beautifully decorated and furnished chamber. As they crossed the threshold, the chanting stopped. The room was white, with shelves upon shelves surrounding the walls. In the centre of the room was a glowing blue orb. This had been the source of the magical light. It emanated a feeling of cold and power. Streams of steam fell from this orb, covering the base of its pedestal with a falling mist.

This must be the cause of the winter, William thought to himself. A large four-poster bed dominated the room. An ornate pine desk was tucked in one corner and in the other was a small, caged beast that chittered with agitation. It looked like something between a bat and a human. It had pasty pale-grey skin. It chattered and scratched against the bars of its cell as the two warriors approached.

"Welcome," spoke a voice. It was a short figure, garbed in a simple blue robe. The figure had been standing next to the orb, but William and Tryrial hadn't seen him. The young Haulfin man regarded them coldly. He was pale with bright glowing-blue eyes, with the fine delicate features and the long, pointed ears of the Aldari. "You have finally come." He spoke calmly, "The humans that come to rape and steal the rest of our lands."

"I have come to free my lands from this torment," William spoke with a quiver. This Haulfin had an aura of frost swirling around him, whipping at his robes.

The short Aldari remained unmoved. "Your lands?" The Aldari released a cold laugh that sent a shiver down their spine. "Your lands!" His voice rose angrily, "The Spine Mountains were Aldari lands long before humans had come down from the trees! We owned this land before you enslaved and slaughtered us! Now all we seek to retake a small part of this world that you stole from us, and you seek to kill us for wanting to live."

"You are choking the life out of the twelve towns," Tryrial growled back as he lifted his crossbow aimed at the Aldari. "End this now!" Tryrial fired his bolt towards the Aldari. The bolt sailed across the room, striking the Aldari in the chest. As the bolt struck, it shattered into a thousand shards with a dazzling white flash. The Haulfin gave a hollow laugh.

"Fool," the Haulfin muttered. Then, pulling his hands from his robe, he cast them in Tryrial's direction. "*Ezilatsyrc!*" the Aldari bellowed out.

Tryrial was hit square in the chest with a flurry of frost that enveloped him. He screamed in blood-curdling agony as the ice encircled entrapping him. The scream stopped abruptly as the air hardened. His body remained standing, frozen ridged, his face a twisted tableau of the agony of his last moments.

William watched aghast as his closest friend was entombed in a frozen grave. Tryrial's body slowly toppled forward, hitting the ground and shattering, casting small fragments across the room.

"You animal," screamed William as he made to lunge forward.

"One more step, and you will suffer the same fate!" The blue clad Haulfin warned, pointing his finger at the young prince. "Your kind has driven my people from this land, slaughtered us in the thousands, desecrated our temples, usurped the teachings of the real gods, replacing it with some unseen forgery that you use as an excuse to torment and enslave us." The blue robed Haulfin walked calmly around the edge of the room to the caged beast in the corner. The small animal chittered as its master approached the Haulfin and rested his hand on the cage.

William seethed in anger, but his mind held him in check. He speculated if he could defeat this Haulfin who could freeze him with a mere gesture. "You must stop this." He ordered, "Your unnatural acts are bringing death to this land."

Drumming his slender fingers along the top of the cage, the Haulfin turned and gave the young man a sideways smile. "You call this unnatural, but this is the power of the real gods." The Haulfin clicked his fingers and muttered, "*Yrrulf.*" Snow began to fall inside the room. William looked around, startled.

"This is the most natural thing ever; these are the celestial grace that formed this world. My goddess, Aurialla of the winter's night, grants me these powers. They are as old as the world." His eyes narrowed at William. "I will grant you a chance to leave. You will tell your humans to leave these lands and never return, or I will freeze them all to death," the Haulfin demanded.

William gasped. There was no way they could get the twelve towns to leave. This man asked the impossible. Not to mention he wouldn't be held to ransom by this Haulfin. The blue, glowing orb in the centre of the room pulsed, it sent a chill through the young man, yet the Haulfin was unaffected by this wave of cold.

Then a thought struck William. "We cannot leave this land," William spoke slowly. "The time of Haulfin and witchcraft is done." He moved with a flash and swung his sword, the blade crashing into the orb. As the sword cut into the crystalline surface, the sphere exploded! The Haulfin screamed as the shattered shards ruptured across the room. The Aldari recoiled backwards, covering his face from the razor-sharp fragments. A chilling blast of ice cold energy struck William sending the young prince spiralling to the ground, his sword scattering across the floor encased in ice.

The tower's walls darkened, the power fading away the magic of the building was broken. The tower shuddered as icy dust fell from the ceiling. The chamber fell deathly silent and plunged into darkness. The light from the Aldari's blue eyes dimly lit the room.

"You will die for this," The Haulfin snarled viciously. He wrenched open the cage beside him. The chattering beast flew out like a savage arrow of fury streaking across the room at William. The young prince instinctively pulled his right arm to protect his face. The creature was a blaze of claws and fangs. It cannoned into William's arm, screeching as it clawed and snapped at William. The beast savaged at him, desperate to get its fangs into William's head and neck, ripping through the mail armour, its fangs slicing through the metal like a hot knife through lard. He cried in agony as the claws rendered flesh. William worked through the torment, thrust his free hand up, and grasped the creature around its neck. His fingers clenched tightly, twisting and with a sickening crack, he snapped the creature's neck.

Struggling to his feet, his right arm hung limply, bleeding freely at his side. William groped for his weapon, fingers fumbling it in the dark as he grasped awkwardly in his left hand. He blinked into the darkness, searching for the light from the Aldari's eyes. All that was left was inky blackness. The young prince swung his sword behind him at a slight noise. The sword whistled harmlessly through the air.

"You may have broken the spell and damaged the dominion of the tower," The Aldari's voice came resonating from around the room. "But I will see you dead, then I will rise again," the voice threatened.

A brilliant-green light exploded into the room, blinding William. Struggled to shield his eyes, he clamped his hand over his face. William waved his sword in a vain effort to defend himself from the attack. His blade found nothing. William braced for the pain of the onslaught he thought was coming. Instead, there was a sound of gasping and gurgling. William blinked, trying to restore his vision. The glaring light faded to a soft green glow. Ailwhyn held her hand aloft, filling the room with the light source. In front of her, Heineroth stood over the body of the fallen Haulfin. Heineroth's, bloodied sword in hand. William smiled and breathed a sigh of relief.

Heineroth glanced around the room.

"Tryrial?" he asked. "Where's my boy?" he asked William.

William looked down at the shattered remains of ice on the floor, chunks of flesh, bone, twisted metal, and cloth was thawing, pooling in a mess across half of the room. He shook his head. "I'm so sorry," William spoke earnestly.

Heineroth looked confused for a moment, then finally understood. His face dropped in horror, but twelve robed figures shimmered, appearing, and surrounding them before he could react. They were dressed in a bright mix of colours, a mixture of Haulfin races. They looked at the fallen body of the Aldari, then glared at the three surviving members of William's expedition.

They spoke in unison, "You have killed our brother, the host to Aurialla, she will live again, but Malek will not."

"Who are you!" demanded William backing up next to Heineroth and Ailwhyn.

They spoke again as one, "We are the eternal pantheon. We are the hosts of the gods," their voices castigating.

"You are going to kill us?" Heineroth barked through gritted teeth; he stepped forward, his sword ready.

Three of the robed Haulfin broke from the rest, one dressed in brilliant white, an Aldari, another in midnight black robe was a strange reptilian humanoid, the last wore a shimmering silver robe that looked like an androgynous human with slightly strange but beautiful features.

The silver robe spoke first. "No, our sister Aurialla sought to drive you from these lands, but she didn't seek to destroy you." The silver one looked directly at Ailwhyn and bowed her head slightly, and she then addressed William, "Your kind have pushed our believers beyond the realms, into barren lands, and yet you still drive us further. We still live. You have systematically hunted and slaughtered our hosts. We still exist. We are of the old religion."

"The old religion died out centuries ago," William countered. "It's time is over."

The reptilian in the dark robes raised his voice with a hiss. "The ancient religion is the land's magic; it is the spirit that unites all things, and it will endure far beyond the time of mankind."

The Aldari in white raised his hand to silence the other. "We did not condone this action of our sister, but we did not prevent it either. We are content to outlive the time of men and your empire. We cannot promise all of us will be of the same mind, but we." She cast her gaze to the black-dressed reptile and the sliver-robed stranger. "We all agree on this. There will be no efforts from any of us to hurt your kind.

"You travel with one of our brethren," the silver robe spoke, looking at Ailwhyn. She still slumped against Heineroth, struggling to hold herself up. "You stand with those that would enslave our kind?" he asked softly addressing her.

Ailwhyn stepped forward, wobbling. "They are not like that, not these men."

She drew herself up. "True, there are others that would kill or enslave us, but not these men. I believe them to be good people."

"They are humans, humans are destructive, they are corrupt." The black-robed reptile hissed, "If the council had listened, we would never have helped them and left them to destroy each other."

"But we did help them," spoke the one in silver. It lifted one hand to silence the others. "Now, we must decide what to do with these three."

"You want to try to kill us like your brethren killed my son! Then try!" Heineroth stepped forward, his face a mixture of anguish and anger as he brandished his sword.

"It has not been decided," spoke the creature in silver, raising its hands in peace. "I am sorry for the loss you have suffered, but this is the way of things."

There was chatter from the rest of the robed figures behind the three. The silver-clad figure looked to its right and left at the two figures in white and black who glared at each other for a long, tense moment. Finally, the figure in black nodded in consent as if some unheard debate was going on.

"It is decided," the silver spoke. "We will allow you to leave, and we will encourage our followers not to interfere with your lands, but we do ask of one thing."

William looked at the silver-clad figure. He felt so fatigued. Every bone in his body was crying out for rest. "What is your request?"

"We ask only that you act kindly to those whom you call Haulfin."

"We cannot agree to anything they ask Will!" Heineroth mumbled through clenched teeth.

Ailwhyn placed her hand on William's wounded arm, "We aren't the demons they are made out to be. They are just seeking peace just like you do," Ailwhyn pleaded.

William felt her fingers against the wound. The bleeding from his injured arm slowed and then stopped with the soft green glow of her magic. She slumped forward exhausted, and William caught her small frame.

The young prince then spoke slowly and calmly, "I need your assurance that your kind will not endanger the lands of Gont again."

"We will not endanger." It waved its hand at the figures behind. "I cannot speak for the others."

"The others?" William questioned.

They spoke one after another,

"We are the council of the pantheon."

"We are the voices of the gods."

"We are not all of our kind."

"For there are many, many more of us."

"Would you be responsible for the actions of every one of your citizens?"

William thought on it for a moment. It had a point. Then the white-clad woman began to speak again. Its voice had a gentle sing-song quality to it.

"This is why we only ask that you, William Nadrog of Gont, be kind to our people. We know you cannot speak for all of your kind, but you will be the ruler of your land. You will allow those Haulfin kept in chains to be free. You will emancipate our people."

"I understand. Then you will leave my lands?" he asked.

It spoke. "We were never here." The Haulfin faded into smoke, leaving the chamber empty save the three.

"Foul magic," cursed Heineroth. He sadly looked down at the remains of his son. Tears began to fall from the old soldier's wrinkled face as he wept freely.

Ailwhyn and William stood beside the old man, not knowing what to do or say. The white tower of the north was silent save the weeping of the old man.

Outside the white tower, the winds had died with the shattering of the orb of power. The blizzard surrounding the spire faded, finally allowing the snow to rest for the first time in many years. A silver moon shone, casting its brilliant white light across the landscape. The stars twinkled in the deep blue night sky.

Chapter 6

The Summer

Six months had passed since the victorious adventurers had returned through town. Weary, wounded, mourning but victorious. The word of their victory quickly spread across the twelve towns. From Holum to Telegos to Reikhaven, the fall of the curse was met with celebrations by all. Except for one man, Raouf. Since news of the victory had spread, the harsh unnatural eternal winter was already fading. Raouf knew what this meant. The sands of time were now seeping through the hourglass as the seasons would march on to spring and then summer, and his debt would be due.

As the days grew brighter, Raouf's mood darkened. Robin first noticed the change in his father. The young lad often accompanied Raouf when hunting or logging. Although Raouf was usually jovial and good-natured, he usually enjoyed joking and playing with his favoured son. However, since the weather was warming, he walked in sullen silence. Robin couldn't fathom the reason for his father's dark mood, but despite this dour demeanour, Robin was always happy to spend time with Raouf.

Jacob attended lessons with the hag daily on the cliff overlooking the bay of Havendale. The young boy's sharp mind grasped the principles and teachings of the witch much faster than Maganwyth felt was natural. This child unnerved her with both his capacity and ravenous craving for knowledge. Jacob had already mastered most of her regular potions, tinctures, tonics, and remedies, and she brewed for her patients in the village, and he was absorbing her books at an alarming rate. Maganwyth would be loath to admit it, but Baron Von Rikton had been right. She would tutor this young man. He was too exceptional to be left to his own devices. Without her training, this young child could become a danger to all around him.

Jacob's time at home hadn't become any easier since the winter had passed. His father's mood darkened, and he took it out on his least favourite, twisted child. Erin, his mother, was a little kinder. She tried but struggled to connect with her smallest child, but Erin doated on Robin, who, in turn, would still be a dominating force in Jacob's life. So, Jacob spent as much time as possible in the witch's hovel despite its often foul and gross smell. A small benefit of this was the long hike every day up to the shack vastly improved Jacob's health.

The family fell into a routine, every morning before dawn, Robin and Raouf would depart on a hunt, Jacob would get up absconding breakfast to traverse the cliff to Maganwyth, and Erin would tend to the house. The huntsmen would return by early afternoon, Jacob would come down from his palace of knowledge before sunset, and they would dine together in the evening.

The quaint little family began a pleasant routine. Every day Jacob would sneak away along the winding path to the hag's hovel. Raouf would go hunting with Robin accompanying him most days. Erin would tend to the house. Then, in the afternoon, the intrepid hunters would return, and just as the sun was setting, Jacob would creep back into the house, trying to avoid his parents' attention.

One evening inside their little cottage, the fire hissed, crackled and popped, filling the family home with a balminess of warmth. Jacob sat in an overstuffed straw chair in the corner. He was absorbed in a thick leather-bound book that he had 'borrowed' from the hag. Raouf had Robin on his knees, and he was in a lighter mood today, enjoying the closeness of his family. Robin was laughing as Raouf bounced him up and down. Erin was tending to the family meal. Raouf and Robin's daily hunt had been good, and Robin had even brought down a brace of snow rabbits with his sling. Logging and hunting had become more manageable as winter finally moved to spring and spring into summer. The land frozen for so long was now giving way to melting snow, and patches of grass were spouting across the land. There were even sapling trees starting to grow. It was almost as if nature had been waiting for the winter to end as much as the citizens of the twelve towns.

"Hungry, Mum!" Robin called as he and Raouf roughhoused.

"A few moments, dear," Erin brushed her hair behind her ears as she dished up the rabbit strew. "Go wash your hands… you too Jacob," she added as an afterthought remembering her other son. Robin ran off to the basin. Jacob grudgingly put the book away. Unlike the books in the temple, although less elegantly written, often scrawled in sometimes illegible handwriting, these books gave much more detail about the world before the empire. They also talked about the gods of the old religion without bias. He slid the text into a small corner of the living room he had made his own. It was his little cubby. It contained some interesting stones, plants he had found, a journal he had practised writing, and now this borrowed book.

Jacob joined his brother at the basin, raising himself on his tiptoes to reach it. His brother got behind and lifted him, digging his hands painfully into Jacob's ribs. Jacob winced but allowed himself to be hoisted up so he could soak his hands.

"Still too short, Jacob," Robin teased.

The family congregated at the table and began their evening dinner.

"Are you all right, my love?" Erin asked, her brow furrowing as her husband stared into the distance.

"Hmf?" He looked around as if breaking himself out of thought. "Yes, sorry, this is delicious, by the way."

"You've not touched it yet, Father." Jacob glared at him, Jacob's' head and arms having to rest high up on the table to reach his food. Jacob knew he was small for his age, which made his life more challenging. Jacob had barely touched his food either. Jacob had never had much of an appetite. He took a small mouthful, chewing on a chunk of rabbit flesh. It rolled around in his mouth before he forced himself to swallow the fatty meat. Beside him, his brother was hungrily and messily shovelling spoonful after spoonful into his mouth, barely chewing.

Raouf pondered his dish for a long moment before pushing it away while Erin continued to talk to her husband and Robin. Jacob's mind was elsewhere. He was going through the passages of his books, expanding his mind with every page consumed. He had learned very little more about his supposed 'gift'. He still couldn't shake the image of the beautiful Aldari maiden's face out of his mind. She had introduced him to his gift and had shown him the potential powers when she had healed his arm. He had learned in the books that gifts differ from person to person. They were supposed 'gifts' from old gods they granted powers. He couldn't understand what his power was and wasn't sure he even had power; he felt the Aldari must have been mistaken. The only gift he had was his mind. He pushed his unfinished bowl away from him. Robin snatched the stew and started wolfing it into his gullet.

"Dad," Robin asked, spraying food across the table. "Would you take me into the woods tomorrow to hunt?"

Raouf returned from his reflections. "Sorry, Robin, I'm heading across the pass towards Woodvale. I've hired dogs and a sleigh, and I'll stay in Woodvale for the night. We have to get a wood shipment out. Now the Everlong sea is thawing. It's time for us to get back on our feet." He smiled across at his wife. Although the last few years had been very harsh, this was the first year they had put a decent amount of food on the table and had more than enough wood to sell.

"Can I get down?" Jacob asked his mother.

"No more books tonight," Erin stated. "You will get ready for bed."

"Aw, Mum," complained Robin. "I wanted to play a game with Dad!"

"You can have one game before bed with your dad." She conceded, "But Jacob, you get ready for bed."

The two got ready while Erin and Raouf chatted at the table for a while longer. Then, as the two young boys came out of their room, the hushed conversation stopped abruptly.

"OK, come on, my little knight!" Raouf smiled and gave Robin a big hug. "One game."

Robin stuck his tongue out at Jacob as he was lifted by his dad.

Jacob looked at the dice on the table. It was a simple sailor's game. Each player rolled five dice hidden by cups and had to guess how many dice of one side were between the player's rolls. Jacob already knew he could beat both his brother and father, which would only make his brother feel bad and wouldn't make Jacob feel any better.

"No, brother, you play with Father," Jacob spoke sarcastically and walked over to the chair by the fire where his mother sat. Jacob sat alongside Erin and gazed into the fire while the clatter of dice rolls, the crackle of the fire, and the occasional whoops of joy from his brother filled the room.

"I told you to go to bed," Erin berated Jacob.

"Just a moment, please," Jacob asked, holding his mother's hand. She relented.

Soon the children were in bed, and Robin was quickly snoring. Jacob contemplated the ceiling. His mind was racing with so much to think about. He could hear his parents talking in hushed tones. His mother's voice occasionally rose to allow him to catch snippets.

"You can't go!" Erin's voice urged.

"I have to," replied the lower, deeper voice of Raouf. "It was the deal."

"You shouldn't have made that deal," she spoke, her voice rising in anger.

"It was the deal or you and the children. I couldn't let you or them die."

"How long will you be gone?" Erin insisted. "We cannot live without you. I'm not strong enough," she pleaded.

"I don't know, but he said I would have to serve him when summer ended. Summer is nearly over." Raouf nodded. "I have to hold good to my word."

"He's not even called for you. Perhaps he's forgotten," Erin pleaded.

Raouf seemed to sigh. "Perhaps, my love, eight years is a long time."

They continued to talk, but their voices had dropped, and Jacob couldn't hear any more. He didn't know what they were talking about, but it sounded like his father was being forced to leave somewhere. He closed his eyes and tried to sleep. Sleep finally came, his dreams filled with words of the books in his head.

Raouf and Erin stayed awake, talking well into the night before retiring to their room to make love. The couple embraced each other passionately. Their love had not faded since the first time they had laid together. Yet, if any one moment in time anchored their souls together, it was this moment as if they knew that this might be the last time, they encompassed one another. With the door closed, every pretence fell away, every kiss had a raw intensity breathing fast, heart rates faster. Their naked skins grinding softly together, like the finest silk, every thrust coaxing moans of passion. Their bodies writhing together. The lovemaking was over too soon, and they slumbered entwined in each other's dreams.

The following day, before the sun had crested the Everlong Sea to the east, Raouf had already commenced his journey. His precious lumber and logs were on the back of the sleigh, securely mounted in gigantic bundles. The dozen enormous sleigh dogs panted as they dragged the sledge through what little remained of the snow. The crunch of gravel ground under the runners and the added weight of the logs made it arduous work. It was usually a day journey to Woodvale, but Raouf would be lucky to get there before sundown despite his early start.

He drove the dogs forward as they crushed through the tracks and trails in the pine, spruce, and fir-mixed forest. Around the evergreen trees, tufts of flowers and grass sprouted up through the now thin snow. By midday, as the sun rose, the air became stifling, and the slurry of snow had melted away. Raouf's winter cloak stuffed at the back of the sleigh forgotten, he rode in just a short-sleeved leather jerkin. A flight of butterflies crossed the path of the dogs, one of the dogs snapping at them playfully. Raouf pulled the reigns hard, keeping them on course.

He mounted a sharp dip on the trail, and the gravel ended, leaving a slick quagmire of mud and water. Raouf cursed and drew the dogs to a halt. In the last ten years, they had gotten so used to using dog sleighs that horses had fallen out of favour. However, he would have given anything to have a good old ox cart or horse-drawn carriage. He dismounted the sleigh and moved up to the lead dog. He pulled a little dried meat from a pouch and gave each animal a small treat. They panted heavily. The hot weather and the heavy load had taken their toll on the giant dogs.

He pulled the lead reign and started leading the way, the heavy sleigh grinding through the mire. Raouf complained to himself as he and the dogs struggled through the bog. It was slow going, but they would make it. After an hour's struggle, Raouf and the dogs took a rest. He was covered to his waist in thick mud, the dogs wholly covered. He gave them another treat and idly scratched one of their ears while he took a small meal that Erin had wrapped for him. In his small lunch pouch, there was a wrapped-up purple viola flower. It was beautiful. He twisted his fingers, looking at the flower and smiling to himself. Viola usually only flowered in the winter months. She must have been saving this since winter.

A twisted voice Spoke. "Don't get up." This startled Raouf. Even though he had only met the creature once, he recognised the shambled form of Vlad, the hunchback crooked man lumbered through the woods till reaching the edge of the treeline, where he stood watching Raouf and the dogs. "It is time," the twisted man slurred.

"Please," Raouf beseeched, looking at the man. "I must make this delivery. My family will need the money if I'm gone for some time."

Ivan paused; he slumped down in a lump sitting next to one of the trees out of the quagmire path, his uneven legs dangling off the verge. Ivan seemed to cock his head to one side, listening to something. "The baron Von Rikton is a considerate person." Ivan drooled. "He will allow you to make your delivery, and then you will come with me."

Raouf breathed a sigh of relief. He looked at the logs. The money from this should last a few months. If Erin could get some work in the tavern or with one of the artisans, it would last even longer.

"But my master's patience is not eternal." Vlad continued, "You better start moving. You will have until nightfall. Then we must be on our way to Rwelvencrest."

Raouf looked shocked. While not an educated man, Raouf had learned a little about the lands away from the twelve towns. Rwelvencrest was spoken of as a land of nightmares outside the realm of the empire.

"Hurry up," Ivan snapped. "Not everything you've heard of my master's lands is true. You will be an honoured servant like myself. I will see you in Woodvale, be there before midnight," Ivan commanded the shambles of a man, then struggled to his feet and lumbered through the forest.

Raouf struggled hard, but he arrived at Woodvale not long after sundown. He had made good time considering. The chill of the evening was setting in. He reached the wood merchant's house and had to rouse him with loud knocks before the man opened and accepted the delivery. He arranged for the payment to be sent to his wife along with a short seven-word message.

'It is time. I love you.

Raouf'.

Once the transaction was complete, he was startled to find Ivan behind him. He hadn't heard the warped man approach, but he had just appeared, standing less than two feet away.

"Come," The hunchback ordered. Raouf cast one last look towards the mountains towards Havendale before following Ivan.

Erin waited a day and a night, frantic for any word of her husband. Finally, a week after Raouf's disappearance, she received the money and the message. Erin sobbed as she read her husband's short words. Try as she might, she could get no word on what had happened to her husband. The last person to see him had been the wood merchant in Woodvale. After that, nothing. No one had news of him travelling the roads or boarding a boat headed across the sea towards Gont. Raouf had vanished without a trace.

Chapter 7

The Family

At first, Erin waited every day on the veranda of their home for Raouf to return. She stared down the path from the village to their cottage, thinking that every figure she saw walking towards the hut was Raouf, only to be hit by another wave of grief when it wasn't. Robin often joined his mother in waiting, constantly asking when his father was coming home, compounding the misery.

Jacob kept up his routine of attending teachings on the top of the cliff with Maganwyth, endeavouring to learn as much as possible. Her initial instructions were menial. She had the young, frail child cleaning her house while she sat smoking her long pipe, occasionally pointing out spots he missed. Jacob quickly understood the trick. She used him to clean her home to avoid teaching him anything of substance. Jacob caught on to this and started planning. He would finish his chores faster, leaving more time in the day when Maganwyth had no choice but to teach the child.

Autumn's chilling winds picked up, howling across Havendale bay. Erin was forced to retreat from her outside perch. She sat opposite the front door on her chair, waiting in suspense for the door to open and Raouf to enter. She held out this hope for many months, every noise she heard sparked a brief hope it was him, but it never was. There were times her longing overwhelmed her driving her to anger. Unfortunately, the anger masked the sadness. She could only hold so much melancholy before it would boil out. When this happened, she would unleash it on Jacob.

Jacob spent increased time up the cliff at the witch's house to avoid this abuse. The more time he spent there, the faster he completed the menial tasks and got to the substantive teaching.

Robin tried to cheer his mother up but was also keenly feeling the loss of Raouf. Erin continued to lie to him, saying that he had been called away for work and would be back anytime. Erin wasn't sure if the lies were to protect her son or for herself. The lies grew more elaborate as time went on. Jacob never believed these lies, he knew his father was gone, possibly forever, yet he couldn't bring himself to feel any loss. The lack of sorrow disturbed the young boy much more than the loss of his father.

The weeks dragged into months, the months into a year. The seasons passed over the small fishing village, and as Erin's hope faded, so did her health. The once young and vibrant woman became bedbound for days on end. Letting the cottage fall into ruin.

The precious little money they had, dwindled, and times became hard. Erin struggled to get to work. Her lethargic and morose attitude hindered any activities. She was able to scrape together a merger living, but it was never sufficient to keep the boys and her sustained. Robin and Jacob were often seen in torn and worn clothes. Luckily for Robin, being the loveable character he was, he was often brought in by kindly neighbours to 'join them for a meal'. Jacob, however, never received such charity. They barely survived on the goodwill of neighbours and the good grace Raouf had built in the village.

The seasons had returned to their usual pattern, spring, summer, autumn, and winter. Throughout all, Robin grew at an unprecedented rate, outstripping any clothes his mother could cobble together. As a result, he often wore britches several inches too short, with patches roughly stitched on. Jacob grew a little as well, but unlike his brother growing into a tall, strapping young man, Jacob was ungainly and awkward.

Throughout the winter, Robin spent his days hunting rabbits and bringing home what lumber he could carry; it was barely enough to keep them alive. When spring finally came, he could gain a few extra coins helping other woodsmen and dock hands in their duties. As a strapping, eager lad, his help was always readily accepted.

Jacob was too frail to help in the same way. Instead, he tried to earn his keep in another way. His lessons with Maganwyth were starting to pay off. He was now preparing most of her remedies and delivering them to town. Maganwyth allowed him to keep some of the payment, which he passed on to his family.

These few coins managed to keep food on the table, logs in the fire, and clothes on their backs, but this was surviving, not living. Times were tricky, though. Erin shrank back from any activities outside her house, stopped attending the temple, and retreated into herself, spending long hours in bed.

Jacob was torn between his duties on the cliff and ensuring he and his brother had clean clothes and a meal on the table. At nine years old, this was a heavy burden.

Robin found the burden equally hard. He would often hunt for hours just to bring home a single cony. As the winter set in a year and a half after their father's disappearance, the family had descended into abject poverty. Often, they sat in a dark, dank empty house with a cold hearth and empty bellies. The winter of the twins' tenth year was the hardest for the family. Raouf's favours had been used up, the rabbits were scarce, and Jacob was the only one still bringing in any money to the family, but it was only pittance. Erin went down sick that winter and didn't rise from her bed till spring was firmly established. Her children tended to her needs as best they could. It was only by the fortunes of fate due to seasonal flu, Jacob became busy, rushing curatives across the town, scraping a few additional coins.

One evening they sat around the family table. It was rabbit stew for dinner; again, there was no money for vegetables or roughage. The stew was boiled rabbit with a few herbs that Jacob had scavenged. It was watery, greasy and without much meat in it. Being hungry is a pang that adults can endure for a few days at least. It is uncomfortable, yet adults can accept these things and continue if it is required when abstaining for the sake of the needs of their children. Erin refrained from eating as much as she could. She was seeing the hunger of her children, especially Robin. Often days would go by when no food was available, so they were even grateful for this little sustenance.

Robin struggled and strived to catch rabbits, but his belly grumbled every day he would come back barehanded. Birel, the tavern owner's daughter, would occasionally slip away from her overprotective mother, having stolen food from the inn and smuggled it to Robin; she did this in the wild hope of an amorous return of her affection. Robin would accept the food, often his hunger outweighing his awareness of his family's needs and consume it there and then in ravenous appetite. Birel would watch the large boy devour the entire pie knowing full well the punishment she would receive, and gladly accept, to see the smile on his molten jam-glazed face. The young girl never understood the harm she was causing, taking away the desperation of the breadwinner of the family and leaving Jacob and Erin to starve.

However, with renewed fortitude, the young Robin would have the energy to go hunting again to bring something home for dinner.

Jacob sat in Maganwyth's hut, his stomach growling. The hag made a 'stew' that simmered with a bluish-green smoke. Maganwyth muttered to herself as she chucked various objects into the cauldron. Jacob saw a rat skull bobbing on the surface. Despite the horrific smell and ingredients, Jacob still yearned with hunger, unable to look away from the pot. The old witch could see the boy drooling.

"You want some?" she inquired, perplexed; most people would baulk at her meals.

"It has been four days since I ate." Jacob apologised, "I would eat anything right now."

Maganwyth paused. She wasn't given moments of empathy. No one had ever given Maganwyth any in her life. Instead, she had been branded a heretic, persecuted as a witch and a monster. However, she felt some pangs of sympathy as she watched her young prodigy, the frail little child, hungrily eyeing her dinner.

"Go home," she snapped. "Don't come back till you've eaten and can think right," she ordered.

The young Jacob looked crestfallen but knew the witch was correct. He couldn't think of anything except the gnawing hunger in his belly.

"I'm not sure how long that will be," Jacob apologised.

"It could be tomorrow or next week but go home. Your belly rumblings are disturbing me, and you are drooling into my dinner," Maganwyth cackled.

The frail young child pulled himself up with all the dignity he could muster and left.

Maganwyth started an argument with herself. *Oh, so you are going to do this?'* one side sarcastically spoke with the voice of her eldest sister.

"Yes, the boy needs it," she countered angrily at the voice in her head.

There was a time we would have eaten the boy.

"Times change."

Maganwyth waved angrily at the fake spirits in her head and gazed deep into her cauldron that held her rat stew. Maganwyth didn't have a gift and couldn't call upon the powers from within. She had had to work for her abilities since she was young; Maganwyth had made deals and bargains with powers beyond her for her capabilities. She investigated the bubbling crock and cast her hand above it.

"Ecnanetsus, wno ym pu evig I taht rof, thginot tae ot elba eb ot ylimaf sih dna Jacob rof ekil dluow I." As she mumbled the incantation of nonsensical words, she drew upon the energy of the pot in front, it hissed and bubbled and evaporated in a puff of smoke leaving only an empty cauldron. This was the basic magic rule for anyone who didn't have the gift; anything given had to be taken. Unfortunately, there was only so much energy in the world, and it needed balance, and her spell had consumed dinner in payment. It had exhausted the old hag, and she retired to bed, hungry. Maganwyth knew she could eat tomorrow, but what she had given would possibly be life or death for the young boy. She felt a moment of pride.

Winter was setting in deep. It wasn't the magical winter brought on by powers but the natural flow of the seasons. Jacob trudged through the thick snow. As hard as he had worked for the hag, she had cast him out with an empty belly. A bitterness of resentment to her indifference to his plight stung hard.

His head was low as he forced his way down the snow-laden track toward home. He didn't notice his brother sneaking up on him.

His brother, renewed by the vigour of having consumed an entire huntsman's pie, a gift from Birel, had been out hunting again. It had been a beautiful pork pie made with seasoned pork, layered with tender chicken breast, and topped with a sage and onion stuffing. The warmth still sat in his belly as he waited by the rabbit holes, his sling in hand. He saw his brother leaving the hag's hovel and had been about to leave his hunting spot when not one, but three rabbits hopped out of the hole! They then remained frozen as if caught in some invisible snare. Robin slung a pellet at the largest of the three. Then as if guided by some invisible force, the bullet bounced off the head of the first, second and third rabbit. Robin was stunned. He had achieved more in the last few moments than he had managed in the previous week. He held three rabbits aloft. They were each a plump specimen. Tonight, they would feast!

It had been an odd course of events for the young Robin. He had spotted the warrant a few weeks ago and staked it out. It was a prominent coven of rabbits, but they had been timid, especially after he had missed his first shot. His patience and skill had finally paid off! He snapped their necks quickly and bound them together.

"Hey, Jac!" he cried out, throwing a snowball at his brother. Unfortunately, the compacted snow caught Jacob unaware, heavily impacting his young brother's face. The colliding snowball knocked Jacob from his feet, and his nose bearing the brunt of the blow, started to bleed. He pushed himself up from the ice looking for the cause of this assault. But, instead, he saw his brother, standing with a beaming smile, holding several dead rabbits in one hand.

Robin called out, "Jac, you'll never guess what!" His voice echoed around the cliffs.

Jacob pulled himself out of the snow and dusted himself off. "You caught some rabbit?" he asked, sarcasm dripping from his every word as he could see the three dead Leporidae slung over his brother's shoulder.

Robin beamed with pride. "Yea, three with one shot!" he boasted.

"Good," Jacob uttered. "We need to make them last," he pragmatically stated.

"Huh?" Robin strained to hear.

"We need to…" Jacob paused. "Oh, forget it." He gave in in frustration.

Robin ran deftly through the snow towards his brother. "Sorry," he apologised. "Couldn't hear you," he explained, jabbing his brother in the ribs.

Jacob looked at his brother for a long moment. His thoughts were in turmoil. His brother was the key to their survival, and his own impotence frustrated him. He hated how much his brother would always be the one who saved the family. But at the same time, he was delighted with the food.

The coneys provided dinner for over a week. Robin's tale of his skill lasted a lot longer. Little was known of the part Maganwyth had to play.

Through the winter, Maganwyth performed the trick several times. Robin was ignorant of this blessing, but Jacob began to suspect mystical play was involved, especially when Robin brought home a wild hog, which had apparently stumbled off the cliff, landing right beside the young boy.

The family survived the winter, but surviving is vastly different from living. Erin's depression slowly consumed her. She retreated from life and her sons. Erin's children had been forced to assume many of her duties, most of which were thrust upon Jacob, who took them on with little complaint.

Why do you look after this child and his family? the imaginary voice of her older sister asked Maganwyth.

The old hag stomped around her place, trying to ignore the voices in her head. They had become a constant nuisance over the winter. Maganwyth didn't know if she was losing her mind or if it was something else.

"I'm doing what your master asked. I'm teaching him," Maganwyth countered to herself.

The voices were not placated. You could let him die... it would be better for all of us if he died.

"Shut up," she snapped to herself.

You aren't teaching him to use his gift, the voice accused.

Maganwyth clamped her hands to her temple, trying to block out the voices. Behind her, Jacob crept into the hut, oblivious to the argument in the hag's head. He began his daily duties. Maganwyth pushed the voices to the back of her mind. She had left that old life behind her many years ago.

The temptation had been relentless, a young child coming to her hovel daily. Maganwyth remembered a time with her sisters, cooking the bones of children ground into a fine powder mixed into beautiful, delicious, sweet rolls. The taste had been beyond this world. It allowed you to escape into an ecstasy of unrealised dreams. The pull of child flesh was an addiction she fought daily. Maganwyth had managed to give that habit up many years ago. She also knew instinctively anything made from Jacob would be a toxic concoction. Maganwyth had, unlike her sisters, realised many decades ago that devouring children drew anger and hate from the world around you. They had been hounded across the known world for their habits. Maganwyth had tried to persuade her sisters that they could survive without children. They had fought till the coven had been forced to schism. They had been in Havendale when her two sisters left for other lands, leaving Maganwyth behind. Now their voices were rattling inside her brain.

Maganwyth never knew why she relented and took the nine-year-old child as an apprentice. She remembered the baron's threat but knew she was beyond his reach. That poor soul was trapped forever in Rwelvencrest. It must have taken significant effort on his part to appear as an apparition beyond its borders.

In the spring, Jacob and Robin took on more duties to service the community gaining more coin. Jacob continued to learn from Maganwyth. Jacob had learnt all the hag would teach him, just not all she could teach him. His hunger for knowledge had overridden his teacher's ability to teach him about alchemy and medicine. His requests for knowledge were now pushing on the heretical teachings of magic.

Chapter 8

The Capital

The capital city of Altran was the wonder of the empire. It was a sprawling warren of thousands upon thousands of people, all blending in a melting pot. It was both the wide avenues and the narrow backstreets, those who wore the finest attires and those who wore the tattered threads. Cobbled pavements flow as a stream of humanity, and the roads were great rivers of people and carriages. The oldest buildings of Altran have seen millenniums pass, standing in silent witness as weathered edifices stretch toward the heavens. This capital was the seat of power for the empire. The great cathedral to the one true God, second in its glory only to the emperor's palace, dominated the eastern side of Altran. The temple city was a city in a city. A two-mile-wide border encircled the small country of religion. It was an independent country unto itself, bordered by a moat and a massive thick wall that cut it off from the rest of Altran. Inside were hundreds of servants of the one true God, all dedicated to his glory and teachings. Ailwhyn felt very alone. She would have been the only Haulfin inside the temple city. Her kind wasn't tolerated here, not even as servants.

Ailwhyn sat in a small antechamber, waiting. She had been sitting for hours awaiting the return of her master, Sir William Nadrog. She sat in anticipation in the dark room, lit only by a single candelabra. The young Aldari was nervous. Any clergyman that passed her gave her an expression of unbridled disgust. They knew who she was, so they didn't openly say anything, but the looks were constant. Ailwhyn smoothed down her simple dress and plucked at lint that wasn't there.

After their expedition, William had been called to make the two-month-long journey to the capital of the empire, Altran. He had been asked to testify before the church leaders to give them the full recount of his adventure. Heineroth and Ailwhyn had also been questioned.

Ailwhyn's question had been very tough on the young woman. While no physical torture had been used against her, the church and Inquisition had been relentless in their questions. She had been kept without food, water, or sleep and constantly questioned by a stream of Inquisitors, priests, and other clergies for thirty hours. They had her pushed to the brink to reveal any knowledge about a Haulfin plot to take over the north. The Inquisitor general of Gont, Talos Tarsus, had led the questioning in conjunction with his superiors. He had felt slighted that such sorcery had managed to exist in his jurisdiction, and he hadn't been the one to rout it out. The stories of the Haulfin mage able to lock an entire region in eternal winter were a cause of great concern to both the church and the Inquisition. Talos's anger had been vented and directed towards Ailwhyn, but finally, he relented that the young servant to the prince had known nothing. The three had told their story a dozen times to various members of the Inquisition and the church.

It had been relentless for a fortnight; however, it would appear an end was in sight. William was meeting with the archbishop. William and Heineroth were being given a blessing from the head of the church of the one true God, one of the most influential people in the empire. Ailwhyn had been told to wait here. The idea of bringing a Haulfin in front of the archbishop was so blasphemous that it hadn't even been broached.

Ailwhyn jumped as the door creaked open, and a dark figure entered. Ailwhyn recognised him immediately. She had seen the face of Inquisitor Talos in the last two months more than she had ever hoped. The man was always prim and calm, watching the world with cold eyes.

Talos loomed over the young Aldari. He spoke simply, sliding into the pew next to her, facing the opposite wall. "I see they are done with you." He didn't look directly at her. Talos' voice sent chills down Ailwhyn's spine as he began to speak.

She kept her head bowed and nodded at the Inquisitor's statement.

Talos spoke, looking ahead. "You know, you will be the first Haulfin to enter this city in the last four hundred years. There was a time when your kind and ours tried to work together. Humans tried to embrace the Haulfin until you betrayed us."

Ailwhyn remained silent, her mind raced with terror, and her soul was shrinking as she wanted nothing more than to run for the door and escape this man. She had thought she would be dragged out for execution for the last two weeks. This constant terror had drained Ailwhyn. Talos was toying with her when she was so close to her liberty from this nightmare.

Talos continued to speak at length. "When the Haulfin betrayed us, it tore the empire asunder. The Haulfin and the foul magicians nearly destroyed us. Now your kind are still here, walking among us. Some, like yourself, know their place, but most would see us murdered in our beds and for the magic to return to the lands. Personally, I believe all your kind have no place in the civilised empire and that you should all retreat to the savage and wild lands beyond our borders."

"Some of us never got the chance to leave." Ailwhyn didn't know what possessed her to speak up. A moment of madness.

"Ah, it speaks." Talos smiled sardonically. "Yes, you are right. So many thousands of your kind remained within the empire after the Great Purge. At the time, it was thought that the skills and knowledge the Haulfin possessed outweighed the threat you demonstrate."

"I possess no threat, milord." Ailwhyn prayed for this to be over,

"I believe you," Talos lied. "But when we return to Gont, I have a favour to ask." Talos didn't wait for any agreement. "You will let me know of the goings on amongst the Haulfin servants in the castle."

"Like what?" Ailwhyn asked.

"Oh, I don't know, just tell me of anything you hear, there are a lot of servants in the castle, and I suspect not all are as loyal to you." Talos rose from his seat, still not looking at the diminutive Aldari. "In return, I will make sure that you are protected." Talos waited for no response, but he swept from the room, his black cloak trailing behind him. As he pulled the chamber door closed, it blew out the candelabra, plunging the small chamber into darkness.

Ailwhyn could hear her heart beating against her chest, blood rushing through her ears. She tried to still her breathing. Her mind struggled to understand what had just happened. She looked down at her hands as her Aldari eyes adjusted to the pitch black. Her nails had dug into the sweaty palms of her hands. Ailwhyn closed her eyes and stilled her heart and her breathing. The door banged open, startling the Aldari again.

"Bloody hell, it's dark in here." The deep, resonant tones of Heineroth calmed Ailwhyn. "What are you doing sitting in the dark, girl?"

Ailwhyn saw the giant soldier standing in the doorway. He still wore his battered armour, now adorned with a golden symbol of the one true God on his right lapel. Heineroth showed it off.

"They've made us knights of the Order of the Sacred Heart," he beamed.

"What does that mean?" Ailwhyn got up and relit the candelabra.

"Not a bloody thing, just another title for Will and a bit of jewellery for me." Heineroth's grin dropped. "I'm sorry that your efforts weren't recognised, but... You know." He waved his large hands across the room.

"It is fine. I just wish to be gone from this place," Ailwhyn iterated.

"We will be gone soon," Heineroth explained. "We have to attend some fancy shindig at the palace."

"With the emperor?" Ailwhyn gasped, "Surely I will not attend."

"I would have thought not, but Will has asked this favour, you will not be at the head table, but you will be allowed to attend. And as a guest, not a servant." The large man's smile returned. "You will see that the emperor and the church aren't the same."

"You know the emperor?" Ailwhyn asked.

"Met him once." Heineroth nodded. "He seemed an all right man. Anyway, got to get you fitted for a fancy frock, I can pitch up looking like I've just returned from battle, but a woman is supposed to look the part of a lady," Heineroth finished guiding Ailwhyn from the dank, dark chamber.

They left the temple city in a horse-drawn carriage. William wasn't with them. He had been called across the city to attend a duty of the emperor.

Sir William Nadrog of Gont was an excellent subject to his emperor, Leopold of the fifth House of Ulis. He could not refuse his emperor. Not even something so mundane as to give a combat lesson for Leopold's son, Karl.

"Aim higher, Karl," William instructed the youth. "Keep the arrow and the sight in line." A straw target had been set up across the courtyard by the palace stables, and all horses and stable hands had been sent away to avoid the often-errant paths of the young man's arrows.

"There!" Karl grunted as he released his arrow. The arrow sailed across the courtyard, clattering against the cobblestones about a foot to the left of the target.

William did not laugh as his father had when he had practised with Heineroth. He had been shown up many times by Tryrial, his boyhood friend whose skill with archery had reached some renown. William briefly lamented his friend's death. Williams' father, Godwin, had often publicly ridiculed his son's lack of skill with the bow. William was endeavouring not to do the same to this young lad.

Karl shrugged and pulled out another arrow. "I cannot keep it straight." The boy complained, "When I pull the string back, my hands shake."

William nodded, the young boy was slight in stature, and the bow was designed for a full-grown man.

If the blessings of the one true God shone upon the young Karl, he wouldn't ever have to use the skills he was practising. However, you never knew what the future might hold. William Nadrog had known his adventure would garner some recognition to secure his position as the heir prince, but he hadn't expected this level of celebrity. William hoped his days of adventuring were now over. Now he could focus on learning the statecraft he would need to bring a fair, just rule to the princedom of Gont. He allowed his mind to wander towards his homeland.

Karl unleashed another arrow with a loud twang, the bow string clipping the young man's thumb. The quarrel hit the target, but it was askew outside the painted rings.

Applause erupted from above. Karl and William looked up to see the Emperor Leopold clapping. William had never received such praise from his father. The man was a lot more stoic than Karl's father.

Karl's face reddened with embarrassment at his father's praise. "It was useless, Father," he called up. "I'm hopeless at this!"

The emperor was a brawny man dressed in the finery of his station. Although, unlike some rulers of the princedoms, he didn't flaunt his wealth. His cloak was made from the finest vermilion. Several bejewelled rings of office adorned his fingers, catching the morning light. Under this finery was a sturdy breastplate, with a finely crafted rapier at his hip. He looked down with kindness on his son. The young Karl didn't have Leopold's martial prowess, but Karl was already twice the statesman Leopold had been at his age. Next to the emperor stood the Inquisitor General of Gont, Talos Tarsus. Rumour had it he was making plays on the position to become the next Grand Inquisitor, head of the Inquisition for the church of the one true God. Talos looked flushed. He had just arrived from the Temple City with urgent news for the emperor.

Despite what William had seen, he still prayed to the one true God but found it extremely hard to trust any clergy member. He had spent the last several weeks in the company of Talos and people like him, being grilled constantly about his adventure. William had come to despise all the members of the priesthood. He felt that the church should be separated from the court, but they played politics with the best, twisting the policies of the princedoms to suit their will. Talos Tarsus, a man who had been a minor member of the Inquisition only a few years ago, was now standing next to the ruler of the empire and had been whispering in the ruler's ear over the last two weeks. Talos's face was unreadable. No one could be as coolheaded and even-tempered as Talos seemed to be all the time.

"William, please do it again," Karl asked, offering William the bow.

William was being shown off like a prize horse. William studied the bow, relieving it from Karl's fingers. It was an extremely well-designed bow, the best that could be bought. It was inlaid with gold filigree along the shaft. It was a fine weapon, far better than William's own bow.

William drew the bow and released the arrow without looking at the target. It sailed across the courtyard. His missile sailed across the quad and split the centre of the target.

Two years ago, when William had embarked with Heineroth and Tryrial to find the source of the eternal winter, he had been a poor marksman. He had been forced to learn the hard way. Their adventure had been beset by multitudes of bandits, beasts, and many others. Shooting at targets didn't mean your death if you missed. You can take a break, wait for your next round and relax. When you are in the depth of battle, you shoot true, or you die. William would never be as elegant in battle as a man trained in the noble practising houses, but he was still alive. Heineroth and Tryrial, along with his bodyguard Abrias and Ailwhyn, had ensured he survived. Unfortunately, too many of the people he had travelled with in his quest were not, Tryrial and Abrias. Their bodies lay forgotten in the Spine Mountains many leagues away.

"Amazing!" exclaimed the young heir to the empire as he clapped. The emperor said nothing but gave William a smile and nod of approval. Then, he left the balcony, returning to the affairs of state. He had many pressing engagements before the celebration tonight, and all called upon his attention.

On the travels across Gont, William was constantly trained in the long bow. He remembered the tight string against his face, the shaking arrowhead resting on his thumb. Breathing out before releasing. Following the arrow with your eye till it strikes the target. Although, as a youth, he had always wrestled with killing animals, now he had taken more lives than he could count. His innocence had long since vanished.

"One more time, then we practice with the sword," William encouraged the young man.

Karl unleashed another arrow across the courtyard. Unfortunately, this arrow shattered against the cobblestones. "I fear I shall never be the archer you are, Sir William."

The heir prince knelt beside the young emperor-to-be. "Time and practice, but a sharp mind will serve you much better than a true shot." He patted the youth on his shoulder. "Now, go put your padding on," he instructed.

While the young man changed into the protective equipment as a carriage rolled into the courtyard. Its large wooden wheels clatter across the cobblestones towards the stables. The massive form of Heineroth stepped out and saw Karl struggling into his padded vest.

"You teaching the lad?" the grizzled soldier asked, crossing the courtyard.

"I was asked to give young Karl a few pointers." William shook hands with his mentor.

"How about I give him a few passes." Heineroth grinned.

"Careful," laughed William. "This could be the next emperor one day."

"A few scars never hurt a lad," Heineroth jested he would never do anything to endanger the young emperor's life.

An array of fine sabres were being brought out by the servants. Heineroth went to look for one that would match his size. Ailwhyn approached Sir William. He looked down at her. "Are you all right?" he addressed the young lady with concern.

"I'll be fine." Ailwhyn nodded. "It was a bit rough."

"Sorry I had to leave you there," William apologised. "I was summoned by our emperor for these lessons."

"I understand." Ailwhyn nodded. "When do we leave for home?" she urged.

William observed as the duel commenced. Heineroth was going easy on the lad; the giant soldier was a veteran warrior of many campaigns. But, while Karl was a better swordsman than an archer, he was no match for Heineroth.

Heineroth didn't fight with a sabre often. It was a weapon of nobility, but he was proficient with its use. Instead, his preferred martial weapon was his double-handed bastard sword, where he could put his significant weight behind each thrust.

In the enormous man's hands, the rapier looked like a toothpick. Yet he effortlessly deflected the youthful heir to the throne's blows.

"That's it, Karl, up and cover, then riposte, aim for my chest," Heineroth encouraged. "Now parry, a little quicker, that's it."

The young man's padding already bore the marks of a dozen blows, where Heineroth struck its stuffing sprouting out. The two danced back and forth. Karl was sweating profusely, but Heineroth still looked calm, hardly putting in an effort. William remembered the lessons he had been given in his youth. Heineroth had been his mentor back then and hadn't been nearly as forgiving as he was to Karl. Nevertheless, those lessons had saved his life many times.

"I was told I need to dress up," Ailwhyn muttered to William.

"Yes, one of the emperor's daughters has lent you a dress." William smiled. "Although I suspect she won't ask for it back." He waved his hand towards some servants. "The lady Ailwhyn Evensong requires attendance."

The human servants exchanged glances—their personal views of the Haulfin in the face of an honoured guest's instructions. The two approached slowly. "Milord?" one asked.

"By order of his monarch, Ailwhyn has been provided residence in the east wing. A noble of House Queen is attending to her. Please see her to her apartments," William said severely to the two retainers.

After much fuss, the two servants guided Ailwhyn through the palace to her chambers. At first, she thought there had been some mistake. The accommodation was a small apartment. It comprised several rooms, a bedchamber, a greeting area, a washroom, and two dressing rooms. Ailwhyn looked at the servants, who gave her a withering look of disgust. As they opened the doors, a toned, battle-dressed young woman sat in her greeting area, busying herself with some needlepoint.

"Ah, you are here finally," she snorted with annoyance. She tossed the needlepoint to one side with frustration. "Now, let's look at you." She flicked her long, dark hair over her shoulder and looked the Aldari up and down.

The door shut behind her leaving her alone with this lady. The woman wasn't dressed like any of the women of the court Ailwhyn had seen. Instead, she wore leather armour, a form-fitting leather bodice, and a thigh-length studded leather skirt cut into strips to allow freedom of movement. In addition, she had metal studded thigh-length leather boots covering her powerful legs. Her hair, like Ailwhyn's, was jet-black, but it wasn't straight; it flowed around her shoulders like a lion's mane. She sprang to her feet and beckoned to the Haulfin.

"Are you simple?" she asked.

Ailwhyn shook her head, stunned by this woman who was so different from anyone she had ever met. This strange woman seemed like a panther coiled to strike at a moment's notice, with a catlike grace that exuded confidence.

"You sure? Right, we've got to get you ready for this ludicrous event, and since most of the noble," She spat the word on the floor. "Ladies are squeamish when it comes to your kind, the duty falls to me." The brash woman crossed the room, looming over Ailwhyn with a crooked smile.

"Who... who are you?" Ailwhyn stammered.

"Catrin Queen," The woman introduced herself. "Not to be mistaken for an actual queen." She smirked, walking around Ailwhyn. "Although I am the youngest daughter of Darla Queen, the mother of Vantoth."

Vantoth was the only matriarchal princedom in the empire. The title of 'Mother' was the sovereign leader of Vantoth, a title that would be passed from mother to daughter or niece. The Vantoth women were known to be vicious and proud warriors. Many times, throughout history, other princedoms had tried to make claims on Vantoth lands, and all had regretted it.

It shared a border with Gont but had maintained a peaceful relationship with its western neighbour. Vantoth, like Gont, also shared a boundary with Rwelvencrest. The two nations served as the protectors of the empire against the horrors of that dark realm.

"You are a princess!" Ailwhyn seemed genuinely shocked.

"No," Catrin corrected, sniggering, tossing her wild mane of ebony hair back. "My oldest sister is. I'm free from that crap. Now, hurry up! You look like you need a week to soak. I've drawn your bath."

Ailwhyn hesitated. Few humans would spend time with a Haulfin, and none so casually as this woman. "Aren't you worried about associating with my kind?"

Catrin smiled crookedly. "I've worked with Aldari and other Haulfin before. I know you aren't any different from us."

"Worked with?" Ailwhyn questioned.

"A story for another time," Catrin dismissed. "Next, I'll teach you how to put on your dress. It's a torture device designed by the Inquisition," she joked. "Go, get yourself cleaned up, girl."

"You know you are gorgeous." Catrin mused as she brushed Ailwhyn's hair. "Your hair is a bird's nest of knots, and that bath was black when you got out of it. I take it you don't get to wash often. Your eyes are amazing, and you look barely in your teens!" Catrin yanked on a stubborn knot in the Aldari's hair, enticing a yelp of pain. "How old are you?" Catrin asked bluntly.

"Seventy," Ailwhyn responded. "They weren't this kind in the Temple City," she mumbled under her breath.

"Yea, the priests are a bunch of old farts." Catrin continued to attack Ailwhyn's hair. "In Vantoth, we have mostly priestesses. They are still a bunch of old farts. Seventy! Bloody hellfire! I'll be thankful if I look as good as you at that age. I don't look as good as you do now!" Catrin continued to ramble on, jumping from conversation to conversation.

"What of your men?" Ailwhyn asked curiously. "Do they not have a problem with this?"

Catrin grinned again, "Nope, some, it's not like we block men from a position of power, but it has just been found that Vantoth women were always more capable than any man."

Catrin was very talkative, filling the air with the conversation even when there was no response from the more taciturn Ailwhyn. She described in detail what was expected tonight, who would be there, and who was liaising with whom. Catrin seemed to know all the court scandals yet not be involved in any. The sun had fallen over the capital by the time Catrin had finished preparing Ailwhyn.

I look ridiculous, Ailwhyn thought as she observed herself in the floor-length mirror.

Catrin was trying to hold back her amusement as the Aldari twisted to catch images of herself, trying to see if there was a flattering angle. The dress was bright pink, with voluminous puffed-out shoulders framing a slender rhinestone bodice that Ailwhyn barely filled. The dress then plumed out towards the floor, ruffles and pink everywhere, and an elaborate pink feather boa formed part of the dress. Catrin had styled Ailwhyn's hair into ringlets that framed her face. Ailwhyn looked desperately across at Catrin.

"I cannot wear this!" Ailwhyn exclaimed in horror.

Catrin nodded. "I will admit I'm glad I don't have to dress like that."

Ailwhyn looked up, shocked. "I've taken all your time. How will you get ready?"

"I am ready." She smirked, "Like the men we are allowed to wear our battle vestiges." Catrin explained with a smile, "Not that we choose to attend functions like this usually."

"So, I don't suppose you have a spare set of armour I could borrow?" Ailwhyn's hope was dashed as Catrin shook her head with a grin.

"This will serve you well." Catrin explained, "You look like a child attending her first party. If you wore armour, you would be seen as threatening. So just enjoy it, but one last thing." Catrin disappeared and returned with another lump of pink frills.

"What do I do with that?" Ailwhyn asked, adjusting the uncomfortable bodice.

"It's for your head." Catrin explained, "We will tuck your ears into it. Not much we can do about your eyes, although the veil will hide them a little." She placed the pink monstrosity on top of Ailwhyn's head.

"There!" Catrin stepped back... "You look..." The warrioress paused. "Well, you look preposterous, but at least no one will want to hang you for being a Haulfin."

Ailwhyn looked at herself in the mirror. She looked like an adolescent being put on display. This was the most elaborate outfit she had ever worn. She would have been happier attending this event in her usual white smock, serving tables. Now she was set to meet her most challenging adversary, the nobility.

Chapter 9

The Ball

The celebration was grand, even by the emperor's standards. Sir William sat at the right hand of the emperor's as guest of honour. Talos sat to William's right. The rest of the table consisted of pompous high-ranking nobles with an overinflated sense of self-importance.

The food was lavish. Dishes from across the empire had been prepared. Royalty from almost every princedom was in attendance. William felt overwhelmed by the pomp and ceremony. A lesser noble, Weasley Weston of the first family of Wayrest in Gont, sat opposite. He was idly regaling the prince with stories from back home. William tried to pay attention to his old friend but struggled to stop glancing at Ailwhyn. She sat at a secondary table. It was a more incredible honour than the young Haulfin knew. She had been seated to the right of Karl, the heir emperor.

William felt he knew what Ailwhyn would be thinking. She had been placed at the children's table. She was many times the sum of the ages of the rest of her table. The children's gossip would be tedious. While she looked like a young child, Ailwhyn had been in this world for several decades. Despite how she might feel about her apparel, William thought she looked terrific; she was dressed in similar pageantry as the other girls around the table. Karl was holding court in a parody of his father. Many potential suitors to the heir emperor were indignant about the young man's attention to the Haulfin woman.

"You will need to watch that," Talos spoke across William to the emperor. "He cannot get attached to her kind."

William felt slighted but knew better than to respond.

"Let the young lad enjoy himself," Emperor Leopold disagreed. "She leaves tomorrow with you to Gont. It is likely he will never see her again."

"The draw of some of the Haulfin is intoxicating. They will poison the minds of the youth." Talos continued, "We shouldn't allow them here in the empire, let alone within your son's presence!"

William had had enough of Talos's poison. He whispered to the emperor, "She has earned her place here. She should have been awarded the same distinction as Heineroth and I." He pointed to his arms master, who sat amongst the emperor's soldiers, loudly recounting them with over embellished stories of past victories.

"You don't reward a demon for betraying its kind," Talos countered. "She is an abomination and should be treated as such."

"Then you know nothing of her or her kind," William disagreed.

"By your words, the plague of ice that infected our princedom was of her kind. Haulfin shouldn't be trusted and never can be," Talos challenged.

A fine-looking woman who sat across the table raised her voice. "They are animals," the woman agreed with the Inquisitor.

It was Margaret Nadrog, William's aunt, by marriage to his father's brother. She was a slender, beautifully dressed woman who caught many eyes in the court. Although William hadn't seen her in several years, she was from the southern princedom of Albian. She didn't often visit Gont. However, she had no qualms about her opinion of what she felt was a backwater savage land. Her hand reached across the table and touched Talos's elbow.

"You are so right," she continued. "They shouldn't be allowed to share the same lands as us. They should go back to where they belong."

"Most of them come from around here," William commented.

The emperor listened but said nothing as they bickered. Instead, he cast his look to his left, where his wife sat and rolled his eyes.

"Stop your bickering," he finally ordered. "This is a night of celebration. The young prince William here has vanquished a foe of the empire, and we are all safe once more."

Talos spoke with sycophantic tones. "Agreed, my lord. But we need to remain vigilant to the next Haulfin threat."

The Emperor Leopold spoke. "I think this young lady has shown she is no threat." The music had started, and he watched as his son offered his hand to Ailwhyn for a dance. Karl led Ailwhyn to the floor. The emperor frowned.

Talos leaned across. "See how she tries to seduce the next ruler?"

William ignored the Inquisitor's provocation. He spoke, rising from his seat. "If you will excuse me, my lord." William crossed to where Ailwhyn and Karl were dancing. William gave a curt nod to Ailwhyn, who was being flung uncomfortably around the ballroom by the young man.

Ailwhyn leaned into the heir emperor's ear and whispered something. Karl turned and looked at Sir William, who smiled and nodded at the heir. Karl broke their dance and bowed to Ailwhyn kissing the back of her hand. The bodyguards of the heir to the emperor relaxed a little as the young man returned to his seat. William approached the cloud of pink that was Ailwhyn. Taking Karl's place. The young Aldari looked up at him with a smile of genuine affection. She was out of breath from Karl's vigorous dancing.

"Hello," she greeted.

"You look… interesting tonight." William grinned back, taking her hand to lead her in the dance.

"I was told that armour was not an option," she jested, jeering at William's clothes.

"Not for most people." William smiled. "Are you doing, OK?"

"I would rather be cleaning chamber pots in Trindon."

"You will be moved to my personal retinue when we return," William promised as they moved around the ballroom. "You will only be required to attend me."

"Will that not draw ire?" she asked earnestly.

"I don't think it's too strange to ask a woman who saved my life many times to become my personal servant."

"Even a Haulfin?" she probed.

"I don't think even my father would object to that."

"I need to tell you something," Ailwhyn urged. "Talos has ordered me to spy on the rest of the household staff of Gont."

"Follow his orders," William advised. "Just be selective," he cautioned.

Ailwhyn nodded, and for a moment, she allowed herself to rest against the chest of William. Here she felt safe, protected against the persecutions of her kind. She let her mind float away from the crowded ballroom filled with nobles, her ridiculous dress, and the scrutiny around her. She got lost the moment held in the arms of the man she trusted and loved.

Across the room, Catrin watched and smirked to herself. The poor girl had no idea that William was interested in her only as a friend. She watched the show with bemused interest. She was broken out of her observation when a shaggy Rhineland soldier slumped over her shoulder. The heavy spirits on his breath stung her nostrils as his hands snaked down to her breasts. Rhinelander's weren't known for their subtly. She reached around and caressed the whiskers on his beard as his hands explored her breasts. Her hands snaked through his hair, and then abruptly, she clenched it tightly and wrenched his face into her oncoming fist, breaking his nose. The drunken man sagged backwards out cold. She glanced over her shoulder as the heavily framed man clanged on the floor.

Heineroth admired her handiwork. "Couldn't' take his drink, I see?" He gave the warrioress a slap on the back. Catrin rounded on the bear of a man at first, ready for another fight. Instead, Heineroth proffered a flagon of ale.

"Drink?" he asked.

She accepted the drink and quaffed it back. "Thanks," she replied wiping her lips with the back of her hand.

A fast friendship formed between the two as they started exchanging war stories, each trying to outdo the other with more embellished tales of heroism on the Rwelvencrest front.

The party continued throughout the night. Ailwhyn was one of the first to leave, making her escape as soon as the opportunity presented itself. Heineroth remained to talk with Catrin till the wee hours of the morning, entertaining the other soldiers of the empire who gathered around them.

"You ever faced a lycanthrope?" Heineroth challenged. "Size of horses, with jaws that will swallow you whole."

"Pah, only if they catch you," Catrin teased. "If you are smart, you keep out of their reach." She punched his arm. "Worse things than wolves come out of those forests."

"Ever been inside?" Heineroth challenged, slurring his words.

"Once." Catrin's face took on a sombre tone. "It isn't an experience I care to repeat."

"Aye, lass," Heineroth agreed. The two seasoned veterans bashed their cups and toasted their fallen brethren.

William woke late the following morning. His head ached from too much wine the night before. He groaned as he turned over in bed, memories flooding back. He must have been approached by more than a dozen minor noble women, all seeking to garner his affection. Weasley Weston, possibly the only noble he wanted to spend time with, had been occupied for the rest of the evening. William had seen Talos doing the political circuit. Any senior member of the clergy and noble of note Talos had brushed shoulders with. William was quickly coming to despise the man.

"Wake up, lad," Heineroth's gruff voice echoed through the heir prince's chamber. "If you can't take the ale, you should avoid it." His heavy shod foot thumped against William's bed. "We are leaving in half an hour."

William rolled over, holding the luxurious pillows against his ears. "Can we not wait till tomorrow?" he pleaded.

"Not if we plan to be on time." Heineroth grinned at his friend's discomfort. "At best, it is forty days to reach Gont. But unfortunately, it will likely be twice that. Your father sent word; they are celebrating your return home on the anniversary of your victory."

"It's already been a year?" William asked.

"Roughly." Heineroth shrugged. "Doesn't feel like it," he conceded. "Come on, lad."

***

The journey back was long and arduous. Talos had managed to organise a whole regiment of Inquisitorial soldiers to guard them on the excursion. Talos rode at the head of their convoy in the centre of the procession. Ailwhyn, by Sir William's decree, rode in one of the carriages. William and Heineroth rode side by side in the middle. Several of the Inquisition that rode along with them carried strange handheld fireworks to fire a projectile across a battlefield. While destructive, they had little accuracy and required an infant's operating skills. Heineroth had asked for a demonstration, and after it had misfired several times, he decreed them inferior to a good old-fashioned bow.

It took two months along the roads towards Gont for the large convoy to arrive, they passed through less than savoury lands where they had to travel cautiously, and they finally arrived at the close of spring.

"Hurry, Hurry! We're going to be late! We won't find a place to see him!" an overly eager young child exclaimed, pushing through the crowds of nobles.

Today was widely anticipated in the Gontish capital city of Trindon, the return of the heir prince! Cheerfulness vibrated in the air. Minor nobles across

Gont and beyond had come to witness the dual celebration, the anniversary of the prince's victory in the north and his return to Gont.

Vendors lined the streets as the wealthy merchants and nobles gathered on this soon-to-be sweltering, scorching day. Children laughed and joked, each jockeying for a position at the front of the precession. The town guards stood in honour, keeping the main precession clear for the prince's return. Bunting hung from every house along the main road, tiny flags flying together on the late spring day.

It was a year ago since he had defeated the evil Haulfin mage plaguing the north with foul magics. William was heralded as a hero by the church and Inquisition in wiping out this foetid menace. The common man and noble alike shared and often overembellished the prince's foray into the north.

The grand prince, Godwin Nadrog, and his wife looked down at the parade from the castle. Prince Godwin was an ancient gruff man well past his prime. Nevertheless, the tales of his son's exploits had warmed his heart. He was proud of the man his son was growing into, not that he would ever tell him. Talos Tarsus, the Inquisitor general of Gont, joined the old prince. He had ridden ahead of the convoy to give the word of William's arrival.

"Looks to be a fine day, milord," Talos addressed the prince.

The grand prince nodded. "Good." His head nodded for a few moments, and a confused look passed across his face.

"Sorry, what did you say, Talos?"

Talos noticed the prince's distraction. It had been happening increasingly. The old man would forget who he was speaking to, use the wrong names and sometimes wander in the castle after dark. Talos repeated himself.

"Ah yes, good day, fine day." The grand prince's wife took his hand and stroked it, calming the flustered prince.

"Come, dear, let's take a seat," she suggested, guiding her husband to his chair. As he passed, Talos gave a curt nod to the old prince, and then he looked down at the crowd. His wife would be down there right now with their son. Talos scanned the public, wondering if he could catch a glimpse of them. He had been away for a long while.

Despite the long journey and the two-month break since the last event, William approached this one with even less gusto. William had found he had little love for the pomp and ceremony. He was heralded with dragon head banners and confetti as the conquering hero over the Haulfin menace. However, William never felt such isolation as he rode down the main road through the parade. He caught a glimpse of the people's reaction to Ailwhyn, who rode at his side. A rotten apple was tossed from the crowd. It sailed past Ailwhyn, impacting the boardwalk, exploding, spraying maggots and apple flesh. William called the parade to a halt.

"Who threw that!" he demanded, his voice filled with anger, "This woman is a hero!" He turned to the crowd bringing his horse alongside Ailwhyn's. "An attack against her is an attack against me!" His eyes flashed with anger.

Talos watched from the balcony of the castle and observed William. This young heir prince had fallen too far. He protected the lesser races. He didn't understand the threat they presented to the princedom and the empire. Also, Talos suspected his passions ran towards the same sex, which wasn't suitable for bringing about a stable lineage. Talos watched the procession. This prince wouldn't' do as the next ruler of Gont. Despite his journey's challenges and experience with the Haulfin mage in the tower, he had grown too weak. Talos turned and looked at Godwin's brother. The man was a fat lecherous slob. However, he had always made his allegiances clear; Renwalt Nadrog was perhaps the better future ruler of Gont.

Chapter 10

The Vila

The twins had turned fourteen years old last winter, it had taken five more years of continuous probing before Maganwyth had finally relented to teach Jacob magic.

"You are keeping things from me." Jacob closed the codex he had been reading and looked up at the witch. He had been pursuing this knowledge for a long time, and Maganwyth had finally run out of excuses. "You know things you keep from me about my gift."

Maganwyth sat in the corner, puffing on her pipe, her feet on a small stool. Her twisted, knotted feet emitted foul dampness that filled the hovel, causing anyone who was not used to the acrid stench's eyes to water. "It's for your own good boy," she repeated, then spat on the floor.

"I'm wise enough to decide what is for my own good." The young man straightened himself up from the table, tidying the books. He had become the housekeeper for the old hag. Her hovel was neater than it had in years despite Maganwyth constantly making a mess trying to keep Jacob occupied. However, Jacob had been unforgiving in his pursuit of knowledge.

"Aye, you are smart young lad, but it takes a lifetime to have wisdom." Maganwyth grinned a toothless smile, she had been palming the boy off for ages, and now she was out of excuses. If she had been honest with herself, she would have delayed obeying Baron Von Rikton's orders forever. But the voices of her sisters in her head had been relentless. She had borne the curse for four years before she relented.

"OK, what would you like to know." She sighed. It had been like this for several years, Jacob constantly pushing. "It's going to be about that bloody Haulfin again, isn't it?" she grumbled.

Jacob nodded. "About the gift, she told me about."

Maganwyth sighed, she had fought this battle with Jacob many times, and she had been considering teaching the young lad about his gifts for a while.

Her phantom sisters urged her daily, and she was confident the boy hosted one of the greater old gods. She really didn't want to open that vein of power. An influential person can make their will known, but those with the blessing of an old god burned like a fire across history. This boy's mind was too sharp. He knew too much, more than scholars twenty years his senior. He had gained more knowledge readily in the last six years than she had managed to learn during the previous hundred. *Admittedly the boy had a good teacher,* she thought to herself proudly.

She started slowly, "You know there was a time when magic was rife in the empire."

"When the Haulfin and the humans lived in harmony," Jacob stated.

"Not just the Haulfin magic, but mostly, as some can live for thousands of years and have time to learn," she mumbled, sucking on her pipe and smacking her lips. "The old gods have always preferred to put their gifts to the longer-lived races, like the Aldari, but it does happen that a human, like yourself, or other races will be gifted. I always suspected it brought about the jealousy of the humans and why they chased the Haulfin away, but the old gods were always strange things, but they all loved the Aldari." The smoke from her pipe filled the room as she waved a hand; images began to form in the blue tobacco smoke. This was magic. In the last six years, Maganwyth had never shown magic in front of Jacob so blatantly, he had always suspected she had powers, but now he could see it with his own eyes.

"The old gods have existed since the beginning of our world and maybe well before. They are not beings like you or me but are aspects of the earth. Anyone sharing their body with one of these gods assumes a bit of their god's personality, becoming far more a part of themselves in the bargain." She paused and waved her hand at the smoke, the image of an Aldari dressed in blue robes hunched over a glowing orb.

"This was Malek," she explained. "He was the host to a goddess who lived here in the Spine Mountains until a couple of years ago, his goddess was Aurelia, she was much worshipped in this region many years ago she was the goddess of the frost."

"The winter goddess?" Jacob asked. "Was it he who caused the long winter?"

Maganwyth smiled. "You are smart, too bloody smart." She nodded. "Yes, it was him. He wanted to drive the humans from these lands and make a haven for Haulfin, I suppose." She waved her hand again. This showed Malek again, a bastard sword thrust through his body. "You've met his murderers." She waved her hand again. Jacob then saw himself and his brother five years ago in the Travellers Rest, standing in front of the Haulfin, the prince and the others. "The powers of the gods vary greatly, there are more gods than we know, but some of the 'greater' ones make themselves known and even enjoy the worship of us mortals."

She waved her hand again, and it began showing temples and churches around the empire. "Once all of these had a gifted priest." She waved her hand again. "Then the Inquisition came, while the powers of the gods were great, the use of their gifts drain those who use them until finally the fay kind were driven from the empire."

"They still live," Jacob stated he had moved to sit near the witch. "Scattered throughout of the empire."

"Some within the empire, most outside. Those in the empire are kept at the church's tolerance for their skills and knowledge. Any that possess the gift are executed just as you would be."

"But the Aldari who healed me?" Jacob interrupted.

"I'm sure she has kept her gifts hidden, and only those she travelled with knew of her secret if it were to come out…" Maganwyth ran a finger across her throat, then knocked the tobacco out of her pipe and placed it on her side table.

She groaned as she pushed herself to her feet. "This is the lesson you must learn before ever trying to use your gift. You must never let it be known." She waved her hand, walking through the images hanging in the air, and the smoke disappeared. "Will you be able to keep it secret?"

Jacob nodded; he was eager to learn. He thrust to the back of his mind how difficult it would be to keep his abilities hidden.

"Not your brother, mother, or anyone. No one must know. Once they know, they will forever mistrust you," Maganwyth warned.

Jacob nodded again.

"Then we begin," she declared. "You need to calm your mind first. Tough for you, I know. Your bloody head is constantly thinking."

Jacob reached into himself, drowning out the sounds of the fire and of Maganwyth's laboured breathing and the foul smell of the tobacco that hung in the air. In his mind's eye, he could see a faint flicker of light in his mind.

The radiance glistened and twinkled, but it was impossible to grasp or hold. Jacob tried to calm his breathing, resting his mind. He could hear Maganwyth speaking, but she seemed distant and far away.

"Raise your hand and concentrate on the fire in your mind," she explained, leaning forward and looking at the young boy. In Jacob's mind, the light flickered, and as he tried to mentally reach out and touch it, it shied away. Finally, Jacob, hearing Maganwyths' instructions, raised his hand.

"Now repeat after me," she ordered. She then spoke some unknown words. Their form and phrase seemed to dance in Jacob's mind as he tried to mimic them. He struggled to cling to those words as they appeared to run from his memory as he reached for them, his mouth working to form the lexes. They were alive in his mind, dancing, moving, changing. The twinkle in his mind flickered, flared and grew into blazing bright light. He outstretched his fingers towards the pipe. The fire in his mind consumed itself in a moment. Maganwyths pipe wobbled. Then was still. Jacob slumped on all fours to the ground, exhausted. The light in his mind dwindled and died, leaving it black.

Maganwyth looked impressed. "That was good," she encouraged, in a rare moment of support. The young man gasped for breath. He struggled to get to his feet. "Easy boy," she laughed. "It's like using a muscle. It needs practice. While your brother builds his physical body, you must build this one." She tapped the side of her head.

"But I didn't do anything," Jacob complained.

"You made my pipe shake." She picked it up, shaking it at the boy. "It was more than I managed my first time. Did you think you would move mountains on your first attempt?" she accused as she stuffed her pipe. "You should come and try again tomorrow, but don't practice outside this hut," she warned. "And you still need to be learning medicine, now bugger off, I need to shit. Tomorrow, I'll teach you about the other forms of magic, not just those blessed by gods," she finished.

With that, Jacob was released for the day. He was glad to be out of the hut. The smell of fresh air was bracing. He had been in the cloistered hovel for several hours. He had felt something move through him even if he couldn't see the pipe sway, but it had been too exhausting to do anything more than move a pipe. He needed to practise. The first steps in Jacob's magic-learning had just been taken.

Across the town, Robin was getting in trouble. To Robin, it seemed like that was all he ever managed to do. He ran as quickly as he could. His accomplice, the tavern owner's twelve-year-old daughter, Birel, had already been caught by her father. Gregor, her father, shouted across the town square at the retreating Robin.

Robin clutched his prize in his arms. Six freshly baked sweet rolls burned his chest as he ran. Robin did feel a pang of regret for Birel being caught. He had planned to share them with her, well, one of them. Birel had allowed Robin to sneak into the tavern's kitchen through the back door. She had shown him where the sweet rolls were cooking. Robin had now made it beyond the village square and reached the docks. He hid in the bustle of the fishermen and dock hands. A smell of fresh fish lingered in the air as the angry calls of his name faded in the distance. Robin ducked between two warehouses off the main street, pausing for breath.

Smiling to himself, Robin opened his tunic, his chest was pink from where the hot pastries had burned his skin, but he had his prizes. He pulled one out and bit into it, immediately burning his mouth with the molten sugar glaze. It seared itself to the roof of his mouth. He chomped away hungrily despite the pain.

"Oi, Robin!" Called one of the dockhands spotting him down the alley. Robin scrambled to his feet.

"Oh, Herod!" he laughed, his face blushing guiltily, spraying crumbs as he spoke.

"You've been stealing Eyias' sweets again!" Herod mocked the boy. "You know one day Gregor is going to catch you and tan your hide!"

Robin swallowed. "He'll never catch me," the young lad giggled before hearing the reply. Robin ran off, not stopping till he reached home. Robin arrived just in time to see Jacob at the door.

"Jacob!" he called out, smiling as he ran up to his brother. With a cheeky grin, he pulled out one of the rolls and threw it hard to Jacob's face.

"Don't tell Mum," Robin implored, giving his brother a painful nudge in the ribs. As Jacob knelt to retrieve the fallen pastry.

Jacob accepted the sweet roll and thanked his brother. "Don't let mother catch you with those," Jacob warned. "She'll send you right back to Gregor."

Robin nodded, stuffing a second roll into his mouth. Jacob plucked off a small section of the treat and ate it.

"Are you getting young Birel in trouble again?" Jacob asked, referring to Gregor's daughter.

Robin blushed. He did feel guilty for that. "She knew the risks, but yea, I'll make it up to her."

"She is sweet on you, brother, don't abuse that," Jacob cautioned. They stood side by side, looking towards the village and the sea beyond it, both eating their stolen goods.

It was late summer now. Soon the cold clasp of winter would be returning. "Did you manage to catch any game today?" Jacob asked, changing the subject.

Robin winced. "No, but we still have a bit left over from yesterday. I'll try again tomorrow; I'm getting better with Dad's old bow."

"You used to be able to bring in lots of rabbits with your sling."

"I'm hoping to get a deer or stag one day. Not many rabbits around these days." Robin smiled at his brother. "Distract Mum, and I'll hide the rolls in our room."

Jacob sighed. He opened the door. Their mother didn't need to be distracted. She sat staring at the fire. She clutched a shirt of Raouf's in one hand, and tears fell from her eyes. As the boys entered, she made a half-hearted attempt to wipe her eyes. Jacob pushed Robin towards their room and moved to his mother's side. He ran his slender fingers over her hair and soothed her.

"Are you thinking about him?" he asked her. She nodded, trembling in his arms. It had been over six years since their father disappeared. Jacob had come to terms with his father's loss, even his brother's hope had finally faded. The twins' recollections of their father had begun to fade. However, their mother endured anguish every day. The old hag had suggested a few things for Jacob to try to help her but had also said there was no remedy for a shattered heart. Jacob reached into his tunic and pulled out a small vial he tried to press into Erin's hand.

"No," she mumbled. "I don't like how it makes me feel. I feel numb when I take it," she argued.

Jacob nodded. He knew the reason. The tincture would do that, rock rose, clematis, impatiens, cherry plum, and summer snowflake, all dissolved in rough fermented grape solution. It would calm her down, but the side effect was a feeling of disconnectedness.

"Drink it," Jacob insisted, pressing the bottle into her hand. Erin nodded and gulped down the solution wincing as the alcohol bit he throat. "You will feel better, Mother. Then, I'll prepare dinner," Jacob stated. He patted her head and hugged her before moving to the kitchen.

Robin came out of their bedroom, his mouth sticky and covered in crumbs, having consumed yet another bun, leaving only two hidden under his bed. He moved on to the seat with his mother and gave her a big loving hug. She looked into her son's eyes and smiled warmly, hugging him back. Robin reminded her so much of Raouf. He was already as tall as his father and almost as strong. He even smelt like his father, she broke the hug for a moment.

"Have you been stealing sweet rolls again?" she asked, looking him square in the eyes. Robin froze. His glaze-covered mouth and his blush betrayed his guilt. Jacob smiled, he didn't know why he enjoyed watching his brother getting into trouble, but as Jacob busied himself in the kitchen, he listened with a small amount of joy inside as his mother berated his twin.

The family managed to get into a routine as spring ended and summer exerted its dominance. Robin would hunt on the days when the weather allowed. Finally, towards the end of the autumn, he killed his first deer. It hadn't been a good kill. It had taken several arrows to bring the animal down, but the hunters took him to the tavern to celebrate. They feasted on the deer and had enough for a couple of weeks.

Under Maganwyth's guidance and in secret, Jacob practised his gifts. It was exhausting but rewarding. In the autumn months, he managed to not only practice moving objects but had learnt how to do several other minor spells. He could now also create small lights and a few other tricks. His knowledge of the herbal arts also increased. Maganwyth also taught him that the gods' gifts weren't the only forms of magic. She explained that her method for calling on magic was immeasurably different from his. In the past, other methods had been widely practised across the empire before the Inquisition and the church. Some could use the powers bestowed upon them by the gods, others could decipher the dragons' ancient languages, others could manipulate the universe to suit their purposes, while others still were endowed with special abilities at birth. Maganwyth decided to show Jacob such a creature one day, so, he could understand the world at large.

One day, he arrived at the hut ready for his lessons to find Maganwyth outside with a small pack on her back,

"Today we do something different." She smiled at the young man. "You have asked many questions about the fay folk. I felt it was time you met some." She stamped her feet, there had been a little snow in the last few nights, and the morning was cold. She tossed Jacob a thick woollen cloak.

"Wrap yourself up," she snapped. With that, she began trudging a little trodden path away from the village. Jacob didn't speak. He knew he would get little out of the hag. She muttered and cursed as she trekked up the path. Jacob struggled to follow her. While his health had improved somewhat in the last few years, he still wasn't as stout or hearty as his twin.

Nevertheless, he fought to ascend the path. The journey took half a day before the witch stopped to take a breath, slumping down on a fallen tree.

Jacob gasped for breath as he finally caught up. His legs and chest burned as he slumped down onto the earth next to the witch.

"If you planned to kill me, you could have just stabbed me in the heart!" Jacob mumbled, clutching his chest.

"You'll live. The walk is good for you, welp," the witch mumbled. "Well, this is as far as I go."

"You said I would see some fay creatures," Jacob asked. "Or was that a lie to get me to go on this awful walk," he complained.

"No, there is fay, but they don't like me," Maganwyth mumbled. She pointed to a treeline where the babble of a watery brook could be heard. "Go to the water and wait. They will come for you."

Jacob got up, feeling the burning returning to his legs, and followed the path Maganwyth had pointed out. "Oh wait," Maganwyth mumbled. She reached into her pack and pulled out a small puppy. Jacob paused.

"Is it dead?" Jacob asked.

"No, just sleeping. It's a gift for them. It was given to me as payment for some healing last week. I have no use for a mutt." Jacob let the small dog be dropped into his cupped hands; it was only a couple of days old. It should never have been taken from its mother this early. "It's the runt of the litter, probably wouldn't live past winter, and wouldn't be useful as a pack dog, but they might like it."

"Who are they?" Jacob asked nervously. The little puppy was fast asleep in his hands.

"You are going to meet the Veela," she expanded. "They are silly creatures, harmless, mostly, but it will be bloody good for you to talk to them. You may learn something."

Jacob left the witch and walked towards the sounds of the babbling brook. This was one of the many streams and rivers that would flow into the Everlong Sea. The path was slippery down to the translucent crystal creek. Runoff from the mountains flowed around him. Jacob carefully made his way down to the water's edge. He clutched the puppy in both hands; the little animal had started to stir. Its little dark eyes struggled to open. Jacob patted his robe. He had nothing to feed the poor animal.

The sisters, Andresila and Jerisavlja watched the young boy and giggled. He wasn't a handsome or comely specimen. Unlike the young man they had seen the other day, Andresila had been about to approach the young hunter until he killed the deer. That had made her sad. This boy had a similar look, but he wasn't as big. Perhaps a younger brother, they mused. As they danced, invisible around Jacob, they saw this young man holding the small puppy. They stopped their dance and looked over the young man's shoulder at the puppy he grasped gently in his hands.

"Aw..." they spoke in unison.

Jacob snapped his head, looking for where this voice had come from, seemingly beside his ears. He stood up, whipping around, trying to see the speakers. As Jacob looked around, his foot slipped on the slick mud around the brook, and he began to fall backward. Four arms caught him and pushed him back to the side of the stream. Jacob landed on his arse in the mud, cradling the puppy in one arm.

"Carefully, carefully, Jacob," they spoke sweetly to the young man. In front of him were now two beautiful women clad in diaphanous gowns. One had blaze-red hair, the other golden. They were slender, their lithe bodies visible for the thin material of their dresses. Jacob watched them, his mouth open, unable to talk.

They started to dance with each other. It took Jacob a moment to realise that their feet were standing above the water as they danced , giggling. "What's the matter, cats got your tongue?" Jerisavlja said.

"Sister, that's a puppy, not a cat," Andresila said. "We love puppies."

Jacob grew worried briefly that they meant to eat, but the way they kept casting adoring eyes at the puppy between their frivolous dance put him at ease. "This is a gift for you," Jacob offered, finally managing to catch his voice. Immediately the two sisters were on either side of Jacob, their arms wrapped around the young teenage boy.

They cooed at the puppy, both women pressing either side of Jacob. He felt their bodies and bosoms pressing against him as they gently squeezed closer to play with the puppy. Jacob, who usually felt uncomfortable with people touching him, felt something different as these two beings seemed to arouse the young man unconsciously. The two women lifted the puppy out of Jacob's hands.

Andresila spoke. "Generally, we prefer not to involve ourselves with human affairs."

"Yet, you are a child who has been cursed by your parents."

Jacob interrupted, "I've been cursed with a gift but not by my parents."

They laughed, pressing their bodies tightly against Jacob. "Even if your parents merely speak in an offhand in a moment of anger, we can feel it," Jerisavlja corrected. "Your parents often felt you were odd."

"We could take you away." Andresila smiled at him, turning his cheek to look at her, her beautiful face inches from his.

Jerisavlja turned her head towards her. "We will feed you honey and instruct you in the knowledge of nature and the supernatural like us!"

Andresila whispered into his ear with a sweet soft voice, "This is what you want most, isn't it, Jacob."

Jacob shook his head. The two were teasing and tempting the young man. He pushed himself to his feet away from the two Veela. The sisters moved together, smiling at him.

"I do wish for knowledge more than you could know." He spoke, "But my mother needs me, and my brother would be lost. I cannot leave them."

The two women pouted, stroking the puppy. "Then Jacob of the Dale, please stay a fleeting time. We would like to teach you something." They patted the ground between them. Jerisavlja took the puppy from her sister, gazing lovingly down at it. She seemed to have a small bottle and was dripping milk into the puppy's mouth. Andresila wrapped her arms around Jacob and whispered into the ear of the young man.

She stroked his hair as she spoke, pulling him into her bosom. "I will tell you something your witch will not. You are blessed by a god."

Jerisavlja spoke, not looking up from the little puppy. Instead, she smiled and wiggled her fingers at the puppy. "It's one that hasn't made himself known for quite some time."

"He's not our favourite." Andresila pouted. "He's too serious. He's cold."

Jerisavlja spoke. "No fun. A bit like you."

"He is called Thoth," Andresila continued. Jerisavlja poked her tongue out. "He is the god of knowledge and learning. He has chosen you to be his vessel." At last, Jacob had a name for the god that shared his soul. "He will help you learn; he will help you grow; he has a thirst for knowledge just like you."

"Should we tell him of his father?" Jerisavlja asked.

Andresila pouted. "I don't think Vlad would like that. He can get so angry."

"Can we teach him a trick then, sister?" Jerisavlja interrupted. "Thoth is boring, but he did like to know good tricks."

Andresila pouted at the interruption but then smiled. "I know!" She clapped her hands, she pulled away from Jacob till both the sisters were in front of him.

"This one." She leaned close to Jerisavlja and whispered into her ear. They whispered for a few more moments before turning to Jacob. In unison, they both began to sing. Their words floated across the river, and as they raised their arms, they appeared to be turning into swans, their clothing changed into a robe of feathers. Their voices mesmerised Jacob. He felt a deep calm wash over him, he couldn't move or speak, but he felt calm. What felt like moments gripped Jacob. He didn't realise he had fallen asleep. It wasn't for long, but the two beautiful ladies were gone. In his mind, their words echoed. They had granted him this spell. He could remember the word of power. '*Rebmuls*'.

Jacob returned to the wooden stump where Maganwyth sat. She was smoking her pipe, the foul blue smoke polluting the air around her.

"So, you met them then," she grunted between puffs.

"What are they?" Jacob asked in a slight daze.

"Silly girls." She grunted, "Some people think they are the ghosts of engaged women who pass away before their wedding night. Due to their inability to fulfil their burning need to dance, they cannot rest in their graves. They also congregate around rivers, seducing young men and dancing them to death. Some people think they are maidens condemned by the gods as atonement for their foolish prior incarnations. According to certain legends, the Vila are cursed never to discover true love, or if they do, that love will pass away horribly." She smiled. "Personally, I think they are a bunch of silly Haulfin whores."

"They are dead?" Jacob asked.

"Undead," she corrected. "They are fay spirits, they can heal the wounded, or they can lure men to their death."

"And you sent me to them?" Jacob asked.

"You were in no danger. You brought them a gift. Those that gift the Vela are known as *Vilenik*. They gave you a gift back, did they not?" She stubbed her pipe out on the trunk of the tree.

"They gave me some knowledge and sang me a song," Jacob admitted.

"Bet they also teased you." She chuckled, "They do that to young men." She saw Jacobs' face blushing. For all his knowledge, the young lad still had a lot of experience to gain. "We best be heading back; at your pace, we won't get home till nightfall."

Following his encounter with the Fay, Jacob understood a lot more, he was able to understand the distinct types of magic, and with Maganwyth's guidance, he even called upon the land's magic and spells of his own, not drawing on the inner god within. The magic from within remained the easiest for him to call upon, though.

Chapter 11

The Inquisitor

The savage crowd was baying for blood. Atop the gallows, six figures stood dressed in torn rags. Three were Aldari with elongated ears, fine delicate features, and glowing eyes. They looked a little out of their teens but would have been many decades old. The other three were shorter, two tubby hobbies and one large muscular Dewar. While the Aldari tried to look as noble as possible in the face of their inevitable deaths, the two short half-men fidgeted against their bonds. The Dewar's head was bowed, and his head and beard had been shaven. His eyes were downcast, all hope lost.

In the crowd, the humans were savage with their hunger for the execution. They yelled and spat towards the Haulfin. They were throwing rotten fruit at the condemned figures.

From the castle, with a clear view over the square, a tall, silent dark-haired figure watched with mild bemusement. Talos Tarsus, Inquisitor general of the church of the one true God, observed the execution with a slight smile. *Six today,* he thought, he would have preferred if it had been six hundred, but he had to work around the laws and the interference of the heir prince. It had been five years since he and the prince had returned from Altran, and the young prince had countered his moves every day. He could, even now, hear the young heir electoral prince approaching his chamber long before he arrived. Talos watched the end of the execution, not moving as his door burst open.

"What in the nine hells is going on in the square?" demanded Sir William Nadrog, Heir Electoral Prince of Gont, as he burst through the doors. The young prince had matured well in the last few years. He bore a long scar down one cheek from his venture into the north, but he had grown taller and more robust, and his once long blond hair was now cropped short. His face was currently gritted with anger. His and Talos' animosity had grown, he knew the Inquisitor was making all efforts in court to usurp him, but he had no proof.

"It's an execution, sire," Talos elucidated, turning around calmly, his fingers steepled in front of him. Talos Tarsus was a tall figure with slicked-back dark hair in a narrow widow's peak. He had a well-groomed black beard with a few flecks of grey. His eyes were crystal-blue and seemed without emotion. His face was marred by only a few wrinkles that showed his age. He wore a simple black smock, with a single adornment around a silver chain around his neck of the symbol of the one true God. On his finger was a single silver signet ring. "They were all found guilty of crimes." He smiled.

"Found guilty by who?" William asked.

"The Inquisition, of course." Talos shrugged and listed their crimes. "Two counts of rape, three counts of theft and one was trying to flee the lower quarter."

William frowned. He knew that most of the charges, if not all, were made up. Yet, despite his best efforts, Talos pursued an increasingly aggressive approach to the subraces. In the last month, nearly fifty Haulfin had been executed for 'crimes'. At the same time, only two humans had been found guilty. Moreover, the guards in the lower quarter were brutal in the execution of their duties.

"Talos, this must stop!" William commanded. "You are persecuting the people of the lower quarter to the exception of everyone else. Yesterday a group of men was brought before the court accused of assaulting and raping a young Haulfin woman. I hear this morning that they have been let free."

"No evidence," Talos stated.

"The woman testified. I'm told she showed the court the damage they had done to her face and body."

"But no one saw the crime, and the six young men each had five alibies," Talos rationalised. "My judges do their duty, sire. We do not persecute the innocent." Talos shook his head, "You simply must understand the Haulfin are just more violent and more prone to criminal acts, milord. This was the reason the empire was forced to all but drive them out of the civilised lands." Talos calmly explained, "We never should have let any remain."

"But we did," William countered. "You need to stop persecuting them over and above other criminals in the city."

Talos smiled a sly soft smile, "Of course, Milord, we will pursue the law of the one true God equally. Your father and I have had many discussions. He has never had cause to question me in the execution of my duties."

"I am not my father," William cautioned, raising a finger to point at Talos.

"I see more of him in you than I think you will care to admit."

"Don't test me, Inquisitor," William stated, pointing his finger at the thin man. With that, William turned his back and stormed out, leaving the door to Talos' chamber open. Talos approached the door and confronted the two guards stationed on either side.

"Well, you are useless," he mumbled to both. "Go fetch my scribe, Carlos," he ordered one of them, who quickly scampered off. He closed the door behind him and returned to his desk. Unlike some in his position, he had a remarkably spartan wooden desk, neatly laid out, a sizable leather-bound black ledger sitting in the middle, and a silver lock kept the book from prying eyes. He reached into his robe and pulled out a minute key. Opened his book and dipping his long-feathered quill into a small pot of ink, he ran a long delicate finger down a list of names in the ledger, stopping six times to strike through monikers, making a detailed note of the date beside each one. Talos sat waiting in his darkened study. He tapped his fingers on his desk as He gazed at the ledger in front of him. The young heir electoral prince's foray into the frozen north had boosted the young man's popularity amongst the commoners, the nobles of the court, and even the subraces. This had made the young man a problem for Talos' plans. As Inquisitor general of Gont, his position allowed him a lot of privileges and power, but, at least by the rule of lore, he was still subordinate to the electoral prince. William's father, Godwin, had been persuaded over many years of pressure and persistence to conform to the church's and the Inquisition's ideals, but the young William appeared brasher than his father, encouraged even further by his valour in the north. Even before he left, Talos noted that the young boy seemed more accepting of the subraces. Now since his return, he was positively championing their rights.

A knock at the door brought his head up. "Come," he snapped.

One of his aides opened the door slowly. The aide was carrying an arm full of scrolls. He was an average-sized, timid-looking man.

"Master Talos?" the aide asked nervously.

Talos Tarsus had garnered an aura of fear in all his subordinates, which he liked to encourage. It helped establish his position as a man beyond reproach. "Place it over there, Carlos," he instructed, pointing to a small end table. *We are allowing too much freedom to the subraces in Gont,* the Inquisitor mused to himself.

"Sir?" Carlos asked nervously, fidgeting, waiting to be dismissed. He kept his eyes down to the floor to avoid contact with the Inquisitor general.

"The young Nadrog has been allowing some subraces to leave the lower quarter."

"Sir." Carlos nodded. Before William had travelled to the north on his quest, Talos had had free reign on detentions, questioning, and even executions. Now he was being questioned. He wasn't used to answering questions, only asking them.

"Take this to the captain of the city guards," Talos commanded, handing a scroll sealed with his personal black waxed stamp. "You will then see to my armour before I visit the prince."

"The prince has been unwell, sire," Carlos nervously muttered.

"He will see me." He waved a hand to dismiss Carlos Talos stated as he straightened up from his desk, closing the ledger and placing his quill in its case before locking the roster and his quill case. All his movements were with exact precision. He walked to the window, looking out over the city.

"Vigilance," he muttered to himself. "The church must remain vigilant against any form of insurrection or heresy." His eyes narrowed to the lower quarter across the city. It was a darkened area, mired in squalor and disease. Even the poorest of humans didn't live in that part of town. Mostly it was just the subraces. The city guards constantly patrolled it. He had memorised the list of potential insurrectionists he would need to deal with to ensure the empire's and the church's security.

He exited his chambers, and as he left, his two personal guards followed a few steps behind, their heavy, full plate boots stomping heavily against the castle stones echoing down the halls. Arriving at the antechamber of the Electoral Prince Godwin, he could see the prince's wife with her handmaiden sitting embroidering. They looked up, startled, as Talos and his guards burst in despite the noise they had made marching down the halls. Talos swept past the wife with barely a glance, although he glared briefly at the Haulfin servant acting as her handmaid. Dressed in only a burlap sack, the young Haulfin kept her head down, trying to avoid the Inquisitor's gaze. Nevertheless, he vaguely recognised her as the same filth that had accompanied William on his excursion.

114

"He's not taking visitors," the prince's wife stated. She was an elderly woman, the prince's second wife, not William's mother. She was quite a few years younger than the electoral princes, but she had passed her prime. She had been a pretty woman in court who had caught the prince's eye after the death of his wife.

"He will see me," Talos uttered. Walking past her, he opened the thick double doors to the prince's bed chambers.

The chambers were luxurious. Heavy wolf pelts lined the floor; thick ancient tapestries of battles fought by Godwin's ancestors lined the walls. A substantial four-posted bed dominated the centre of the room; thick gold-rimmed velvet curtains were drawn around the bed. An elderly physician was snoozing in a chair beside it. He woke with a start as Talos entered the room, fixing the older man with a baleful eye. The blue-robed physician said nothing.

"Wake him," Talos ordered.

"B... B... But s... s... s... sir," stammered the physician. He was an old balding man dressed in the long blue robes of his order, technically the physicians were a part of the church, and so they had been allowed to practice simple alchemy, but the blue-robed healers were a fringe part of the church, and as such, one of the lowest orders. Talos waved the man away and approached the bed pulling aside the curtains.

Lord Godwin Nadrog, Electoral Prince of Gont, was dying. The once powerful man was now a shrivelled shell. His skin clung to his skull like wet rice paper, and his eyes were greyed over and blind.

"William, is that you?" Godwin asked. "What are you doing making such a racket, boy!"

"Milord it is Talos." Talos took the old prince's hand. "I'm sorry for disturbing you." Talos stroked the old man's hand. Talos spoke with a soft, soothing voice. "I wouldn't disturb you, but I worry for your son. I feel he is too young for the burden you are leaving upon him."

"Son? What son?" the old man asked.

"William, sir, your son," Talos soothed. The old man's mind had gone the way of his body and was deteriorating fast.

"Oh, him," the old man mumbled under his breath. "He's a Nadrog! He will do fine."

"I was thinking of another Nadrog who could hold the reigns for a few years until your son is ready." Talos continued, "Your brother Renwalt perhaps?"

The old man's wrinkled face crinkled even more, and his voice crackled as he spoke, "He's a cad! A liar and a thief! He stole my horse!"

"Sire, that was many years ago, when you were both children." Talos continued coaxing, "He has grown much since then." The prince's mind seemed stuck about sixty years ago when his brother had stolen a wooden horse from him.

The old prince looked up at Talos as he continued to talk. It was dull stuff about the city, the church, and other tedious stuff. The old man's mind began to drift until he mentioned a name, 'Leopold' the words rang back a memory in his head.

"I remember Leopold! Young lad, we fought together against the southern princedoms! Good warrior for a youngster." The princes' eyes seemed to lighten for a second.

"Yes, I believe you and the emperor did fight in the southern campaigns thirty years ago."

"No, not the emperor!" The old man tried to salute, "His son! I was his guard for that campaign." Instead, the old man began rambling about old stories, his voice slowly fading into snores.

Talos pulled himself away from the bed, pulling the curtains back. He glared at the physician. "Was our chat being eavesdropped on by you?" Talos inquired, his eyes narrowing on the old man.

"No, Milord" The old physician was visibly trembling. He spoke honestly. "I heard nothing, just something about the prince's brother, nothing else, Milord."

"Good," Talos bade. "You can bear witness to his last statement. Follow me."

"I must stay here, my lord," the physician protested. "The prince might need me."

"He is sleeping, and his wife can tend to him. It will be but a moment." Talos marched out of the bed chambers. The healer followed, shuffling behind him.

Two hours later, Talos Tarsus returned to his chambers. He was in a foul mood. The foolish physician had taken ages to put his pen to paper. He had been so intimidated by Talos that his feeble old fingers had kept dropping the quill. Word had come that the old prince had woken again. The blue-robed physician's testimony would now be useless. Talos took a moment to calm himself before he entered his dwelling. He removed his leather gloves and stuffed them into his belt. He let out a breath to relax. He pushed open the door, and a young boy charged across the room, cannonballing into Talos' chest. Talos' stern frown broke into a warm smile. A slender woman stepped out from a second chamber with a cloth wiping her hands.

The woman spoke with a smile. Konrad, leave your father alone. You would have thought he hasn't seen you in a week."

"He misses his father when he's at work." Talos knelt next to the child. "Have you been a good boy today." The six-year-old nodded. "Done your chores for your mother?" Another nod. "Finished your studies?" Shake. "We cannot have that," Talos playfully warned, "Go to your books, and I'll join you shortly." Talos rose to his feet and moved to his wife, kissing her on the cheek. Talos' wife was a slender young woman. Her fair hair was primly knotted in a simple plat. She wore a simple white dress. The two had been together for eight years, and their love had never faded.

Talos' chambers were almost juxtaposition from what many would have expected, having seen him in his duties. They were spartanly decorated, but with a warm, friendly atmosphere, Konrad's toys littered the living area around the warm fireplace, and several simple tapestries covered the otherwise bleak stone walls. There were plush furnished chairs and a simple dining table. While Talos' duties kept him busy, he never missed a family meal. He considered it a cornerstone of his life.

"Please give me a moment, my dear," he apologised to his wife with another kiss.

Talos crossed to a small alcove. Upon a small pedestal was a symbol of the one true God. In front of it was a small kneeling cushion. Talos approached it and made the sign of the one true God before kneeling in prayer. He spoke quietly under his breath.

"Please revive me and give me the energy I need to take care of my family. You already know how much I adore them but managing everything may be challenging. Teach me how to interact with my family more effectively and to lead them correctly. Give me the encouragement I need to press on, the direction I need to follow, and the fortitude I need to carry out

117

your mandate and defend us against heresy and Haulfin demons." He closed his eyes a moment and gave a silent thanks.

Talos rose to his feet once finished. He unclipped his long black cloak and hung it by the door before he returned to his wife, bereft of his vestments. Talos showed an impressive physique despite his age. He embraced his wife warmly and kissed her passionately.

"Talos! I'm filthy!" She laughed, showing her flour-covered hands.

"I don't know why you don't let the castle cooks prepare our meals," he joked, breaking the embrace and dusting the stray flour off his tunic.

"A family should cook together, eat together, and pray together." She smiled, touching his nose. "Speaking of which, dinner is almost ready. Are you hungry?"

Talos grinned. "For your cooking, I'm famished."

"Father," Konrad's soprano voice echoed from the other room. "Can you help me with my studies?" the young six-year-old asked. Talos looked at his wife, who nodded.

"Sure, then we have supper," he replied.

Talos went through to the young boy's room. Konrad had more the look of his mother, with fair hair and a slender face. He smiled, gazing lovingly at his father with his large blue eyes.

"What are you studying today?" Talos inquired, taking a seat and pulling the young child onto his lap. Konrad held a slim book in his little hands. "It's the story of how the first emperor came to be." Talos raised an eyebrow.

"It's good to learn history so that we aren't doomed to repeat the mistakes of the past," Talos commented.

"I don't get what happened to the Haulfin?" Konrad asked. "From what this book says, they used to be our friends."

Talos's face dropped. He would have rather his young child didn't have to learn about this part of history, but it was good to teach them young. But, on the other hand, he would hate if his son turned out to be as weak-minded as the fool heir prince.

"It is a long and sad story," Talos explained. "Emperor Sigmund Von Ulis, before he was the emperor, was a king of a large kingdom, but back then, the world was a lot wilder than it is today. There were many more Haulfin. Most were savage tribes." He continued, "Sigmund was constantly waging war to keep his kingdom safe, then the one true God took form and came to

118

him. The one true God guided Sigmund to raise a powerful army, the army of the church, and he tamed the lands around his kingdom, but as he did so, more and more of the Haulfin, and human tribes grew jealous of his successes. He was forced to conquer more lands. Rhineland, Altran, Hebon and Albian. Sigmund spent most of his life trying to bring peace to the empire's lands, but whenever he tamed the savages, more savages attacked his lands. Sigmund formed the council of princes as it is today."

"Were there Haulfin in the council?" Konrad asked.

"Yes, there were, and that was Sigmund's greatest mistake and downfall. He wanted to share his power amongst the princes and made the council of thirteen."

"Why thirteen?" Konrad asked.

"Sigmund had spent so much of his life at war. He had never had time to raise a family, no children, no wife. Sigmund knew he wouldn't live forever, and he wanted his fledgling empire to continue well past his life, so the council of thirteen would, upon his death, vote in the new emperor from amongst the nobles, and thirteen can never be split evenly so this meant there would always be a clear winner, or so Sigmund thought." Talos face went momentarily cold. "Alas, he was wrong. Upon his passing, the council of thirteen squabbled and fought amongst themselves. The Haulfin wanted to install one of their kind on the throne, which would have dominated the world for a millennium. The other lords felt different, and the empire would have crumbled had that chaos been allowed to continue. Fortunately, the church saw this oncoming pandemonium, and they raised the army of the Inquisition, who brought the princes to order and then the Devout House of Hartford was voted in."

"What happened to the Haulfin?" Konrad asked.

"Oh, they accepted the new rule for a time. It wasn't until many years later that their true treachery was revealed." Talos Tarsus closed the book and turned to look his boy in the eyes. He spoke firmly. "Konrad, the Haulfin races don't accept the love of the one true God as you or I do, they are devious and treacherous beasts, you may see them in the castle from time to time but do not approach, do not speak to them, their mouths are filled with lies, and they are dangerous."

"Why do we keep them in the castle, then?" Konrad asked.

Talos sighed, "Unfortunately, the compassion the one true God teaches us is also our greatest weakness. We allow them here because many believe they can change their true nature. They can't, and they will betray us. Listen to me, Konrad, never turn your back on a Haulfin."

The young boy nodded, and Talos gave him a warm hug. "Now go wash your hands. Your mother is calling us."

Fatherhood was an aspect of Talos that only came out when he was with his child, and it did so because he loved Konrad so very, very much. He relished his company. Talos watched his young boy rush to the chamber room to wash his hands. He looked at the book. Steinhardt, the old court vizier, had been teaching his boy stuff well beyond his years. He would need to have a word with the old man. Steinhardt was responsible for the heir prince's foolish tolerance of the Haulfin. He wasn't going to allow the old fool to infect his child.

The family ate together, smiling and laughing around the table. One could almost forget for a moment that at the head of this table was the Inquisitor general of Gont. When he entered this room, he was no longer. Inquisitor Talos was a father, husband, and family man.

Chapter 12

The Agent

Leaving his wife to clean their dishes, Talos put Konrad to bed. Talos read his child a story, one he had heard many years ago:

"There once was a great hero.

"He was a fierce warrior that never ran from any challenge.

"He lived in a village of nearly one hundred people and was loved by all.

"One day, a messenger came into town with word of Haulfin beasts heading towards the village.

"These Haulfin were vicious and vile creatures that had destroyed many other mighty warriors.

"They went by the names 'Doubt', 'Fear', 'Doom', 'Grief', and 'Loneliness'.

"Word of the beasts spread fast, and the village was worried the hero would not be able to conquer these beasts.

"Our hero visited the priests, who were the wisest people in the town.

"The priests had been our hero's teachers since he was a child.

"The hero arrived at the priest's church and asked them if they knew about the Haulfin beasts.

"The priests were aware of the threat and knew the way to fight them.

"The first beast would be Doubt.

"This Haulfin caused uncertainty in its foes; without conviction, the hero would falter and miss their strikes.

"The second Haulfin will be Fear, the most powerful of the beasts, it can break any man, and the hero would need courage in the face of Fear.

"The third beast is Doom. It is a vile creature that casts darkness upon its foes, consuming them with despair! To fight against this, the brave warrior would need hope.

"As hope will shine through any darkness.

"It is easy to face challenges that come at you head-on, but these beasts were sneaky.

"Loneliness and Grief.

"Loneliness is a beast all warriors must face.

"It drains your soul slowly, but you must remember the love of your comrades.

"Grief is a demon we all will face.

"It is a leach that sucks away at your will to continue.

"To fight this, the hero must use joy to remember the good times of those who have gone.

"The hero faced the horrific Haulfin, and with conviction, courage, hope, love and joy, the hero defeated the foul beasts casting them back and saving the village."

Talos finished the story. It was a story he had told his child a hundred times. The soft blanket of a story soothed the ears and wrapped Konrad in a peaceful world. Talos leant forward and kissed his son on the forehead. He lingered on the edge of the bed until his son's eyelids fell shut. The silence was the loudest sound, the moon was the brightest light, and his son's chest's rhythmic rise and fall were the only movements.

Talos left his child's bedside, leaning against the door frame, watching Konrad in the dim candlelight of the room. Satisfied, he let out a sigh. This was his world. The outside world was for a different man. The windowpane cast dancing shadows across young Konrad's face, almost like the bars of a prison keeping him safe.

The was a clatter from the next room. Talos approached the kitchen area, watching as Olivia, his wife, stacked the dishes. Talos approached her and hugged her from behind, kissing her neck.

"Bad day?" she asked.

"It's nothing that you should hear," he whispers in her ear.

"Tell me," she demands, leading him into the brighter light of the living room, sitting her husband down on the long-cushioned chair. Talos slumped into the chair like he had no more strength, his mind spinning. It was this backwater of Gont, he had been sent here six years ago by the church to ensure the sanctity of the church, but the people of Gont were so 'fair' to the Haulfin that it made his job almost intolerable. He looked deeply into Olivia's eyes, seeing nothing but love and support.

"It is nothing you can help with." Talos smiled.

"Please," she whispered, tightening her grip on his arm. "How can I help."

He spoke softly, stroking her hair. "You can be here for me when I get home. You and Konrad"

Talos pushed himself off the couch and walked to the window to stare at the city lights. He took a deep breath and calmed himself.

He turned to look at his wife, who was watching him with concern, her perfect cheeks, the paleness of her skin, the delicate features, scrunched up with worry for her husband.

A harsh knock came to the chamber door, and beyond the portal, a soft voice called, "Milord."

Talos's face immediately hardened. His attendance knew never to disturb his time with his family. It was sacred. He gritted his teeth and flung open the door. Standing in the archway was the small clerk, Carlos.

"What!" he demanded.

"Milord..." Carlos faltered. "You... you must come, sire! I have news of the heir prince."

Talos sighed. Drawing upon his inner strength, he pulled his cloak from its perch and clipped it over his shoulders. He turned to face his wife and offered her a half-smile before Talos slipped away. She returned the smile.

"I don't know how late I will be, don't wait up." He gently closed the chamber door behind him to avoid disturbing Konrad.

With that, he was gone, following the scribe.

"This had better be important." Talos swept down the dimly lit castle corridor.

"I would never have disturbed you otherwise, sire." Then, Carlos muttered, "We have a Haulfin who has some information you will want to hear."

The Inquisition hold was a short walk away from the main castle. They kept it that way to prevent the noises of the inmates from disturbing the lords and ladies of the central court. The top rooms housed an enormous collection of paperwork with notes on many citizens of Gont; it was significantly more in-depth information than Talos held in his private chambers inside the castle; it filled several rooms. Below the record rooms were the cells in which the questioning of the heretics was done. A dozen or so clerks looked up as Talos entered the upper rooms. Upon seeing their lord, they scrambled to their feet. Talos waved them to sit down with an annoyed flick of his wrist.

"Take me to this Haulfin."

A heavy metal door barred the entrance to the lower chambers, it did little to stifle the din of the Inquisition technicians working hard to extract information from the inmates, but it did a little. From the top of the stairs, Talos could hear the agonised screams of several prisoners below.

Carlos led him to one of the chamber doors, opening it for his lord. Talos dismissed him.

"Go, but I may require you later." He waved the clerk away.

Two people were in the room; Talos recognised one of them as one of his most excellent intelligence gatherers. He was a short, wiry man, and he was standing next to the chair. The man loved his work. His mind wasn't all there, a simpleton by all accounts, but one with his uses. The man had a dysfunctional brain. He derived pure pleasure from his work. Had he not been recruited by the Inquisition; he would have ended up on the streets a murderer with no sense that what he was doing was wrong. Instead, this man had been brought into God's service.

The second figure was a Haulfin. Talos struggled to recognise the exact species. The torture had gone quite far, the beast had had two horns, but only one remained. Fur covered parts of his body, but his face wasn't that of a man. Instead, he looked like a devil. *He was a devil,* Talos reminded himself. The devil was slacked jawed and unconscious from the pain.

"Wake him!" Talos demanded.

The animal came to with a thudding headache and closed its eyes in defiance of the numb agony when the tormentor flung a pail of ice water at its face. The beast chewed out a snarl and attempted to move his hands, clinking against the chains. The back of his skull pounded. Talos could see that the beast's eyes were swollen under its blindfold. It was terrified, confused and confined. Talos wondered if the Haulfin knew he was a lamb waiting for the slaughter. The chilly air of the basement steamed with its laboured breaths. "Can you hear me?" Talos inquired.

The beast yanked against his metal chains; the rings cut deep into his flesh and fur. It howled out in agony and kept struggling at the bonds. The animal's every instinct told it to flee to escape . Talos nodded, and the torture placed a red-hot brand onto the beast's chest, summoning an excruciating, tormented howl.

"I asked. Can you hear me." Annoyed at having to repeat himself.

The beast snapped his head back, still unseeing. It spoke with a lisped, misshapen mouth. "I hear you." Its throat was raw from shouting, and its lips were parched.

"I am told you have an interesting tale of our prince." Talos pulled a chair opposite the beast towards him. The chair's metal legs screamed painfully as they were dragged across the stone floor. Talos calmly sat opposite the Haulfin. "I wish you to tell it again."

"W… water," the beast managed.

Talos nodded, and with a disappointed pout, the torturer raised a small cup to the beast's lips wetting its lips. Then whether by purpose or accident, spilt the rest of the water into the Haulfin's face.

"Now speak," Talos smiled, ripping off the beast's blindfold. Its eyes were swollen shut. "If I am pleased with what you tell me, I might be able to do something to help you." He spoke calmly, "We can put you in a nice warm cell, get you more water… something to eat."

The beast listened to Talos and nodded, anything to stop the constant pain. Finally, with heroic effort, it forced one eye open. The beast looked at the man seated opposite him. Calm and neat, Talos watched him with his remarkable eyes.

"I… I've heard the young prince had gone to the lower quarter." The beast croaked.

"Why would he do that?" Talos inquired.

"He seeks to forge an alliance," the beast struggled.

"With whom?" Talos urged.

"A man named Balis Gestalt."

"The Haulfin thief?" Talos raised an eyebrow. "Where did you hear this from."

"No." The beast slumped his head. "I cannot tell you."

"Sure you can," Talos soothed. Then he nodded at the torturer who branded the Haulfin's chest, repeatedly, summoning another cry of pain. "Tell me."

The beast remained silent for a long moment catching its breath. "Someone, I don't know the name!" Finally, the beast sobbed. "Please, please, just kill me," it implored.

"I want a name," Talos insisted.

"I don't know her name," the beast begged. "I was just asked by a woman to help the prince find Balis."

Talos sighed and leaned back in the chair. He knew when a man was broken. "Can you describe her? And then you will get your wish."

"She wore a hood, she... she was kind." The beast shook its head. "I never saw her face."

"Human?" Talos pushed.

"I don't know, please, please no more," the beast begged.

This was all he was getting. He nodded towards the torturer. "Give him release," Talos commanded.

With annoyed frustration that his latest toy needed to be put away, the torturer slowly drew a blade across the beast's throat. The jagged edges of the serrated knife slowly opened the Haulfin's' gullet. A gurgled sound came as the blood from the throat began to gush. As blood trickled and pooled down the front of the beast, Talos straightened up and moved away from the gore.

He scowled at the tormenter. "You've created a mess. I expect you to clean it up," he ordered as he left the cell.

In the castle of Gont, Talos paced back and forth in his office. This had turned out to be a frustrating day. First, the fool of a physician hadn't confirmed Godwin's instructions to allow stewardship of the princedom to fall to Renwalt. Then he had learnt the heir prince had visited the lower quarter to make some sort of deal, and worst of all, his time with his family had been disturbed.

Talos Tarsus had already decided for the physician to be found in possession of magic relics. It was more out of spite than anything else. He knew it to be a trivial action, but it would make him feel better. He had to find a way to rally the people of Gont to the church and understand the Haulfin menace for what it was. He did have a tool that could easily show the princedom the wickedness of witchcraft. However, he dared not release such a plight, not so close to his own family. He gazed at his locked cabinets. It was an artefact he had confiscated from a grove of pagan druids, or *doire* as they had called themselves. He had set them all to blaze and sword but had kept the trinket. They had apparently been guarding it for many centuries. Before he had killed the archdruid witch, he had extracted much information. Inside the bauble was a spirit, a demon of the old religion. The archdruid had called it a god who must never be released upon this world.

A scheme started to form in Talos's mind as he opened the secret drawer in his room and pulled out the artefact. The artefact was a sizeable metallic urn. He placed it on his desk. The large metal urn was laden with symbols, a few holy symbols of the one true God, and the other markings were of other older gods. Talos ran his fingers over the side of the urn and shuddered to feel a cold sickness flow over his body.

Carlos entered the room timidly. Talos had summoned him. The man was a bit of a weasel but a useful weasel, Talos thought. He wore a long grey robe, the vestments of the order of the scroll. An arm of the Inquisition that kept the records. While many may call the Inquisition cold or cruel, no one could call them inefficient. Talos looked the man up and down. He was pale-skinned, deep sunken eyes from lack of sleep, and had greasy, matted hair.

"Carlos, how long have you been in my service?" Talos inquired, rapping his fingers against the old urn.

"Five years and three months, sire," the scribe recited back.

"I bet you could tell me how many days and hours as well," Talos mused, and Carlos nodded. Then, Talos beckoned for the scribe to approach closer. "Now, Carlos, tell me, what do you truly desire?" Talos' eyes locked on his clerk as he fixed him with a penetrating stare.

Carlos tried to return the look but found he had to look away, fearful of what would happen if he did. "I only wish to serve the church, milord," he managed to mumble.

"You are the only one of my scribes and attendants that has never asked me for a favour," Talos mused. "Most ask for a relative who has breached the law in some fashion or to request a position or recommendation, but not you."

"I believe in the way of the one true God, sire. While he has never talked to me, I have heard the priests' and clerics' lectures and am familiar with his path. I also no longer have any kin, sire."

A true believer, Talos mused, "You are from Sintra, are you not? The capital of the princedom of Belize." Again, Carlos nodded. "You studied at the church and the university before taking your vestments." Carlos nodded again.

Talos paused. It was time to evaluate this man's faith. "Like myself, I'm sure you have read the book."

"I have read the holy book, sire, and the *Vedas* and *Zabur,* sire," Carlos proudly beamed.

Talos nodded; not many would read the additional texts. "Then, like me, you will have noticed many contradictions in the books, even amongst themselves. How do you reconcile these words of the one true God when they even argue against themselves?"

Carlos paused. "I... I..." He stammered, "Permission to speak without repercussion, sir." Talos smiled and nodded. "The books were written by a man," Carlos explained. "They were transcribed from the words of the one true God over two thousand years ago. Man is flawed. I believe that the words of God were too much for a man to understand. Man wrote what he could understand."

Talos nodded; that was a valid point. However, he had always assumed the book was constructed from various ancient religious scriptures. Scriptures that had become muddled during the purge. The old priests had then shaped a book to control the populace.

"You have never heard the voice of God?" Talos inquired.

"Only through the priests', sire and those who have heard his voice." Carlos looked uncomfortable. This wasn't a topic he enjoyed, especially in front of a man whose sole purpose was to find deviations from the faith and resolve them.

"Would you like to?" Talos inquired, catching Carlos's eyes.

The younger scribe's eyes went wide. "God only speaks to who he chooses."

Talos shrugged. "This is true. However, the holiest of his servants can be brought to his attention." Talos continued to wrap his fingers against the metal urn. "However, it comes with a cost. Those who become the prophets of the one true God don't remain on this plane of existence for long." Talos again locked his gaze on Carlos. "We would elevate your position to the rank of priest, you will don the black robes, and you will take the holiest of orders. Then you will spread the word of the one true God to the Everlong Sea and the Spine Mountains."

Carlos nodded. "It is my duty to follow the will of the church, milord."

Talos smiled. The fanatics were the easiest to guide. "Then I will leave you here," Talos cajoled. "You are to open the urn after I leave and commune with God," he instructed. Rising from his desk, he passed the young scribe a key. "Here, use this to open the urn. Once you have spoken to God, you must travel to Wayrest and beyond, do not delay, do not tarry, and spread God's love to the godless lands of the north." He walked past the scribe and out of the room.

Carlos was left in the room. The urn stood on the table in front of him. It had an ominous presence. Carlos gingerly touched the metal urn. He felt a chill run through his body, and a voice spoke in his head. *Ah, my child, you have come to me.*

Carlos froze. The voice was soft and welcoming. "Are you God?" Carlos asked.

I am your God; I am the beginning and the end, the alpha and the omega, the voice continued to speak in Carlos' head.

Carlos slipped the key into the lock, his fingers shaking. Was he about to meet God? He had lived a pious life, wanting nothing more than to serve in the name of the one true God. Carlos felt a flutter as the key clicked open the top of the urn. His fingers still shook as he twisted the top. A thin layer of rust cracked as the top broke free. Carlos placed the top of the urn to one side with reverence. Then peered into the urn... to see nothing. The jar was empty. Carlos tilted the container to get a better look, the inside was coated with rust, but there was nothing else. The young scribe looked confused. *Had he imagined it?* he thought.

A voice spoke in his head. No, I am here with you, my child.

At that moment, the pious scribe, the man who had dedicated his life to the church and the one true God, Carlos of Sintra, died. His body remained standing, his eyes flared with a greenish-yellow glow, then faded to a soft brown. His skin soured into a waxy yellow. The god had overtaken his body, but it wasn't the God that Carlos loved. This was something else. The god remembered the last command, "To the north to spread my 'love'." It grinned. It wanted to spread its own love. The body of Carlos lurched towards the door. A figure barred its path. The god relished tasting its first victim in a millennium.

129

"Stay where you are, demon. I have a gift for you," Talos offered. In his arms, wrapped in soft leather, was a long rod of ebony topping one end was a gloriously brass crafted pair of lion heads.

"*Maahes,*" The body of Carlos slurred.

"Only fitting for someone of your station," Talos explained. "However you must follow my instructions."

He looked at this thin, hawklike man in front of him. He could kill him, take the staff and be done, but something stayed in his hand.

"What do you desire?" The god requested of the Inquisitor.

Chapter 13

The Lower Quarter

Sir William Nadrog walked through the streets of Trindon, the capital city of Gont, his only companion, his bodyguard and mentor, Heineroth. The two strode through the cobbled streets heading down the hill.

Heineroth was an old man who had lost his son a few years ago in an almost forgotten expedition led by the young prince. In the years since, he had adopted the young Nadrog as his son, giving him the love, he never received from his senile old father. The large bearlike man mainly had recovered from his grief and appeared to be his old gruff jovial self.

William had noticed that occasionally Heineroth would stare off into the distance with a tear in his eye, but he would soon snap himself out of it. He had other children, but none had been as close as Tryrial. Dealing with the loss of a loved one takes time. You never get over the grief. It is like an open wound, constantly hurting. However, you learn to live with the pain and adapt to continue your life.

"Will, why in all that is holy are we heading down to the lower quarter?" Heineroth asked, shifting his sword belt around his ample belly. They passed a patrol of Gont soldiers who saluted Heineroth, their general. He tapped two fingers to his forelock. He had earned his position through feats of great valour and had been recognised across the princedom, but Heineroth always felt himself to be more of a sergeant, not an officer. He disliked all the pomp that came with his rank. Although he did enjoy not having to take the orders of idiot lords any more.

"I've made arrangements to meet someone," William explained. He wore at his side a sword and a simple breastplate for armour. It was good armour but more functional than eloquent. Heineroth had trained William not to go for the flashy armour like his peers, but to look and dress like a solider just like himself. *In battle gold armour means easy target, you want to dress like one of the boys like me, they will also respect you more and know you mean business and not all show.* The words of Heineroth rang in his head.

"I have quite a few soldiers. I trust they would be happy to head down instead of us," Heineroth grumbled. "Chef is making pheasant pie tonight, and we are missing it."

William laughed, "You could do with skipping a few meals." He playfully slapped his old friend's belly. "However, this is a meeting I need to take care of myself."

Heineroth gave a chortle. "Maybe." He smiled. "I don't get out much these days. Being general means most of my time is spent at a desk with bloody paperwork."

"You wish for another lengthy campaign?" William winked. "I could demote you to captain and send you to the Rwelvencrest front."

"You know, give me a few more months of doing accounts, and I might take you up on that," Heineroth grumbled. On his return from the north, Heineroth had been promoted to general by Godwin Nadrog, William's father. The promotion was supposed to be a reward for protecting his son in his adventure and compensation for losing Heineroth's own son. While Heineroth was an excellent tactician, he had little patience for the logistics and number crunching. Nevertheless, he had enjoyed the field of battle. The only fighting he did these days was with numbers and bits of paper.

"Talos has said the Haulfin that live in the lower quarter are nothing but criminals, drug dealers, rapists, thieves, and murderers. I do not believe this; I have met several members of the other races, and only one was evil. Some have been strange, but I've met more evil humans in my life."

"You're talking about the warlock that killed my boy," Heineroth grumbled.

"Er... yes. Sorry, I shouldn't have brought him up." William raised his hand to apologise,

"Don't apologise," Heineroth grumbled. "I cannot say I'm a fan of any Haulfin I've met, save the witch that travelled with us. Most of them seem too arrogant for their own good. In the border skirmishes with Rwelvencrest, I learned never to trust any Haulfin."

"The beasts of that land are quite different from the ones we have in the city. I've always wondered why the Inquisition never purged that land," William mused.

"You've never been there, have you?" Heineroth asked as they walked through the merchant's quarter. "A foul magic surrounds that land, a mist that hangs over it. So many soldiers enter, never to leave. Armies approach the high walls surrounding the land only to become lost and march back on themselves right out." Heineroth shuddered, "And some of the beasts that come out of that fog, the foulest things I've ever seen. Wolves the size of wagons that can take apart an entire regiment." Heineroth shuddered. "Makes the Kubra we fought in the north seem like puppies in comparison. So very few people who have travelled in and out of Rwelvencrest at will, there are a strange bunch of nomads called the Tzigane that do, they tell tales, but they are known to... embellish their stories."

William was drawing attention from a few of the merchants, his face had become recognisable in the town, a fact that Heineroth hated, but for the most part, the heir prince was well-liked in the city. William stopped to talk to a few merchants they passed. He would ask them how their day was and what wares they were selling. He had ingratiated himself well with the city folk of Trindon.

"Wish you wouldn't do that," Heineroth grumbled, standing beside his prince. "Anyone of them could be an assassin in the service of our enemies."

"You mean the baron of Taros?" William asked.

"Him, yes, and others."

"This walk was unplanned. No one knew of it, not even you." William explained, "And the people should see their future prince." William added, "If I am to rule these people, I should know as much about them as I can."

"Is this why we are heading into the bloody slums?"

The two walked through the city square, where the gallows stood. Six bodies still hung from them swaying slightly in the late afternoon breeze. Their eyes bulged, their Haulfin features twisted as they had gasped their last, leaving a gruesome frieze on their faces. William stopped briefly and looked up at the figures as they dangled. The bodies would be left until tomorrow morning, where no doubt the Inquisition would have found more sedition or heresy.

"I don't like this Heineroth. The people of the lower quarter are being persecuted unfairly." They continued past the stage of execution towards the lower quarter.

"You don't know it's unfair. Perhaps the Inquisition is doing the one true God's work wiping out these beings."

"I cannot believe that a god that is supposed to be as benign, forgiving and loving as the one true God would warrant acts of such barbarism."

The lower quarter wasn't a quarter of the city. It was barely a minuscule fraction of about two square miles of run-down derelict slum, surrounded by a guarded wall. Anyone trying to get in or out without a permit or permission usually wound up dead or hanging from the gallows the following day. A few Haulfin were allowed to leave to work the merchant's quarters. Some even worked in the castle as life long indentured servants. However, most of the Haulfin would be born, grow old, and die within the confines of the small section of Trindon.

The houses near the wall against the lower quarter were all dilapidated old and worn. No human would live this close to this area of town if they could help it. But those that did had little choice. This would be the only housing they could afford. As they walked down these streets, the cobbles ended in rough gravel. Young rag-dressed children played in the gutters.

"Paupers alley." Heineroth smiled and waved at the children. "Many years ago, I would have been one of those sprogs."

"I'm not sure the empire had been formed when you were a child," William jested.

"Oi lad, watch it." He playfully thumped the prince's arm. "Must say I was glad to get out, joined the army as soon as possible. Served fourteen campaigns as a grunt, don't think many can boast that."

"How did you become an officer?" William asked. He had heard the story several times but knew Heineroth liked to tell it.

"Well, it was the fourteenth campaign I was serving in. I had made it to full-colour sergeant, the highest rank for a commoner. We were in open war with Taros." Heineroth started to ramble on, "Surrounded and outnumbered, all our officers were dead or wounded. The enemy wanted to negotiate our surrender. For a grunt like me, to wear an officer's colours would have been a court-martial offence. I served in the Lightfoot's back then, under the young Richard Lightfoot, a good man, a little idealistic back then for war. Despite his injuries, he wanted to be the one to go to meet the enemy. Well, knocked him out and nicked his kit." Heineroth smiled. "Then some of the lads and I pretended to surrender and caught the bastards unaware, ended up capturing their officers. Well, I had put Hawkwood in a bit of a bind. So, he and Lord Lightfoot decided that, since they didn't want to court martial me for impersonating an officer, they made me one." Heineroth grinned. "Since then, I never stopped moving through the ranks."

At the end of Paupers Alley, they approached four fully armoured guards. These wore the black armour of the enforcers and soldiers for the Inquisition. They blocked the gates that barred the lower quarter from the rest of the city. Two carried halberds, long spearlike axes, and beside them were two other guards in lighter armour carrying crossbows.

"Quite a heavy guard," William noted.

"I don't have any say on the Enforcers movements," Heineroth rationalised. "They fall under the Inquisition's remit."

"I've never liked how much say the Inquisition has in running our lands."

"Me either, lad, but them's the facts."

"When I'm running the princedom, I will be much firmer with these thugs."

"You are already pretty much running the princedom, lad."

"I wish. There is so much that is hidden and blocked from me." William gritted his teeth in frustration. "I've tried to ask the Inquisitor, but he gives me nothing, and neither will the bishop. The church directs our princedom against our wishes."

"You will always be dealing with people who have their own agendas. So, you shouldn't trust anyone," Heineroth stated.

The guards stopped them as they approached the gates.

"Halt," The lead guard spoke with authority. The two brought their halberds forward, the sharp tips pointed towards William and Heineroth and the archers brought their crossbows up to bear.

"Do you lads have any idea who this is?" Heineroth tested. He noticed atop the wall two additional crossbows were pointed in their direction. "This is the heir prince. Now you will stand down and let us pass."

"I'm sorry, sir, but we have strict orders from Inquisitor Talos. No one is to pass these gates after nightfall." The guard stumbled, "By the orders of the Inquisition."

Heineroth looked up at the dusky sky. "Good thing, looks like we have a few minutes then."

"This is my city." William stepped forward. "If you are going to try to stop me, then you will have to attack your prince," he continued on until the halberd point clinked against his breastplate. Then, he gave a winning smile at the young guard. "Are you willing to do that?" he asked, his hand idly resting on the pommel of his sword.

"You are not my prince," The enforcer stated. "I am in the service of the Inquisition and the holy church of the one true God." The guard's confidence wavered, sure he had been given orders from the captain of the city enforcers, but he was also sure that a prince outranked any captain, not to mention the general of Gont was right beside him.

"They don't recruit them for brains," Heineroth complained under his breath. He stepped forward, brushing the point of the Halbert to one side till his face was close to the Enforcer's dark helmet. He started using what Heineroth liked to call his sergeant's voice. It was a rough series of snapped, barked orders, "The prince has important duties in the lower city. I'm here to ensure he doesn't get into trouble. Your orders weren't to let anyone in after dark. We have a few minutes before sunset so step aside, or you'll feel my boot in your rear." Heineroth's eyes flashed with anger.

The guard raised his weapon out of the way. "I'm sorry, sir. I was only obeying orders, sir."

William was about to speak when Heineroth interrupted, "You did just as you were ordered, nothing more, but if you want to get anywhere, you need to learn when to follow orders and when to think, lad." As he walked past the guard, he slapped him on the shoulder.

The towering gates opened a crack to allow Heineroth and William through. There were four more guards on the inside of the gates. William and Heineroth exchanged glances, even more enforcers.

There was a distinct change in this area of the city. There were no cobbles, only mud, leaving very rough narrow streets. There was sewerage and waste everywhere, piled up against the walls of the houses. These houses were made from garbage; a few long-standing buildings had fallen into complete disrepair gaping holes in their roofs and the walls, their former glory crumbling and dissolving with time.

The streets were almost dead, abandoned. The only sign of life was vermin scavenging amongst the refuse. William wrinkled his nose at the smell.

Heineroth could feel eyes watching them from the shadows, but he couldn't see them. He loosened the clasp on his sword.

"You get used to it, lad, after a few battlefields," Heineroth grinned. "We better move on. This isn't safe."

"I was told where to meet our contact, four streets ahead and on the left."

"How can you tell what a street is?" Heineroth complained. "This place is a hive."

They picked their way cautiously through filth-laden narrow streets. Unlike in the merchant square, there was no sound of revelry, just an eery quiet with only the chatting of tiny, clawed feet. The air grew thicker with the foul stench as they got deeper into the lower quarter. They passed a thin Haulfin slumped against a wall dressed only in a burlap sack, an empty bottle still held in its limp fingers. It snored loudly, dead drunk from whatever it had consumed.

"I think it's just round here." As the two slid between two buildings, the gap was tiny. They had to walk in single file, turning sideways to make their way to prevent their shoulders from scraping against the sides of the buildings.

Heineroth's large gut touched both walls as they slid between the narrow gaps. "Hurry up, lad," he grumbled, forcing his way between the buildings.

"It's not far." William pushed through till he came out in a tiny courtyard. As he came out into the small square, several little Haulfin children fled. Grumbling and swearing came from behind William as the hefty old soldier forced his girth through the tiny passage.

"We are here?" Heineroth grunted as he forced himself out of the gap.

"No." William shook his head. "There is supposed to be a door with a small red cross on it."

"Are you sure your contact hasn't led us into a trap?"

"Would you trust me if I said Ailwhyn set this up?" William asked.

"The witch?" Heineroth paused. He had fought and bled beside the young Aldari. She had put her life on the line for his, but she was still a Haulfin and a witch. "Maybe," he conceded.

"Come on, this way. Perhaps it is further down." William started moving down a similar small passage, slightly broader, and Heineroth could proceed unimpeded. They entered another small courtyard, a group of figures huddled down an alley off the square. Heineroth turned around and could see some shadowed figures approaching from behind.

"To arms, lad!" he warned, drawing his sword. His large bastard sword wasn't the best weapon for alley fighting. A dagger would have been more suitable. He squared his back against the young prince. Seven figures approached them, surrounding them. They all wore faded grey hoods and cloaks, each carrying long knives.

"Well, look what we've got here." A weaselly voice, "Looks like we got some guards who wandered into the wrong neck of the woods."

William pulled his sword free. "We are no guards." In the fading light, his features shone clear. His eyes flashed with steel. "I am seeking Balis Gestalt."

"Lots of people are seeking the boss." The leader grinned, it was a taller Haulfin, but with its hood, it was hard to make out its features. The would-be muggers eyes saw a heavy-laden pouch at the heir prince's waist. "You want to be handing those coins to me now, and no one will get hurt."

"You want them, come try to take them," Heineroth bristled.

"We don't wish to kill anyone here," William explained, trying to placate the attackers. "I have a deal I wish to offer Balis Gestalt."

The seven thieves acted in unison, and as if by some unspoken command, they rushed the two warriors. Heineroth was a survivor of many battles and hadn't gotten this far by not knowing how to fight. As the first one charged, he thrust his foot into the man's groin, leveraging his kick by bracing against the prince's back. There was a sickening crunch as his metal-plated boot connected squarely with the lead attacker's groin. William had braced himself for this and used the added weight of Heineroth to lend weight to his meticulously crafted sword. The tip sliced neatly against an attacker's face causing him to flinch. He then used the blade's pommel and cracked it against the man's skull. The body fell, obstructing the next attacker. This one was a squat man. He tried to lumber over his fallen comrade, only to be met by William's flashing blade slicing against his chest, leaving a deep wound. William stepped backwards, his back against Heineroth again. The large man was using the reach of his sword to poke and prod to keep the next attackers at bay.

The thieves still outnumbered the two defenders by two to one, but this wasn't how it was supposed to go. They had ambushed enforcer groups who had tried to invade their territory before, but those bullies were all might and had no skill. Heineroth gave a battle-tongue command to William, and with ease of movement, the two swapped places, William darting deftly under the left arm of Heineroth to catch the next attacker square in the shoulder, the blade sank deep and slid out, leaving a trail of green blood. Heineroth had used the switch to bring his sword above his head and brought it down with all his strength. The startled mugger raised his arms to prevent the blow, and the mighty bastard sword cut deep. This was enough for the robbers, five of their number down in moments, the remaining two fled into the warrens. Heineroth picked the long knife from the man he had just maimed.

"He won't be needing this." The wounded, seeing their friends flea and faced with the great grizzled old warrior brandishing a long knife, scrambled for their freedom, leaving the first attacker still writhing in the muck in agony, blood leaking from his groin.

William knelt by the man, rolling him over. He clutched his family jewels, whimpering. "I'm sorry it had to go this way," William spoke genuinely. "Now, would you be able to tell us where Balis Gestalt is, please?"

Chapter 14

The Den of Thieves

They reached the end of another narrow alley; it hadn't been far from the attack, only one street over. There had been no other incidents, although they had noticed an increased number of figures watching them cautiously down the narrow backstreets and alleys. This alley halted at a dead-end. There was a small rough wooden door with a small red cross staining its upper corner. Night had now fallen, and thin trickles of light escaped around the broken edges of the frame. William knocked against the door twice, then after a second pause once again, and after another break, another two knocks. He hoped he had remembered the secret knock better than the directions.

"Who's there," a grizzled voice spat as if it was chewing on gravel.

William spoke. "A friend."

The wooden door slid back, and at knee height, a tiny little creature popped out its head. The individual was barely over a foot tall and looked like a bearded old man with a hunchback. It looked up at the two towering humans. The Haulfin spoke. "You are humans."

"But I am still a friend." William continued, "I was sent by Ailwhyn Evensong."

The Haulfin, a Gnomus, looked up sceptically. A voice came from inside, again soft-spoken, "He was expected." The Haulfin looked back inside and then up at the two. "You sure?" the tiny Gnomus asked inside. "They look like fucking guards."

The voice spoke again. "Let them in, Gneth."

The little Gnomus moved the door aside to allow the two large humans to enter what looked from the outside to be a squalid shack. Inside, surprisingly, it was immaculate and well-kept. It was a much larger room than it appeared. It must have gone through several of the adjacent houses. At the entrance, there was a small desk behind which a fat Aldari sat. It was rare to see a fat Haulfin, especially those who struggled to survive in the horrific conditions of the lower quarter, and unique still to see a fat Aldari. As a breed, they were known to be a slender and graceful Haulfin race. However, his large glowing eyes and pointed ears confirmed his Haulfin breed. The hunched Gnomus assistant, Gneth, had a tiny stool and table beside him. Behind them were several small rustic tables where a few people were murmuring. There were a couple of bottles on each table.

The Gnomus closed the door behind them, sat back at its table, and started smoking a tiny pipe. Heineroth found he was staring at the little figure. "What? Never seen a Gnomus before?" Gneth sneered.

"No," Heineroth admitted. "You are so titchy."

"And you are a fat oaf," the Gnomus shot back.

William interrupted, "I'm sorry, he didn't mean to stare."

"Figures, no one notices us until you need your chimney or privy unblocking." The figure grunted and crossed his arms. "I've seen you two before."

"There are a couple in the castle, but as he said, they are often in a place you wouldn't go," William explained to Heineroth. "I saw one once when I was a child." William turned his attention to the sizeable Aldari man. "I had some questions and an offer," William began.

"Not so fast." The Aldari tapped the palm of his hand. "I'm sure your slave told you I would need coin before I spoke."

Heineroth leaned over the table. "How about you answer our questions, and then we decide how much it's worth." If the old soldier had been hoping to intimidate the Aldari, it failed, the large Aldari leaned back slightly to put some space between his face and the grizzled old man, and he nodded backwards. Heineroth looked behind the Haulfin. Two dozen of the patrons had drawn crude, rusted weapons.

"You may have been able to take care of some malnourished street thugs on your way here, but you will find my boys are a little more adept." The Haulfin grinned.

William interjected, pulling Heineroth away. "Now, my friend here is just a bit overeager." He then tossed a small pouch onto the Aldari's desk. "Fifty guilds," he offered.

The fat Aldari looked at the pouch and then up at William. William was calm with a slightly crooked smile that endeared him to the large Aldari.

The Haulfin spoke, waving his hand, and the patrons settled down. "Fine. OK, ask your questions." The Haulfin didn't offer them a seat.

"The people executed today…" William began.

"Murdered," corrected the Aldari. He was poking the pouch of coins.

"Fine, murdered. Were they guilty of heresy or sedition?" William asked.

"They were guilty of the same thing we all are guilty of." The Aldari waved his hand backwards. "Living, they had planned no sedition or heresy unless it's heresy to live, same with the group yesterday and the day before. You people must know this. Why are you spending coin on answers you already have?"

William watched the large violet eyes of the Aldari, looking for any sign of deception. "I seek confirmation of information for the betterment of the princedom. I know that you are Balis Gestalt, leader of the underworld in the lower quarter."

Balis Gestalt smiled. "Seems you already have some information." His grin creased his chins. "Fine, I'll tell you what you need to know. Look, very few of my men are foolish enough to get caught by the enforcers, those that know the bribe of ten guilds will usually get them out of trouble."

"So those who have been tried and killed were innocent completely?"

"Not involved in any crime I know of." Balis shrugged. "They were only guilty of trying to survive. Survival in this part of town means very few of us have clean hands."

A lizard-like creature approached the table carrying a tray with a bottle and three wooden mugs. It reminded William of the vision he had seen in the ice tower many years ago.

"Five guildersss," The reptile hissed at William. The prince looked at the bottle and guessed diplomacy would catch more flies than vinegar. He paid the barkeep and sat at the table opposite the Aldari without an invite. He popped the cork in the top of the bottle and left it on the table for the Haulfin. Heineroth scowled and didn't sit. He kept his arms crossed, standing behind his prince, one hand resting on the long knife he had acquired. The fat Aldari Balis Gestalt leaned forward and poured himself a generous portion from the bottle. William took the bottle from him and filled his mug. He sniffed the liquid as he watched Balis take a huge gulp. The ale was strong, giving off a fortified smell of roughly distilled spirits. William took a tentative sip, his lip went numb almost on contact, and the strong liquor burned its way down his throat. William suppressed a cough and gag on the ale.

"Haulfin spirits take some getting used to." Balis smiled, taking another gulp. "OK, what else, Prince."

William looked startled. "What makes you think I'm the prince?" William asked.

Balis laughed. "Information is my business. I knew you were coming even before you were through the gates. I know who you are. Heck, most of us do. Even those thugs who attacked you outside knew who you were." He waved around the bar. "We also know that you have been trying to help our kind. Which means on your visit here, you have my word that no harm will fall you, at least this time."

"Wish we could have had that promise before we had to cut those thugs down," Heineroth commented.

"They are a young gang of fools who thought they could make a name for themselves. They were, of course, wrong." Balis sipped on the mug.

"I wish to make things better for all of Gont," William began. "To do that, I need information and a deal."

"So, you wish me to be your spy in the lower quarter?" Balis laughed, taking another sip of the foul spirit.

"No, but with change comes resistance, and as I ease the restrictions on the lower quarter, the humans will feel threatened. I will be banning the slavery of the Haulfin, and many will fear the loss of profits." William kept his eyes locked with the Aldari as he took another sip of his spirit. The burning wasn't as bad the second time. "My father will soon pass, and with that, the full power of the princedom falls to me." William paused for a moment, while he and his father hadn't been close for many years, he would still mourn his passing. "As I try to implement changes, many on both sides would seek to gain opportunities. I would ask you not to be one of those and perhaps let me know if anyone seeks to cause trouble."

Balis thought about this for a moment. He prided himself on being a good judge of character. This prince seemed to be telling the truth. He was naïve but believed what he was saying. "OK, here is the deal." Balis leaned forward. "I will do as you have suggested, but I want one thing, not coin, as I will always be able to get that, but I want a place in your court." Balis Gestalt smiled. His violet eyes seemed to flash a little brighter.

William frowned. Easing the persecution of the Haulfin had been his promise to those who called themselves gods in the north, a promise he intended to keep. William was happy to uphold that promise but allowing an Haulfin in the court of the princedom would be an intriguing challenge. He thought about it. "It couldn't be a prominent position." The prince pondered, "A courtier, or perhaps an almoner."

"The Almoner is determined by the church," Heineroth reminded William.

"So, a courtier?" William asked.

Balis shrugged. "The title matters little to me, but to have a voice." William extended his hand, and the deal was sealed.

The inn door burst open, and a short slender Haulfin ran in. He rushed to Balis' table, and Heineroth drew his blade.

"Easy." Balis calmed the boy down. "What boy?" he asked the newcomer.

"Balis, they come!" This one looked about six years old, but with Haulfin, it was hard to tell. "They pulled Hagar off the street. Now a platoon of hard heads is coming this way."

"Who?" William asked.

"The fucking enforcers, your people," Balis grumbled.

"Not mine." William iterated.

"Well, regardless. You must hide. If enforcers catch you with us, the Inquisition will find a way to ruin our deal." The large Aldari grumbled, "Kill the lights and out the back anyone who isn't ready," he announced loudly. "Follow Gneth." He pointed at the small Gnomus, who was already struggling off his perch.

The tiny Gnomus ran with surprising speed for one so small, out through the room towards where there was a back door. William quickly ducked into the small room, but Heineroth had to carefully ease himself through the small frame. Once in the back room, the lights went out, plunging them into darkness.

"Follow my voice. You big folk can't see in the dark." The grizzled voice led them forward. They were led through more backrooms guided by the little Haulfin and occasional bumps and bashes as they struggled through the darkness. Finally, they were led out into a narrow street, crawling on their

144

hands and knees through the filth. Through the warrens, they could hear the shouting of the enforcers. It seemed to be several streets away now.

"This way," Gneth instructed. "Oi fat man, keep up." He called back to Heineroth. In the pale moonlight, they could see the diminutive figure of the Gnomus scampering down the streets. "I'm going to take you to the southern gate. You'll have to talk your way out from there."

Back in the dark tavern, Balis Gestalt remained seated with his desk facing the entrance. He could hear armour scraping against the walls as the enforcers approached. There were four... no five of them. If a platoon had been sent into the lower quarter, that would mean about thirty. They would break into five or six units to search the lower quarter.

The Aldari was calmly sipping his drink when the enforcers smashed open the door. Balis had arrangements with some enforcers to turn a blind eye to his activities. Most of his associates would 'escape' the iron clutches of the Inquisition because of the greed of a few officers. He recognised none of these five. He hoped he could get them in his pocket.

"In the name of the Inquisition and the church, you will come with us," the first one announced, stooping into the room.

"Welcome, officer," Balis smiled. "What am I supposed to have done?"

"You are charged with hosting an illegal drinking establishment." The enforcer shone his blazing torch over the desk of Balis, who was calmly drinking. Balis carefully moved the Dewar ale away from the open flame.

"Come, Officer, have a seat and share a drink with me." Balis grinned. "But I wouldn't put that flame too close to this."

The officer bristled, "I would never drink with a Haulfin scum."

"Now, that is quite rude." Balis Gestalt grinned. He raised an eyebrow and looked the enforcer dead in the eye. His violet eyes flashed. "There is more than one kind of ambush, officer." Balis continued, "You break into my home hoping to catch me unaware, trying to ambush and intimidate me. But I make ambush an art form. I will take you down from every side, pick your men apart until you are alone. Because here I am the predator of the predators, the protectors of the lower quarter."

There was a silky sound as a dozen blades were unsheathed in the darkness. The enforcers were suddenly surrounded by a brace of daggers. From the night of the inn, a dozen Haulfin emerged with cutlasses and other weapons drawn. The enforcers were suddenly encircled, outnumbered and in unfriendly territory.

"I ask you again to sit down," Balis asked, this time with more menace.

The guards looked around for a moment, they were outnumbered, but these were only starving Haulfin from the lower quarter. They wouldn't dare attack the soldiers of the Inquisition. The soldiers gripped their heavy metal clubs tighter, ready to fight back.

"You will all of you submit to the will of the church," the lead enforcer commanded; he looked to his troops. "For the one true God!" he cried out, brandishing his heavy mace at Balis. The oversized Aldari rolled his chair back out of the way of the clumsy swing.

"I'm sorry you couldn't be reasonable," Balis grunted, rising from his chair. The fight was swift, bloody, and brutal, the enforcers stood no chance, and the blades from the dark quickly made short work of the small patrol as the Haulfin stepped forward, blades sliding between the folds of the armour of the enforcers. Balis straightened his chair.

"There will be five or six more patrols out tonight." He grinned a wolfish grin. "I want there to be less." The Haulfin left the inn and were sent like wolves to hunt in the night.

Twenty enforcer bodies were found the following morning, floating down an open gutter, unceremoniously disposed of, a gruesome reminder of the dangers of the lower quarter.

Chapter 15

The Hunter

Jacob had been out collecting herbs, it was nearing winter, and he needed to stock up. When he returned home, he found the house silent. He called out for his mother. She hadn't left the house for any length of time in almost six years. She had become a hermit entrapped in her own home.

He called out, "Mother." Into the house. As he looked around, he briefly let part of him hope that she had gone out, finally sick of the four walls of their little hut. He called out for her again, hearing nothing. Jacob smiled to himself; he rarely got peace in his own home. If his brother wasn't badgering him with questions, he often tended to his mother's needs, housework or preparing curatives. He decided to check his mother's room and poked his head through the door.

Lying on the floor beside the bed, he saw her body, face down. Jacobs' heart froze. He hesitated; he called out again, this time with a slight tremor in his voice.

"Mother?" The body on the floor didn't stir. He rushed to her side and rolled her over. Her skin was pale, her lips tightly clenched, and her eyes half-open, showing only the whites. Once Erin had been a flower of beauty in the village. No trace of that beauty remained on this body Jacob cradled in his arms. He placed the back of his hand to her mouth, feeling for any breath of life. It was there, faint. He searched her for any marks or injuries, finding none, he began a diagnosis, glancing across the room for any other cause to her malady. Several vials lay scattered next to a pile of unwashed clothes. They were small vials of the tincture he had used to treat her depression. She had poisoned herself by overdosing. She had drunk enough to put herself into an unconscious stupor. Jacob listed the ingredients in his head. Some could be deadly if taken in sufficient enough quantities. Jacob pulled a pillow from her bed. Propping her head up, he rushed to his little corner in the kitchen where his supplies were kept. He pulled bottles of herbs from their shelves, scanning the labels.

"Dried rhizome." Jacob placed it to one side, checking each bottle and discarding the useless ones. Finally, he found what he was looking for, root of ipecacuanha, he clutched the bottle. Jacob sprinkled it into his pestle and mortar, frantically grinding them to a pulp. He needed to make an emetic. Jacob spread ground mustard and salt into the mix before topping it up with water to form a syrup. The cure in hand he stumbled back to her side. He lifted her head from the pillow dripping a few drops of the liquid down her throat.

Erin began vomiting immediately. In Jacob's rush, he had forgotten to get anything to catch the vomit; it splattered across the floor. Large chunks of her half-digested lunch splattered across Jacob's lap. He could smell the alcoholic vapours of the tincture she had taken. Jacob cursed his buffoonery. His mother had fallen into a profound depression since Raouf vanished. He cradled her head in his lap as his mother repeatedly wretched, expelling the poison.

Jacob heard the front door open. "Robin," he called out. "Get a pail."

His brother sauntered through the house carrying the latrine bucket. "Will this do…" He paused at the bedroom door. He dropped the bucket spilling the last day's filth over the floor and rushing to his mother's side. "What's wrong with her?" he asked, panicked.

"Shut up and pass me that pail," Jacob snapped. Robin grabbed the foul-smelling bucket and helped Jacob prop up their mother's head. "OK, now help me get her on the bed," Jacob ordered. Jacob lacked the strength to lift his mother, but Robin effortlessly managed.

It was a long night as Jacob tended to his mother. Erin twisted and tussled with a night of fitful sleep. Jacob knew what he had to do, the words of Andresila and Jerisavlja, the Veela he had met at the mountain stream, came to mind. He closed his eyes, imagining the light in his mind. It had become more accessible the more he had practiced. As he spoke the words of the old religion 'rebmuls' drawing on the spark of magic, he felt its flare igniting and flowing through his body, and then it faded. Erin fell into a restful sleep her breathing returned to normal. Jacob felt a wave of nausea wash over him. The effort to summon the magic had drained him. He pulled himself from the bed and slumped to a chair beside his mother. Still awake, Jacob could hear his mother finally resting. Next door, the loud snores of his brother reverberated through the house as sleep overtook him.

The following morning Robin found his brother dosing in a chair. Robin blundered through the door and kicked his brother's foot. Jacob jumped, "Shh, you clot," he barked at his brother. "She needs rest."

"Will she be, OK?" Robin asked, his face filled with worry.

"Yes, but we need to watch after her." Pulling himself out of the chair, his back hurt from the awkward position he had slept in. "She did this to herself," Jacob added with a worried tone.

"What do you mean?" Robin asked, confused.

"Never mind, brother," Jacob answered. He glanced at the vomit and mess on the floor, he would need to clean it, and his eyes fell to the collection of vials. "Don't worry, we just shouldn't leave her alone." He darted a look at his sleeping mother, and a thin smile crossed his lips; he had cast a real spell last night. *True, it left me drained and fatigued, but I did it!* he rejoiced quietly in the confines of his head. He briefly wondered about sharing the experience with the hag but thought better of it. Jacob rubbed his brother's back, gently coaxing him out of the room. "I'll clean this up," Jacob offered.

Erin woke late the next afternoon; her stomach ached, and her head was spinning, but worst of all, she was still alive. For the briefest of moments, she had hoped that death would finally take her.

The light burned her eyes as she forced them open. She saw her son, Robin, perched on her bed through the blinding haze. *How selfish of me,* she thought to herself. She reached out and touched her son.

The young man looked at his mother as she rose in the bed. "Mum," he cried, giving her a big hug. From the living room, Jacob heard the commotion. He stood up, approaching the doorway. He watched as his mother and brother shared a hug. Jacob nodded with satisfaction, closing the door, and giving them privacy. He continued to clear away the mess in the kitchen. In his frantic search to treat his mother, he had demolished his collection, and it would take him most of the day to reorganise it.

Shortly, Erin and Robin left the bedroom. Robin helped guide his mother to the dining table. She followed him like a lost child. Jacob brought over some stew for his mother.

"Come on, Mum, eat," urged Robin, he lifted the spoon to her mouth. He looked worriedly across at Jacob, who calmly handed him a bowl before getting one for himself. They sat around the table in silence while Robin tried to spoon-feed Erin. The food occasionally found her mouth, but most was dribbling from her slack jaw into the bowl.

"Brother," he admonished. "You're making a mess." Jacob wiped his mother's chin with care then carefully and tenderly fed her while Robin devoured both his own and Jacob's food. As Jacob fed Erin, he stroked her hair.

After clearing away the bowls, he watched his mother. She just sat at the table, staring vacantly off into the distance. Jacob felt a twinge of apprehension that his mother wasn't there any more. He worried that perhaps his spell had caused this. He shook his head, the magic had had no such effect on him, but he would bring it up with Maganwyth tomorrow.

"Bring her to the fire," he ordered his brother as he prepared her chair, tidied up her pillows and moved the foot stall closer. Robin gently guided his mother across the room onto her favourite chair, easing her into it with Jacob's aid. She sat, scarcely blinking, looking into the fire, her fingers locked on the chair's arms.

Robin danced from foot to foot nervously. "What's wrong with her, Jacob?" he asked. "She isn't speaking."

Jacob turned with a soft glare. "Do the dishes," he ordered, causing Robin to slink away.

Jacob stroked his Erin's hair, checking her temperature. She had a mild fever but nothing too wrong. He looked into her eyes; they were unfocused, the fire glistening in her eyes, but there was no spark of recognition.

Robin was clattering and bashing while cleaning the dishes and somehow managed to break a pot in his fumbling. Jacob closed his eyes and breathed slowly, imagining the light in his mind, but the light struggled to ignite. He was still exhausted from the previous night's exertion. He concentrated on his mother. He reached out to her, touching her forehead, a soft dark aura emanating around his hand as he stroked her head. He could feel the misery and darkness that filled his mother. In Jacob's mind, a voice with echoing hollowness sounded.

The voice spoke, it was ladened with grief and sorrow, and its' words hung heavy like lead in the air. *Hello, uncle.*

Who are you? Jacob asked in his mind.

The voice spoke. It sounded hurt and wounded. I am called Penthos. I am in here with your mother. I have come to her. She called to me.

What are you? Jacob asked. Are you doing this to her?

I am what you call a god, although my father was a true god of old. Then, her voice seemed to quiver with a sob. I am here because of your mother, she called to me.

Jacob thought to himself, *So the gods have family.*

The voice spoke. Yes. We have family. Some of us are greater and older, and some of us are younger. I have been with your mother for several years now since the disappearance of your father.

So, you have done this to her? Jacob countered in his mind angrily.

The voice seemed to sob as it spoke. No, she was like this, so she called me.

Can you leave her? Jacob asked. She is dying.

The voice uttered softly between sobs. All I live with eventually fades. I cannot help her. It is my nature. It is their nature. Then, it paused for a long moment. I can bring her mind back a little, but she will still dwell on the sorrow.

With that said, the connection was broken. Jacob was kneeling next to his mother in the warm cabin, the fire crackling in front of them. He blinked twice, had it been his imagination, *No!* Jacob knew what had happened, and he would trust his own mind if nothing else. *Uncle?* The voice had called him Uncle. He thought about it for a moment. Then he noticed his mother's eyes had focused a little, and she was blinking away tears. He wiped them away from her cheeks.

"I'm sorry, Robin," she apologised, clinging to Jacob.

Robin hearing his mother's voice, rushed over and roughly pushed Jacob away, hugging her. Jacob was caught awkwardly between the two. Jacob extracted himself, leaving his brother and his mother to embrace. He looked over at his family, cuddling each other. He allowed himself a brief smile before turning away, leaving his mother and brother consoling each other.

I'm not the only one with a god's gift then, he mused to himself sarcastically. He felt tired. The effort to speak to that sad spirit in his mother's head, combined with the poor night's sleep caught up with him. He returned to his own room, slumped onto his bed, and a peaceful slumber took him.

***

The following day when Jacob rose, Robin had already left to go hunting, leaving Jacob to tend to their still-ailing mother. Since his father's passing, Robin had been pushing himself to be the best hunter in the village, but he was far from there. Robin felt his brother was useless. Jacob spent all his time on the cliff with the mad old hag. At least right now, he was looking after their mum, the first valuable thing he had done in a long time. Robin was fourteen now, soon to be fifteen with the coming winter but was already as strong as any half-again his age. Despite his size he moved faster and quieter than most. Robin had been practising with his father's bow daily. Although he hadn't had much luck hunting deer or elk, he could bring down rabbits with his sling, as sure a shot as any, but rabbits would barely keep the family alive. Sure, Jacob was brilliant, but smarts didn't put food on the table. Nearly six months ago, at the beginning of the summer, Robin had been approached by one of the oldest of the hunters in the village, Laban. Laban had been one of the old men who had taken Robin out to celebrate his first kill, he had insisted on teaching the young boy.

"You brought one down, but it was a sloppy job," Laban berated Robin in the tavern that night. "Almost a quiver of arrows, and it was a young buck." He pulled the young man aside on the night of his celebrations. "If you are going to do this, you will do it with me. I'll show you how to do it so that the rest of us have something to hunt next year." The other hunters cheered and celebrated the young lad's first blooding. Laban had been true to his word. For the last six months, he had been training Robin. Robin's skills had improved, but he had yet to take down a second animal.

"You are fast and strong." Laban imparted, "But you continue to be bull headed, rushing when you should sneak, shooting when you should wait." He continued to lecture as they left before dawn. "A hunter is calm; a hunter takes his time."

Over the last half-year, Laban taught him what to hunt, when to hunt and when to protect your 'flock' as Laban called them. "You hunt too much, weaken the flock; hunt too little, starve. There is a balance." The lithe old man seemed to have no end of words and continued to talk as Robin dutifully strode beside him. Robin wasn't a fast learner like his brother, but after six months, the stories had sunk in. "Good hunters are the honey and milk of the land, for they are sensitive to its needs and balances. A bad hunter is the poison of the land, with sick addiction to death. If you find you fall in love with the killing, stop. You don't hunt any deer younger than…"

"… Three years because you need a good breeding stock," Robin repeated in a monotone. He was fed up. He could swear the old man had been speaking for hours, and dawn hadn't even broken. The first sunrays of the day were gently caressing the heathland. The greys melted away into the dawning sun's greens, purples, and oranges. It was drawing to the end of summer, and the morning was cold. Their breath misted up around them, and morning frost crunched underfoot. The deer and stags would look for a deep thicket to bed down for the day. The best time to catch them was early morning, during the dawning hours.

Laban smiled as Robin repeated his words, "There is another reason we don't hunt the young, a hunters secret." Then, he smiled. "I'll tell you someday, but let's just say the spirits of the forest can get annoyed if you kill the wrong deer."

Robin laughed. He couldn't believe this old man would fear the fairy tales and superstitions of the old.

"Quiet lad, we are near the flay." The two hunters dropped low, coiled like springs. Robin was able to scramble stealthily through the thicket. With a few more decades on his joints, Laban took a little longer to catch up. They gazed out over the open field. Finally, in the growing light, there was some movement.

Their game would flee into the forest at the first disturbance. So, Laban and Robin spent some time quietly observing them. Laban grinned as he saw the lovely creatures grazing, admiring the beasts, even though he would hunt and kill them, he still loved the natural world that provided for him.

A low fog hung over the flay, shrouding the creatures. Silently Laban pointed to one of the animals. It was a little larger than the others, walking slower. Robin observed the beast. The animal was the oldest and the slowest. He rolled on his back and strung his bow biting his lower lip as he strained to bend the wood to attach the bowstring. His father's weapon was built for a fully grown man. It was a fine bit of craftsmanship. Laban left his own bow unstrung. He signalled to Robin to take the shot. Robin snapped a piece of grass and dropped it. There was almost no wind.

The young lad slowly rose to his feet in the rapidly growing light, making no noise. Robin drew a single arrow fitting it to the bowstring. *Aim for the heart,* he thought to himself as he notched the arrow and drew it back, pulling in a huge breath. He drew the weapon; the taught string tortured his muscles. His father's bow was an impressive hundred and fifty-pound weapon. He gritted his teeth and focused on the old deer in the mist. His target moved into the thickest fog; he tracked it in his mind. In the morning light, he could imagine the deer's hide, exhaling he unleashed the arrow. A loud crack of the bow disturbed the morning stillness. A faint whistle of the shot disappeared into the mist. The deer scattered, darting in all directions, sent into a mad panic losing themselves in the woods.

"Did I get it?" Robin asked eagerly.

"You tell me, lad; you are the one who fired the bow." Laban grunted as he pushed himself to his feet. "Let's go see."

The two walked through the mist on the flay towards the deer. There were sounds in the mists of a dying animal. Robin had struck the beast, but it hadn't been a clean kill. The arrow had embedded itself through the animal's lungs. Laban winced. He hated seeing an animal suffer. He pulled out a long knife and handed it to the young boy. "Shit, do it, boy, finish him."

"But…" Robin paused, still holding his bow.

"Quick, don't let him suffer," Laban urged, thrusting the knife at Robin. The boy took it, looking at the blade, feeling uncomfortable weight the heavy wooden handled knife. The beast was struggling on the ground gasping for breath and baying with panic as the hunters neared. Robin knelt by the animal's head, its large black eyes staring up in a frenzy, unable to breathe or move. Robin placed the tip of the knife against the animal's chest where the heart was, where his arrow had meant to hit. Robin pushed the knife down hard, cutting the animal's heart and ending its pain. Robin stayed by the animal as the large black eyes dulled as death took it.

Robin remained watching the dears' eyes for a few moments. This seemed much more substantial than when he killed rabbits or fish. This animal, still warm under his touch, he had just killed.

"Right, let's get him back to Havendale," Laban said finally after a few moments. Robin pulled out a rope to hitch up the deer wrapping the hemp around the hooves. The beast looked to weigh about two hundred pounds.

"Can we carry it together?" Robin asked hopefully.

Laban laughed. "When you make a clean kill, I'll help you carry it."

Chapter 16

The Wolves

Robin trudged down the hill, the full weight of the beast on his back. Laban carried both bows and quivers, whistling as he walked ahead of the young man. Dawn had broken, and the warmth was spreading across the land. As the forest woke, the birds began to chirp.

"Now, lad, that wasn't a bad hunt. Although you've got to be a better shot," Laban instilled. "You do well to draw this bow of yours," he mumbled as he continued along the trail, inspecting Robin's bow. "Are you sure you don't want to trade it for a smaller one? I've got a few light bows that will serve you well."

"It is my father's." Robin grunted, "I would rather get used to it."

"It will take time," Laban stated. "You'll need to practice every day."

"I do." Robin breathed heavily as he hefted the beast. "I can draw it, but I quiver slightly at full draw."

"Hence why you missed your..." Laban paused. "Hold up!" He raised his hand in the air, dropping low.

Robin knelt on the ground slumping the weighty beast behind him. Laban handed Robin back his quiver and bow. He made a face as he did so, baring his teeth. Robin guessed that meant predators. Robin hadn't heard anything over the sound of his own heartbeat. He tried to still his breathing. The strain of carrying the heavy deer had taxed even his muscular physique. Robin's arms burned and his back ached. He tried to follow Laban's gaze to spot the threat. Laban had drawn his bow and was at the ready.

Then he saw it. It darted through the forest in a flash of white-silver, fur glossy and thick and then another, their paws touched the earth silently. Robin knelt still, as did Laban. Robin stilled his breathing. He counted four creatures snaking through the woods. In the half-light of the morning dawn, they could have been dogs, but dogs didn't move that way, in quick motions moving as one, like a family of dancers stalking their prey. There's an intelligence in the eyes and a wariness of the hunters.

The wolves are not the devils of fairy tales. They are not aggressive, and they usually avoid humans. However, this pack of wolves had seen better days. Their fur was thin and clung to their bones. Even from this distance, Robin could count the ribs of the closest animal. Their bodies bore the scars of age. These wolves were desperate, starving, and cunning.

Near Havendale, wolves were a hazard to any livestock or a lone person who strayed too far away from the village. There were two humans here, not easy prey. However, they could smell the blood of the fresh kill held by the hunters, and hunger was about to overcome reason. Starvation had all but driven these wolves to the edge of madness. As the summer had reached its zenith, the increased hunting from the village had forced the wolves into harsher lands. From their razor-sharp teeth, saliva drooled. They could sense the blood in the air, wanting it, tasting it. Their claws pawed at the ground; their feet honed into deadly claws sharpened on the rocks of the mountains.

Robin dropped his bow and drew Laban's heavy knife. He raised one hand to ward off the approaching wolves, and he began to cut away one of the deer's hind legs.

"What are you doing?" Laban asked, keeping his arrow notched. Even if he drew as fast as he could, he couldn't shoot four wolves before they were upon him. As frail and weak as these creatures looked, he knew their jaws had a strength that could rip through his flesh and bones. One of the wolves howled, its cry echoing through the forest, striking fear into anyone who heard it. In the distance, there were howls of replies.

"Give me a moment." Robin frantically used both hands to saw through the deer's leg, cutting a large haunch off the animal. It dragged into a long, tense moment as the wolves circled, their hunger driving them forward. There was a ripping of skin and flesh as Robin tore one of the deer's legs away. He stood up; the wolves backed away as Robin drew himself to his impressive height. He then hefted the leg, throwing it as far as he could. The chunk soared through the air, leaving a blood trail behind it. It collided with a tree and crashed to the ground. The wolves scrambled around it, joined by two more that had been hidden pouncing from bushes either side of the hunters. The pack of seven fell upon the discarded leg tearing at it with fangs hungrily. There wouldn't be a lot of meat for seven wolves, but it would be more than they had eaten in weeks, and by the time they had finished, Laban and Robin would be long gone. The two hunters hefted the deer between them and started running. Robin's strength and stamina far outpaced the old hunter as they sprinted, dragging the heavy deer. After what felt like too fewer moments, a howl behind them indicated that they had run out of time. The chase brought on a primal fear that pushed every ounce of reserve Robin and Laban had. Robin could feel his heart pumping. He imagined he could hear the patter of feet chasing him, growing closer. Robin pushed himself to his limit. He couldn't outrun a wolf, even alone and not carrying a heavy deer.

"We should drop it!" Robin cried, running as hard as he could.

"Not on your life." Laban huffed, struggling to keep up. "This is the first decent catch you've had since I started training you."

They weren't far from the edge of the forest. Once they were in the clearing near Havendale, the wolves wouldn't dare approach. Another howl echoed behind them, striking that primal part of the brain, they were the prey, not the predator, in this chase. Robin glanced over their shoulder but couldn't see anything. He stumbled briefly over a hidden root but managed to keep his footing. Laban felt like his heart was about to break out of his chest. They broke the clearing, running through the fields putting a hundred feet from the edge of the forest; the two hunters fell to the ground. Laban lay on his back, clutching his chest. Robin tumbled, unable to carry the weight of the deer by himself. The young man struggled to his knees and readied his bow, scanning the forest for any sign of pursuit. Blood pumped in his ears, a steady thumping drum of his heart. He wiped the sweat from his forehead with the back of his hand to clear his eyes. He could see the silver-white streaks, weaving like dancers between the trees, but they didn't break the treeline. Robin fancied he locked eyes with the alpha. They gazed at each other across the field. Then, after a tense moment, the wolves slinked back into the forest. Their hunger somewhat sated, and the madness no longer driving the pack.

Robin let out a sigh of relief. Laban and Robin laughed for a few moments. "Well done, lad." Laban laughed; He slapped the side of the deer, still trying to catch his breath.

***

Laban stayed on as Robin's trainer until winter hit, and then he left, travelling to the east, apparently to rest up for the next season. The village hunters slaughtered the rogue wolf pack, removing the threat to the village, and the winter came and went, and the twins celebrated their fifteenth year.

Even over the winter, Robin made a name as an accomplished hunter. He was now stalking and taking down bucks alone with relative ease. Jacob continued to hone his skills and powers; Jacob eventually forced the old hag to explain more about the gods of the ancient religion. He continued to grow in capabilities to the level where he could practise on his brother and mother without their knowledge. Once, Jacob used a spell to calm Robin's incessant snoring, another time he used his power to comfort his mother's spirit and commune again with the being inside her. He also used other less magical practices to treat his mother. He had also taken on more duties with the witch and had begun helping Maganwyth tend to the villagers.

Erin hadn't been the same since the winter, despite Jacobs' efforts. Penthos, the entity inside her, kept her in a gentle melancholy, and sadness continued to haunt her eyes. She slept long hours, barely spoke to anyone other than Robin, and never left the hut. Finally, again, winter passed, and the spring dawned, the frozen sea melted, and the trade ships began arriving in Havendale. Robin was invited to participate in the great bear hunt. It was an old Havendale tradition, he was the youngest person ever to be included. He came back with a giant bear skin, which the tanner turned into a cloak, after his bow, this was now his most prized possessions.

With the spring came more opportunities for Jacob. He began to work with more patients under the watchful guidance of Maganwyth. He even began to get a few callers of his own, either not wanting to make the long hike up the cliff because of their malady or because they feared the old hag.

In the summer, puberty hit the twins. Robin grew another few inches and filled out, even more, becoming a young Adonis of a man. His voice broke, and the young man found hairs in many places that were a surprise. The winter and spring of hunting and tracking through the forests had helped tone his muscles and tanned his skin. While the young women of Havendale had always paid the young hunter interest, many were more direct in their advances. Birel, the young daughter of Gregor, the tavern keeper, had a crush on Robin and followed him everywhere around the village, but he was ambivalent to her advances, seeing her more as a little sister. On the other hand, he wasn't so oblivious to the amorous advances of some of the older girls, most notably Celina.

One of Havendale's most alluring women, Celina, was the daughter of the town's blacksmith. She had huge blue eyes and gorgeous blonde hair often fashioned in ringlets. She had started developing womanly curves throughout the winter, something none of the village's young men – including Robin – had failed to notice.

When returning home from a hunt, Robin often found Celina and her younger sister, Falia, gathering spring berries on the edge of town. Neither Robin nor Celina was practised in the art of seduction; the young lovers would awkwardly share small talk but quickly find they had run out of things to say before gauchely bidding each other farewell. Celina was a year older than Robin; her father was one of the wealthier citizens of Havendale, and as such, she was highly sought after. The blacksmith would have been pleased if he had found out about his daughter's dalliance with Robin. The young lad was becoming a prominent figure in the community in his own right and would have been a suitable match to any family.

It had been a light hunting day in the early summer when Robin was returning through the forest. As he reached the clearing close to the village, he noticed Celina was on her own, her sister absence.

"Afternoon." Robin smiled at her as he detoured slightly to pass near her. She wore a simple pale-blue summer dress; her hair was bound up and matched with a simple silk bow. She carried a basket half full of berries.

She blushed as the strapping young man approached.

"Hello." She smiled at the young man as he stood next to her. "Would you like some berries?" she asked, offering him one in her dainty fingers.

In the falling shadows of the sun, their faces were so close together as Robin devoured a berry from her hand. Robin could smell the sweet fragrance of the summer fruit on her skin. Then Celina's tongue was in Robin's mouth. Robin had not invited the kiss; he had just wished to look closely at her beautiful face. So spontaneous and urgent was her tongue probing his mouth, exploring like some writhing sea shape into his own. Robin felt stunned, feeling her slender body next to his as he shaped into the embrace, their bodies entwining.

Robin and Celina stayed together till the sun fell in the sky, touching the mountains, their mouths rarely parting. They fell in each other's arms onto the grassy fields, their hands teasing and touching each other as their maws locked in an enthusiastic osculate. The sun had long since fallen when they realised the time. Few words were spoken between the couple, and the heady desire to be with each other had overridden their senses.

Robin skipped his way home, his heart filled with the joys of life. Arriving at the dour squalid residence didn't dampen his spirits, even when he saw Jacob working in the kitchen preparing dinner. Jacob's snide remarks couldn't impact his brother's euphoria.

Robin tossed across a snow hare he had caught to Jacob with a sizeable stupid grin. He collapsed in the chair beside his mother and started to tell her all about his day. First, he told her about Celina and their afternoon together. She mumbled a few words back to Robin but wasn't truly engaged.

Jacob listened to his brother's gossip as he worked. Jacob rarely had time for idle chit-chat and never shared anything he knew about peoples' maladies. Besides that, Jacob rarely had anything that either Erin or Robin would find interesting. Jacob found their conversations tedious and banal. He still took the time with Robin, trying to teach his brother basic math, reading and writing. However, the young hunter had little patience for it.

He wasn't surprised about Celina and Robin's dalliance. He had observed most of the young ladies in the village yearning for his bigger, stronger twin brother and even quite a few of the older women. Maganwyth confided to Jacob that several of the young maidens had visited her, pleading for an elixir of love. The old woman had given them mandrake root extract and henbane and told them to mix it with the blood of their menstruation before giving it to the object of their desire. The old hag had laughed, the concoction had no real power, but she gained a few guilders for her deception. After Maganwyth had told Jacob of the ruse, he had taken great delight in warning his brother and then watching with glee as the large handsome man panicking whenever he was offered a drink by a young woman.

Jacob hadn't been immune to the effects of puberty either, he had grown a little, but he wore his height with an ungainly, slender awkwardness. He had also started to have the urges of a young man. His encounter with the Veela had awoken something inside of him. For the last few weeks, he wanted to spend more time with Falia, Celina's younger sister. He had never been confident enough to speak to or ask her to walk out with him. He occasionally saw her while delivering medicine to her father for rheumatism. She had always been sweet to him, inviting him in, offering him a drink and even taking the time to talk to him. He always struggled to talk back, save a few stammered words. Whenever she spoke to him, or if their fingers accidentally touched when she handed him a mug, he felt his cheeks flush and his heart pound. She was a year younger than her sister, the same age as the twins, a green-eyed red-haired slender girl, her face was dappled with freckles; she seemed timid compared to her older blonde sister, but whereas Celina wouldn't even look in Jacob's direction, Falia took the time to be kind to Jacob.

Jacob listened to his brother's story as he finished preparing supper. The meals prepared by Jacob was significantly more nutritious than what Erin used to concoct. Jacob had spent time learning about the benefits of a balanced diet and trying to keep the family as healthy as possible. As a result of which, Jacob, Robin and Erin all benefited. He spooned out the roasted rabbit and the fresh blanched vegetables onto three plates.

"It's ready," he mentioned.

In a well-planned routine, Robin helped his mother to the table as Jacob laid out the food. Erin could feed herself these days, but Jacob knew that the god of sorrow was still inside, working its poison into her mind. There was no way to cure her. The hag on the hill had explained that the 'God's gifts' were permanent.

"The old gods find hosts that match their domain." Maganwyth explained, "The old gods of war would find great warriors and make them greater; the old gods of healing would find apothecaries or physicians helping them heal and so on. They come in all shapes and sizes, the weaker gods could go unnoticed, but the greater gods, you only have to look at the history books to see their impact." He recall her saying, smoking her pipe as she sat, her withered, crusted bare feet adding a feted smell to the air. "The old gods are like any mortal being. Some are stronger, some are weaker, some tend to chaos, others to law, and some look to malice and others benevolence." She scratched her feet, flaking off chunks of dried skin. "From what you tell me, I suspect your mother is host to a minor god of sorrow, and there is nowt you can do about it."

"How are you doing today?" Jacob asked his mother placing his hand on top of hers. She looked down at him. His delicate fingers clutched her hand. "Yes, Robin, I've been OK," she mumbled, using the wrong name yet again, her eyes locked into the distance. She got increasingly confused these days. Muddling the twins' names. Jacob worried her mind was withering away as he withdrew from her. The twins shared a worried look and ate their supper in silence.

Chapter 17

The Plague

A loud knock echoed in the small hut of the twins an hour after daybreak. Robin let out a startled cry from his room. He had been down the tavern the night before. Since becoming an established hunter and celebrating his fifteenth year, Gregor had allowed the young man to have a few ales. The hunters enjoyed slipping him a few more to see the boy acting a fool. Last night had been a heavier night than usual. On days like these, Robin usually wouldn't rise before midday. Erin, would sometimes rise, sometimes not, her mind never fully waking from her mourning.

Jacob, on the other hand, had been up for hours; He didn't like sleep. He felt sleep was a thief that stole hours from the day. Even though Jacob knew not to push himself too much due to his weak constitution, Jacob enjoyed staying occupied. He had finished his housekeeping and was preparing breakfast. Opening the door, Jacob was greeted by a cool summer morning breeze that rushed into the house with a fragrance of life and flowers and a vision of beauty, Celina.

The blonde-haired young woman was in a panic. Her hair was loose and free, and she wore a green woollen cloak covering what appeared to be a nightgown. Her eyes were rimmed red; she had been crying and her cheeks were still stained with dried tears.

"Father is sick. Please come!" she pleaded.

Jacob looked her up and down. The young beautiful woman gazed at him with pleading eyes, hovering on the edge of crying.

"I will come." Jacob stated, "I need a moment to gather my stuff."

Robin chose that moment to exit his room. He was naked. "What the hell is this noise, Jacob!" he deep voice rumbled, his bleary eyes struggling to focus. He then saw Celina. Despite her worry and concern for her father, her eyes couldn't help but drift to admire the young man's body.

"Get dressed!" Jacob called back to his brother. "Then come help me with my stuff."

Celina's eyes lingered, watching the young man's rear as he left. She chewed thoughtfully on her lower lip, leering at him as he returned to his room.

Jacob packed a small satchel with some herbs and potions. He then ran his fingers along his herb collections and packed a few more vials in his pack.

"What are his symptoms." he asked Celina.

"Er…" The young lady paused. "He won't wake, and he is sick," she fumbled.

"Robin, please carry this," he asked, handing his brother the heavy pack.

The sun had risen high above the sea as they left the small hut on their way to town. As they strode towards the blacksmith's, Jacob looked behind him and saw that Robin held Celina's' hand. The young lady was distressed but found comfort in Robin's grip.

They arrived at the blacksmith's house; the forge was joined onto the side. Two colossal barn doors were flung open to allow the morning air to cool the sweltering heat of the furnace. Along one wall, the old blacksmith was slumped. His precious tools were scattered over the floor. His breathing was laboured, and he was sweating profusely. His skin was pale, and his eyes only showed the whites.

Jacob took his time. He remembered Maganwyth's training. *Observe. Jacob looked around the room to see any cause.* Upon the anvil was a strange lump of metal. Blue light pulsed from the unknown object. "Don't touch that," he warned, pointing towards the anvil.

Jacob knelt next to the blacksmith; he ran his hand over his forehead. He was sweating profusely. Jacob tried to rouse the man with no effect. He then took a moment to inspect his patient. Jacob saw that under his heavy leather gloves, his arms were covered in strange red sores. "Pass me my bag," he ordered Robin.

Jacob rummaged for a moment, then pushed a small vial into the blacksmith's mouth and emptied the liquid down the man's throat. Jacob then pulled the gloves off the man's hands; they were covered with scars from burns acquired working on the forge, but there were more of these strange red blotches.

Jacob realised he had an audience. He pivoted and found the blacksmith's wife, two daughters, and youngest son at the entrance.

"We need to get this man to his bed," Jacob demanded. "I can treat him better there." It was a struggle to lift the blacksmith. Even with the power of Robin's muscles, he was a dead weight. It took the whole family struggling to drag him through the house. Finally, they had him in his room. "You must not let anyone in here," he warned the family. "Now you all need to go wash your hands." He cautioned, "You too, brother. After, I need you to go up to the cliff and ask the hag to come here." Robin backed away and made the sign of the one true God. "Oh, don't give me your superstitious crap," Jacob snapped. "I need her help."

Celina, Falia, and the rest of the blacksmith's family made a sign of the one true God at Jacob's blasphemy, but they quickly left the room to wash as he had ordered. Falia quickly returned. First, she clutched at the doorway, enthralled watching as as Jacob worked. Jacob could feel her eyes on the back of his neck.

"How long has he been like this?" Jacob asked.

"We found him about half an hour ago," Falia stated.

"Aside from my treatment for his rheumatism is he taking anything else?" Jacob asked.

Falia shook her head.

"Has anything happened in the last day that could cause this?" Jacob quired.

Falia shook her head again.

"What about that rock in the forge?" Jacob asked, moving from his patient to stand next to Falia. It was strange, but, at this moment, he didn't feel the same burning shameful desire when he talked to her. Instead, he was a professional needing information.

"It came several weeks ago, Father was very excited about it, but it has been with us for ages."

"Has anything else changed?"

Falia slung her head. "No," she mumbled.

"What is it?" Jacob demanded.

Tears were falling from the red-haired beauty's eyes. "This is my fault," she whimpered. "I missed church three days ago."

Jacob sighed. "Trust me, that isn't the reason for this. Is anyone else suffering any symptoms?"

Falia bit her lip, trying to fight back her tears. "Er..." She paused, hiccupping as she fought down her sobs. "My little brother..." her voice trailed off.

"Fetch him," Jacob ordered.

The young boy was four years old, and sure enough, he had similar symptoms. While he hadn't succumbed to the fever, his arms showed the same red welts.

Jacob sent the young boy to his room. "Get him to rest and make sure he has plenty of clean water but spend very little time in the room with him."

"What is causing this?" The mother asked once he had the women reassembled in the kitchen.

Jacob was honest and confessed, "I don't know. The hag will know more. However, it appears to have had an impact only on men. What do they do together on their own time?" The women shrugged their shoulders.

"I have given them something to sleep and rest," Jacob lied; he had actually used magic to put them into a restful slumber. "Leave them be and let them rest," he instructed. "The hag will be here soon. Hopefully," he added, wondering how his brother was getting on.

***

Robin had arrived at the top of the cliff; he had only been up here a couple of times. He and other boys from town would dare each other to be the one to get the closest to the witch's house. Last time they had thrown stones at the place. Robin hoped the witch didn't recognise him. Robin pushed his dark hair back away from his face and brushed down his clothes, making himself as presentable as possible. He knocked softly on the door, almost hoping she couldn't hear him. A strange green light seemed to come from the windows fighting against the now glaring sun. The whole hut felt spooky and foreboding. The garden was an overgrown mess with vines wrapping around the stone base of the house. The windows were smeared and oily and only allowing the strange green light to glow through them. He knocked again a little louder, not wanting to disappoint his brother.

"What fucking time do you call this!" growled a voice from within. The roughshod door was wrenched open. The old woman peered up at Robin with a scowl. "Oh, it's you!" She sneered. "Come to torment an old woman some more?"

Robin nervously fidgeted under the old hags' gaze. "No, ma'am," he mumbled. "My brother has asked me to bring you to the town. The blacksmith is very sick," he answered.

Maganwyth glared up at the young boy in front of her. While Robin was taller and more robustly built than Jacob, he had similar looks to his twin. However, whereas Robin wore his fine features well, Jacob just appeared emaciated and wain.

"What's wrong with 'im?" She barged past Robin.

Maganwyth was already powering ahead down the cliff. Robin scrambled to catch up. But, despite the old woman's stooped back and old age, she had a surprising turn of speed, and even Robin struggled to keep up. It took them less than an hour for the two to cross the league into town.

By the time they arrived at the forge, the young boy had succumbed to his fever. As yet, none of the women were showing symptoms. Jacob took time to explain the malady to Maganwyth as they checked on the patients.

"You were right to call me," Maganwyth agreed. "I've not seen something like this for years."

"You have treated this before?" Jacob asked. "What is the cure?" he insisted as they sat in the blacksmith's kitchen. Robin hung to one side, consoling Celina.

"It was many years ago," Maganwyth mumbled. "Last time, my sisters and I found and destroyed the source. So first, we need to find the cause," Maganwyth mumbled.

"I saw something strange in the forge," Jacob noted. "It looked like an odd rock or metal."

"Show me," she asked.

They entered the dark smithy. The fire of the forge had died. Just the coals gave off a soft orange glow. There was the strange lump on the anvil in the centre of the room. It was glowing with blue veins running across its shape.

The witch spat on the floor. "Adamantine," she grumbled. "I was hoping it was something else," she complained. "That is a rare metal, known as the metal of the gods. It's not usually known to cause any sickness, quite the opposite," she grumbled. She moved close to the metal and held her hand over it before snatching her fingers back. "Get rid of it," she ordered Jacob. "But don't touch it, just in case."

Jacob took a pair of long plyers used for handling hot metal and gripped the metal. He could feel the power emanating from the stone. It was a familiar power. He knew this power. He could feel the strength of this stone. He had read that Adamantine was one of the rarest metals in the world, used to forge some of the most extraordinary items, the weapons of the gods, or so it was alleged. A gram of this metal was worth more than Havendale and probably more than the whole of the frozen north. "Where can we put it?" he asked.

Maganwyth looked around the room. "Stick it in that box." She pointed to a rough iron box filled with slag and cut-off bits of metal. "Then get your brother to take it out to the forest and bury it."

***

Maganwyth and Jacob worked with the family throughout the day and night. It was early in the morning when more reports started coming in of people around the town falling ill with the same affliction. Both were exhausted. Neither had slept.

"Sean, the son of the verger, has fallen sick," Robin rudely interrupted as Jacob and Maganwyth were trying to recharge themselves.

Jacob looked up with bleary eyes. "I will attend." Casting a glance over to Maganwyth. The haggard old witch looked the same as usual, perhaps a little more withered than expected, but with her face, it was hard to tell.

"Fine, go." She muttered, "I'm going home, nothing more can be done for these folk right now, and I need a shit and a kip." She gave Robin a sly wink. "Hopefully, in that order."

Jacob went to the verger's house; it wasn't far from the towering temple building that dominated the town square. The Sean displayed the same symptoms as the blacksmith when Jacob found him. Unconscious, sweating, with strange red marks on his arms.

Jacob went to work to raise the victim's body temperature by applying cold towels to Sean and cleaning the weeping sores on his arm, he wanted to cast a sleeping spell on the poor young boy, but the verger didn't leave his son's side for a moment. It was late afternoon when Jacob noticed that the verger had also developed the tell-tale red welts on his arms.

By the second evening, Jacob was forced to rest having been working for more than thirty hours. Five more cases were reported. He had pushed his body beyond exhaustion to treat the sick, but it had finally given out. He woke on the third morning of the plague to find himself in his own bed. Robin had discovered his brother slumped over the kitchen table of the seventh victim and had carried him home.

The plague of Havendale spread slowly over the following days. Jacob and Maganwyth went from house to house, trying to treat the symptoms of the ill but unable to find the root cause. Eventually, the village priests issued a decree that the illness was due to the sins of Havendale against the one true God and that they needed to pray and repent. This dogma went quiet when Father Yusef, the oldest of the priests, fell sick. The rest of the clergy had become ill within two days, along with four others. Jacob laboured from before noon until well after the witching hour, treating the victims. Maganwyth had also moved down from her cliff house to address the sick. She had been given a small alcove within the temple to set up as her temporary home. The priests that had damned her and insulted her now cried out for her help. The plague quickly spread across Havendale indiscriminately. There was no apparent link between the victims, the young, the old, the rich, and the poor all suffered.

Jacob worked continuously for more days than his sleep-addled brain could count. With little or no rest, his frail body was beyond exhaustion. Maganwyth and Jacob had set up a quarantine in the temple, a centralised point where all the victims could be brought for treatment. Celina and her mother were brought in on the tenth day by Falia. They were both unconscious with the fever. The church was quickly filling up with the sick.

Jacob sat in the temple's vestry, his eyes drooping with fatigue. He and Maganwyth had done all they could to discover the source of this infection but to no avail. There were now victims lying in the church who had never been in contact with any from the village. These people came from small hamlets west of Havendale, seeking treatment for the malady.

With each victim of the plague, the symptoms were the same, at first, there were unnatural welts on the arms and hands, blood and pus seeped out of these strange swellings, which were followed by a host of other more unpleasant symptoms—fever, chills, vomiting, diarrhoea, terrible aches, and pains.

The first deaths came in the early hours of the twelfth morning; Sean, Robin's boyhood friend and the verger's son. Next was the blacksmith. While both had drunk heavily and wasn't the apex of human health, it didn't bode well for the rest of the infected.

When the fifteenth day of the outbreak came, the bodies were piling high. Maganwyth and Jacob had tried every cure they knew and even thrown some old wives' tale remedies into the mix. Nothing had helped.

Robin brought Jacob a meal when he took a short break from tending to the sick. Gregor and Eyia supplied food to the temple and to the others who were now housebound in their homes where infections had broken out.

Jacob struggled to stay awake as he read his notes. He barely touched his food and slowly dozed off his plate, resting on his knee.

A voice spoke in his head. Jacob, the cause of this is a lot darker than you think.

Jacob's sleep-deprived mind struggled to identify this voice. It seemed to come from his head. "Who are you?" Jacob asked the voice.

I am you, the voice answered. The voice spoke. It was hollow and without feeling. It said with calm unfeeling coldness, We are together. I am Thoth, we have never spoken, but I have been with you since the day you were born. I will be with you forever. We are one.

Jacob nodded to himself. He had known about this 'god' in his mind, this gift. "You are with me then." Jacob paused. "What is causing this?"

The voice in his head paused. He could tell the apparition was thinking. I could tell you, it continued with that hollow emotionless tone. You know I have the knowledge of the ages from all of time. I could give you the answer, but it is always better to learn the knowledge yourself.

Jacob sighed; it would have been better if he… A loud clang startled him awake. His plate had fallen from his knee, crashing on the stone floor of the antechamber. He looked up to see Robin rush in.

"I'm fine." He waved his brother away. He then noticed Robin's hands were covered with tell-tale red welts. Jacob looked up at his brother, and a sudden rush of fear hit the pit of his stomach.

"You aren't." Jacob pointed to his brother's hands. Robin looked down, seeing the blotches.

"Oh God, oh God!" Robin panicked, the strong young man had never had a day of sickness in his life, and this terminal plague was claiming him.

"Calm down, brother," Jacob reassured. He sombrely pulled himself up from the chair. "Go to the hall, find a bed and rest," he ordered. "I will not let you die."

Jacob took his brother through to the church's main hall, which had been set up for the treatments. There were cries of the dying and the sick. With most everyone else avoiding the church, it left only Jacob and Maganwyth to tend to the dying. Only those suffering from this malaise dared approach this house of worship.

The people of Havendale showed great concern as the sickness spread unabated. All over the town, friends would avoid any gatherings, and many wore wrapped cloths around their faces and mouths, it might have protected them from spreading the illness but wouldn't protect them from protracting it. The old superstitions arose, people stuffing their pockets with crushed poppy petals to ward off the sickness. On the twentieth day, there was no more admitted patients to the church, and rumours began to circulate the distemper was easing despite Meganwyth's and Jacob's warnings. The priests took credit for this pause claiming their prayers were defending the citizens of Havendale; even from their sickbeds, they still touted their rhetoric.

This turned the people's opinions against the hag and her young apprentice. Soon rumours were flying that it was her who was making people sick, and that they should avoid their care.

This had only stemmed the flow of people into the temple but hadn't stopped the spread of the plague. Jacob and Maganwyth falsely hoped, ever so briefly, that less patients indicated an end to the plight, but on the morning of the thirtieth day, after the blacksmith had fallen ill, a house was discovered filled with the bodies of the dead. Each bearing the marks of the malady. No one had heard from the Greyson family for two days. Finally, Gregor, a leader in the village council, had ordered every house to check in and report any incidents of the illness and had instructed several young men and women around the village to check on the residents.

Young Wilfred was such a volunteer. Most of the villagers he went to wouldn't open their door to him for fear he would bring the plague inside. Wilfred didn't like this duty, but as a dutiful and God-fearing community member, Wilfred felt bound. So, with trepidation, he approached the Greyson house. Yesterday Wilfred had tried to call on them, but there had been no answer. He had received a clip around the ear from Gregor for failing to be thorough. So today, Wilfred would execute his duty without excuse.

He knocked at the door, hoping to get a quick answer and be on his way. No reply. He hammered on the door again, but still no response. Finally, he pushed the door open without waiting. The stench of death struck him immediately. Inside he could hear crying—Wilfred wretched at the stench which assaulted his senses. Flies buzzed around the house; the sickness was pervasive in the air. The young lad's courage began to falter. He didn't want to get ill. Only the crying of a mewling infant drove him on. He saw the family's father slouched in a chair, his jaw slack, flies dancing in and out of his mouth, his wife beside him. The crying came from the first floor. Wilfred dared push himself onwards. On the first floor was a large open-plan dorm where the family rested. The shrieking came from a cot beside the window. On the large double bed, the grandmother rested motionless, dead. Wilfred approached the cot. The tiny infant son was bawling, the baby's skin was a sickening greyish hue, and seeping pus-filled welts formed on the distressed child's arms and face. His eyes were leaking blood as he cried in the agony of his final moments. Wilfred fled the house forever, scarred by what he had seen.

The sickness wasn't abating. People were now hiding the illness, choosing to remain in their houses and avoid the church because of rumours. Upon hearing the news, Gregor and the rest of the town council proclaimed that all in the village must be checked daily for symptoms. Those who couldn't leave their houses would be inspected.

"Fools!" Maganwyth cursed as she inspected the bodies before people carted them to the pits dug at the edge of town.

"They are fearful," Jacob qualified, washing his hands in a basin next to her.

"Fearful fools then." She grumbled. "But fools nonetheless."

Chapter 18

The Pirate

Yusef, the old priest and the adoptive grandfather of the twins, passed away on the thirty-fifth day. A steady stream of those showing the symptoms had resumed arriving at the church. Jacob and Maganwyth had tried their best, the old witch had worked tirelessly alongside Jacob, and villagers who had treated her with scorn and hatred for many years were the first to beg for her help when the red welts appeared. The witch did what she could. The young blacksmith boy had been deathly ill for over a month, barely clinging to life. Jacob had worked especially hard to save this child. Falia had been the only member of the family not to fall ill. She stayed by her family, assisting Jacob however she could.

Like everyone else, Robin's condition began to worsen. A day after Jacob had noticed the red blotches, Robin fell unconscious. Jacob attended to him as much as possible, but he couldn't ignore his other patients. The evening after Robin had fallen cataleptic, Jacob sat exhausted in the vestry that Maganwyth and he had made their temporary home. They had lost four more patients that day, including the blacksmith.

"How many dead?" Maganwyth asked.

"Three score that we know of." Jacob sighed, "Twice that number are sick. What is causing this?" Jacob asked the old hag.

She shook her head, sucking on her pipe, filling the small room with thick, foul-smelling blue smoke.

"Buggered if I know, I'm sure it's magic, though." She put up her feet, her thick-soled boots rested beside her chair, and her malodorous socks laid over them. Her twisted, cracked, thick yellow toenails were at the forefront of Jacob's vision. He hadn't seen anything as gross and malformed in his short life.

"I spoke to a few people, aside from that adamantine that had been brought in by a trader a couple of months ago; the fool had no idea of its value," she added. "Nothing else I can tell has changed in the village. There is no rhyme to this, some families get ill, others are fine, people living on their own are falling ill, but then Gregor and his family are fine, and they've been coming in and out all week." She grumbled and spat some dark spittle onto the floor. "You and I have been around all the sick people, but we aren't affected. In most plagues, it's the carers who suffer first."

"What about food or water?" Jacob thought out loud, "Anything that they share? Anything that could have been cursed?"

Maganwyth paused, sucking on her pipe. "Nope." She grumbled to herself, blowing out a plume. "The only link I have deduced was that the first to fall sick had all come to the temple for last month's sermon, but others have started to fall sick now, even those who never attend church."

"Did Falia not attend?" Jacob pondered; he thought her whole family to be amongst the most devout in the village. "She always attends, but she isn't sick."

Maganwyth gave a toothless smile. "You're sweet on her." She chuckled. "No, she had to run an errand for her mother, delivering some fabrics to the fletchers or something."

Jacob thought for a moment, exhaustion still filled his body, but his mind buzzed. Finally, he pushed himself out of his chair and approached the door. "Where are you off to?" Maganwyth asked.

"I'm going to get answers from the priests. They usually refuse to speak to me, but they will tonight," Jacob spoke with conviction.

"Most of them are down with the sickness," Maganwyth glumly stated. "And as I said, others are now sick who aren't even from this village."

Jacob spoke with determination. "I will find out if anything happened a month ago in that sermon. The illness may have spread to the others, but I suspect the epicentre was here."

Jacob entered the main temple worshiping hall. The large, cavernous room was filled wall to wall with cots having been turned into a hospital. Large wood-filled braziers leapt with great reaping fires. All candles of the hall were lit so those volunteering to help the sick could see to make their way from cot to cot.

The room was filled with the coughs and groans of the sick and the dying. Jacob picked his way through the makeshift hospital, stopping to see his brother. Robin was still unconscious, twitching in his sleep, and his breathing

174

was laboured, but he was doing better than most. His fitness and physique fighting the illness. His next stop was at the blacksmith's family. The empty cot of their father hung in Jacob's mind. Falia sat on a stool. Her eyes were red and raw with tears, having been crying for days.

Jacob spoke softly to her. "I'm sorry for your loss. We will find the cause and stop this. Please trust me." She looked up, her red-rimmed eyes gazing at his. She reached up and touched his hand. Despite the horror of this situation, Jacob felt a thrill from her soft touch.

She spoke earnestly. "Thank you." She leaned forward and kissed Jacob on the cheek.

This was his first kiss from someone other than his mother. Even his mother's kiss was barely a buss of lips against his forehead. Falia's lips pressed against his cheek, and then the moment passed too soon, leaving only a memory of her soft lips on his skin. He felt the smouldering of arousal in his loins. Embarrassed, he turned away.

"You are welcome." He coughed to cover his embarrassment turning his back on the beautiful young girl. "I will be back to check on them later." He could still feel the touch of her lips pressed against his cheek. He couldn't help but grin while he continued his search amongst the bilious masses.

His search came to fruition at the back of the cavernous temple hall, he finally found the cots he was striving for. The heads of the priesthood in Havendale were all cloistered together. Like all the other temple leaders, the head priest's cot had been set up some distance away from the rest of the ailing masses. The beds in this section had been dragged through the temple and were more comfortable than the makeshift cots. The abbot was an obscenely obese man. He was clean-shaven, with piggy eyes and a bulbous chin. He had red blotches on his arms but hadn't yet fallen into the deep slumber. He looked at Jacob with those narrow piggy eyes filled with unabated and undisguised hatred and disgust.

"What do you want?" the large man growled. The abbot had always disliked Jacob intensely since the day he was born. He had seen the child have the mark of a demon about him. Little did he know how close he was to the truth. Father Yusef had always protected his surrogate grandchild, but that protection was gone with his death. Aside from Yusef, none of the other priests had liked Jacob, very few in Havendale did. He didn't need their love and had never expected it. However, he hoped, by his actions, he would garner some respect. He also anticipated his service throughout the plague might earn him some protection from persecution as it did the hag.

He spoke with a command to the old priest. "I've come to check on you and ask you some questions." The large man writhed about in his luxurious bed, so Jacob stepped in. "You need to lay back and rest; drink water while you can." He stood beside the large wooden ornate bed that had been dragged from the abbots private chambers into the temple's main hall.

"Bah, you and that witch aren't able to help us. Only faith in the one true God can do that," the fat man spat out. "I will fight your foul treatments as long as my body allows." He swung his large arm toward Jacob, trying to ward off imagined evil.

Jacob shook his head. "Faith and dogma will not help you now. I need to know if anything was different when you held the sermon a month ago." He looked around the room. "Everyone who attended is now sick or dead. What was different?"

The abbot turned his head and looked away from the young man. "No, nothing," he stumbled, giving a slightly too-long pause. The laborious fat man rolled over on his bed, turning his back on the young boy.

"What were you just thinking of," Jacob insisted, his eyes locked onto the back of the priest's head. "Tell me," he ordered, his voice taking on a darker tone. A brief flare of magic sparked in his mind as Jacob spoke in the old tongue, "*Yticarev.*" The priest's willpower dissolved, and he began to talk earnestly.

The anger and passion dropped from his voice as he rolled over to face Jacob. "We had a guest speaker, Carlos of Sintra. He came from Telegos. He is a prophet of the one true God." The priest's own will reasserted itself, "Which you would know if you ever attended you heathen." Jacob shook his head and stepped back. *Could a man cause this?* he asked himself.

The voice of Thoth spoke in his head calmly. He a host of one of the gods. He is one of my brothers, not an affable one, my brother and I have met in conflict before.

"Where has he gone now?" Jacob asked forcefully, directing his voice to the priest, the magic flaring in his mind again.

The priest spoke, his voice taking on a monotone as he continued before he fell into a coughing fit. "He is travelling to the twelve towns bringing the

light and glory of the one true God. He would be nearing Holum by now."
Jacob left the abbot to rest.

Holum was the most remote of the twelve towns. Before coming to the unending ocean, it was the furthest town to the west. Holum was once a military fort centuries ago. Now it was known as a haven for pirates and smugglers who used the Everlong Sea to smuggle goods across the empire. Jacob had never been that far. When the hag had asked him to deliver some medicine, he had once been to Woodvale, the closest neighbouring town. Holum was more than a week's travel over land, significantly less if he had a horse, but he couldn't afford one. It was maybe a day by the sea.

He returned to Maganwyth, who was snoozing in the vestry. He woke her and explained what he had learned.

She spat on the ground. "I bet it's Irra or someone like them," she grumbled. "Old chaotic gods of sickness and plague."

"Who is Irra?" Jacob questioned.

"Bah, a minor old god of pestilence." Maganwyth griped, "A foul little shit if ever there was one." She paused, lighting her pipe. "A few hundred years ago, Irra was here in Havendale. He spread a plague like this one. Oi never met him myself, but my sisters did." She chuckled to herself. "Baba cast that spirit out and banished him. She left him with a curse of his own," she chuckled.

Jacob cocked his brow. Maganwyth never revealed her age or ever mentioned her sisters. The previous several days' exertions had let her defences down. "What else can we do?" He asked.

Maganwyth thought. "Last time, the plagues were stopped when he was killed." She looked at Jacob. "None of our healing will do much to help these people. When the Haulfin collaborated with humans, they made talismans to ward off this sort of magic, but now?" she griped to herself for a moment. "We can give comfort to those dying." She shrugged.

"That isn't good enough," Jacob firmly demanded; his mind focused on his brother. "We have to help."

"Some will live." She shrugged. "Your brother is more likely than most."

Jacob shook his head. "No, I need to find this Irra and stop him."

A hissing came from the old woman. It took Jacob a moment to realise she was laughing. "You are no match to fight anyone, let alone kill a god." She crossed her arms. "Irra was a minor god of pestilence. Who isn't to say this is something more powerful? And it took both my sisters, who were much more powerful than you." She cackled, "Now get some rest. We have a long day tomorrow." She got up from the chair, shuffled over to a small cot in the corner and slumped down into it with a groan. It didn't take long for her loud snores to fill the room. Jacob had tried his sleep spell on Maganwyth to stop her constant wheeze, but his magic had no effect for some reason.

Jacob couldn't just leave it. Sitting on his cot, he decided, he couldn't do nothing and let his brother die. The journey to Holum was exceedingly long, far further than Jacob had ever travelled in his life. The trip would take more than a week over land, but around the coast would be much faster. Jacob had little experience in sailing, nor did he have a boat.

He thought long and hard about the problem, the night wore on, and the loud grumble of Maganwyth's cacophony of snores filled the small antechamber. Jacob's mind rattled off several solutions. *I cannot let my brother die,* he thought firmly to himself. *I cannot let Falia down.* In his mind he added, the thought of the kiss made him blush again.

The voice spoke in his head. *I can help.* He had started to get used to hearing this voice in his head. It often talked to him when he was deep in thought, sometimes offering him advice, sometimes guidance, he wondered if the voice had always been there, but he hadn't 'heard' it before, now it spoke to him more regularly. *I need a boat,* he stated to the voice. *Robin is well-liked. So many owe your brother a favour,* the voice concluded, and with that, a plan formed in Jacob's mind.

***

At night the docks were deathly silent. Jacob tried to remember where his brother's friend lived. A young dockhand named Herod hadn't been admitted to the temple yet. Jacob hoped Herod had avoided the plague as many were choosing to stay in their homes, afraid entering the temple would worsen their condition.

He knocked at what he hoped was the young sailor's door. Herod took a few minutes to answer. The young man was blatantly drunk.

"You're Robin's brother, aren't you?" slurred the young man.

"Yes, I'm Jacob."

"Wat yeursh doing out so late?" Herod bumped against the door.

"I need to sail to Holum, and I was hoping for your help," Jacob stated firmly, using the magic in his mind to try to bend the drunk man's will.

"Wut?" Herod's eyes seemed to bulge at this suggestion. "Why the fuck does you want to head to that shithole?" He slumped against the door frame. The magical flare in Jacob's mind seemed to come up with a foggy resistance. The magic fluttered and failed.

Jacob spoke calmly, trying to keep his words simple for the alcohol-laden mind of this dock hand and resorted to diplomacy rather than magic. "There is a chance a cure to this plague can be found there."

"Pah, come back in the morning!" Herod went to close the door, but Jacob jammed his foot in the door.

"Please!" Jacob begged. "Walking would take me over a week. You could be there in less than twelve hours," Jacob insisted. "My brother might not have that long." Herod's eyes rolled back; Jacob wondered if a drunk man would be able to sail.

A voice spoke from behind Herod. "Let the boy in." Herod slumped back, letting the door open. The second man in the hut was dressed in once fine colourful clothes stitched in many places. A patch covered his left eye. His face was fine and delicate but was covered with scars and a jagged beard. He gazed at the young boy under the brim of a wide tricorn hat.

"Do you really think a cure can be found there?" he asked. His voice had an almost sing-song quality to it. Along the side of his neck, there were some weeping sores. It wasn't the marks of the illness that was plaguing Havendale. It was a disease much more mundane, often suffered by young men and women who weren't so picky on whose bed they shared.

Jacob pushed past the drunken Herod stepping over his slumped body. "It might be, I can only hope." He stood in front of the man. "Who are you? I don't recognise you."

"I'm from here and there, don't come this way often." The man waved a hand holding a bottle around the room. "I came in on the evening tide. I know of your brother; he gave me a hand loading my ship once. I sailed here when I found out a friend of mine is one of the sick," he stated glibly. "Couldn't bring myself to go up to the temple." He shrugged, "I don't have time to be down sick."

Jacob looked the man up and down, he was shifty, and there was something odd about this person. Jacob repeated, "You didn't answer my question."

The man paused. He cracked a grin showing several golden teeth. "You are right." He took a swig from the bottle. "My name is Loth. I'm just a simple trader trying to make my way in the world."

"Do you have a ship?" Jacob asked.

The man's eyes narrowed. "Aye, a small cutter, but a far better rig than this lad." He pointed at the now snoring Herod. "Why?"

"You will take me to Holum," Jacob ordered. He tried again to make his mind flare with magic. This time instead of fog, the man's mind danced away from the flame. Jacob sighed. He guessed he was too tired.

The man raised an eyebrow. "Why would I do something like that, boy? It would take me a day there and back. Time is money." Tapping the table with his bottle before taking another swig.

Jacob didn't look away from the man's eye. "You could take me to save your friend, the one you mentioned who was sick. What is their name? I have been treating those in the temple."

The man spoke with a burp. "Let me get this straight, you want me to get in my ship, wake up my crew, sail through the night to get to Holum by morning, on a chance you might be able to help my friend."

"To sweeten the deal, I will treat your pox," Jacob offered, pointing at the man's neck.

"I've got no pox." The man defensively waved his hands.

"You do," Jacob insisted. "And within a few months, if left untreated, it can cause tumours, blindness, and paralysis, damage the nervous system, brain, and other organs, and may even kill you." He gave the sailor a stern look. "But it is straightforward to treat."

Loth paused as he looked the young man up and down. "Hmm, we would have done it for my friend," he explained in the end. "Wouldn't we, Bob?"

Jacob looked around the room to see who he was talking to; he then noticed an elderly fat overfed wharf rat peeking out over Loth's tricorn hat. "Are you speaking to that rat?" Jacob asked.

Loth smiled. "This is Captain Bob." He reached up and took the fat rat out of his hat. "My companion and the ship's captain."

A moment of worry gave Jacob pause. This man was obviously insane, probably from the pox, but there were few other options.

"Can we leave now?" Jacob urged. "We have lost so many people already."

"No time to waste!" The man sprang to his feet, swigging down the last of the bottle and slamming it against the table.

"But first, we must put this young man to bed." Loth pointed towards Herod, who was still slumped against the open door holding a bottle of rum cradled in his arms. The Sailor staggered a little as he walked, but he managed to guide the young drunk dockhand to his bunk. "Right onwards to the Lorelai," Loth proclaimed, referring to his ship. Loth staggered ahead of Jacob as they walked toward the docks. Loth was singing an old sea shanty.

"According to what my mother

"Told me when I was a little boy,

"Remove, drag away

"We'll remove Joe.

"If I didn't kiss the gals.

"My lips would get discoloured,

"Remove, drag away

"We'll remove Joe."

Jacob trailed behind as the sailor sang this tune, shattering the dock's serenity. Loth continued to sing all along the docks till they reached the boat, where he tried to straighten himself up. The Lorelai was a single-masted boat with two headsails. It had two mast stays running fore and aft. It was one of the larger ships in the small Havendale harbour, about fifty feet long; its figurehead was of a mermaid. It was painted gold that was now flaking, giving her a ghastly appearance. As they got to the side of the boat, Loth stopped.

"Now we need to come up with a good reason for our crew to head back to Holum." Loth paused. "It's not really going to be for money, and we haven't even offloaded our haul from our last trip, so It'll have to be a good reason," Loth slurred.

"Could you not tell them it was for the greater good?" Jacob asked.

Loth laughed as he swung himself over the gunwale. He helped Jacob over, then called out below the decks.

"Listen up, you lazy bunch of dogs!" he shouted loudly, his voice echoing across the still waters of the Everlong. "We have a mission of mercy to help this town!"

There was some grumbling from below; finally, three figures emerged. The first was short and stout, with a beard almost reaching the ground. The second was dumpier and fatter. The last was a tall Arbay man who ducked out from the cabin standing double the height of his two companions, his black as ink skin as dark as night. The smallest of the three spoke up first, stepping onto the deck.

"What in the blue blazes are you talking about!" it demanded. As it stepped into the dim light offered by the moon, Jacob could see that he was a Hobby, a breed of Haulfin similar to humans but half their size. "What's the payment?" he asked.

"Trigger, my old friend, when have I ever led you astray!" Loth gave a sly leer,

"Many times," Trigger responded, crossing his arm.

"We ain't getting paid for this?" spoke up the second short figure. It stepped forward, standing beside the Hobby, Taller and more heavily set; this was another Haulfin, a Dewar, Jacob guessed.

Loth smiled charmingly. "Ah, maybe not with coin, but we will be paid with the goodwill of all." He looked sideways towards Jacob. "This young lad is a local healer. He believes we can help the pleasant town of Havendale with a short-day trip back to Holum."

"Is that true?" Trigger asked Jacob.

Jacob nodded. "Yes," he explained. "There is a man who might be able to help the village."

"No coin?" the Hobby pressed.

Jacob shook his head. "No coin, but I will…"

Loth interrupted, "He will see what he can do to compensate us. We need to set sail now!" he barked more orders. The crew begrudgingly began to respond.

"You have crew that are subhumans?" Jacob asked Loth quietly.

Loth looked around and spoke quietly into Jacob's ear, "Don't speak too loudly. Also, don't use that word here. If you must call them anything, call them Haulfin, but," he mumbled. "Trigger is the short fat one, the strong fat one is Kazun, and the Arbay man is Aibois. They prefer it when you use their names."

"Doesn't that get you into trouble?" Jacob asked.

"With the Imps?" Loth laughed, "They would need to catch us first! We keep our heads down in the port, and there aren't too many Impy ships here in the north. So, we try to avoid them when we see them." The cutter creaked and groaned as it slipped moorings and drifted out into the still sea of the Everlong.

Chapter 19

The Journey

The seas of the Everlong were calm, and the boat rocked gently as they pulled away from the harbour. The moon glistened over the bay, sending a shimmering light on the Lorelai as it ploughed through the still sea. A gentle lapping sound of the water kissing against the boat's hull. As the cutter crossed the Everlong Sea, Loth had settled himself behind the wheel. Jacob gripped the gunwale despite the calm seas, heaving his guts over the side. "It happens to most people their first time at sea!" Loth laughed, "There are two stages of sea sickness, my lad. You are at stage one."

"What's that?" he asked.

"You are at stage one, which is feeling like you are going to die." Loth laughed, "Stage two is worse. It's the realisation that you ain't gonna." He turned and smiled. "Haven't you got a fancy potion for it?"

"White hellebore," Jacob mumbled. "But I didn't bring any with me, and it would take hours to prepare properly, if I didn't want to poison myself."

"Now about my pox," Loth asked.

"That I can treat." Jacob was finally glad for something to concentrate on other than the decks moving under him. Jacob opened his pack between his legs. "You will need Griseofulvin," Jacob muttered. "I have a small amount here." He handed over a small glass bottle inside what looked like mouldy bread.

"What is it?" Loth asked.

"Mouldy corn starch." Jacob mumbled, trying to keep his stomach in. "You best wash it down with this." He handed him another small bottle which contained a green liquid. "It's eucalyptus extract."

Loth swallowed both making a face. "Ugh!" Gulping back the bitter taste. "You sure this will work?" Loth asked.

"It won't cure you straight away. It will take another treatment or so. I'll give you more when we return to Havendale." Jacob offered.

Trigger waddled back to the upper back deck. "We are on course, Captain." The short Hobby stopped next to Jacob. "Suffering, lad?" His fat face wrinkled into a broad grin. "Don't sweat it, lad. You should have seen Aibois on our first trip. He was paler than you are now!" The Haulfin slapped Jacob on his back. "Go below and get your head down. You look exhausted." He pointed towards the cabin. "You can use my bunk."

Jacob stumbled to his feet, struggling to keep his footing as he made his way to the cabin. "Thank you, Trigger," he mumbled. The shifting decks gave the young man trouble as he staggered from support to support. He staggered down the stairs entering the darkened lower cabin. A single lantern shielded with red-tinted glass cast a dark maroon glow around the lower deck.

Below decks, Kazun was sitting at a table carving a small cork with a little knife under the gloom of the red light.

"Trigger's bunk is that one," the Haulfin growled, barely looking up. Jacob nodded at Kazun. He had never seen a Haulfin like this before. He was sure this was a Dewar. They were said to be a vicious greedy breed of Haulfin. Jacob had always guessed that the history taught by the priests was tainted by their spin.

"Thank you." He struggled to get into the bunk. It must have been past midnight, the last week of constant work trying to keep the village alive, and the illness he felt from the sea travel all piled up. This was the first time Jacob had closed his eyes without interruption in several days. Sleep took him quickly. His dreams were troubled with the world spinning, images of Thoth, the god in his head. The moon god, sacred writings, science, magic, mathematics, the recorder of the gods, the master of knowledge, and the protector of scribes. His old name had been Djehuty, which means, 'He who is like the Ibis'. He had vivid images of Thoth surrounded by a vast library, halls upon halls of books and scrolls. He laboriously was hunched over a desk writing.

The words danced across Jacob's eyes; he couldn't recognise each word, but he felt something in his mind. He could then see a male figure carrying a mace topped by a double lion's head. Thoth stood facing this figure, holding just a quill and an open book. The male figure was yellow and sickly, fat rolled over his trousers, he had double chins, and its skin was pocked marked with boils and sores. It raised its lion-headed mace to strike at Thoth. The blow struck an invisible barrier, and the impact caused Thoth to stumbled backwards, sinking to one knee. Jacob's dreams continued with this troubled turbulent battle between Thoth and this unknown figure.

Up on the deck, the crew were relaxing; the sails were set. Now it was an easy straight run with the wind behind them to Holum. They would need to change tack in several hours once they rounded the bay, but they were on course for the moment. Trigger had caused a lot of fuss over the unnecessary trip to Holum, but he didn't really care. Trigger, Kazun, and Aibois all owed their lives to Loth. Loth had busted Trigger and Kazun out of an Inquisition prison several years ago. They had been caught trying to flee the empire. Aibois had been on the wrong side of a mutiny of one of Loth's rival traders. Loth had managed to fish the half-dead Arbay man from the southern sea.

"Why are we helping the lad?" Trigger asked, looking up at Loth, whose eyes gazed out into the dark sea. "Honestly, Loth?"

Loth grumbled to himself. "Should we tell 'em, Bob?" Loth spoke to the rat in his hat. He seemed to listen to a voice only he could hear. "Oh, all right... a friend of ours is one of the sick people."

"Wanda." Trigger rolled his eyes. "I would hardly call her a friend of ours. Didn't she slap you last time you saw her?"

Loth shrugged. "It was a playful slap." He grinned, "You know she's one of the good ones who look after our kind."

"She sells us food and supplies overpriced," Trigger mumbled.

"Still a better deal than in any major ports." Loth smiled.

"Fair enough." Trigger offered, "Want me to take the helm for a couple of hours?"

"Nah, I'm good." Loth waved his hand. "I'll get us past Telegos, and then you can take over."

***

Jacob woke up as dawn was breaking. His stomach churned still, but this was the most rest he had gotten in many days. Jacob tumbled out of the hammock, crashing to the ground. He heard a rumbled laugh from the bunk one over. Kazun was chuckling at Jacob's awkwardness.

"There is a knack to it."

Jacob gathered himself up and scrambled onto the deck. Once he was in the open air, the fresh morning air filled his lungs. The Lorelai was making excellent speed through the sea. They had already passed Pine Run Bay and were halfway across the next bay that would lead them to Goodmead. The crisp, clean air filled Jacob's lungs. He closed his eyes.

"You are best off looking at a point on the horizon, lad," Trigger mumbled behind him. He turned to see the Haulfin holding the wheel. Jacob looked around. "Loth is below sleeping." Trigger noted.

In the morning light, Jacob got his first good look at the Haulfin. "You are a Half-man?" Jacob asked.

"Oh really! That explains why I'm so short," the tubby sailor shot back. "Yea, Hobby, Haulfin, half-man, we get called a lot of things."

"I didn't mean to be rude," Jacob apologised. "I've just never met one before."

"You are unlikely to," Trigger mumbled. "Most of my people went into hiding, or died."

"But not you," Jacob added.

"I was born in Altran." Trigger pouted. Trigger spoke the words laden thick with venom. "The first city of the empire. I was born a slave in the emperor's palace. They kept us penned in the worst areas of the city. I was kept as a kitchen skivvy. I was forced to work day after day; eventually, Kazun and I had enough."

"You escaped?" Jacob enquired, sitting on the wooden plank near the Haulfin.

Trigger nodded. "We almost got away. After several months evading imperials patrols, we were caught by the Inquisition outside Wayrest."

"That's the major port in Gont," Jacob noted.

"One of them, it's the main link for Gont to the Spine Mountains," Trigger agreed. "We were fools trying to escape that way. Instead, we should have travelled into Rwelvencrest. The Imperials would never have dared enter that land."

Jacob nodded. "I've heard that is a dangerous place."

"For us, it would have been no more dangerous." Trigger shrugged.

Jacob talked with the Haulfin for the next few hours. He was learning much about the empire, things he had never heard from Maganwyth or the temple priests. The empire was always painted as a glorious harmony of thirteen electoral princedoms unified behind the emperor of Altran. Trigger painted a much different image. According to Trigger, the princedoms were constantly arguing and warring with each other. The emperor, who oversaw this, was the corrupt elected ruler who kept the princes off balance, pitting them against each other for his favours.

Loth, Kazun and Aibois joined the rest of the crew on deck. They passed very few other ships along the Spine Coast; they kept their distance. "You will find a few of the ships which operate along this coast have non-human crew members, but you can never tell,"

Kazun cleared their throat with a sound like gravel in a mill, "The reward for our kind is enough to tempt anyone, Trigger and I got away. But unfortunately, my husband wasn't so lucky." Jacob looked confused and then realised that Kazun was a woman.

Loth laughed, seeing the boy's confusion. "Hah, with the Dewar it is hard to tell the difference between the genders unless you know what you are looking for. Kazun is a bit of a beauty."

The gruff Haulfin blushed. She brushed her beard out of the way. "Don't feel bad, human. We find your bald faces quite disturbing as well." She handed Jacob a small object. It was a carved cork, a tiny, beautifully crafted dragon. Jacob looked at the exquisite handiwork; the dragon almost seemed alive.

"This is amazing!" Jacob muttered.

"This is why the humans keep us alive. We have skills." Kazun shrugged.

The crew and Jacob chatted and joked for the rest of the journey. The only one who didn't speak much was Aibois. He busied himself with the sails of the ship. They were about an hour away from Holum when Loth ordered Trigger and Kazun to get below decks. "While Holum is a bit of a mixed bag, and probably the most remote part of the empire, there aren't too many friends of the church and inquisition, but regrettably, there are still a few here who would try to turn us in," Loth explained.

"What about you?" Jacob asked.

Loth gazed at him astonished.. "Clever boy." Loth smiled, "True, my great-grandmother was an Aldari." He lifted his hat off carefully, showing his slightly pointed ears. He smiled and winked before putting his hat back on. "I'm passable as human. Holum is a rough town. Have you been before?" Loth asked.

Jacob shook his head. "No."

"It's very different from Havendale." Loth looked Jacob up and down. "Well, no one would mistake you for having the coin to rob, but that doesn't mean you won't find trouble. Do you know who you are looking for?"

Jacob shook his head seeming to listen to a voice in his head. "He is pretending to be a priest of the one true God. He will probably be staying at the temple."

Loth laughed. "There is no temple in Holum. So, if he's trying to pass as a priest, he will be in the upper quarter. When we make land, I'll take you up there, lad." Loth shrugged. "Sooner you find this guy, the sooner we get back."

From the bow of the boat, the harbour of Holum came into focus. Above, the gulls swooped, crying in repetitively. The houses were a mishmash of shapes and sizes, and no two were the same shade. They were yellow, lilac, blue, red, orange, brown, and every shade in between. Jacob couldn't see the fish shops from here but could already smell them lying on those tables. Silver scales turned to the sun the morning's catch would be displayed. The dock of Holum was much more extensive and busier than Havendale, several large cutters dwarfed the Lorelai, and there was even a galleon. Jacob marvelled at the size of the large ship. Loth explained that it was one of Gont's naval ships, a military vessel probably running the flag to the remote sections to show that it still held power in this remote part of the princedom. He nodded to Aibois, who acknowledged him, turning the ship away from the galleon towards a far-end dock. A small pilot ship ran out to guide them as they dropped the sails.

The smell was the first thing, aside from the noise, that struck Jacob as they approached the docks. Havendales docks had a strong fish odour, but it was nothing compared to this. Jacob felt his stomach churn again. The air had a rotten, dirty, squalid, quality.

"Ah, smell that!" Loth smiled. "The smell of civilisation, finally!" He turned to Jacob. "OK, lad, when we get in, keep your head down and don't speak."

"Understood," Jacob agreed.

Once they had tied up the Lorili, Loth vaulted the side of the boat, his boots landing heavily on the dock. It creaked and wobbled under his weight. Jacob scrambled over the edge.

"Boss," Aibois called as he tossed Loth a wrapped-up bundle.

"Ah, yes." Loth caught the package and unwrapped it; it was two rusted sabres. "Wouldn't want to be in town without these." He slid the two sabres into his belt.

"Should I be armed?" Jacob asked.

"Probably." Loth grinned. He took on a swagger as he walked the docks towards the town. "First stop the Comely Wench." He smiled, showing a few golden teeth. The port was busy. There were Gont soldiers all around the pier. They walked in pairs patrolling the docks. If the smell had been bad while still on the ship, it was almost overpowering as they approached the central part of the town. There was human sewerage running down the sides of the cobbled streets. By the docks, several scantily clad women waved at Loth.

"Ladies." Loth smiled at them. "Halie, Tracie, Lucie," he named them all as he passed. Then, he leaned to Jacob's ear, "Never known why all of them have names that end, 'ie'." Jacob noted that all the ladies bore the same tell-tale sores as Loth on their necks.

"You should tell those ladies to see an apothecary; they will need the same treatment I gave you," Jacob warned.

"Oh, they know, I'm sure." Loth waved away Jacob's words.

Near the docks was a tavern called The Comely Wench. Outside were additional women who addressed Loth by name, and he welcomed each of them individually. "I have an important assignment, and the lad is too young. Consequently, there is no time for fun today, ladies," he teased.

They entered the tavern. It was filled with raucous laughter and angry shouting. There were groups of sailors fighting, some laughing, some with women on their laps. It was a spectacle unlike anything Jacob had ever witnessed.

A large man squared up in front of Loth. "Oi!" A hefty, meaty hand shoved Loth pushing him back.

"Hi, Felix!" Loth laughed. "How's the wife?" he asked, stepping backwards.

The man's substantial greasy face erupted in anger; the large sailor's flabby arm swung towards Loth. Loth brought his knee up quickly, ducking under the man's swing and striking the attacker between the legs. Loth stepped back as Felix groaned and toppled over falling to the floor. Loth stepped over the prone man. "Bye, Felix."

Jacob looked around the tavern in wonder, then looked down at the supine figure, who was still wheezing. Jacob stepped around the body and rushed to keep up with Loth as he pushed his way through the crowded tavern. A crash behind him caused him to turn as another man was thrown through a table.

"Is it always like this?" Jacob asked Loth when he finally caught up.

"It's a bit quiet today." Loth shrugged, ignoring the mayhem around him. "Ah, there she is!" He pointed across the bar towards a large buxom lady who was laughing with several other dock hands. "Mable!" Loth shouted.

The woman's face dropped as she saw Loth. She glanced around nervously. "You aren't welcome here, Loth, you pox-ridden water rat!" she cursed at him.

"I'm getting the pox treated." Loth held his hands up. "I just need some information."

"You still owe me for the last favour." She approached him, fists clenched, her fat face red as she got closer.

"Mable, Mable, Mable, you know I'm good for it!" Loth lied. "Also, it's not for me. It's for this young lad." He stepped aside to show Jacob. The young boy looked so out of place, with the chaos of the bar erupting all around him. He looked calm. His hands were clasped in front of him, his fingers interlaced.

"Why are you bringing a child into my bar," Mable mumbled, her anger broke. "This is no place for a squab." She pushed her huge body towards them, barging several patrons out of the way. As she got close to Loth, she looked up at him, and her face broke into a grin. She grabbed Loth by the neck and pulled his head into her sizable bosom.

"You rascal." She smothered his face against her body for a moment or two. "Well, bring the squirt round the back!" she ordered, releasing Loth's head. The sailor gasped for breath as he was removed from the monstrous mammaries. She bustled the two visitors into a small back room, her little living area attached to the tavern. It was a poky little room. It had a large double cot, and the rest of the small room was packed with dressers and drawers. A small table was jammed into one corner, and a powerful, invasive spell of perfumes cloyingly hung in the air.

"OK, well, out with it!" She demanded after she had closed the door behind her locking out the din from the tavern hall.

"I need help finding…" Jacob began before Loth cut him off, pushing the small child back into the corner. Loth stood in front of Mable, smiling with his charming golden smile.

"You see, this poor lad is tracking down his father," Loth interrupted. "He is a man who pretends to be of the cloth." He got remarkably close to Mable and leaned till his lips were next to her ear, giving a loud whisper, "Poor lad's mum was done wrong by this man."

Jacob looked incredulously at Loth as he told the blatant lie. "I'm not…" Loth waved his hand at the child.

Loth continued again, "He's not going to settle for anything else than confronting his father face-to-face." Loth broke out his golden grin, "Now, Mable, no one enters Holum without your knowledge. Have you heard of any such 'holy' man who's arrived in the last couple of days?" Loth asked.

Mable paused. She looked at Loth, then at the young Jacob, and pushed Loth to one side. "Is that man actually your father?" Mable asked the young boy, her voluptuous body towering over Jacob.

Jacob spoke slowly, looking up at the woman's face, her impressive bosom uncomfortably close to his countenance. "No." He was trying to avoid looking her chest. "He has, however, wronged my village," Jacob added.

She didn't miss a beat and slapped Loth. "Don't try pulling my heartstrings, Lotheran!" she snapped at him. Her manner calmed immediately as she turned back to Jacob. "I would leave that man well alone if I was you. Take your loss and go," she advised.

"I cannot," Jacob uttered flatly. "Please, Ma'am, I need to find him."

"He's a polite boy," Mable mused. "And tells the truth when asked! Unlike you, lying dog." She clipped Loth around the head, dislodging his tricorn hat.

"Oi steady on, you could have hurt the captain." Retrieving his hat and Captain Bob, the rat, who had been woken from its slumber, Loth placed both back on his head.

"You still have that disgusting rodent with you?" Mable tutted, "OK young man, he's staying at a fancy place called the Golden Horn up on the hill. His name is Carl or something like that. He's been holding sermons up in one of the old grain stores for the last few nights, swindling some good folk out of money, no doubt. He will have made influential friends if he's in that part of town." She added, "Bet he's trying to form a proper church here in Holum."

"Do you know where this Golden Horn is?" Jacob asked Loth. The vagabond nodded. "Loth, let's go. Thank you, Ma'am." He gave her a short bow.

Mable blushed. "Such a polite, nice young man. You look like you could do with something to eat before you go."

"I would be honoured, but we have no time." Jacob gave another short bow.

"That's right, we must be off; wrongs to right!" Loth chirped in, straightening his hat and belt as the two rusted rapiers rattled. Mable looked at him with suspicious eyes.

"You need to be careful lad," Mable cautioned, her face becoming serious for a moment. "That Carl has been making a name for himself." She rounded on Loth. "You don't let this lad come to harm." She pointed a finger right up the nose of Loth. While she stood a little shorter than him, she used her impressive body to push the man against one of the walls. "Now give me a kiss before you go, you scoundrel." She grabbed the back of his head and pulled him into a kiss. Loth was helpless as the large woman gripped his head, thrusting her tongue down his throat. He flailed his arms, trying to pull away. Jacob watched the exchange and raised an eyebrow. Loth managed to break free and dislodged himself from her cloying embrace.

"Right lad, let's go," Loth ordered slightly flustered, grabbing Jacob and pulling him through the door. The deafening revelry of the inn hit like a thunderclap; without Mable's management, several more fights had already started, and significant damage was being caused to the inn's furnishing. Felix was leading the battle, but he broke it off when he saw Loth back in the room. "OK, we need to leave now!" Loth demanded, grabbing Jacob's arm roughly and yanking the young man out of a side door into the streets. This door led to a small alley between the tavern and the next building. This alley was narrow and filled with refuse. The smell smashed his senses causing Jacob to wretch.

"Come on, lad!" Loth continued to half-drag half-lead Jacob up the alleys at a hurried pace. Once they were several buildings away, Loth shortened his strides.

"Right, lad, are you sure we need to confront this, Carl?" Loth's face took on a moment of grave concern.

Jacob thought about it. "I believe so. I believe he has magic and has been causing this plague," Jacob explained the whole situation.

"So, it's only a chance he's involved?" Loth asked, glancing up and down the alleys slightly nervously.

"No, I have it on authority that this man is the cause," Jacob explained, thinking about his conversation with the otherworldly presence in his thoughts. He avoided telling Loth about the voice in his head. He was sure that even the drunken mad half-Aldari would find that crazy. "Remember, this is probably the only way to save your friend and my brother."

"Wanda." Loth nodded. "Bah, plenty of doxies around," he lied; he could see Jacob's expression. "I guess you are right." Loth poked his head out of the alley and scanned the surroundings. "Right, we've got to keep our heads down." He turned back at Jacob. "We've got a couple of issues. First, we need to avoid the military in town, and while I don't think I've got any outstanding warrants or bounties, the guards are often less than discriminating with whom they detain, especially in a town like this. Second, I might have a few local competitors who might want to make a run at me."

"You are a criminal?" Jacob asked. He had guessed as much, but Loth had finally confirmed it.

"No, no, no, not normally." Loth shook his head. "But sometimes misunderstandings happen. So, it would be best to wait until dark."

"We cannot. We need to save Havendale," Jacob insisted.

"Then we will need to take the back alleys up the hill then." Loth sighed.

Chapter 20

The God of Plagues

It took them over an hour to pick their way across the streets. Jacob was not as adept as Loth at sneaking around, but the young lad didn't attract much attention. He looked like just another street urchin.

They arrived in an alley just opposite the Golden Horn. It was a sizeable ornate inn. The smell in this part of town was not as pervasive. All the open gutters were leaking down to the bay and the docks. Outside the tavern, there was a large, armoured man. He had a long pike and stood lazily leaning against the entrance. The guard yawned and scratched his arse. Loth turned to Jacob. "We will sneak in the back. I know one of the servants here."

They snuck around the back of the large inn. Loth ordered Jacob to hang back as he approached the servants' entrance. He knocked on the door till a young waifish-looking lady opened it. Jacob couldn't hear the conversation, but he noticed the young lady blushing. Loth kissed her hand, smiling at the obviously enamoured young lady. He gave her a rakish smile. Loth looked back to the alley and beckoned Jacob towards the door. He rushed across. "Don't let them know I let you in, Loth." The young lady blushed shyly.

"Oh, Yvette, I won't." He smiled and kissed her hand again. "Stay beautiful, my precious flower." He winked at her before escorting Jacob into the back door. As Loth and Jacob made their way through the lavishly stocked kitchen, they walked by several other drudges hunched over superfluous chores who didn't glance up. "Now Yvette told me that he's staying in the penthouse, it's the largest room on the top floor," Loth explained as they progressed through the kitchen. "Now we are inside; we should be OK. While we aren't dressed like most people, no one questions guests. If anyone does, just act natural."

The tavern's interior was lavishly furnished; expensive tapestries and paintings adorned the walls, and the flooring was covered with crimson carpeting and rugs. Jacob could see the mast of the Lorelai and the other ships in the harbour, including the enormous war galleon, through the large windows that offered panoramic views of the bay. The whole bay seemed to be opened to the vista of the tavern. Thick felt red curtains were tied back to leave the scenery exposed. From the ceilings, beautiful gold and crystal chandeliers hung, lighting up the decadent opulence of the inn. The guests sat chatting in drawing rooms on each side of the main entrance. Some were enjoying mid-morning refreshments, and others were talking away. Jacob spotted two very well-dressed men in naval uniforms casually speaking with each other. Loth turned his back to them so they couldn't see him. "We will need to avoid those guys," Loth warned. "Let's head upstairs." They walked up a large split staircase. An impressive portrait of the emperor hung at the top of the stairs. It showed him atop a white stallion in full military armour inlaid with gold.

There weren't too many other patrons on the second floor. Those that Jacob and Loth did see were all wearing fine silks and jewels. Jacob had never in his life seen so much wealth in one place. All the patrons had white powdered wigs and painted faces. They picked their way through the tavern, and Jacob noticed Loth would occasionally brush past the guests. Jacob's keen eyes saw that he was taking the opportunity to lift a few items, purses, and bracelets. Jacob kept his head down and followed the pirate.

"Loth, what are you doing?" Jacob asked as they got up to the landing of the third floor.

"What do you mean?" Loth feigned innocence as he stuffed a blue gemmed necklace into his coat pockets. He shrugged. "I'm just making sure this trip will be worth my while."

"Stop it!" Jacob snapped. "If we get caught, we won't be able to confront Carlos." He looked around and pushed Loth up to the third and top floor, this had no social areas. Instead, it was lined with row after row of doors. "Which one is his room?" Jacob asked Loth.

Loth shrugged, "I don't know, we could poke around a few rooms, and if there happens to be anything lying around that isn't being used, we could…" He spotted Jacob's scathing look. "OK, OK, no more liberating."

One door was more significant than the others. It was a heavy dark wood with ornate brass hinges. Jacob knocked on the door, but there was no answer. Jacob waited a few moments before he pushed at the door. It was locked.

"Keep an eye out," Loth advised with a smile barging in front of Jacob. Loth knelt by the lock, rummaging in his pockets. He pulled out two small rods and started to manipulate the lock. After a few seconds, there was a satisfying click, and the door opened. The room was darkened. No candles were lit. The thick heavy curtains were pulled close, leaving no room for any light to penetrate the room. Jacob entered the room, whispering to himself, "*Etanimulli.*" He felt the glow in his mind spark and erupt. A small ball of shimmering light irradiated from the ceiling casting the room in a soft-yellow haze.

Loth looked at the young man. "Been hiding that trick up your sleeve. Guess now we all have something to hide from the impys." He smiles, following Jacob into the lit room. He pulled the door closed behind them. "Are we sure this is the right room?"

Jacob looked around the room. While it was beautifully decorated, there wasn't much in the way of personal effects, only a small backpack. Its contents were neatly folded beside it. A heavy steel chain necklace with the symbol of the one true God was laid on top of the clothes.

"I think so." Jacob looked around. "*He was here.*" The cold, unfeeling voice in Jacob's head confirmed.

Loth paused, glancing around the bedroom, "Not much in the way of stuff to liberate," he complained as he poked around; he pulled open the wardrobe and saw a heavy metal box. "Ah, here we go." Loth lifted the metal box and placed it on the bed. It had a heavy clink. Loth grinned. "Jackpot!"

Jacob rolled his eyes. "Open it. There might be a cure inside."

The voice spoke. The cure will only come from the defeat of Carlos.

Loth popped open the lid, "A nice haul." He smiled, eyeing the chest filled with coins.

He approaches,' the voice in Jacob's head warned.

Jacob turned around just as the double doors opened. Standing in the doorway was a man wearing the simple black robes of a priest. He wore a heavy chain necklace with the holy symbol. He gripped in one hand a staff; the head of the pole was adorned with two finely crafted lion heads back-to-back. The man's face was impassive, and his skin glistened with a yellowish tint. His eyes were a greenish hue.

The man spoke. "Thoth." He stepped into the room and raised his hand. The heavy wooden doors slammed shut behind him.

"It's Loth," the thief uttered, mistakenly thinking the priest was talking to him.

The priest cast an annoyed glance at Loth. "Not you. You are insignificant."

"You are Irra?" Jacob asked, squaring up to the man.

The man laughed. "Irra is one of my children. I am in the embrace of the great Nergal, the old father, the oldest and the original. I am afraid no longer, for, with his pestilential favour, I have become death that which I once most feared." The man appeared surrounded by a black swirling shadow. "Do you still recall what you told me, brother? Do you recall what you said to me during our confrontation at the front of the Pyramid of Imona? Do you remember the words you used? I do. As I recall, your face was tortured. Imagine that—the master of knowledge, your intellect twisted into grief. Nevertheless, you carried out your obligation. You always followed through on expectations. Very devoted. You were steadfast enough to keep writing about the gods' conflict. You did not enjoy what you did. Both then and today, I was aware of that. But my brother, everything changes. I'm not the same person I used to be, and as for you, let's not bring up where you are right now." He cast a scornful glance over the frail body of Jacob. "You will not stop me or my plans." He pointed the lion-headed staff towards Loth.

"Hey, don't mind me." Loth held his hands up.

"Why do you two stand against me?" The man asked. "You, a bastard Haulfin, an outcast of society, and you, Thoth, inhabiting a frail human boy."

"You are also human," Jacob mentioned.

"Oh, this body?" The priest spread his arms. "This is a temporary vessel, the mind of Carlos has long since rotted away. He and I are one. I will now use the corruption of this one true God to kill the heathens."

"But why do this?" Loth asked. "You are responsible for infecting all these people in the north?"

"I am the god of the end. I am where you will all end up. Even now, you bare my mark as your body rots! I do this for the gods of old. So that we may return to control this world and drive this false god from the world, I will thrive over the rotting corpses of their congregations."

"Most of them are innocent," Jacob stated. "You need to stop this, brother." He wasn't sure if it was him speaking or the voice in his head. At this moment, they seemed to be talking as one. "A pact was made."

"Pah, the pact of cowards," snapped the priest. "It was a pact made because they are cowards. They fear the humans, but we are more powerful and greater; we shouldn't be cowed by their spinelessness."

"The pact was agreed by both sides of the pantheon." The words came out of Jacob's mouth, but they were not his words. Jacob looked across at Loth, who had begun to edge around towards the side of Carlos.

"Not by me." Carlos' eyes flashed green and a spray of thick green smoke erupted towards Loth. Loth ducked and rolled away as the thick green smoke sprayed across the wall.

Jacob rushed forward, raising his hands to bring the light into his mind and focusing his power to try to stop this priest. White light erupted from Jacob's fingers; it slammed into the priest, knocking him back against the door. The priest let out a cry of pain, part of his flesh peeled away, showing pulsing yellow sinew underneath. He turned a hand towards Jacob, and a green bolt of energy shot out of his fingers. It hit Jacob in the chest. Jacob let out a cry of agony. The young man doubled over, struggling to breathe; a violent coughing attack wracked his frail body. He couldn't stop coughing; blood splattered on the ground as he tried to cover his mouth; lights and spots danced in front of his eyes as he struggled to catch his breath. He couldn't; he gasped, choking and coughing.

"Sorry, brother," Carlos stood over Jacob's prone body. "Time to find a new host." The double-headed lions appeared to roar as the god of plagues lifted his staff and slammed it down with great force. The lion heads impacted a white light barrier. It was blocked by Jacob's uplifted hands as he called upon his magic to shield his body.

"*Reirrab,*" Jacob cried out in panic. He struggled to keep the light in his mind as his body failed. Jacob could feel his arms shaking, straining to remain conscious. He could hear screaming; it took him a few moments to realise it was coming from his mouth. "I will not fall!" Jacob's eyes started to bleed, tears of blood dripping down his cheeks, the metallic taste of blood and bile in his mouth. Jacob's eyes darkened as he fought for consciousness. Strength from within was helping him, driving him on with borrowed power.

Loth rushed the plague priest; he had drawn his rusted sabres and struck out with a savage speed. The priest pulled his staff around and blocked and parried Loth's attack, moving with a speed that matched the sailor. The two danced around, blocking and attacking each other. Loth didn't let up, not giving Carlos a single moment to use any magic. Then, with two sabres whirling like a dervish, Lotheran struck out. Each strike was parried by the lion-headed staff.

Jacob watched as Loth and Carlos danced around each other, both nimble and agile, Carlos had strength and speed, but Loth moved with the agility of one who had survived many battles. Jacob pushed himself onto his knees. He closed his eyes, trying to control his breathing; he focused on the light in his mind, gritting his teeth he dug into the reserves of his soul.

"*Nergal!*" Jacob called out. The light in his mind began to flare and a white glow formed around the young man. His eyes sparkled with the white light, and his bloodstained cheeks and mouth sprayed spittle as he opened his mouth, letting out a scream of pure white energy.

The energy surge splintered against a sickly green magical barrier. Nergal extended a palm and waved the stream of energy aside with a gesture. Jacob yelled with all his strength, but the barricade was too powerful. However, Nergal-possessed body of Carlos had forgotten about Loth while his attention had been subverted. A sabre came down, slicing deeply into the plague god's chest. The second sabre thrust forward through the priest's neck. The priest's eyes went slack, as thick yellow puss-infected blood sprayed from the wound. The putrid green barrier failed, and the priest was struck by the faltering white energy erupting from Jacob's mouth. The young mage pitched forward, his power finally spent, consciousness fled his mind, and Jacob fell face-first onto the floor. Carlos' body sank to the floorboards with a sickening splat. The lion-headed staff fell beside them. The staff clanged loudly against the stone. Despite being unconscious, Jacob's hand shot out, gripping the long staff with a vice-like grip. The artefact had found a new master.

Loth looked over at the fallen body of Jacob, now gripping this ornate staff. Loth paused, catching his breath. He rolled the tiny body of the young mage over. Jacob was still breathing; his face was deathly pale, and streaks of grey marked the young boy's hair.

"What the hell was that?" Loth murmured to himself, looking at the putrid mess that was Carlos. He would have to rouse the young lad or carry him. He was sure the commotion of the fight would have disturbed the entire inn.

Loth pulled the limp body of Jacob up onto the bed, the young man wasn't large, but the dead weight made him awkward to lift. Loth thought for a moment just to leave the young man behind and make his escape. *The artefact with the double lion head and the frail young man sprawled beside it would be cumbersome,* Loth thought to himself.

A noise behind him startled Loth as the door to the room burst open. Two figures framed the doorway, swords at the ready. They were half-dressed soldiers, each gazed at the scene before them, a figure on the floor in a puddle of oozing puss, another laying on the bed and a roguish man brandishing two rusted sabres.

"Halt," one of the guards commanded. The roguish man paused, realising how the scene looked.

"Look, I can explain," Loth started.

The guards didn't listen. Instead, they approached, stepping around the fallen body of Carlos. As they danced around the mass of the decomposing body, it began to twitch and move.

"He's still alive!" One of the guards shouted in alarm as the form of Carlos roughly pushed itself up, and the horrific visage of a man lurched to unsteadily to its feet.

"By the god!" One soldier gasped as the melted face of Carlos turned on him . Then, with surprising speed, it struck out with a swing of its fleshy stump of an arm. It caught the first soldier round the neck and dragged him into a fatal embrace. The soldier screamed as rotten teeth sank into his flesh. The other soldier remained stunned.

"By the hells," Lotheran cursed. He flourished his sword towards the living dead form of Carlos as it grappled and sunk its teeth into the second guard letting the body fall to his feet.

The creature that once was Carlos tried to speak. With its slashed throat, it came out in a burbling cackle of blood and a hiss of air. It rushed towards Loth. Loth danced out of the creature's reach, swinging up his blade and severing the creature's hand; the hand landed on the floor with a wet splat as it lurched again at the sailor. Loth slashed and parried against the oncoming monster, cutting off rotten flesh parts at a time, but the beast didn't stop. Behind him, the soldiers' fallen bodies began to lurch to their feet.

Loth was slowly backing into the corner. No matter how much he cut the oncoming body, it kept coming. The two other soldiers swarmed the sailor. Loth felt fear. This isn't how he wanted to die, not like this. He cut at the outreaching limbs that were trying to drag him down.

Jacob's grip tightened around the staff and he sat up. His eyes flashed open, showing pure black, *"Nurgal!"* His voice echoed, resonating around the room. "Your time has come!"

The rotting dead forms stopped their assault on Lotheran and slowly turned towards Jacob on the bed. Jacob pushed his body up, but this wasn't Jacob. Thoth was moving the body of Jacob. *"Etacidare,"* The echoey voice of Jacob spoke and from the top of the staff a flash of light filled the room. Loth covered his eyes as the brilliant white light filled the room. Gurgling hisses of searing rotting flesh filled the room. Stars danced in front of Loth's unpatched eye. He used the back of his hand to flip his eye patch up. He was trying to blink vision into his blinded eye.

The walls of the room were scorched, blackened by some magical flame. Jacob lay resting on the burned bed, still gripping the staff. Three piles of ash had replaced the attacking figures. Yet Lotheran was unscathed. Slowly the stars faded from Loth's eye. He sheathed his swords and pulled his patch down over his recovering eye.

There were sounds of more people approaching, more guards. Lotheran looked around the room for another means of escape. He stopped and looked at Jacob, then at the window.

"Fuck it," he grumbled, retrieving his swords and sheathing them. He approached the bed and lifted the young mage over his shoulder. "I cannot believe I'm not being paid for this shit."

Chapter 21

The Pact

Jacob came around in a darkened room; the floor rocked and creaked, his whole body ached, his chest was tight like a vice seizing his lungs, and he struggled to catch his breath. A spasm of coughs wracked his body. His arms were weak, and he couldn't move.

Then, from the darkened rocking room, a gruff voice called out, "Lotheran, the boy is awake." Jacob recognised the voice of Kazun. The Haulfin stood next to Jacob's cot. Jacob tried to speak, but his voice came out as a weak croak. "Don't try to speak." Kazun ran a wet cloth over Jacob's face, it stank of rotten sea water, but it was cool and refreshing. "You're lucky Loth was there to save your arse, boy." The Haulfin grinned through her thick beard. Jacob struggled to focus on the light. It was a deep red glow, but Jacob couldn't sit up. He couldn't move. He could feel his body trembling. His once black hair was now marred with grey streaks matted across his head.

"Rest easy, boy." Kazun stepped back, giving Jacob some room, Loth loomed over him, and his pockmarked, scarred, and bearded face looked over the young man.

"Well, well, well," Loth smiled. "You're alive, good." Jacob tried to speak, but again he couldn't catch his breath; it came out as a rasping wheeze. "Whatever that bastard hit you with almost killed you."

Jacob shook his head. He tried to bring his hand up and found it grasping a long staff. He managed to raise his head slightly. His fingers were gripped tightly around the shaft of the artefact.

"Yea, you gripped that and wouldn't let go." Loth smiled, "I managed to get you out, but you wouldn't let go of that bloody thing. Carrying you with that bloody staff made it impossible for me to take the coins you owe me, lad." He handed him a small cup of water.

The water was oily and smelt bad, but it soothed Jacob's sore throat.

"What happened?" Jacob managed finally, his voice weak and cracked.

"Well, that priest Carlos hit you with some mojo, and then I stabbed him. You grabbed this staff and wouldn't let go." Loth pointed to the rod that Jacob's fingers clutched around like a vice. "You were out of it, and we had made enough noise to wake the dead, and we attracted some unwanted attention." Loth winced. "What was that thing?" he asked Jacob.

"It was a god possessing a priest," Jacob managed to croak.

"Oh, just a god then." Loth shrugged. "What do you mean a god!"

"It's a long story, but with him dead, the plague will end," Jacob finished.

"We are having to take a bit of a longer way back to Havendale," Loth advised. "We sort of picked up some unwanted attention from our actions in Holum. We will arrive back the day after tomorrow. You had better rest; you've been coughing up blood."

Loth left Jacob in the cabin. Once alone Jacob looked down at the staff, he was holding with a death grip. He tried to flex his fingers; it took all his effort to unfurl his clamped hand. His fingers ached from griping the staff so hard. He turned it over, looking at the twin-lion heads. He could feel a power in this relic. It was an old power.

The voice in his head spoke, it was still cold and spoke with no feeling, as if reading from a book. It is the staff of Maahes. He was one of the oldest of us. He was destroyed by Nergal during the war of the gods many millennia ago.

What happened when we fought him? Jacob asked the voice in his head.

The voice spoke. You were the fire. I was the fuel, you and I worked together and defeated Nergal..

What has happened to me? Jacob asked.

You were struck by a blast of pure disease. I tried to protect you, but it was too strong. Your body has been shattered. It is only your will and my power that keeps you alive.

Will I recover? Jacob asked.

No, your body is broken. Every day of your life will be pain and anguish, you will not die, but you will never be the same. The voice went silent.

Jacob's hand ran his fingers along the lion heads. A tingle of power arched against his fingers; he could feel its power channelling through his body, adding to the light in his mind, he and the relic were one.

The Lorelai was one of the fastest ships in the Everlong Sea. It quickly outran the slow sluggish galleon that had given them chase. The skilled crew of the skiff had led the galleon south for half a day on a wild goose chase before turning east along the northern coast of Taros, a neighbouring princedom to Gont. The two princedoms had been hostile towards each other for generations, and the galleon wouldn't come this close to the Taros coastline.

Jacob's health did not improve much over the next two days of travel. His body was wracked by coughing fits, sapping his strength. While the sickness did not leave, Jacob was able to get used to his disability. Two days into the trip, Jacob rose from the cot and ate some fish caught by Trigger with a running line from the stern of the boat. By the third day, they sailed into Havendale bay just as the sun was receding behind the Spine Mountains. Jacob had spent most of the afternoon staring into the sea on the deck. Despite his broken health, he glad when he saw the lights of his home as the Lorelai sailed into the harbour. Jacob was still having trouble breathing and periodically suffered from horrible coughing episodes. Jacob's spirits increased as he anticipated seeing his mother and Robin. Trigger was piloting the ship toward the bay. Loth sat close to the young lad.

"Remember our deal, lad. You will heal my pox."

Jacob managed a weak smile; the fresh sea air helped his breathing somewhat, but his chest was still tight. "I remember. When we get to port, I'll send some more griseofulvin."

Loth made a face remembering the taste. "Yea would you mind giving me a few extra doses."

Jacob nodded. "You can have treatment from me whenever you are in Havendale."

Loth spoke seriously for a moment. "We are going to have to leave before the morning tomorrow, we are going to have to head out of the Everlong for a few months." His face creased, all his scars crinkled together. "Might try to head south to Arbay, I'm sure Aibois would love to go back to his homeland."

The towering black man only grumbled in response. "We couldn't take Trigger or Kazun, so we don't go there," he warned.

Loth waved his hand. "I was joking! OK, lads, we are coming in. You know the drill."

Trigger and Kazun nodded and headed towards the cabin. They bid Jacob farewell. "Won't see you again, lad. I hope you get better." Kazun slapped Jacob on the back, Trigger gave the boy a nod, and both headed below decks.

Aibois readied the dock and spring lines. Loth skilfully brought the Lorelai alongside. The docks were busy despite the fading light.

***

Three days ago, most of the sick had begun to recover. It started the moment Carlos' body hit the floor. Maganwyth had claimed responsibility, coming up with a new cure, but she knew the truth. A few more of the weaker people had passed away, including Erin,. Robin had been in a cot next to her but hadn't been awake for his mother's passing. The twins were now orphans. Maganwyth had covered for Jacob, claiming to have sent him to deal with another outbreak in Woodvale.

Jacob walked through the busy docks; they were catching up with weeks of work that had fallen behind during the plague. Jacob could see those still recovering were working slower than those who had avoided the sickness. Behind him, he could hear Loth calling to a young dark-haired woman called Wanda, his friend who had recovered from the malady. Jacob walked as fast as his broken health would allow him. He used his new staff to prop up his weight as he struggled to ascend the steps from the docks towards the temple. Despite the early evening, there were still crowds of people milling around outside the church. Jacob could see the blacksmith's wife and children. Jacob approached them, and Falia ran to him. "Oh, Jacob, I'm so sorry!"

The young girl ran up and hugged him all under the scowl of the blacksmith's wife. Jacob could feel her lithe body pressed against his. Despite his shattered health, he could still feel the warmth filling up, starting from his loins. Then he made sense of her words. "Sorry for what?" Jacob asked. "Is my brother OK."

Falia broke the hug and stepped back. She was crying. She wiped her eyes. "Oh yes, Robin is fine, he is helping with the…" She paused, her voice caught in her throat. "He's helping with the burial."

"What are you sorry for?" Jacob asked again, insistent he gripped her arm. "Tell me," he pushed.

"Ow." She pulled her arm away. "It's your mother." The words struck Jacob like a hammer to the chest. He felt the colour drain from his face. His mother. Erin's will to live had long left her body, but the actual news of her death still struck the young man hard.

"Where is she?" Jacob urged.

"On the upper field," Falia mumbled, rubbing her arm where Jacob had grabbed her. "We were just heading there to say farewell to father."

Jacob took a deep breath, summoned what little of his strength remained, and pushed towards the upper fields. He leaned heavily on the staff of Maahes as he climbed the slopes. Reaching the plateau, Jacob could see the start of a large fire. The glow of torches and the large fire filled the upper field. From this distance he could see one of the young priests speaking before a gathered crowd. As he approached Jacob observed several dozen bodies lying next to the large fire. His brother stood next to one. His face was sunken and low. *No,* He thought as he scrambled forward, using the staff to propel himself. The crowd turned as he arrived. Robin saw his brother appear and rushed to Jacob. Jacob fell to his knees weeping; he was crying tears of blood. Robin grabbed his brother and hugged him with all his strength. The hug hurt, but it made Jacob feel alive. He could feel the warmth of his brother's body next to his. His brother's chest was heaving as Robin sobbed. "I'm sorry, Jacob."

Jacob patted his brother's back. The twins wept together over their mother's death.

The funeral was a traditional northern funeral with the priest's speaking words about the warmth passing onwards towards the love of the one true God. The voice was a drone in the air. Jacob couldn't help but feel anger at the priest's words. The one true God had never done anything and never showed itself, yet his mother's death was the cause of one of the gods, a real god, one Jacob had seen and killed.

One by one, the bodies were cast onto the pyre. They were wrapped in linen soaked in alcohol to help them burn quickly. The stars were twinkling as the night had fallen. The moon shone brightly over the field. Jacob and Robin clung to each other as Erin's body was cast onto the flames to be consumed. Robin lifted up Jacob as they watched the flickering flames consume their mother's body. Jacob spoke in his head to the voice. *Did you know she would die?* he accused angrily.

Yes, the hollow voice came back echoing. I knew she would die. Everyone will die eventually.

Could I have saved her? Jacob asked. Was there any hope.

The emotionless voice spoke. No, not since my niece, Penthos, was with her. Poor Penthos, any she binds with will lose all hope and fade.

Jacob leaned against his brother as the ceremony ended. He looked across the gathering at Falia. She, Celina, and their mother clung to each other as they watched their father enter the flames. Held tight by his mother, the blacksmith's youngest child looked back at Jacob. He whispered to his older sister, and Celina walked with the young boy towards Jacob and his brother. The young boy stood before Jacob. He looked up at the young man, "Thank you," he spoke with a lisp.

"For what?" Jacob asked, confused.

"My sister says you looked after me when I was sick," the young boy stated. "She says I would have died if you hadn't helped me."

Jacob thought back to when he was working in the temple fighting to save everyone. He hadn't managed to keep the blacksmith alive but had healed the rest of the family.

Jacob spoke with a nod. "You are welcome, child."

Celina cast a shy smile at Robin, her eyes were rimmed red from crying, but she still looked like a vision of loveliness. Robin gave a short smile back at her.

"Come, brother, I need rest." Jacob leaned on Robin. Robin broke eye contact with Celina and supported his brother, as they left the field and headed towards their house.

The house was as Erin had left it. Unwashed dishes covered every surface, the water basin was dry, and there was nothing in the house to eat. Jacob didn't feel hungry. He felt almost nothing. With the death of his mother, he now felt hollow. Robin started the fire and helped Jacob sit in his mother's old chair.

"Sit with me, brother," Jacob asked, pointing to the other chair next to the fire. He laid his new staff down beside his chair.

Robin slumped into the chair; he was exhausted but hadn't wanted to stop. "I'm hungry," the large man mumbled.

"Later," Jacob dismissed. "I need to speak to you first." Jacob stared into the flames framing the words in his mind.

"What is it?" Robin asked.

Jacob spoke slowly. "Brother, it is only the two of us now. And I need to be honest with you."

"Jacob, you are always…" Jacob cut him off.

"Listen, brother, it is hard to speak." Jacob paused to catch his breath. "I need you to trust me." Robin nodded. "I'm going to reveal something to you, but before I tell you, I need your word that this stays between us."

"Of course," Robin promised.

"I need you to give me your word," Jacob insisted. "I need to swear on the body of our dead mother."

Robin looked hurt, "I swear."

"What I'm going to show you will probably scare you, brother, but you need to know, as I'll need you from now on, brother." Jacob slowly explained, "I have powers... magical powers."

Robin let out a laugh, "Don't be silly, Jacob. Only the evil Haulfin have magic."

Jacob raised a hand and, in his mind, called on the glow of light. "*Steppup wodahs,*" Jacob's voice formed the strange words. It was a simple spell, and a small ball of orb danced around his fingers, casting flickering images on the cottage walls. He could hear Robin gasp in horror. Robin made the sign of the one true God.

"This is not evil, Robin," Jacob explained calmly. "The rise of the empire and the competition between the various branches of the churches in the early days enhanced the blood lust for the witches and Haulfin's with no distinction between the good and those who harmed. They slaughtered everyone without distinguishing between heroes and killers and then questioned why society and the natural world had become so unstable. Negative chaos will overwhelm all without the practitioners of good chaos. It's that straightforward." He looked over at Robin's confused face. "They have been telling stories to make us think that the Haulfin are pure evil. They have trained their flocks to fear magic to control us."

Robin shook his head. "That isn't right,"

"Think about it, Robin," Jacob explained. "It was Maganwyth and me that protected the village, not the priests, and not the one true God. We fought that disease. We cured it." Jacob sent the light to dance in front of Robin, and the light weaved around and changed colour. "The magic is not evil, no eviller than a sword or knife, it is a tool, and it depends on how you use it," Jacob explained. The light vanished in a puff of bubbles. "I need you to understand this, brother." Jacob then began telling him the story of his travels to Holum. He left out the parts about the voices in his head and brushed over some details of the fight with Carlos, the false priest. Robin asked a few questions and looked in wonder at his brother. Jacob had never lied to Robin; he had always tried to teach him since they were young. Robin wasn't a quick thinker like his brother, he had always just taken what the priests told him to be true, but as Jacob talked, he began to understand that the world might be more complicated. Jacob finished the story with his arrival back at Havendale. "My health is shattered, and I struggle to draw each breath. I will need your help."

Robin rose and moved to his brother. "Oh brother, anything." Robin vowed, "Of course."

"Thank you, brother." Jacob clasped his brother's hand. "On that note, I need you to do something for me." He pointed to one of the shelves. "Grab three of the blue labelled bottles and the other with the green liquid." He brought them to Jacob. Jacob checked they were the right items. "Please take them down to the docks to a ship called the Lorelai. Tell the captain, 'Thank you' from me." Robin nodded. "Also, on your way back, please bring us some water. We will need some."

Chapter 22

The Betrayal

The small satchel clinked as Robin walked towards the town. He could see the glow on the upper field as the funeral pyre burned low. Robin was thinking deeply about his brother and his mother. Jacob had always struggled to accept the teachings of the priests; he remembered Jacob had always argued and questioned their lessons about the one true God. Robin hadn't ever thought about it much. It was just what he had been told. He was lost in thought as he made his way through town. He waved to a few other villagers mindlessly as he made his way towards the docks.

"Robin," a sweet soft voice called. It was Birel, the inn master's daughter. She ran up to Robin and grabbed his hand. "I'm so sorry," she apologised, giving Robin a big hug. Robin looked down at the young girl. He knelt, so they were at eye level.

"Thank you, Birel." He gave her a grin. "I've got an errand to run now. I'll see you tomorrow."

She smiled weakly and gave him another big hug. "Here, this is from my mother." She passed Robin a wrapped-up package. From the smell, Robin could tell it was a sweet roll. He smiled at the young girl and accepted the package.

"Thank you." Robin got to his feet.

"Oh, Celina has been looking for you." Birel pouted. "I told her you had gone home after the funeral."

Robin nodded. He continued to the docks; a tall, dark-skinned man was preparing ropes on the deck of the Lorelai. "Ahoy," Robin called up,

The large man nodded. "You're Robin?" he asked in a deep voice.

"Yes," Robin admitted

"Loth!" the man called down into he decks..

A scandalous man sprang out of the cabin. He hung to the side of the boat, looming over Robin. "Ah, my little friend came through." His golden grin flashing. "I assume this is for me?" Loth asked; leaning over the rail, he snatched the satchel.

"Er yes, my brother says…" Robin started.

"How is he?" Loth asked, his face showing genuine concern.

"He… he is struggling," Robin admitted.

Loth nodded. "Give him my best. I hope he survives."

"Loth," came a womanly voice from the cabin below.

"Ah, duty beckons." Loth gave the young lad a wink. "Be there in a moment Wanda," he called back towards the cabin. "Just one last thing." Loth paused, he jumped off the boat to stand next to Robin on the side of the dock. He placed a hand on his shoulder and gazed deep into the young lad's eyes. Loth spoke slowly and clearly. "Your brother is a hero, you need to look after him, he will protect the village with everything he's got and more, but he needs someone to look after him." Loth finished and jumped back up onto the boat. "Anyway, I'll see you around." With that, the sailor dropped down into the cabin.

Robin turned from the boat, the docks were quieter now, and a few people were heading home. He was still deep in thought. The words from Loth ran in his head, along with the revelation Jacob. He made up his mind long ago and would protect his brother with everything he had. As he walked through the village square, he caught sight of Celina. Robin ran to her calling her name, "I'm sorry we had to go earlier," he explained. "I wanted to stay longer… with you," he added.

The young lady blushed. Robin was emboldened by sorrow and needed something simple in his head; grasping her hand, he pulled her away from the main streets. He pushed his body against her and kissed her passionately. The young woman at first didn't respond, but after a moment her hands moved up and held Robin's body against hers. Jacob's quest for water was forgotten, and the two young lovers snuck into an old hayloft near Celina's house. They lost themselves in their combined grief and took the temporary comfort of each other's physical bodies. Every nerve in Celina's body and brain were electrified in that split second before Robin's touch. They shared the anticipation of being together in a way that's more than words, in a way that's so wholly tangible.

In the hayloft cast in twilight and shadow, Robin stood close to Celina, he pulled his shirt over his head and revealed his well-toned body. Celina breathed in his scent. It was a deep musky forest scent, tinged slightly by the smell of fire. His arms wrapped around her, and in one gentle pull, their skin touched. Robin ran his hand through her long blonde hair pulling it free of her braid, watching it tumble as he released it, cascading like a golden waterfall. Robin loved the soft feeling of her skin and hair in his rough, calloused hands. Then his hand moved down Celina's cheekbones to her lips. That was when the kissing started. They moved like partners in a dance that is written in the stars. Their bodies fitted together as if they were made just for this. Falling into one another, to feel a natural rhythm. With a laugh, Robin lifted Celina into his arms, carrying her toward the hay. He gently placed her into the rough straw. They locked eyes, excitement and chemistry passing between the two of them for a moment and for that moment, their grief was forgotten. He rapidly peeled off her dress and started kissing her legs his lips moving up, his hands on her legs, sliding higher and higher with each planted kiss. Celina's head rocked back against the rough hay as he reached her nether, the first moan escaping from her lips. In the twilight loft, their fingers caressed each other's skin as if afraid a heavier touch would break the heady magic. Instead, they became one mind with one goal and purpose, each utterly drunk with lust for the other. The act didn't take that long. The passion and pent-up frustration for Robin exploded in a fleeting moment. They collapsed together, entwined in each other's limbs. The moons rose in the night, creating a shimmering silver light across Havendale.

***

It was nearly morning when Robin returned home with a beaming smile. He couldn't help but grin until he entered the home, he saw his mother's old chair, with his brother slumped in it. His brother was struggling to draw breath as he slept. The fleeting memory of sex with Celina fled his mind.

Robin picked up his slender brother and placed him on his own bed. Returning to the living room, he slouched by the fireside. While he was exhilarated by lovemaking with Celina, Robin's mood was tempered by the sorrow for his mother's death. He briefly attempted cleaning up and then cried over the dirty dishes. His shoulders shook as his grief came in waves. At first, the waves were so strong Robin felt like he was being swept away into an inky void, removing him from the world. Robin felt lost. He struggled to reconnect

213

and weave himself anew into the fabric of living. The one focus he had now was his brother. Robin would have to look after his little brother. Finally, after half an hour of sobbing, Robin pulled himself up, rubbing his eyes red raw; he finished cleaning and went to bed.

Erin was gone now, and the home felt lifeless. Without their mother, the twins felt lonely. While Erin had only been a walking shell for the past few years, her absence left a void. Riding the waves of loss together, the sorrow bore testament to the love connection that endures even after death. The twin's bond grew. While Robin's sadness was apparent, and he could express it freely, Jacob suffered his profound grief in silence. Both of them felt they were consoling the other's loss.

***

As the year dragged on, only time allowed the pain to lessen. After months, days when they didn't think about their mother, became more frequent. Jacob had earned a reputation during the plague and had almost supplanted Maganwyth as the village's go-to healer. He still used to visit the witch, but there was little she could teach him about medicine now. Robin had returned to hunting and logging. He and Celina had continued to see each other, grabbing moments whenever they could. Much to the jealousy and envy of many of the village's other women.

The twins still were coping with their mother's absence, the months passed into winter, and the twins grew into a routine. However, the sorrow did lessen little by little over time.

Jacob was doing his rounds. He walked leaning on his staff around the village, the first snow had fallen, and it crunched underfoot as he went from one house to another, giving of his patients their weekly medicines. Jacob had improved on some of the old remedies the hag had used to make. Jacob was almost welcomed as he arrived at the houses. The most welcoming was always Falia. She not only came out and greeted Jacob, but she took the time to talk to him. He found he could chat with the young lady; she didn't seem revolted by his frail visage, pale skin, or sunken eyes.

On the contrary, she was always welcoming. Jacob had a genuine affection for Falia. On rare occasions, she would converse with Jacob the entire time they walked back to his isolated cabin. She could lighten Jacob's usually dark mood. They would even laugh together. When he struggled to breathe, she would pause and help him. Jacob felt that they were becoming close. He couldn't ever understand why she chose to be around him.

One day after his rounds, Jacob was at home. Robin burst into the house in a mad panic. "Jacob, you've got to help!" he asked urgently.

Jacob looked up from his book. He closed it, placing it beside the chair that had once been his mother's, which he had since adopted. Robin stood over Jacob, his eyes wide, darting around as he fidgeted from one foot to another.

"Be still, brother," Jacob cautioned. While Jacob's health had never returned from his adventure in Holum, he had learned to measure his energy to cope with the day. He used his staff to steady himself. "What is it?" He looked his brother up and down. It was obvious that Robin was upset about something.

"They are going to kill me," Robin repeatedly mumbled to himself.

"Start from the beginning," Jacob instructed. "What is wrong."

"I, we, she," he stuttered and mumbled. "I'm too young!"

Jacob precisely realised the problem. A sly smile crossed his lips. Ah, so his brother had impregnated Celina. "I'm guessing Celina is now with child."

Fear crossed Robin's face; he managed a nod.

"Oh, dear brother." Jacob got to his feet. "I can help, brother, but only if both, you and Celina agree."

"She will agree, her mother will kill her, and the village will kill me!" Robin urgently fretted.

"You will probably need to bring her here," Jacob explained. "But before that, I will need some herbs from the forest. I've only had to make a couple of these potions before." Jacob thought about Wanda, a lady who worked down the docks. She had made a few visits to Maganwyth and later to Jacob's when Maganwyth had inappropriately offered to buy the remains of the unborn child. "I have pepper and Birthwort, but the myrrh will be harder to find. The Commiphora, in which it grows, isn't native to the north. Go to the tavern, Eyia. She usually has some." Jacob moved to the kitchen and picked up a couple of bottles that held a few potions. He handed them to Robin. "Give these to Eyia in exchange."

Robin hurried off, still frantic. Jacob smiled to himself; he loved his brother, but he would need to teach him a few preventatives. Such as using honey, acacia leaves, and lint to make a rudimentary cap. He would probably have to teach Celina. Robin returned in short order, out of breath. He must have run the whole way. "Put it on the side," he ordered Robin. "Now you have the challenging task of bringing Celina here." Jacob turned. "She will become sick once she has taken this, it will take her several days before she feels better. During that time, you cannot bed her again," Jacob explained. "Now go and get her."

It took Robin an hour to return with Celina. She was as nervous as Robin, standing by his side clutching his hand. Jacob had finished mixing the potion. He looked her up and down. "Now I need to make sure you are sure about this," Jacob asked, gazing at the woman with his dark eyes. The young lady shied away into Robin's arms.

"S," she managed to mumble, clutching onto Robin's firm chest.

Jacob nodded. "You understand this will make you unwell," he explained, holding the bottle. "You will be unwell for several days, and you will lose the child." He spoke softly and calmly. "This cannot be undone if you change your mind."

She nodded again.

He looked at both. "Now, while my brother hasn't given me the details of your dalliance, I will need to show you some ways to prevent this from happening in the future," Jacob explained. He went on for several minutes explaining ways to prevent the pregnancy before administering the mixture to Celina. As she drank the potion with a single motion, with practised skill Jacob pulled a small bucket in front of the woman and steadied her as she vomited.

"You're going to have to take her home," Jacob instructed. Celina staggered, clutching Robin. The hunter effortlessly supported the woman as they left the hut. Jacob cleaned up his tools. He would need to check on Celina tomorrow.

***

The morning after, sure enough, Falia knocked at Jacob's door. Her little fists hammering frantically. He opened the door warmly, greeting the young lady. "Good morning Falia." Jacob blushed as he greeted her with a smile.

"Morning, Jacob," She spoke sweetly. She tried to peer past Jacob into the hut but then turned her attention to Jacob. "My sister has been sick in the night. Mother is distraught."

216

Jacob nodded. He had been expecting this. "I will be along directly," Jacob agreed. "Unless you would like to wait and walk with me?" Jacob offered; this was the boldest he had ever been with Falia. The young lady still unnerved him, stirring the young man's loins in ways he only had a practical understanding. Falia nodded as she walked into the hut. Jacob went to the kitchen area to pack his satchel. Having prepared the night before, he filled his bag when his brother came out of the bedroom wearing only a towel.

"Oh, hi, Falia." Robin grinned at the young girl,

The young girl said nothing, her face flushed. Robin's charm washed over this woman. Jacob felt a burst of jealousy and anger boiling in his chest. "Go get dressed, brother," he ordered. "Celina is unwell. I'm going to see her."

"Oh no." Robin feigned; his acting was awful, but it appeared to be ignored by Falia, who was leering at Robin's half-naked body.

"Would you come with us?" Falia asked. "Seeing you would cheer her up."

Robin shook his head. Jacob stepped in to avoid more awful acting. "I'm afraid my brother has to go hunting this morning." He looked at Robin and shooed him away.

"Tell Celina I will stop by later." Robin shot over his shoulder returning to his room.

Jacob led the way, Falia hovered for a moment until she followed Jacob. "When was your sister unwell?" Jacob asked as they walked the long path back to town.

"She came home from an evening walk last night, then she complained about feeling faint, in the night, she wouldn't stop groaning. This morning, she was very sick."

Jacob nodded. "I understand."

"You don't think the plague is back," Falia asked nervously.

"We dealt with that." A brief flash of memory of the death of Carlos flashed through Jacob's head. "I suspect it is something she ate," he clarified.

Falia nodded, "Thank you for this." Taking Jacob's hand as they walked. Jacob felt her small hand gripping his as they strolled down the long path. He propped himself up with his staff and walked, holding the hand of this beauty. Jacob's cheeks burned with desire as he sauntered towards the village. As they got to the outskirts, Falia dropped his hand. Jacob felt the loss. Falia broke away and ran ahead. Jacob admired her as she ran towards the blacksmith's forge. The forge had been handed over to an apprentice who paid the family for its use. A young man was working in the forge, hammering away. He waved at Falia and Jacob as they arrived.

The scene in Celina's bedroom was as Jacob expected. The woman was retching into a bucket. Her usually well-kept blonde hair was matted over her face, and her nightdress was covered in vomit. Celina's blue eyes were rimmed red as she had been crying. Instructing Falia to wait outside, Jacob took Celina's temperature. She had reacted to the concoction more severely than he had foreseen. She looked at him with baleful eyes.

"I am sorry about this," Jacob spoke earnestly. He dipped a cloth in a small water bowl beside her bed and cleaned her face. He sat at her bedside. He spoke softly. "Now I'm afraid you are reacting badly to this." He looked at the sheets bunched between her legs. He nodded slowly; he could see the tell-tale tint of red stains on the sheets. "It would appear the deed is done," Jacob explained. "May I?" he asked politely. She nodded, crying as he pulled back the sheets revealing a lot of blood staining them. Jacob found a small bean-sized blob that had been the child. Her night dress was ruined with blood. "You were further along than we thought, probably about nine weeks. I'm going to dispose of these," Jacob offered. "Where are your fresh sheets?" he asked. He tended to the young lady with care. After a few more potions, she had stopped vomiting but was still weak. He bundled up the nightdress, along with the bedding stashed it hidden outside. After freshening her bed and allowing her to redress, he put her back in the room. "I'm leaving you with two more potions. If you start to vomit again, you will take one. If it continues, take the second one," Jacob instructed. She was quietly weeping the whole time Jacob tended to her.

He was there for most of the day. Robin arrived late in the afternoon; he didn't stay for long, just long enough to give his best wishes. Jacob stayed until the sun was low over the mountains. Finally, Celina fell asleep, and Jacob returned home with the stained sheets stuffed into his satchel. She had begged him to hide the sheets from her mother. He had obliged. He knew that Maganwyth would love to get hold of the remains. He was tempted to head straight to her hut, but it was getting dark, and the long trek would take a toll on his poor health. He decided to head home. As he approached the house, he heard a noise. He slowed his steps coming in the darkness keeping to the shadows.

The sound was giggling, coming from the side of the house. His curiosity piqued; Jacob approached. He wondered if some of the younger villagers had decided on having a dalliance near his home. He crept around the side to get a better view taking every chance not to make a sound. The light from the moon reflecting on the snow lit up the figures. The first figure, a man, was tall and well-built. Jacob immediately recognised his brother. Jacob shook his head, thinking, *How many women do you have on the go, brother!* He allowed himself a sarcastic smile. *Another foolish woman attracted by your charms,.* The couple were kissing passionately, his much larger form engulfing the more petite woman ardently.

. Jacob was briefly tempted to interrupt.

"Oh, Robin," moaned the voice. It was a voice that previously sent shivers of excitement down Jacob's back. He knew who it was at once. The couple rolled against the side of the hut. Her face was briefly caught by the moonlight, the long red hair, and the delicate features of Falia. Jacob felt his soul sinking away, his teeth clenched with anger. *How could he?* Jacob struggled with his wrenching gut. He staggered backwards as if he had been hit by a hammer. His chest felt tight. Every woman loved Robin! He was tall, handsome, charming, known and loved by anyone who met him. Now the only person in this village who had ever shown Jacob even the slightest romantic affection he had taken. Jacob turned and ran.

His feet crunched through the snow, he didn't know where he was running, and his chest was tight and clenching. He coughed and spluttered blood that speckled his lips. He wiped it away, annoyed. He kept running until finally, his legs gave out, and he slumped to all fours kneeling in the snow. He wept blood, staining the snow under him. His body shook, tears of blood falling from his cheeks.

"I hate you," Jacob gasped between sobs. "I hate you!" he screamed into the snow.

The voice spoke in his head calmly. *You don't.*

Shut up! Jacob shouted back. You don't know me.

I know you; I know you better than you know yourself. Thoth continued to speak, You have been distracted by these feelings, these hormones. They have called you away from your true calling.

What is my true calling then? Jacob asked,

Ultimate knowledge, Ultimate power. Jacob heard a trace of emotion in his voice for the first time. It sounded hungry, lustful. Seek not the lust of the flesh, only the lust of knowledge.

Jacob's frail body collapsed onto the snow; tears still fell from his eyes, leaving trails of blood along his cheeks. It took him several minutes, slouched in the freezing snow, for Jacob to pull himself together. He wiped the blood from his face. He pulled himself to his feet, propping himself up with his staff. The voice was right. He had wasted his time. He had wasted precious thoughts. All women were the same, turned by the slightest smile from tall, handsome strangers. Jacob gritted his teeth. Anger burned and seethed in his soul. He began the long trudge home.

He arrived at the cottage. Only an hour had passed since he had witnessed the betrayal of his heart. Falia had left, and Robin was in the kitchen burning some food. Thick black smoke filled the kitchen area.

"What are you doing?" Jacob asked as he opened the door.

Robin turned to face Jacob with a charming smile. "Hey, Jacob." Robin had a big stupid grin on his face. "I'm just making dinner."

"You are burning dinner, you buffoon." Jacob dumped the satchel beside the door and pushed his way past his brother to the hob. Robin, while a considerable eater, was a terrible cook. Jacob removed the large slab of stag meat that Robin had sitting almost on the flames. He started slicing it up with a knife, his back to Robin. Jacob gritted his teeth. His brother began rattling off something about the hunt and how he had found this old stag stuck in the frozen fens. Jacob tried to drown out what Robin was discussing. He interrupted his brother as he dumped the salvageable parts of the flank into a skillet with some vegetables and herbs. "Celina will be OK.,"

"Oh, that's good," Robin mumbled idly. "I'm not sure we should see each other again."

Jacob turned around and faced Robin. "Why?" he asked, his curiosity piqued.

"Oh, I don't know," Robin spoke idly. "After this whole thing, I'm not sure about her."

"Has someone else drawn your eye, brother?" Jacob probed.

"Maybe," Robin blushed. "When I was at Celina's earlier, her sister told me she liked me."

With a bit more venom and a slipping hold on his rage, Jacob spoke through clenched teeth, "Is that so?" As he scraped the meal onto the two plates. "Anyway, I've had a long day; eat up." Jacob violently thrusted the plate at Robin.

As per usual, Robin was oblivious to Jacob's emotions. Robin continued to speak as they ate, unaware of Jacob's tortured stares across the table. The next morning Jacob took the messed sheets to Maganwyth. He didn't want to know what the hag did with the remains. Only she was delighted with the present.

That winter, the twins celebrated their sixteenth birthday. It was their first birth year without their mother. Jacob continued his duties as the town healer but avoided Falia. He couldn't trust himself not to let out his anger towards her. The dalliance between Falia and Robin lasted until spring, when his eye wandered to a new woman. Robin left a trail of broken hearts throughout Havendale, not just among maidens. Many a married woman had a flirtation with the handsome young hunter.

Chapter 23

The Council

Balis Gestalt was true to his word.. He fed the heir prince information, and in turn, William had done all he could to protect the denizens of the lower quarter. Lord Godwin Nadrog of Gont had lasted many more months than anyone had anticipated. The old priest that had been treating the prince had been charged with witchcraft and consorting with the Haulfin. A new younger physician had been brought in. Talos used this to cement his stance on who had access to the prince. Balis Gestalt had whispered into William's ear that no one he knew had ever had dealings with the older physician, but it is hard, if not impossible, to prove something never happened.

Godwin's health had improved with the younger physician's care, but the man's mind was long since gone. Renwalt, Godwin's brother, had muscled in on the prince's duties taking over the treasury and the city guards and, in turn, had control of most of Trindon. William had tried to assert his claim, but even with the backing of Heineroth, the general of the army, his control over the city and the rest of the princedom hung by a thread. For as long as his father lived, he couldn't push his claim as he was only a steward and heir prince, not the electoral prince.

William had deliberated a few times to ask Ailwhyn, his Haulfin servant, to try to heal his father, but as the young Aldari woman had stated, if she were to use her gifts, it would undoubtedly be discovered, and she would be hanged or burned. And, as much as he loved his father, he wouldn't risk his friend's life.

Stories from the northern and other boarding lands had also helped sow the distrust of the subraces and magic. There had been a magical plague in the north, the murder of a profit of the one true God by a band of Haulfin's in Holum, creatures from Rwelvencrest were becoming bolder, and other evil creatures seemed to be plaguing the lands. To the south, there had been rumours of a Dewar miner rebellion quashed by the Inquisition's forces. It felt that Gont was besieged from all sides. These stories sowed fear in the population, and William felt helpless.

Six people sat around a large table in a darkened chamber under the castle. William had worked with Heineroth to get this hidden chamber ready. This section of the castle had once been an old grain storage many centuries ago but had been abandoned, and the whole sub-chamber had been locked off. So, William had set up a shadow council to help him in his efforts to secure his princedom. Around the table sat William, Heineroth, Ailwhyn, Balis Gestalt, and two others. Weasley Weston of Wayrest, an influential noble and long-time friend of William, had joined the council and Gneth, the small Gnomus friend of Balis.

"Why do we keep gathering?" Heineroth complained. "There is nothing we can do." He had been growing more complacent about these meetings in the last few months. "We are risking life and limb to meet up just to discuss fuck all."

Sir William ignored his old friend's foul language. "We gather here to share what we know," he explained clearly. "Renwalt now has complete effective control of Trindon and the surrounding villages. Talos has been sending his Inquisition to the furthest reaches of Gont, bringing every thane, burgomaster, lord, and councillor under his heel."

"Wayrest will always remain loyal to the true prince," Weston snapped.

"While Wayrest is an important port in the princedom, it alone cannot ensure our control of the outlying regions." William nodded, "To the south, they have fortified our military under the guise of preventing raids from Taros, as even Taros wouldn't dare attack the members of the Inquisitor's army. There is also a sizable number of agents on our western border with Taros. They have a sizable force to send north and given how much they have been raising fear of the Haulfin hiding in the northern territories, it will only be time before they flood that area with their troops. Finally, to the east, Vantoth has been quiet, aside from the stories of the Haulfin miner rebellion."

"I've heard something about this." Balis smiled as he tapped a knife against the table, chipping the ancient wood. "Rumours reached my ear saying that the ration for the slaves was cut in half. They protested and were slaughtered. It wasn't a rebellion. It was an orchestrated massacre."

Heineroth nodded. "It would be an effective way to justify such a thing, I can only state it wasn't any of my troops involved in that. My captains would have informed me."

"This all means the south lands will probably support Renwalt if he makes a play to usurp my position." William nodded.

"Can he do that?" Ailwhyn asked quietly, speaking for the first time. "The line of succession has always been a father to son."

"There is precedence; in Taros, for example, the baron has declared his nephew his successor over his son. In Vantoth to the east, it has passed down the female line."

"Odd bunch, the Vantoth," mused Heineroth. He was met with a slightly critical stare from Ailwhyn. "Got drunk with one of their battle sisters in the capital, fine figure of a woman, but she was odd."

"What would it take for Renwalt to take your position?" Gneth asked; due to his diminutive stature, the Gnomus sat on the table on a small stool. His arms were crossed, and he was puffing on a small pipe.

"If he rallied enough landholders to his command and had enough support from the church and the emperor, he could get it decreed, or if my father declared it so."

"Talos has been trying to get your father to disinherit you for several months," Ailwhyn stated. "He visits the prince's chamber daily, but the prince's mind is gone. He is stuck in the past."

William rubbed his eyes; the last few months had been gruelling. The tale of his adventures to end the eternal winter had lost its value over time and his support was waning. "There is too much for us to take on all at once," William complained. "We need to focus on what we can."

Gneth smiled grimly. "You could just kill another monster."

Heineroth nodded. "Not a bad idea Gnomus," He grinned over at the tiny hunchback. "Got any you can think of?"

Gneth grinned. "Too many, old man." They shared a glare between them. An odd friendship had formed between the Gnomus and the old soldier. They shared a macabre sense of humour, and both had a love of ale.

Balis banged his knife on the table bringing the meeting to order. "There are still daily executions of our kind." He looked at William. "You have managed to slow the unlawful detentions, but still, at least one of our kind per week is dragged from their home and faces the Inquisition."

"The sessions of the Inquisition are closed," Weston muttered. "We do not know what goes on inside."

"We can guess." Balis shrugged, "Torture, interrogations and false confessions."

"I like this idea of finding a monster to slay." William mused, "If I could rally the support of the people, the lords would follow. The church wouldn't stand against someone actively hunting those it considers unholy, and the Emperor Leopold wouldn't support my uncle against both the church and the lords."

The other five around the table nodded. "Balis, Heineroth, I want you to find such a creature causing a considerable vexation, one that everyone, including Haulfin, will be glad to be rid of. Gneth, keep me informed of what your people hear. Ailwhyn, you will continue to aid my stepmother to keep my father alive. Finally, Weston, I would suggest you return to Wayrest. The Inquisition will likely send troops north soon, and Wayrest is our main port. You need to tell me if they send troops to the Spine Mountains." Everyone around the table nodded. Then, there was a noise that caused everyone to freeze.

"What was that?" Heineroth asked. He pulled back from the table, getting to his feet.

Balis also drew away, dagger in hand. He cocked his head to one side, listening. "Seven, no ten men approach."

"Ailwhyn, the lights," William warned.

With a wave of her hand, "yrtcurbso" she muttered, and the lights died, plunging the large grain store into pitch black.

"We cannot see a blasted thing now," Heineroth grumbled.

"Neither can they," William shot back.

"Speak for yourself, human," Gneths gravelly voice came out of the darkness. "The Aldari and I see just fine."

Emerging from the solitary entrance in this long-abandoned section of the castle, a dim radiance from flickering torches became discernible. Echoing through the corridor were the clinks of metal meeting metal and the muffled thuds of boots treading lightly, steadily advancing.

Soon enough, ten figures entered the darkened grain store, and the dim flickering torch lights kept William and the others hidden.

225

"You sure this is the place?" one asked the other. "It's a fucking maze down here."

"This is where we were told to go. He is supposed to be here," the other answered.

"Perhaps we are too late."

In the darkness, William could just make out the ten figures. They weren't dressed as either palace or city guard nor did they wear Inquisitorial soldier uniforms. They were wearing dark black leather with deep hoods to hide their faces. Most carried long daggers, not swords. A couple had light crossbows. The metal was dulled with oil to prevent a glint in the night. *Assassins,* William thought to himself,

The ten figures began to fan out. William clutched his sword. Instead, he felt a soft, gentle hand lay against his. In the dim light, he turned and saw Ailwhyn beside him. She shook her head and pointed at the assassins. Sure, enough, two more slipped from behind the others. These two wore long dark-grey cloaks. They had been almost invisible in the darkness. Ailwhyn then made a deliberate blink showing William should close his eyes. William shut them tight.

"*Ssendnilb,*" Ailwhyn whispered in a voice that echoed with power. In an instance, a brilliant white light erupted into the grain hall, and cries of agony and surprise erupted from the assassins as the light blinded them. Ailwhyn's hand released William. Around her, an aura of green radiated. She thrust her hands forward, and a wave of force hit five men, knocking them off their feet. William charged forward. His sword was through the first assassin before they could recover. Heineroth also taking his cue to attack took another blinded attacker down. Weasley wasn't a fighter, having spent most of his life in luxurious courts, he cowered as the violence erupted around him. Balis wasn't a fighter, he had people for that, but he knew his way around a blade, he took his opportunity gripping the head of one of the assassins and thrusting his dagger into the attacker's throat; blood spurted out as he severed the jugular. William and Heineroth both charged the two holding the crossbows. They hadn't recovered their sight, trying to back away, only to be slammed against the wall, swords thrust through their chests. Gneth was slitting the throats of any who had fallen. One managed to get to his feet, dazed and now outnumbered. He wiped his eyes, trying to see again. Heineroth was on him, knocking his daggers from his hands and slamming him down against the floor. William signalled Balis, Gneth and Ailwhyn to leave, and the three slipped into the shadows.

"Who hired you!" Heineroth growled, kneeling on the assassin's chest, all his weight crushing the attacker's ribcage. His sword was at the man's throat. The man refused to speak. Heineroth smashed him in the face with the pommel of his sword. "Speak, or I'll slit your throat."

The assassin shook his head. Heineroth grunted and sliced deep; gore gushed, covering the grizzled soldier's face. "Pah, fool." Heineroth got to his feet. He looked around at the twelve dead assassins laying around them. He spoke with a grin to William. "Forgot how much a good fight gets the blood pumping."

William picked up one of the fallen torches and scanned over the fallen bodies. "Someone knew we were here." There was no livery or marks on any of their equipment. He pulled off a few hoods to see if he could recognise any of the faces.

"Good thing we had the witch with us," Heineroth mumbled. "That trick of hers really is a good ace in the hole." He kicked another one of the fallen bodies. "I'll get a few of my trusted boys down here to clean up." He grumbled, "We need to find a new meeting spot."

William agreed, resting against the wall, "We also need to know how they found us down here."

"It's that cursed Talos," Heineroth muttered, "He's got eyes everywhere." They each took a torche and left the bodies.

***

The following day, Talos Tarsus saw the young heir prince at the breakfast table, beside him his bodyguard and general, Heineroth. His eyes narrowed, and he gritted his teeth. As it arrived, the moment of frustration passed.

"Good to see you well, Milord." Talos took his customary place to the left of the head of the table opposite the heir prince.

"Oh, Talos, good morning," William greeted, looking up from his plate. "I'm glad you here." He smiled with a disarming smile. "We got lucky last night."

"Lucky sire?" the Inquisitor asked innocently. He waved away a plate of food one of the servants brought before him.

227

"Eleven assassins breached the palace walls last night. It would have appeared they were after my father," William lied, his eyes scanning Talos for any tell.

"Eleven? That is a considerable number to breach our walls with no one noticing," Talos repeated. He knew there had been twelve. *Had one got away?* he thought to himself.

"Heineroth's men responded quickly and killed them as they crept through the halls." William continued, "They made short work of them. I'm commending the young men later today. I'm sure you will be in attendance."

Talos nodded. "Of course, sire. Are any of your men injured?" he asked Heineroth.

The shabby old soldier was not a good liar, so he had left most of the speaking to William. Finally, however, this is something he could answer honestly. "Not a scratch," he grinned. "They are well trained."

"They were human, not Haulfin, probably hired by Taros." William continued, "We need to respond to this aggression."

"Oh, sire, you cannot be sure it was Taros. The baron's troops have been quiet since we placed several Inquisition troops with yours on the border."

"It has only suspended the raids. Taros and Gont have been at war since before my grandfather was born." William looked at Talos. "The hatred between our countries has been eternal. Your troops may have merely forced them to change their tactics. Now they choose to hire assassins to strike at the heart of Gont."

The Inquisitor nodded. "Excuse me, milord, it would appear I'm not hungry." He pulled away from the table and marched away. Behind Talos' back, William shared a grin with Heineroth.

"Why did you say only eleven?" Heineroth asked.

"To keep him on his toes." William explained, "He will be wondering what happened to the last, especially if he is responsible." He took a bite out of the chicken leg. "What did your soldiers do with the bodies."

"Nothing much," Heineroth shrugged. "I would guess they took the opportunity to steal the weapons to sell, but they will have dumped the bodies in the lime pits beyond the wall."

"Good, there will be no way for him to verify the numbers." William smiled.

Talos stormed into Renwalt's chambers with no ceremony. The fat man was still in bed, with two whores. All three seemed to be struggling with a hangover.

"Get out!" Talos barked angrily to the whores, who struggled to untangle themselves from the sheets. Renwalt groaned, grasping for the young ladies.

"What the fuck are you doing here?" he demanded of Talos.

The Inquisitor strode across the room. Gripping the curtains, he yanked them open, flooding the room with daylight to an anguished cry. The whores scurried out of the room, grabbing their clothes.

"You've chased away my bedwarmers," Renwalt complained, pushing himself up. Talos looked up, seeing they were alone.

"Why did you try to assassinate your brother," Talos demanded. "He is nearly dead anyway. You have but to wait a couple of weeks."

"I never sent anyone to attack my brother," Renwalt sat up in bed. He was a large fat man with a grease-covered beard, his lips were stained from excessive red wine, and his eyes were blood-shot. Talos couldn't help but sneer in disgust at this abomination of a man. The obese figure took several attempts but finally managed to pull himself into a sitting position. He pulled the stained sheets to cover his expansive gut. Renwalt rubbed his head and reached beside his bed where a goblet of stale wine sat. He drank the sour drink. It dribbled down his chin onto the sheets.

"I wanted to catch my nephew plotting against me," he finished.

"You fool." Talos cursed, "We have slowly been undermining his position. You have the support of the lords to the south and the west, I would have brought you the support of the church, and the emperor would support whoever has the most control."

"You underestimate my nephew, he is determined, strong-willed, and well-liked by the people, plus he has Heineroth who commands the army." Renwalt muttered, "He is stronger than you think."

"He certainly is stronger than you thought. He killed your assassins." Talos hadn't for a moment believed that some unsophisticated soldiers had killed eleven well-trained assassins.

"All of them?" Renwalt gasped. "I hired a dozen to make sure."

"I'm not sure. The prince claims that a few of Heineroth's guards killed eleven of them. The good news appears to be he doesn't suspect you. He suspects Taros."

"That isn't good." Renwalt shook his head. He swung his fat pudgy legs over the side of the bed, pulling the stained sheet with him as he walked towards the latrine. A simple stone hole with a seat. He grunted as he sat down and began to relieve himself. Talos turned his back.

"I know. You and I have been making inroads with the baron. Hoping to put these years of fighting to rest between the two nations." Talos muttered, "We need to be more cautious. If word of this assassination attempt should become public, the lords could turn against you."

Renwalt grunted as he finished his ablutions. "Fine, no more attempts." He called for his servant to dress him. "Have you seen Steinhardt?" Renwalt asked Talos.

"The court vizier?" Talos inquired. "He's been keeping to himself since Godwin took ill."

"He could be our route to the throne." Renwalt mused, "He oversees the succession line."

"Pah, the old fool knows nothing but the lore and what is in his books. He plays no court politics, only recites precedent."

"He would be perfect to bring on to our side." Renwalt shrugged. "If he states it is the lore, not one of the nobles would dare argue."

Talos thought about it. "You may have a point," the Inquisitor mused as the servant entered the room.

"Where the hell have you been?" Renwalt cursed the young boy, giving the servant a harsh slap on the back of the head. "Get my clothes!"

Talos turned and left the fat man to get dressed. While Renwalt wouldn't have been his first choice for ruler of Gont, it was undoubtedly the one he preferred over the available options. The heir prince was too naïve, too headstrong, and wouldn't be easily controlled. Godwin's other children had died in infancy leaving no other potential heirs to groom. Renwalt was the younger brother to Godwin and, had been given a life of luxury with none of the responsibilities. For the last few years, he had been draining the coffers for his own personal pleasure, wine, women, and gambling. Talos would have to keep an eye on that. The church wouldn't want Gont to become a bankrupt state like Quorth, a backwater princedom boarding the lost kingdoms that could only keep itself going from its Haulfin slave trade and the illicit goods smuggled through its lands. Talos had never been that far east, but he had seen the reports. In Talos' brain turned cogs within cogs, as he planned. Finally, a strategem clicked into place.

Chapter 24

The Death

Two weeks later, in the darkened throne room, midnight approached. Sir William was hunched over a command table, Heineroth standing next to him. *How had they missed it? Why had no other reports made it back?* Taros had invaded. The small fortified village of Hrafnborg had apparently been destroyed as a column of twenty Taros regiments marched across the southernmost frontier. One messenger, bearing the missive, had been riding hard for two days when he collapsed before the castle gates. 'Taros invades', those two words brought a shiver down William's spine. Heineroth had quickly issued a call to arms rallying troops from the rest of the princedom. They were to assemble south of Trindon and march to meet this invading army.

"I still don't understand how they assembled such a force," William cursed, removing a small scout piece from the battle map. He slammed his fist against the table, causing the candles to flicker. Reports had come that Taros' troops turned north, cutting Trindon off from its southern border towns.

"We will leave it till after this war is over, we don't have to second-guess our defences right now," Heineroth muttered. "It appears from the latest reports they are raiding the farms and villages and moving to cut us off our border fortifications," he grunted. It was a good plan, especially if Taros had a second army, they could use to re-enforce the first. They will encircle the fortifications protecting Gont's eastern and southern borders and leave the capital defenceless.

"What about the Inquisition troops?" William asked, turning to face Talos. The sly dark-haired man stood a distance from the table detached. The Inquisition always made its stance between warring princedoms clear. It didn't approve, but wouldn't get involved unless it suspected heresy.

"I'm afraid our orders from the church were clear; We are there as a deterrent, but we are not to engage in any combat with any princedom's forces." Talos looked over the map. He idly picked up a piece representing a battalion of Inquisitorial soldiers. "I have sent word that they are to make their way across the border into Vantoth. They will be crossing the Rhineland and returning to Altran." He placed the piece off to the side. "Unfortunately, my lord, you will have no support from the Inquisition or the church in this."

Heineroth cast a glance at Talos. He would have loved to wring that snake-like man's neck with his bare hands. He spoke loud enough for Talos to hear but ignored the feigned reaction from the tall, dark-haired man. "Fucking Inquisition, always around when you don't want them. Come to a real fight, and they run to the hills."

"We will have to ride out to meet them," William demanded. "We can muster six hundred mounted soldiers, twice that number in infantry, and twice that again in militia." Pulling several pieces onto the map. "Can we get word to the remaining fortifications?" he asked Heineroth.

"I've got agents who can get through the lines. Once we get word to one of the towers, we can light the beacons," Heineroth mumbled. "But if we send everyone to engage the Taros army, we leave nothing to defend Trindon."

"It would take only a handful of men to defend this city for a week from any army that gets passed us." William noted. The walls of Trindon were a hundred feet high, built from solid granite. Its star shape and double moats made it one of the most defendable cities in the empire.

"Us?" Heineroth gasped. "You're coming with the army, lad?" William nodded.

Talos smiled to himself. This was working out better than he had planned. He had hoped the invasion would draw Heineroth and his army from Trindon, but for the prince to leave was a bonus. He glanced across at Renwalt, who sat in the only other chair, aside from the throne, in the room. He had a bottle of wine in one hand and an overflowing goblet in the other. "You are a braver man than I am, Will." He raised his glass, the red wine slopping over the edge. The man had been drunk since sundown, and his eyes were bloodshot. His bulbous red nose seemed glowing as if filled with wine, and thick blue veins pulsed along it.

William ignored his uncle. He looked across at Steinhardt, the court advisor. "Any words of wisdom?" he asked his old tutor.

The old man had served the court for many, many years. The man's hair was thin like straw, his skin a ghostly white, his body was bent low, all the weight of his years resting on an ornate golden cane, a gift from Godwin many years ago. Steinhardt had been old for as long as William had known him, and now was decrepit, but death seemed to have passed him by or just didn't want him. The old man shook his head. "Sire, I've always been more inclined to diplomacy and scholarly pursuits, not the marshal skills of war, sir."

"Renwalt, get up and join us," William ordered. "Allow Steinhardt to sit."

The fat man struggled to his feet, waddling and staggering towards the war table. He reached the table, his large belly jarring it knocking several pieces over. William sighed. "Uncle, if we travel out to engage Taros and the baron's men, you will need to rule in my stead." William plucked the wine from his uncle's hand. "And this needs to stop until this crisis is over." He passed the goblet to Heineroth. The old soldier looked at the glass. He gulped it down in one shot and placed the goblet on the table. William pulled away from the table, "Rest well this night, for tomorrow at dawn, we ride," William firmly proclaimed. Heineroth nodded and left the room; he had a lot of preparations to make before he could rest. The boy's plan was bold, but it would force the hand of the Taros' army.

William waited in the room for a little longer. Looking over the map, he wondered if the baron Harkeeth of Taros rode with his men. William doubted it. He had once met the baron in Altran when he was young. Eight Arbay slaves were chained to his golden, jewel-encrusted litter as it was borne into the emperor's hall on a massive, elaborate palanquin. Around the chair had been a dozen guards.

On the other hand, his own father had arrived with only two guards, his wife and William. Taros was known to be one of the wealthiest princedoms in the empire, made rich by its expansive network of gem and gold mines and it's lucrative trade in Hurk slaves. The baron was so paranoid about his safety even in the capital of Altran he was not a person who would put himself on the front lines. Sir William made his way back to his chamber. Sleep wouldn't come easy that night for the young heir prince.

***

The sun hadn't finished cresting over the plains to the east as the knights of Gont mounted. Several hundred men and horses milled around behind their captains, awaiting the signal. The young heir prince stifled a yawn as he adjusted his reins.

"Not enough sleep, lad?" came the gruff voice of Heineroth. The large man sat on his imposing war horse. He was wearing half-plate armour that made the substantially sized man look even more impressive.

"I tried," William apologised.

"Don't worry, boy, we've got half a day's ride for you to wake up." He grinned. "But now is the time for you to rally the men."

"I don't see Talos or my uncle here to see us off," William noted, looking back towards the castle. There was a large crowd of citizens waving. News of the invasion had spread throughout the city as all men of fighting age had been called up. The irregulars milled about disorganised. Heineroth had ensured at least one trained soldier per dozen irregulars. While numbers were often helpful, the irregular militia would often turn, flee and shit themselves at the first sign of actual combat, not always in that order. The plan was classic. With Heineroth and the prince, the cavalry would ride ahead to harry the invaders. Driving them towards the infantry and continuing to attack them from the rear and sides to disrupt their advance as the main bulk of the army moved to intercept them head-on.

William spurred his horse ahead. Heineroth had chosen this as the mustering ground. There was a small hill where the prince could ascend so more of the assembled troops could watch him give a speech.

The young prince atop his white horse crested the hill. All the cavalry, the regular soldiers and the militia could see the young prince, the dawn rising behind him as he held the banner of Gont aloft. He shouted, his voice carrying across the open plain.

"Taros have encroached on our territory for the first time since my father rose to the throne! When our forefathers fought Taros, they lacked the resources we currently enjoy; they gave up everything they had. Then, they drove back the foreign invasion and established our city of Trindon and the princedom of Gont as what it is today. They did this through force of will rather than luck or strength. We must uphold the standards they established, fend against our enemies in every manner possible, and work to leave a tremendous legacy for those who will come after us. A leader's place is in the thick of battle! I will live or die among you and sacrifice my blood for my princedom and my people. I am not among you for my amusement but for the honour of Gont. Should we permit our brazen opponents to invade Gont's area without consequence? Will you allow the enemy to flee after it terrorises your family and the families of your countrymen? No, you won't! So then, to meet them, we march. Educate the enemy about the consequences of violating Gont's domain. Our efforts will lead to clear glory and enduring peace!" His voice echoed across the plains, and a cheer erupted from the troops.

Heineroth smiled. The young prince knew how to give a speech. He looked to his battalion of troops before adding his own remarks, "We are not holding a fucking thing. I'm not a speaker like our prince, but I don't want to hear any messages that say, 'I am holding my position,' or 'trying my best.' Leave that up to the enemy. The only thing we'll be holding is the enemy by his balls; else, we'll be moving forward constantly. We will twist his balls and kick the living shit out of him. My plan is to advance and keep advancing regardless. Whether we must go over, under, or through the enemy. My preference is through their guts." He made a growl thrusting his double-handed bastard sword in the air. His troops gave a laugh and cheer of approval.

"Now, let's ride!" he ordered, spurring his horse.

The cavalry rode off, leaving the infantry to trudge behind them. The seasoned soldiers started singing a marching tune to keep the ranks in pace as they followed the path set by the knights.

"The one God has arisen

"From the painful prison of death.

"Thus, we shall all be rightly glad.

"God, our comfort now will be.

"The world would be imprisoned

"In death if He had not risen.

"We now give thanks

"To our one true God

"Since He did indeed rise.

"God be praised!"

The army began its march, the heavy feet churning up the plains, and a convoy of supply wagons rode between the troops. The regulars and the militia were inspired by the princes' words. He was heading off ahead of them to face the enemy first, and not one of them wanted to be the one to let their country down.

From the castle's battlements, Ailwhyn, Balis, and Gneth watched the army leaving the city. They wouldn't have long before they would need to return to their duties or slip back into the lower quarter.

"I hope he will be safe," Ailwhyn muttered to herself.

Balis put his arm around the young Aldari woman in a rare display of affection. "Don't worry, lass, that boy leads a blessed life."

"Yea, plus he's got that oaf Heineroth to keep him safe." Gneth sneered, lighting his pipe. He hopped down from the parapet, grunting as he landed heavily on the stone floor. Ailwhyn bent over and helped the Gnomus to his feet.

"I hope you both are right." She sighed, "I must return to Godwin. He sickens daily." Bowing her head. "His physician is a fool, but luckily, he is a negligent fool who would rather spend time in the court seeking a patron, and I have time and freedom to ease the prince's symptoms."

"I, too, must get back to the lower quarter." Balis Gestalt smiled, "Criminal empires don't just run themselves; you know." He bowed and left the Aldari maiden and Gnomus.

"I suppose I've got shit pipes to clean," Gneth grumbled. He shifted his belt above his waist and hobbled off, disappearing quickly.

***

Two days had passed, and Ailwhyn and the others had received no word from the battlefield. Ailwhyn and the others couldn't meet without the prince's protection. They had been randomly setting up meeting places since the incident in the grain room. Since Weston had left for Wayrest, they now had no ear in the court. Gneth managed to glean some information when he was cleaning latrines or fireplaces. In the evening of the second day, Lord Prince Godwin Nadrog of Gont died. Ailwhyn had been in attendance when the prince finally passed away. Ailwhyn had made his last moments a peaceful dream of his glory days, but she could do little to stop his death.

"Gyia, help him pass," she pleaded, praying to her goddess as she cast a soft magical glow rest over the body. The old man breathed his last breath, his body resting, his spirit departing. Ailwhyn wiped a tear from her cheek, Godwin hadn't been a kind ruler to the Haulfin, but any death was a sad passing. She got up and exited the room. The prince's widow sat outside embroidering with a tambour frame. Her handmaid, another Aldari Haulfin, sat beside her meekly.

"I'm sorry, Milady, he has passed." Ailwhyn bowed her head.

The following morning an army of the Inquisition troops arrived at the capital. The gates of Trindon were cast open, and they were welcomed inside by Renwalt with Talos at his side. With Sir William away and a peaceful coup, he was usurped. Renwalt was declared the crowned electoral prince that evening.

Chapter 25

The Inquisition

Maganwyth was hurriedly packing her house. She knew what was coming, Jacob had given her the means to divine the future, and the future had been bleak, especially for her. The casting of the spell carried a profound cost, an irretrievable fortune relinquished. She had chosen to employ the minuscule embryo bestowed upon her by Jacob. It possessed potent potential for various other purposes, yet she found solace in the decision to channel its power for divination, rather than consuming it as she had initially contemplated. In hindsight, she now recognized the wisdom of her choice and felt a sense of gratitude for the insight it had unveiled. She had chosen the Spine Mountains when the empire had first purged the fay-races as it had been remote. Most of the Inquisition's power had been focused in Altran, the first city of the empire. She had reasoned it would be centuries before the churches power stretched this far, if ever. Even while the empire's influence had expanded and enforced the will of the one true God, she still had hoped for a few more decades. She had scried the future.

As soon as the Everlong defrosted, the ships would arrive here. She reminisced for a few moments. She should have followed her sisters to Rwelvencrest. There was no chance the Inquisition would enter that cursed realm. She finished stuffing her pack with the last of her goods. She had a long journey ahead of her. She was leaving many precious things behind. Casting a final glance around her hut, Maganwyth had been tempted to let Jacob know of the upcoming event, but that wasn't her way. She briefly contemplated leaving Jacob a message but decided against it. Swearing to herself as she left her hut for the last time. Maganwyth Puzzlecrow left Havendale with no word and no trace.

It took several days before anyone even noticed the hag had left. The only person to even feel the loss of her departure was Jacob. He expected her to return, but after several weeks even Jacob gave up hope. The town had become used to Jacob being the healer anyway and hardly notice the change. Jacob continued to serve as the village healer. Then the day came when five huge black-sailed galleons sailed into Havendale bay.

During the winter, there had been talk of war striking the lands of Gont. Rumours and hearsay had spoken of Prince Godwin dying and his brother taking the throne, and he had decreed that all the lands, no matter how remote, must pay fealty. Part of this decree was to send missionaries of the holy church to the far reaches of the princedom to teach any in the north who had frayed from the path of the one true God. The rumours were few and far between, but there were stories of the priests rooting out heresy, witches and Haulfin, who had been hiding in the villages and bringing the church's glory back to the frozen north.

Jacob had heard these stories through Robin every evening for a week. These were stories and rumours Robin had picked up in the tavern. Usually, after his brother rolled in drunk after his latest conquest. Jacob listened but didn't pay heed. Jacob hadn't noticed the five tall, black-sailed ships sailing into the bay until he was in the village square.

The galleons were too big for Havendale's small docks, so they anchored far into the bay. It didn't take long for half a dozen rowboats from each Galleon to be moored alongside the jetties. It took even less time for the Inquisition troops to move through the village, rounding up the villagers to the centre square. The heavily armoured, black-liveried enforcers of the Inquisition were cold, efficient and quiet.

It felt like an invasion, but no one from the village resisted. Soon hundreds of villagers were gathered in the village square. The soldiers surrounded them. They encircled the hundred or so villagers boxing them in.

A few men had been out hunting or logging, including Robin, but everyone else was gathered, the old, the sick, and the young. They huddled together in family groups mumbling amongst themselves. They looked at each other nervously.

A makeshift stage was quickly built, and a tall, thin dark-haired evil-looking man stood atop the platform. Beside him stood the priests from the temple, their presence calming the villagers. Most looked dishevelled as they had been dragged from other duties. They seemed dumbfounded, and confused staring at this tall, dark man with a mixture of awe and fear.

The man began to speak, his tone building with each word till he reached an angered crescendo. "I am Talos Tarus Inquisitor General of Gont, Your gradual and subtle loss of your purity marks the beginning of the path leading to Haulfin rule over the empire. And the loss of the desire to preserve the purity of our lands! People's best intentions have helped to pave the way for this particular horror on us. You have placated and tolerated all around you. One who truly believes in the one true God is a person of peace. Therefore, this appeasement strategy is not just a result of one person's acts; rather, it is at the core of our most significant cultural cornerstone. We are at the very beginning of a very terrible and deadly struggle. We must not just stand with our views but fight for our beliefs against this new barbarity, if we don't it will literally wipe out all we have built over the past two thousand years." He paused for a breath, his spittle forming in his mouth as he yelled out at the corralled audience. To Jacob's horror, he saw many of his neighbours nodding in agreement. There was, and always would be, an underlying fear and apprehension of magic and the Haulfin, but in Havendale, it had been burried deep under the surface. The villagers knew or suspected some of their neighbours of having fay race heritage, they had even tolerated Maganwyth, a witch, for many years. This man's words were speaking to a profound seeded intolerance. He was finally saying the words they had wanted to say for years. Jacob could feel several eyes on him.

The priest continued, "But we are in an outright war against fanatical Haulfin fascism. And this war is escalating far quicker than the church alone can manage... We have witches, warlocks and other Haulfin that will eventually join forces, becoming a greater threat to your lives. Sadly, we must deal with it now, and it will not be pleasant."

He turned with a waving hand. Jacob had to admit the man was speaking with skill at rallying the crowd, speaking to the base fears of the average man. Jacob tried to edge towards the side of the group, but he was penned inside. He wanted to get away from this place. He desired to find his brother and leave town.

The priest continued his sermon, "The old religion is not a religion of peace. The old religion is a religion of submission to the old gods. It is a religion of possession and subjection. Its means to submit to these false gods! They aren't gods. They are parasites. We are at war and take care of this hidden enemy. There's a hidden agent of evil here in Havendale that needs to be dealt with immediately." The man's eyes scanned the crowd. "The Inquisition is here to protect you!" He scowled, "We know there are agents of this hidden empire amongst you, your eternal winter, your plague. These are all proof of this and symptoms a greater disease. We are the cure."

He signalled with his hands. "My men will be taking you to your houses and take a census, those who aren't guilty have nothing to fear, but we need to find out who are the demons in this village."

There was a rumbling amongst the crowd. The man's speech had split the audience in two. The more pious and simple-minded of the mob nodded in agreement. The more liberal and less devout, or were suspected of having Haulfin heritage, seemed nervous. Jacob shared worried glances with a few others from around the town, Wanda the prostitute, Eyia and Gregor and their daughter, Birel, and even Falia and Cecilia were nervously clutching each other's hands while the widow blacksmith shouted agreement above the crowd. The Inquisition enforcers started to peel off the villagers guiding them to their homes.

"This interruption to your lives will be short!" the man cried out from the platform. "Comply with the guards, do not resist. The sacrifice of a little freedom will guarantee a lifetime of security."

The guards were firm as they pushed the villagers away. There was no arguing. The Inquisition enforcers outnumbered the villagers by half their number again. The heavily armed troops quickly and efficiently guided family groups away from the huddle. Jacob was politely but firmly gripped by his arm and dragged away. He stumbled a bit, leaning on the staff of Maahes as he was guided towards his house.

In the centre of the town square, Talos was directing his troops around Havendale. "I want a census of every man, woman and child; take family names, and we will begin questioning them separately." The old temple priests watched this Inquisitor expertly give instructions before he rounded on them.

He spoke, his dark eyes focusing "Now you, you who have allowed corruption to seek into the lives of your flock," he accused; he loomed over them. "You who have tolerated evil to walk amongst you, I will deal with you first." He clicked his fingers, and four Inquisition enforcers dragged the priests towards the temple. The old men protested as they were bundled off. Talos followed his cloak sweeping behind him.

Inside the temple, Talos had set up a tribunal. He sat at the podium, looking down at the three cloistered priests with the guards surrounding them. "You have failed in your duties," Talos stated. The priests cowered as the inquisitor general berated them. The halls of the old temple felt cold and empty.

"However," Talos continued, there was a visible look of relief on the priest's faces. "I believe you have been allowed to stray from doctrine in this remote part of the empire. Your passion and zeal have been weakened by the cold. You have allowed things to pass when you should have acted." Talos looked down at some notes he had placed before him. "I see here that you have allowed a witch to live!"

The leader of the temple stammered something, mumbling nervously. Talos raised a hand to stop his blabbering.

"Where is this Maganwyth," Talos inquired. "Was she taken by our soldiers?" He asked.

The youngest of the priests stepped forward he spoke more clearly. "The hag lives on the outskirts of town, milord, on top of the cliffs." The older priest stepped away from this young initiate. "She has been gone almost ten days. No one has seen her, even the boy."

"What boy?" Talos inquired, making notes.

"A young man named Jacob has been our town healer for a few years, taking over from the hag," the priest explained.

"Family name?" Talos inquired, writing his notes.

"Apologies, my lord. We don't have family names in Havendale. We are a small village."

Talos sighed. He had encountered this situation before. Everyone in the civilised world had family names, but many remote backwater towns hadn't developed that far. "What does the family do?" Talos inquired.

"The family were hunters sire."

Talos scratched down the name 'Venator' using the old naming convention. "Fine," Talos finished. "Who else in town has strayed from the way?" he asked, his eyes glaring at the novice.

The Inquisitor continued his questioning of the acolyte for many hours until he had a list of names. He ran his finger down the list. It had six people on it who needed to be interrogated. Their heritage, their beliefs or their actions Talos considered heresy. The young man's voice was hoarse after speaking for so long. Talos finally dismissed the Havendale clergy, and poured over his notes. It was clear to Talos that magic and blasphemy was at work in Havendale.

It was a pity the witch had fled already. That would have been a good opening act for the masses. Clearly, she was despised, and it would have been easy to manipulate the village to support the trials. On the other hand, this Jacob was not well liked, but he was respected, and his services were also valued by the village. Talos made a mark by the name. He would lure the young healer into his clutches. But first, he needed an easy quarry, someone that wouldn't be missed by the village. He looked at his notes. There was a woman called Wanda; he had added the family name Meretrix after some thought. It would be easy enough to turn the pious women of the town against her. She was a whore and trader who worked on the docks. He needed to emphasise that heresy would not be forgiven.

***

That evening, Robin and several other woodsmen were returning from the hunt. He was joking and laughing with the others when he noticed something was wrong. Smoke rose from the top of the cliffside.

The hag's house was ablaze, a black fume billowing up into the air. Robin's keen eyes could see twenty black armoured figures near the hovel holding torches. Robin struggled to understand what was happening. There were five imposing galleons filling the small bay. Large black flags emblazoned with the symbol of the one true God. Chills ran down Robin's spine. Jacob had told him stories of the Inquisition and its harsh and cruel judgments. The other hunters cautiously returned to their homes, but Robin hung back. He watched as the hunters were intercepted by Inquisition enforcers. Robin remained hidden; he was worried about his brother, but Jacob had been teaching Robin caution.

The sun had fallen below the mountains and the temperature was dropping rapidly. Robin pulled his bearskin cloak tight around his body. Taking a longer way round to avoid being spotted, he pushed stealthily and cautiously through the brambles and thickets till he got round the back of the house. Robin could hear voices inside, he recognised his brother, but he couldn't identify the others. Robin crept around the back of the house and peered through the window. In his mother's old recliner, Jacob sat composed and calm. Two men stood over him. One was dressed in a plain black robe, the other wore thick black plate mail and a black helmet that covered his face. Robin listened at the window.

The tall, dark-haired man was speaking. "Mr Jacob Venator."

"Just Jacob, yes," Jacob replied.

"I am a representative of the church of the one true God." The man spoke. "Do I understand correctly that you serve as the physician of this town."

"I'm the doctor if that is what you mean," Jacob responded. "Can I help you or your men? Are any sick?"

The man turned to the enforcer standing beside him. "You know what to look for." The large, armoured thug roughly and clumsily started routing around the house, pulling books and bottles from the kitchen. From his viewpoint, Robin gritted his teeth, wanting to rush in to protect his brother.

"What are you looking for?" Jacob asked calmly. "I will gladly direct you to it."

"Silence." The dark-robed man spoke.

"No." Jacob calmly locked eyes with the Inquisitor. "Not while your man ruins my home. Tell me what you seek, and I will help you."

The man spoke. "With Haulfin sorcery, no doubt. I don't think so."

"I think you must be mistaken," Jacob countered.

The enforcer had finished trashing the kitchen before returning. "There is nothing here, sire. Just some bottles and flowers."

"Are you sure there is no work of magic?" the man asked the enforcer.

"It is science," Jacob enlightened. "Nothing magical."

"Do you pretend that these things are not witchcraft?" the man demanded.

"This is simple alchemy and medicine. It is a medicine from older times lost to history. I've studied times past and relearned these methods to treat my patients better."

"Haulfin heresy." The man snapped.

Jacob spoke clearly "No, it has nothing to do with any god, I know not of any acts against the church of any of my neighbours."

"Nothing to do with God?" The man looked at Jacob harshly. The man's look softened. "What of Wanda Meretrix?" the tall, dark-haired man asked.

"Who?" Jacob responded.

"She is a young woman who works at the docks." The man explained, "She has been reported to take men into her bed for money."

"I don't get involved with the rumours of the town." Jacob shrugged, "And I find it odd that you would give her the last name Meretrix. I believe that means prostitute." Jacob kept his calm, "I have treated her for some ailments over the last few years, but other than that, I do not know the woman."

The dark-haired man stroked his beard, thinking for a moment. "And these…" He paused, waving his hand at Jacob's bottles that littered the kitchen. "Things of heresy?"

Jacob spoke, rising from his chair. "They are just tinctures for the treatment of my patients." He leaned on his staff and walked over to the wrecked kitchen. "I could go through them with you if you like?" Jacob offered and looked the dark-haired man square in the eyes.

Talos glared at the staff beside Jacob; the double lion head was unmistakable. "What a remarkable walking stick," the Inquisitor stated. "Where did you come by it?"

"A gift from a patient," Jacob lied, staring the Inquisitor down.

Robin couldn't see clearly towards the kitchen and tried to shift his position, adjusting his longbow and arrows, so they didn't rattle. He could see the dark-clad enforcer looking around their hut. Robin could hear the mumbles of conversation but couldn't hear clearly. He listened intently into the cabin, crouching low, hiding behind a bush. Robin watched the tall, dark-haired man leave, followed by the enforcer. Waiting for a few more moments till they had disappeared into the night, he approached the front door and rapped on it. He heard shuffling, and Jacob opened the entrance. Jacob spotted his brother. "Ah, Robin."

Robin always found that Jacob spoke weirdly formally all the time. He never seemed to relax. "Who were those two?" Robin asked. He lifted his bow from his shoulder and his quiver of arrows and placed it beside the fire.

Jacob returned to his brother, handing him a small bowl of food. Jacob knew that Robin would be ravenous; he always was. Jacob spoke slowly. "The Inquisition has arrived in Havendale, and they have burned down Maganwyth's house."

"I saw." Robin glumly apologised, "I'm sorry."

"She had left. It was just a house." Jacob shrugged.

"Do you think she knew they were coming?" Robin asked.

"Probably, although she never informed me," Jacob sneered. "Still, we need to be careful, brother. All are supposed to remain in their houses until dawn."

Robin thought about this. "We could run away," he suggested.

"I had thought the same thing myself." Jacob nodded, "However, where would we go?"

"We could head down to Woodvale or travel east to the mainland?" Robin suggested as he ravenously consumed his food.

Jacob looked at his brother and cocked his head to one side. "I fear the Inquisition will be sweeping across the Spine Mountains." He took his seat by the fire. Taking a small bowl of his own, he nibbled away. "I'm going to ask you to prepare packs for travelling," Jacob warned. "But we will see what the morning brings." Jacob handed Robin his unfinished bowl and retired to his room.

Robin continued to eat, staring at the fire. Robin's face remained impassive as he was thinking. Many believed Robin to be a simple man, and he was, but that didn't mean Robin couldn't think deeply. Robin was concerned for his brother. He had never told anyone about his brother's magic. He had learned much more about magic under his brother's guidance. Magic wasn't something to be feared as many believed, Jacob had used his powers to help the weak and the sick subtly, but it was still feared by the church. He gazed into the fire, deep in thought. The firelight glistened off his tanned skin, his shoulder-length dark hair still grubby from his day's hunting. He hadn't caught any quarry today. The deer he had spotted had been too young. He thought of his mentor's lessons teaching him about the ways of the forest and nature. He thought about this Inquisition. With deliberate grace, he slowly ascended to his feet, dutifully following the command as he meticulously readied two compact travel packs.

Chapter 26

The Barkeep

The following morning, the sky was overcast with sprawling, dark clouds. It set an ominous tone for the day to come. Robin and Jacob travelled into the town. Near the temple, a crowd was gathering; hordes of people were milling around, oblivious to their daily responsibilities. The children remained patiently by their parents' sides. While they couldn't understand their parents' worry, they could feel the tension in the air. Robin looked up at the darkened sky, it would probably rain later. Small patrols of enforcers moved around the village. They hadn't rounded up the villagers like the previous day, but they were making their presence known. Robin and Jacob saw Celina, Falia and their mother near the forge. Celina bowed her head slightly to Jacob as they approached. All the women still cast lustful looks towards Robin. He flashed them a smile and approached.

"Good morning, ladies," he greeted them. He noticed Jacob standing back away from the gathered women.

"Nothing good about this morning." Celina bowed her head. While she was still a beautiful woman, she had lost some of the lustre of her youth. Since her treatment from Jacob, she hadn't been as much of a hell-raiser. Her sister, Falia, was taking on the mantle. Falia was still stunning, Robin thought to himself. Her beautiful crimson hair flowed like lava across her shoulders. She wore a simple green gown. She smiled at Jacob and then at Robin. Her mother pulled her back as she approached the young hunter. Robin winked at her, he and Falia still occasionally enjoyed each other's company, but Falia had a string of young men with whom she revelled in intimate relations.

Neither she nor Robin was committed to any single lover. Nevertheless, Robin thought to himself once this Inquisition business was over, he would definitely call on her again.

The mother spoke up. Finally, she was a handsome woman with a stern face that looked like it was constantly sucking on a lemon. "They have arrested that harlot," she muttered.

"Who?" Jacob asked, approaching the gaggle.

"The wench, Wanda," Celina muttered. "They say she has been leading the men of the town astray from the teachings of the one true God." She made the sign of the one true God as she spoke his name.

Jacob sneered and snorted derisively, "I'm sure she will not be the last they find who has been firing the lust in men." His gaze fell on Falia, the red-haired young girl remained oblivious. "But I'm sure they will find others, not just the promiscuous."

A group of enforcers marched past the forge. They had a woman shackled between them; Jacob recognised Eyia, the landlady of the Travellers Rest and wife to Gregor. Behind her, Birel, her young daughter, was being dragged along. Robin saw this and immediately approached the guards. "Don't do anything foolish, brother," Jacob warned, but it was too late.

Robin was a huge man, he stood almost two meters tall, and his arms bulged like barrels. He stood in front of the enforcers barring their path.

"What is the meaning of this?" he demanded.

The guard looked up at the considerable hunter. "Move aside, boy, in the name of the church," the soldier snapped back.

"Not until you tell me what is going on." Robin flexed his arms. Jacob moved beside his brother, placing his hand on his brother's shoulder.

"Come, brother, we shouldn't interfere," Jacob warned.

"No, these men are dragging two good friends through the streets in shackles," Robin demanded. "Why have you taken them?" he asked. Eyia and Birel looked at Robin both with pleading eyes. He made an awe-inspiring figure standing up against a dozen armed men in defiance. He stepped forward. The enforcers brought their spears up aimed at Robin. He felt a point rest against his chest, but he didn't back away.

"Brother, please listen," Jacob insisted.

"You should listen to him." The captain of the enforcers nodded at Jacob. "The lad knows the score."

"They are being taken to a tribunal Robin," Jacob explained. He gripped Robin's shoulder harder and pulled him away. Robin yielded to his brother, who swiftly moved him aside. The enforcers raised their spears and continued their precession towards the temple.

"This isn't right." Robin shook his head.

"You are right about that, brother," Jacob agreed. "We should see this Tribunal." He pointed towards the church.

"I'm not sure I want to see that." Robin looked nervously at Jacob.

"We need to learn what we are up against," Jacob compelled; he leaned against the staff of Maahes. "Come, assist me," he demanded, relying on his brother's shoulder for support. In unison, they proceeded toward the church. Just outside its entrance, a resounding hammering echoed through the air, marking the construction of a platform. Robin's gaze settled upon it, a mixture of curiosity and bewilderment painting his expression.

"It's a pyre," Jacob explained. "They are planning a burning."

Robin gritted his teeth. This was unbelievable, crime was almost unheard of in Havendale, and most disputes between neighbours were resolved with either the town council or the church. It had never resulted in someone's death; they would never have delved out this sort of punishment, it seemed barbaric.

Jacob muttered, "It's the usual practice of the Inquisition."

The entrance to the church was guarded by several dozen enforcers. They all stood to attention, checking the villagers as they arrived. Gregor was trying to gain entry. "Please, they have taken my wife here!" he begged. "Please, she is innocent."

"That is not for us to judge, sir," the enforcer stated. "The Inquisitor will make that judgement later."

"Please," he begged repeatedly. Jacob moved up beside him.

"Gregor," Robin offered. The barkeep turned around to see the twins, Gregor was one of the town councillors, and even his family hadn't been protected from the Inquisition.

"They've taken Eyia and Birel!" Gregor's eyes rimmed red he was near tears. Robin gripped the man's shoulder in a manly hug.

"We saw, Why have they taken them?" Robin asked.

"They... they believe her to be a..." He paused. "Haulfin," he sobbed.

"Oh," gasped Robin, sure he had heard the rumours that Eyia was part-Haulfin. It was kind of an unspoken secret. He wasn't sure he believed it, sure she was a good-looking woman for her age, but she didn't look like a Haulfin.

"They are holding her and Birel. They are going to interrogate her!" he cried.

"I'm sorry" Was all Robin could say.

Jacob looked around. The guards were still impassive, "Who is on trial now?" Jacob asked the guard.

"You can attend the tribunal," the guard responded. "But you must not speak." He nodded. He beckoned for Robin to follow him.

"Gregor, go home. There is nothing you can do here," Jacob stated. "Get some rest. I'll send Robin to fetch you before her trial." Using his staff, he walked through the doors into the fortified church. The church was never a warm building, but now it felt colder than ever. A sizeable baroque chair sat on the podium, Talos sat on the chair, two scribes were seated on either side of him, busy hunched over their writing, and guards lined the walls. The woman Wanda stood off to one side, where the village choir would sometimes sing. Her arms were bound in chains, her dark hair matted across her head failing to obscure the black and blue face of a once beautiful woman. There was a sizable audience in the church.

"By her hand, she has confessed to being a succubus!" Talos held up a scroll. "She has used her foul magic to seduce the men of this town, extracting coins and driving the men from their faithful, loving wives." There was a murmur of agreement from the women in the court. "This is an affront to our holy lord," Talos calmly stood up from his throne and glared at the beaten woman. Talos spoke in a low menacing voice. "Your crimes are the work of foul demons, and no other punishment can be handed down, tomorrow morning, you will be taken from your cell and burnt to death."

A sob escaped Wanda's cracked lips as the guards on either side roughly gripped her arms, dragging her away. "No, my lord! Please," Wanda begged, struggling as they pulled her away. "I've been true to the faith; I don't want to die." Her pitiful pleas echoed through the halls of the temple. There was a murmur from the court as the women booed the broken woman.

"Why are we allowing this?" Robin whispered to Jacob. "Wanda has never hurt anyone."

"No," Jacob nodded. "But prostitution is considered an affront to the one true God." He sneered, "This is just the beginning."

"We cannot let this go on," Robin insisted.

"There isn't much we can do." Jacob shrugged.

They watched as the young wench was hauled away. She was crying, kicking, and screaming. Robin felt a stirring, burning sense of shame at his helplessness.

"Order!" Talos's voice boomed through the congregation hall. "We have found one person guilty of heresy. However, this succubus alone is not responsible for the plights of the north. The plague, the eternal winter, all the foul magics permeating this land." Talos sat back down. "In order to rout out this evil, we need a few of our good citizens to testify before this court." He waved a hand, a well-dressed young man was guided by enforcers to the choir box. "Please state your name," Talos inquired.

The man spoke. "Samuel."

Jacob looked at his brother. "Do you know him?" he inquired.

Robin nodded, "He's the dockmaster's boy, bit of a welp." Robin shrugged. "Never had much to do with him."

"You are Samuel Hagemeister," Talos corrected.

Jacob understood why people used a family name in big cities, but in Havendale, it wasn't required. He guessed that the Inquisition and church were trying to bring this practice to the north to keep track of its citizens. Robin looked at Jacob, confused, so he explained the reasons for the family name to his brother.

"What's ours?" Robin asked, still a little confused.

Jacob thought back to the previous evening when Talos and the enforcer had visited him. "I believe he called us Venator. It means hunter in the old tongue," he explained.

Robin made a face. *Robin Venator, could have been worse,* he thought to himself. He focused on this Samuel Hagemeister as he spoke. He was discussing temptations, something about being a well-behaved chaste boy led astray by a devil's daughter. The young lad talked about this for a few moments before Robin realised who he was discussing.

Robin spoke loudly. "He's talking about Falia!" Jacob nodded. While he held love no more for the former blacksmith's daughter, he hadn't wanted her dead.

Samuel was dismissed as another youth was brought to testify, followed by another. It was a similar story that the men, before they had met her, had been good, chaste, loyal members of the church, falling to her wicked temptations. Robin blushed when he realised how many lovers his former paramour had conquered.

Robin nudged Jacob. "Should we go warn her?"

"It is likely we would end up burning alongside her," Jacob whispered back.

"This isn't right," Robin repeated. The last man had left the stand, after being dismissed by the Inquisitor.

"There is another daughter of the devil in this town. She has tempted and drawn these men away from the pure path! Leading their souls to be damned for all eternity!" Talos waved to one of the guards as he wrote a message down. "This temptress will be brought before the court," he ordered, handing over the missive. "The court is dismissed," Talos slammed a gavel onto the podium.

Jacob and Robin waited outside the church; other throngs of villagers were huddled together in groups casting looks at each other but not talking outside of their family groups. Robin wondered how safe it was for his brother to be here. Jacob hadn't been well-liked in the village. Sure, they respected him after the plague. He had spent ages tending to those who struggled to recover, even while his own health had been shattered. He spent weeks following the epidemic nursing those scraping to get back on their feet, but he had never been liked. The priests often called him the cursed child, and most found Jacob off-putting. His sarcastic superior attitude never helped.

"We should leave, brother," Robin suggested.

Jacob thought about it for a moment. His brother's caution wasn't misplaced. Jacob stared up at the cliff. There was still a faint trail of smoke rising from Maganwyth's burned hut. In times like this, Jacob would have sorted the council of the old hag, but now she was gone, He felt isolated. Robin urged him again, bringing him out of his melancholy thoughts.

"You are right, Robin," Jacob agreed. "Let's go see Gregor. I feel he might need friends right now."

The tavern was empty except for Gregor who sat alone on a table, an tankard in front of him. His face was downcast, his eyes staring blankly at the wall. The large man was broken. He looked up at the towering frame of Robin as he loomed over the table.

"They have taken my family!" he mumbled. He looked up with pleading eyes.

"Here, take this." Jacob offered, pulling a small vial from a pouch. Gregor took it with limp fingers and gulped it down without question. Jacob slid onto a seat next to the barkeep. Robin paced awkwardly back and forth.

"We cannot let this go on," Robin demanded. "Perhaps we could break them out?"

"Don't be a fool, brother. There are hundreds of enforcers in the church," Jacob cut in; he saw a flash of hope light up in Gregor's eyes. "The accused will be well guarded; it would take the entire village to revolt to save those poor souls." Jacob tapped his fingers on the table. He noted Gregor seemed to be responding to the sedative. "It's only a few hours before Eyia and Birel are on trial. You need rest," he soothed.

Gregor looked up bleary-eyed. "We will have guests in for lunch," he mumbled. "I cannot..." His voice trailed off.

"I will tend the bar," Robin offered.

"It can be closed for a day," Jacob waved his brother's suggestion off. He suspected his brother would drink more than he sold. "No one would expect otherwise." He turned to his brother. "Robin, help Gregor to his room."

Robin helped the man to his feet, guiding him to the second floor. Jacob remained seated in the empty tavern; he consulted with the unheard hidden voice in his head. Thoth, a god of wisdom, learning and knowledge, he would have an answer!

The voice spoke. I am here, I am always here, I have no answers now, just as I had no answers two thousand years ago.

Two thousand years ago? asked Jacob in his head.

This Inquisition rose two thousand years ago with the teachings of this false god, I was with a young Haulfin at the time, a brilliant-minded young man, and he pleaded with me to find an answer. There is little wisdom can do against hate. Logic, reasoning, and information hold no strength against the power of this fanaticism. At first, I thought we could reason with them, we tried, but my host was killed.

Should I flee? Jacob asked.

The voice was silent.

Jacob winced at the information. He heard the loud hammering footsteps of his brother coming down to join him. He looked up at Robin as he neared the table.

"I'm lost, brother," Jacob admitted. "I have no answers, no solution to this." Jacob felt deflated. "We can only hope that this is over quickly."

"But Jacob!" Robin protested. "They are going to burn Wanda, Eyia and Birel and probably Falia!"

"And probably others," Jacob added. "I fear more will suffer the same fate."

"What about you?" Robin asked. "And your…"

"I am at elevated risk staying here," Jacob muttered. "However if we leave, they will come after us. They will use that as proof of guilt. We've seen that they want confessions. They are looking for people to damn themselves by their own hand."

"But they beat Wanda for that confession!" Robin protested.

"You noticed," Jacob nodded. "They are determined."

Robin slumped next to Jacob. He idly picked up the tankard that Gregor had been drinking from. It was empty.

"What do we do if they come for you?" Robin asked nervously.

"When they come for me." Jacob thought. "I will hold out. I will try as much as I can not to confess. With no confession they may choose not to prosecute me."

"Can you not use your powers?" Robin asked.

"To do what?" Jacob asked sarcastically. "Blast past the troops, rescue the prisoners and then what?"

"We could worry about that after we get them out."

"My power is not infinite." Jacob frowned. Robin's thoughts had some merit, but he doubted he had the power to take on an army.

The door to the tavern erupted open startling both twins. "We are closed," Robin spoke automatically, not turning to see who had come in.

"We aren't here for a drink."

Robin looked up. Standing in the tavern doorway were two huge enforcers carrying large maces. Outside behind them, several others milled around. They marched in, flanking the twins at the table.

"We have come to question Jacob Venator." The two patted their maces into their mailed fists. They were trying to be intimidating.

"So, the time has come when the church mistakes medicine for witchcraft." Jacob shook his head. "It is a sad day." Using the staff of Maahes,

Jacob pushed himself to his feet, facing the enforcers. "You wish to take me? To torture me. To break me?" Jacob's eyes flashed with anger.

Robin stood up, his impressive height towering over the two enforcers. Robin crossed his arms, presenting an even more imposing figure. "How about you don't," Robin warned menacingly.

The two enforcers exchanged glances, the young healer seemed calm, and his brother looked dangerous, but neither was armed, and they had orders from Talos himself. "You might have the wrong person?" Robin suggested. "Perhaps you should go check?"

"Er…" The guard stammered.

Jacob let his magic flare inside his mind and used it to plant a suggestion in their heads, *You are wrong* Jacob's words echoed his brothers, and he nurtured the seeds of doubt, they had elementary brains, he could see their whole life history in his mind, they were little more than bullies who enjoyed the violence. Even more so than Robin's, their heads barely contained the essential thoughts. Jacob reflected, like other bullies he had faced, the intimidation and prospect of violence prompted them to back down. The seeds of doubt planted in their mind by Jacob's magic, combined with the bearlike presence of Robin, allowed these seeds to flourish.

"Yeah, well, we might be wrong," they hesitated.

"Yeah, we will just go check," the other mumbled.

"You do that." Jacob shuffled away from the table. "Go speak to your boss."

The two enforcers left the tavern, and as they got outside, neither could be sure why they hadn't brought Jacob out, only thinking to themselves that it must have been a mistake. They had seen the wrong man.

"We must leave now," Robin counselled firmly, placing his hand on the table.

"We cannot," Jacob explained. "If we leave, we both will be hunted." The young mage shook his head. "We need to help not only ourselves but also others."

"I won't allow you to be taken," Robin insisted, slamming his fist on the table.

"I feel you must," Jacob stressed. "I've got a plan. They will be coming for me, and if We're not careful, they will also come for you." He sighed. He wasn't looking forward to what he knew he had to do. "Do you remember the adamantine?" he asked as he explained to Robin his plan.

Chapter 27

The Trial

Jacob arrived at the church on his own that afternoon. He walked unaided by his staff, alone. Jacob wore his most formal clothes, having taken his time to carefully prepare his appearance. He strolled into the church just as the trial of Eyia and Birel was concluding. He glanced at Eyia; she had received a similar treatment to Wanda earlier that day. Her pleasing face was black and blue. She was trembling as Talos was giving the verdict.

"It has been proven beyond a doubt that you have hidden your heritage as a Haulfin. You have lied to your husband and even hidden from your child the truth of her lineage," Talos scowled at Eyia as she wept. "For this, there is no excuse," he growled. "However, the court is not without its compassion," Talos continued. "We understand that your husband was ignorant of your nature, and the child didn't know of her heritage. As such, we will not hold him responsible. However, the mutant spawn of your kind cannot be allowed to stay unchecked in the village."

There was a gasp from the audience as Talos raised his hand to quiet the audience.

"We would never execute a child, even a spawn like her."

Talos rose to his feet to speak above the audience. "She must be taught her place in this world; she will be taken from this town to the city of Trindon, where she will stay with others of her kind." He nodded to the guards as Birel, and her mother were torn apart. Birel was known to everyone as a sweet, timid, but lovely child. The enforcers pulled Birel away from her mother. Eyia was too broken to fight. Birel cried and struggled to reach her mother.

"Mama!" she cried as she was hauled away. The young child kept screaming over and over as she was dragged away. Gregor stood up and tried to rush to his wife and daughter, but two enforcers intercepted him, pushing him back roughly. Jacob watched the scene from the door. The screaming child was dragged from the temple to the docks to one of the row boats, while

Eyia was led defeated into the back rooms of the church. Talos looked up as Jacob approached the podium.

"I believe you summoned me," Jacob asked. In his calm, passive voice, his dark eyes locked with Talos. There seemed to be an unspoken battle of wills between the two.

"Yes," Talos recovered. "The enforcers were to bring you to us earlier, but there appeared to be some… confusion," he finished.

The audience had fallen silent. Only the sobs of Gregor could be heard. Jacob approached the barkeep.

"Gregor, my brother waits for you outside to take you home. He will look after you," Jacob instructed. The mage looked up at Talos. "I will take my place on the stand."

Talos felt annoyed by this young man. He didn't have the respect or fear in his eyes that he expected from those who entered his tribunals. On the contrary, this physician appeared calm and collected. He was even trying to dictate the order of the service.

"It is late," Talos excused. "We also would like to ask you a few questions first in private."

Jacob smiled. "I will happily answer all questions here before my neighbours." He turned and looked at the audience. "They all know me. I have cared for most of them, treated their most embarrassing conditions. I have brought lives into this world." He nodded at a woman carrying a child he had delivered barely three months ago. "I have seen lives leave it." He nodded towards Falia, Celina and their mother, remembering the blacksmith's passing. "I have no secrets from my neighbours."

"We shall see," Talos responded grimly. He looked down at the paper on his desk, "You've been accused of performing unnatural acts, consorting with a known witch, heresy, and witchcraft." Talos read off the allegations. "I have statements from your neighbours, evidence of your crimes. So, there is no doubt in this court's mind that you are guilty, Jacob Venator."

"It is just Jacob," Jacob responded. "And I am guilty." There was a loud commotion in the church, people rising and shouting and booing at Jacob as he spoke. Jacob raised his voice, "I'm guilty of nothing more than looking after the well-being of this town." He continued, still calm but with a raised voice, "You charged me with performing unnatural acts." Jacob smiled. "I have done these acts if the natural thing was to let them die. You accuse me of consorting with a witch. Maganwyth was her name. She taught me medicine only to help the village. Heresy." Jacob laughed, "I have never broken a commandment. I have learned more about our god than anyone in this village, including those that pass as priests. Witchcraft…" Jacob paused. "Now that, I cannot prove I have never done," Jacob smiled at the church. "How can anyone prove a negative?" He glanced around the room. "If I accused someone here of using god's name in vain, how could you ever show that they hadn't ever in their lives?" he asked.

"I ask the questions here, Jacob Venator!" Talos demanded, nodding to the enforcers flanking Jacob. The young man gave them a wicked smile as they hesitated to restrain him. These were the two he had encountered in the Travellers Rest earlier. They kept as much distance as they could between them and Jacob. Jacob raised his arms towards one of them.

"I believe you need to shackle me," he suggested. The guards paused before placing the heavy iron cuffs limply around his skinny wrists.

Talos continued once Jacob had been detained, "You say you have been here to help your village." He paused, reading. "But you have committed acts of murder of the unborn." He glanced up. "Is it not true that, on several occasions, you have deprived this village of a new life. For example, poisoning young women to end the lives of their children?"

Jacob raised an eyebrow, wondering who would have told him that information. This act alone would damn the person in the eyes of the church. "I would guess that Wanda would tell you this?" he asked.

"The source is irrelevant," Talos snapped. "Answer the question."

"I have treated many ailments of Havendale," Jacob calmly answered. "Always for the betterment of the village."

"You don't deny it?" Talos demanded, his voice raising with frustration.

Jacob nodded, smiling. "I would guess you 'extracted' this information from the poor woman Wanda."

"Answer the question," Talos interrupted. The guards on either side of Jacob jabbed him with the pommels of their maces.

Jacob winced as the heavy handles pummelled into his back. "I cannot confess to something I have not done."

"You lie!" Talos demanded. "Here in the house of our true God!"

"It is true, I have not attended the sermons held in this house, but my grandfather, Father Yusef taught me that the one true God is everywhere." Then, calmly continued, "Everything is part of his will and…"

"Silence!" Talos interrupted. "We will continue your trial in the morning." He slammed his fist onto the podium. "Perhaps a night in the cells will change your mind." He waved at the guards.

Jacob continued to smile as he was led away. Despite his rough treatment, he had shown this Inquisitor up in court. It wouldn't do anything for his treatment later, but it had weakened the crowd's resolve. When he appeared beaten tomorrow, it wouldn't be with a confession. He had slipped himself a small bottle of valerian root crushed with other anaesthetics of his own creations, gulping down the vial and letting it fall the floor unnoticed. The potion would numb his body. No matter the pain caused, he wouldn't feel it. He felt the concoction hit him immediately, a wave of numbness sweeping over him as he was led away. To get a confession, they would have to kill him. He was led to the tunnels that wormed under the church. There were several cells down here. Two of them were already locked. In his numbed state, Jacob had trouble focusing. He guessed that one contained Wanda and the other Eyia, but he couldn't be sure. He hadn't planned on the numbing effects on his mind, only his body as he was dragged into a room.

He was thrown onto a chair, his shackles bound to a table. Jacob slumped down. He let the effects of the valerian wash over him. It was a numbing feeling; he flexed his fingers in the bindings and tried to relax.

***

Meanwhile, across the town, Robin was pacing back and forth. He was trying to comfort Gregor and doing a poor job. He was agitated. He didn't like leaving his brother like this.

"Will you sit down," Gregor demanded. "Get yourself a beer. There isn't anything you can do this evening."

Robin looked at the wooden keg. He walked over, filled a flagon to the top, and took a large gulp. "Tomorrow morning," Robin cursed. "Tomorrow morning, Eyia and Wanda die."

"Yes." Gregor nodded. The large barkeep had given up hope. This idea of a grandstand of defiance against the Inquisition seemed to be a last-ditch effort.

"You have spoken to everyone?" Robin finished the ale and placed his flagon back on the bar.

"Yes, tomorrow." Gregor nodded. "Everyone will be there."

Robin didn't like Jacob's plan. Too much was left up to chance, too much relied upon Jacob holding out the night, and too much could go wrong. He loved his brother; he had grown to understand his power, but he felt this plan was too risky.

"It is all we can do," Gregor grumbled. Robin paused and looked at his bow and quiver sitting on top of a rusted metal box. The plan relied on a lot of things going right. If enough of the town stood up to the Inquisition, they might leave, if it was done peacefully, and a compromise offered. The bow and arrows were just in case. Robin had spoken to the other hunters, and they were ready. Gregor had spoken to many villagers, sending word to everyone who owed him a favour. Gregor was admired, as was Robin. Together they had managed to gather a crowd. Word came to the tavern that Falia had also been taken to the church. There had been no word of Birel. She was now onboard one of the galleons.

"We will get her back," Robin comforted. "Birel is my friend as well."

"She's sweet on you." Gregor smiled at the handsome, towering hunter. "You should spend some time with her you might learn to love her. You are a good lad."

Robin shook his head. "Nah, Birel and I are just friends." He smiled.

Gregor sighed. His ability to argue had been taken out of him with today's exploits. He felt exhausted. On the other hand, Robin was still alive with energy and righteous zeal. He wanted to storm over to the church and free his brother. He gritted his teeth in frustration.

***

Underneath the church, the torch lights flickered, and the room was kept in a partial gloom. Even in his drugged state, Jacob could tell this was a tactic to intimidate him. He had been left in this room for about an hour now. He could vaguely hear sobbing from the next cell.

"Who is that?" Jacob called out.

There was a long pause, and finally, a voice came back. "It's Eyia," the voice mumbled, sounding distorted.

"How are you coping?" he asked. He felt dumb for asking such a question. He had seen her in court, and his mind was muddled.

"They've taken my baby," she sobbed through the wall.

"I'm sorry." Jacob winced; he didn't want to give away his plan. He was about to ask her something else when he heard the heavy footfalls approaching his cell. The metal cell door screamed as it opened, causing the torches to flutter. Jacob raised his head. In the entrance, Talos loomed. A small, wiry man peered around from behind the tall Inquisitor. He carried with him a leather satchel that clinked with metallic instruments.

"You have caused me a great deal of trouble," Talos stated, approaching the table. He closed the cell door behind him. It groaned and creaked, complaining on long-since-used hinges.

"The feeling is mutual," Jacob mumbled, his addled mind trying to focus. He looked sideways at the small man as he began to pull items out of the satchel. There were knives, hammers, and other twisted implements of pain.

"You are an insolent young man, have you no respect for the church?" Talos asked. "Don't answer that. You soon will." Talos took a seat opposite Jacob. "My friend here will ensure that you learn some respect."

Jacob looked at the little man. "Is this how you get people to admit to things they have never done?"

"You are an educated man," Talos stated. "By your own words, you have read the books of our lord. You should know that no means will extract information from the demons of this world."

"I am no demon," Jacob mumbled. The thin man gripped his hands and laid them flat on the table.

"We shall see." Talos glowered at Jacob. "We shall see."

The thin man slammed a hammer down onto Jacob's hand. The ball pin hammer cracked the bones. Jacob let out a howl of pain as the heavy hammer crushed his slender, delicate fingers. The agony rang through Jacob's body, his hands unable to move as the thin man slammed the hammer down again. The numbing effects of the valerian antithetic eased the pain, but the pain was brutal.

"Would you like to confess now?" Talos inquired coldly.

Jacob looked up, his dark eyes returning the Inquisitor's stare. "Confess to what?"

"To it all, that you are a host to a demon, you are the cause of all of the north's ills, you are the reason your town suffers so." Talos loomed over Jacob.

The youth gritted his teeth. "You will need to kill me for me to confess to something I've not done."

"Very well." He nodded to the man who slammed the hammer down again, eliciting another agonising scream from Jacob. "If you confess, this pain will be over," Talos urged.

"Never," Jacob snapped back.

"Very well." Talos turned to the small man. "Continue, but make sure he can still speak and write his name." The vicious man nodded. "We probably should have checked to ensure he was right-handed first." He sneered, looking at Jacob's crushed left hand. "I'm going to be with the young slut. She will be easier to break."

Jacob could not see through the pain, but he heard the heavy metal door creaking in protest and slamming behind him. Jacob's eyes became alive again as soon as the door closed. Despite the searing pain in his left hand and the numbing drugs, he sparked the magical fire in his head. It was a dwindling flicker. He struggled to get the light to erupt in his mind to flare. The sadistic man struck the side of Jacob's face with a knuckleduster knocking a tooth loose. Jacob fought to stay conscious, struggling to focus on the light, the flame in his mind. Finally, the light flickered to life.

"*Dloh peels!*" he called focusing his will on the small torturer. Jacob shook his head, clearing his mind as much as he could. He looked at the man who now stood motionless beside him, unmoving. His eyes had rolled back unseeing. "*Kcolnu,*" Jacob muttered, and his bindings cracked open, clattering to the floor. He took a moment to take a few breaths before pulling himself to his feet. He felt naked without the staff of Maahes strength to draw upon. Cradling his crippled left hand close to his chest he calmed his breathing.

"*Senob dnib,*" he muttered. The pain eased, but his hand was still severely battered. He tried to flex his fingers, wincing as he tested them. He realised even his magic had its limits when it failed to fully heal his hand. He would need to keep up the pretence of being tortured for a while. Closing his eyes, he focused on his inner light. He had only cast three spells, but he already felt

264

weak. This was the greatest weakness of magic, why the subraces had lost the war. The powers only lasted as long as the strength of the wielder, and each spell required a toll. It didn't matter whether it was the inborn magic like Jacob's or the ritualistic magic of old. They all had a price.

Jacob sighed and slumped into the chair. Unbound, he tried to relax and rebuild his strength. The throbbing from the side of his face and his hand hindered his thoughts. He breathed in slowly, trying to let the effects of the valerian ease away the pain. It took a few moments before he could stand up again. He looked at the small torturer, who remained entranced. Jacob began to probe the man's mind with his using his magic. It was a void of blackness; this shell of a man had a single focus in his life; get confessions for the Inquisition. He enjoyed the pain he caused; he revelled in it. He hated when his victims talked. It ended his fun. Jacob was weak, but with a man with such a limited mind, he could easily plant a seed of suggestion drawing from so many memories of torture. Jacob spoke. *You have tortured me for hours, but I have not broken. You have used every method you know, and I have not broken. I will not break.* He used his will to bend the man's mind. He called upon every experience the man had used to elicit information and substituted himself in the victim's place. A huge grin spread across the small man's lips. Jacob didn't have the energy to fake the screams. He could hear the cries of a young girl somewhere down the halls. *Falia,* he guessed. Jacob briefly wanted to break out of his cell and save the young girl. If he did that, he would give away the plan. He closed his eyes, trying to block out the screams. "*Gniyd smaercs,*" Jacob whispered under his breath. His cell was filled with the sound of screams in his own voice. This should hold the ruse for a while. Jacob returned to his chair and slumped down. He wondered how long it would be before Talos returned. He looked at the confession that Talos had left on the table. It was unsigned and would remain so. Jacob closed his eyes and tried to rest too restore his energy. If Talos were to return, he would wake the torturer.

***

It had taken longer to break the red-haired slut than Talos had thought, she had remained defiant in the face of threats against her sister, and her mother. It had taken using pins under her fingernails before she had finally cried out a confession. Talos wiped his hands on a bloody rag and threw it away. He could

265

still hear the screams coming from Jacobs' cell. His young pet torturer did enjoy his work. He was tempted to interrupt but knew his man would get a confession. He always did. It had been a long day for the Inquisitor; three agents of the devil had confessed, a spawn was to be shipped home to the church pending execution, and a warlock was about to be broken.

Chapter 28

The Execution

It was a gloomy morning that greeted Havendale. The skies were dark, heavy, and ominous. A smattering of drizzle peppered the ground. The galleons rocked in the dark waters of Havendale bay. There was no morning bustle of the fishers or whalers getting ready to leave. Instead, the streets of the small town were sedated. The only disturbance was the screams echoing from under the church.

The magical fake screams of Jacob Venator had echoed through the halls of the church throughout the night. Meanwhile, Jacob recovered his strength sleeping uncomfortably in the chair he had been shackled to. The effects of the valerian sedative had finally worn off, and his mind was clear again. His injured hand and face ached in the freezing damp air. Dawn was about to break when the young mage woke. The torches in the room had burned down to nubs, and his would-be torturer still stood in a daze at attention beside him swaying on his feet. The spell would wear off soon, Jacob could end it with just a wave of his hand, but Jacob was content to let this animal remain frozen. He would have been happy to leave the man standing frozen until he died. Jacob slipped his wrists back into the cuffs and with a whisper, used magic locked them again. His left hand was still mangled. His spell had knitted the bones but hadn't repaired all the damage. His jaw ached from the punch he had taken earlier. Jacob couldn't see his reflection but knew he looked a mess, but not rough enough. Jacob mumbled to himself, flaring his magic again. "*Inoisulli.*" He focused his mind on what he wanted his face to look like, covered in bruises and blood. His face shaped into a battered, beaten mess as he finished uttering the words. The features of his face distorted, his eyes swelling almost closed, his pale skin now shades of black, blue and red. His lips appeared thick, cracked and bleeding.

In the courtyard outside, the villagers had begun to assemble as planned. Organised by Gregor and Robin, it had taken a lot of work and many favours being called in, but they had managed to gather almost half of the abled-bodied towns folk. Only Robin wasn't with the group; he was elsewhere. Gregor carried a heavy metal box, slung in a leather strap over his shoulder, as he led the march on the church. They weren't angry or yelling; the towns folk were determined. They walked silently, stopping only a few meters from the church doors. As they arrived, four pyres were being prepared by servants of the Inquisition. These weren't the heavily armoured enforcers, but acolytes dressed in simple grey-black robes. As the crowd approached the servants, one took flight into the church.

The villagers began to chant in unison. "Let them go, let them go," was a repeated chant. It started low as people got into the rhythm, but the loud echoing chant soon carried over the village. It hadn't been the most creative, but it was all Gregor had been able to think of at the time.

Several enforcers resting inside the church made their way outside, drawn by the ruckus, only to be greeted by the mob.

Unaware of the commotion outside, Talos walked through the lower church's halls. He entered the cold, gloomy cell where Jacob was being held. Jacob quickly and silently ended the spells holding his torturer, and the small man awoke swaying on his feet, exhausted from having remained standing all night. Talos looked at the man and then at the slumped Jacob.

"Has he confessed?" he asked.

"Sire, I've tortured him all night," the man mumbled, seemly unsure. "I've used everything." He cast his hands towards his tools. They were surprisingly clean. "He refuses to confess." The torturer could remember using them but couldn't remember the specifics., almost like he had been in a dream. Blinking at Jacob, he tried to understand his confusion. The young boy's face was a bloody pulp. *I must have tortured him,* he thought to himself.

Talos was shocked at Jacob's resolve; this agent had never failed him; even Talos lacked his aptitude for extracting confessions.

"Nothing?" he asked. The man shook his head.

"You can go," Talos ordered as he sat opposite Jacob. "You are stronger than any I've seen in a long time." Talos was impressed. "You've chosen not to confess."

"I did nothing," Jacob croaked feigning exhaustion, putting on a slur to match his split lips.

Talos nodded. "I would have preferred a confession," he admitted.

"I cannot confess to what I've never done." Jacob raised his head, meeting the Inquisitor's gaze.

"Confession is good for the soul. You might still earn a place in the one true God's good graces even with your wicked ways." Talos lowered his voice, "If you confess, we will end your suffering. He reached forward and gripped Jacob's injured hand. He squeezed hard, causing the young man to groan. "It will protect your family, your brother, your village." Talos insisted, changing tactics. It was clear the stick hadn't worked. Now time to try the carrot.

"I cannot confess to something I haven't done," Jacob repeated. "However, you have a way out of this without losing face."

Talos almost laughed at this man's audacity. "A way out?" Talos cocked his head. "I am not the one that needs a way out of this."

"Are you sure?" Jacob asked, glaring at the Inquisitor. "You put on a good show yesterday, beating a confession from Wanda and Eyia and taking Birel away from her family, but that will not have sat well with the village. After a night's rest they will realise the horror they have woken up to. They will rise up."

"They also seek the purification of this town," Talos boasted. "They know to defy us would be a fool's choice."

"You underestimate this town," Jacob stated. "Yesterday you may have called upon those base fears that sit within the heart of man, but that anger has faded when they saw you dragging a mother and child apart, the beaten face of a defenceless woman, and my defiance." Jacob looked him in the eye. "You will find you have stretched yourself too far and too fast." Then, Jacob added, "The people will rebel."

"Then they will die. They are clearly under the influence of foul magics." The Inquisitor smirked.

Jacob lowered his head. "I believe you would destroy a village to prove your point. In your mind, you feel it is better to leave no sign of rebellion or defiance. The truth is we aren't to blame for the magics that have plagued this land. It is not the doing of the Haulfin, the result of Maganwyth or any witchcraft. It isn't the fault of Wanda, Eyia, Birel or Falia." Jacob gritted his teeth. "This isn't even my doing," His voice remained calm and level. "A rock was brought to this town years before I was born." Jacob lied, "This rock was said to have been magical."

"What bargaining is this?" Talos cocked his head to one side.

"No bargaining, just the truth." Jacob managed slowly, "I was told the story by Maganwyth. It is an old mystical metal called adamantine."

Talos' eyes lit up. He knew there was no magic in adamantine, but it was known to be the metal of the old gods. A pound of it was worth more than most princedoms had in their coffers.

"We were told this metal was evil by Maganwyth. So, she ordered the village to bury it far away."

"Where?" Talos inquired. The greed was evident in his eyes.

"I could tell you, but I want you to guarantee the release of all of the villagers and the return of Birel from your galleon."

Talos mused. He could quickly go back on his word. "I give my word," Talos lied.

Jacob gave him a weak smile. "Of the two of us, I'm the one whose word we will be trusting."

"What's your plan then, young man," Talos inquired.

"You will announce the exoneration of all those so far tried." Talos scoffed. "You will release them, returning the young Birel." The Inquisitor shook his head. "Then, when they are back with their families, you will release me, and I will give you the rock."

"What is to prevent me from torturing you until you give me the location," Talos inquired.

"Firstly, I can hold out against pain as you assessed last night. For the last few years, I have lived with pain; it has become my friend; since the plague wracked my health, I have lived in agony, and more of it cannot break me. Secondly, I don't know where it is at the moment." He gave a sly smile. "I asked for it to be moved." Jacob took a moment to pause. He could see Talos' mind working. His mind was clearly too sharp. He wouldn't want to try his magic on this one, he would be caught.

"Describe the rock to me so that I know you aren't lying," Talos demanded.

Jacob described in detail the glowing veins along the rock, how it had been sealed in a metal box just in case it was dangerous and buried away in the woods.

"You assume, of course, that your village hasn't accepted its place," Talos muttered.

Jacob smiled as a booming knock came against the metal door echoing through the cell.

"Come in," Talos called. The old iron door creaked and squealed on tortured hinges with a wail. It allowed the admittance of one man in full plate mail. He hovered at the door, not wanting to interrupt.

"Yes, what is it?" Talos inquired.

"Sire, it's the villagers. They are…" He paused, trying to think of the word, it was more than a protest, but it wasn't a riot… "Restless," he finished.

Talos looked over at Jacob, who gave him a sly smile with an 'I told you so' look on his face. Talos felt anger bubbling up inside. How could this one village yokel have predicted all of this? Talos briefly suspected actual witchcraft. It was unlikely. There were a few mages around, but not here. This was little more than a very intuitive boy.

"Very well." Talos feigned defeat. "I will release the others, but you will be strapped to the pyre. Shackle and gag him," he ordered the guard.

A wave of fear washed over Jacob. The gag hadn't been part of Jacob's plan. While some magic could be cast with thoughts or gestures, the spell Jacob had intended to use would need him to be able to speak. Jacob was dragged roughly from the chair. His feet were limp as he was manhandled through the church.

Perched high atop the spire of the church, Robin's vantage point was unrivalled. The brisk morning air was a biting embrace on his skin, as he nimbly clung to the edge of the spire. Robin had managed to scale the back of the church to reach this point, the climb had been arduous and now his skin glistened with a sheen of sweat which was cooling against his body, sending shivers down his spine. Jacob had instructed him to wait, only to act if absolutely necessary. From his perch, Robin could hear the frenzied cries of the villagers begging for the release of their people. He wiped the sweat from his eyes and tied a rope securely around the spire, coiling it around his waist for added safety. Years of climbing trees and roughhousing with his friends had finally paid off. Jacob had always belittled Robin's youthful pursuits, insisting they were a waste of time. Looking down, Robin could see the guards below growing restless. The villagers were making no aggressive moves, yet they were still outnumbered two to one, as most of the enforcers had returned to their galleons for the night.

'Robin steadied his breathing and focused on his task. He couldn't let his emotions get the best of him. He knew that he had to act quickly and precisely. He pulled an arrow from his quiver, feeling its weight in his hand, and notched it onto the bowstring. As he drew the bow back, his muscles tense and ready, he felt a sense of determination well up inside him. He would do whatever it took to protect his brother and these women.

Meanwhile, down below in the courtyard, the enforcers were preparing for a fight. Their weapons glinted in the sunlight, and their armour clanked as they moved. Suddenly, a tall figure dressed in black emerged from the church. Robin recognized him as the man who had been passing judgment the day before. The man stood in front of the crowd, and the enforcers parted to make way for him.

As the man approached the mob, the enforcers dragged out three figures. They were barely recognizable as human, their bodies beaten and battered beyond recognition. Robin felt a surge of anger and disgust at the sight of them. Their faces were swollen, and their clothes torn and bloody. He couldn't imagine the kind of cruelty that could inflict such violence upon innocent women.

Then, to his horror, he saw his brother being dragged out from behind the women. His mouth was gagged, his hands bound tightly behind his back. Robin felt a cold rage grip him. He knew that he had to act quickly if he was going to save his brother and these women from the clutches of these brutal enforcers.

Talos took a stand in front of the restless mob. His face remained calm and passive as he scanned the crowd.

"Silence!" he called in a loud voice that echoed from the town's cliffs. He raised his hands until the chants of the mob slowly faded. He waited a few more moments allowing the public to mill about restlessly. "New evidence has come to light." Finally, he cried out to the masses, "Evidence that could exonerate these women." There was a murmur of approval from the audience. "To get this evidence, they are being released to their families." With a nod from Talos, the women were released. The three women staggered across the courtyard.

Robin saw Falia and Eyia return to their families from his vantage point. Wanda, who, like Robin, was an orphan, stumbled to the ground alone. It took a few moments as she whimpered on the wet cobblestones before a kindly soul helped her. Talos continued, "This young man, an accused warlock," gesturing to Jacob. "Has brought information that is the cause of your village's ruin." He gestured towards the pyre. The guard dragged Jacob onto the stacked wooden platform and tied him to the middle post. Robin watched helplessly as his beaten brother was bound tight to the bonfire.

"Don't forget the child." Jacob tried to mumble through his gag as he was lashed to the beam. "She needs to be brought back."

Gregor shouted out about his daughter from the crowd. Talos raised his hand again as the group grew restless. "I have ordered that the child be returned to her parents," he stated calmly. "However, this warlock!" he announced, pointing to Jacob. "Must reveal the source of the corruption."

Jacob's eyes widened as Talos' rage began to boil, his tall, dark figure towering over him like a black storm cloud. The air crackled with the intensity of his anger, and Jacob could feel the heat of his breath against his face. He fought to keep his composure, but his body trembled with fear.

Talos pointed a shaking finger at Jacob, his voice booming across the courtyard. "You will reveal the source of your power, or you will burn!" His eyes blazed with fury, and Jacob could see the veins bulging in his neck.

Robin watched as Talos had turned his wrath on Jacob. This was not part of the plan. He saw Gregor begin to waver, clutching Erin tightly in his arms. Jacob had never been popular, but he didn't deserve this.

His fingers were trembling with rage. His nocked arrow shaking, its point glinting in the dim light. He took a deep breath, trying to steady his nerves. The Inquisitor's back was turned to him, and Robin was tempted to let the arrow fly. He wanted to end this madness once and for all.

Jacob mumbled into the gag. Gregor raised his low rumbling voice carrying it over the crowd's noise.

"No," he stated, clutching his wife. He stood, turning to face the Inquisitor. "You have accused my family of being Haulfin, these women of being heretics and succubus; you accuse this man of being a warlock!" he growled. "I do not like this man," he declared, pointing at Jacob. "And he doesn't like me, but when I was at my lowest, he came to help me. He cared for me." He turned to look at the audience. "All of you have, at one point, owed this man a great deal. We have all jeered and ridiculed him for being frail and different, but he has looked after all of us. I, for one, do not believe he is a warlock! He is being used as a scapegoat for this man." Gregor pointed

273

his finger at Talos. As he turned to point, Talos saw the metal box hanging from a makeshift sling around Gregor's shoulder.

Talos guessed, correctly, this would be the adamantine.

"Enough of this. The witch must die," Talos snapped. He then grabbed a torch from one of the guards and chucked it at the bottom of the pyre. "Bring me that box," he ordered to the Inquisitors.

The villagers had the upper hand in numbers, and the enforcers were struggling to keep them at bay. More enforcers were on their way, rowing in on boats, but they were still a few minutes away. The situation was escalating quickly. The enforcers charged forward towards Gregor, their maces raised and ready to strike. The tension was palpable as everyone held their breath, waiting for the next move.

At the same time, the whale oil that had been spread across the base of the pyre ignited with a deafening roar. The flames licked at the wooden structure, quickly consuming it in their inferno. The heat was intense, and the acrid smell of burning oil filled the air. Jacob, still bound to the stake, cried out in agony as the grease rendered his flesh. The crackling of the flames drowned out his screams, and Robin felt his heart break as he watched his brother burn.

Chapter 29

The Fight

The fight erupted quickly as the enforcers rushed the villagers. Sickly blows in sickly death came the fists and maces that made fissures in skulls beneath bruised skin. The combat was bloody and primitive, all the worst ways a human can endure and inflict. Each stood upon the hallowed ground before the church, the enforcers, and villagers the same, fighting for survival each in their own way, the excruciating deaths of screaming souls of hell, made a human hand. Maces hammered into the skulls of the villagers, but they outnumbered the enforcers and were overwhelming them, ripping their halberds and maces from their hands and turning their own weapons against them. Throughout this orchestra, the high-pitched soprano of Jacob's screams of agony echoed across the town.

As Robin took aim, his senses sharpened to a razor's edge. He focused intently on the fleeing figure of the Talos, his breath coming in short gasps. With practiced ease, he notched the arrow and drew the bowstring back, feeling the sinew stretch taut against his fingers. The ancient wood of the longbow creaked and groaned, protesting the incredible force required to bring it to full tension. Robin's muscles bulged as he fought against the bow's inherent strength, his fingers white-knuckled against the pressure. The leather of the bowstring grated against his fingers, tearing at the soft flesh, and sending sparks of pain shooting up his arm. Despite the agony, he held his stance, waiting for the perfect moment to release the arrow and strike down his target.

Robin's biceps bulged and his forearms quivered as he held the bowstring back, feeling the strain of the powerful weapon in his grip. His mind raced as he calculated the perfect shot: considering the distance to his target, the wind's speed and direction, and the trajectory of the arrow's flight. He adjusted his aim, raising it ever so slightly to compensate for the arrow's natural arc, then finally released the string. The bowstring snapped forward with a deafening 'twang,' the sound echoing through the courtyard as the arrow flew towards its target. Its speed was remarkable, and it sliced through the air like a knife, a blur of wood and steel hurtling towards its mark. The arrow sang through the air, the feathers on its shaft rustling with the force of its flight.

Robin's eyes narrowed as he watched the feathered shaft hammer into the backplate of one of the enforcers, burying itself in the now prone body. For a moment, time seemed to stand still as Robin realized what he had done. He had taken a human life. His heart pounded in his chest as he stared at the fallen man, his thoughts racing.

But there was no time for hesitation. He could see others rushing towards his friends, their maces held high. Without a second thought, Robin quickly notched two more arrows and drew back his bowstring. The leather sinew creaked and groaned under the intense pressure as he aimed and fired with deadly accuracy. The arrows flew through the air like deadly missiles, finding their targets with unerring precision. Two more enforcers fell to the ground, their bodies writhing in pain as Robin's arrows found their marks.

The bow in Robin's hands felt heavier as he aimed at the incoming enforcers. He remembered his mentor's words about the gravity of taking a life, and the bow seemed to echo them. Robin's heart weighed heavily in his chest as he prepared to release another arrow. He knew that he didn't enjoy this, that it wasn't a game, but he also knew this was the only way to survive.

His arrows flew with deadly accuracy, finding their targets one after another with sickening thuds. Robin felt the pang of guilt and sadness with each successful hit, but he pushed them aside, focusing on the fight at hand.

He took a deep breath and readied himself for the next salvo. This wasn't about fun or enjoyment; it was about survival, and he would do whatever it took to protect his brother.

The piercing screams of his brother's agony shattered Robin's concentration, snapping him out of his trance. He jerked his head towards his brother, his gaze locking onto the towering pyre. The damp wood was now engulfed in flames, belching out thick, choking smoke that made it difficult to see. Through the hazy veil, he could hear the raspy, hacked coughs of his brother, struggling for each breath as the smoke choked the life out of him.

With a rush of adrenaline, Robin's mind kicked into overdrive. He knew he had to act quickly if he was to save his brother.

His heart raced as he checked the rope around his waist, ensuring it was secure. He peered over the edge of the roof, down at the courtyard below, and his brother's writhing form on the pyre. He picked up his brothers staff, he could feel the weight of the Staff of Maahes in his hand, his brother's had made him swear to bring him the staff. Taking a deep breath, he steadied himself, listening to his brother's words ringing in his mind.

"Calm thought over action, brother."

Robin knew he had to act quickly, but he had to do it with a clear mind. He slung his bow and quiver over his back and grasped the staff, wrapping it tightly around the thick rope. With one swift movement, he leaped off the edge, the staff rolling with the rope as it tried to uncoil. Robin gripped it tightly, releasing it little by little, allowing the staff to unwind and slow his descent.

The wind whipped past his face as he hurtled towards the ground, his heart pounding in his chest. He hit the hard ground with a jarring impact, rolling to lessen the blow. His brother's staff clattered to the cobbles beside him, and Robin lay there for a moment, catching his breath, winded.

He could feel the adrenaline coursing through his veins as he scrambled to his feet, his mind focused on his brother and the desperate need to save him.

Around him was chaos. The villagers had overwhelmed the few enforcers. Some of the Inquisition had fled into the church, others towards their long boats. Robin stood up amongst the chaos. He tried to rush to his brother, whose screams were becoming weaker. An enforcer stood before him, trying to bar his way, swinging a heavy mace. Robin caught the mace with his left hand, it gave a sickening thud, Robin then twisted it from the enforcer's grip. He switched it to his right hand and swung it in a heavy arch back at his would-be attacker. The enforcer's helmet caved under the blow, and the body fell limp to the ground, the metal of his armour clanging, blood leaking from the crushed helmet oozed onto the floor.

As Robin charged towards the pyre, the heat of the inferno singed his hair and clothes. The roaring flames drowned out all other sounds, save for the occasional pop and hiss of burning timber. Through the smoke and flames, he could barely make out his brother's slumped form, his head drooping lifelessly. The acrid scent of burning oil and wood filled Robin's nostrils, stinging his eyes.

Undeterred by the danger, Robin swung his mace, sending splintered beams of fiery wood flying in all directions. But it was too slow, and he knew it. With a fierce determination, he hurled the mace aside and lunged onto the platform, ignoring the scorching heat that seared his skin.

Using every ounce of strength, Robin gripped the pillar to which Jacob had been bound and tore it from the frame, splintered wood exploding under his bulging muscles. Once free he jumped from the pyre free of the flames. He hit the cobbles hard, the flesh on his legs and arms slapping against the hard stones. But he pushed through the agony and began pulling his brother's lifeless form away from the burning post.

With sweat pouring down his face, Robin knelt beside his brother, his fingers burnt and raw as he fumbled with the thick hessian rope. He begged and prayed for his brother's survival as he worked to free him. Finally, Gregor appeared at his side, offering a sharp blade to cut the bindings.

Together, Robin and Gregor sliced through the ropes, freeing Jacob from the smouldering log. Jacob was still and unmoving in Robin's arms. "Live!" The words came out in a desperate, guttural cry from Robin, his eyes red-rimmed and swollen with tears. He pleaded with Jacob, as if his own life depended on it. "Please, Jacob, don't leave me here alone. You have to live!"

Jacob lay on the ground, his body wracked with coughs that sent droplets of blood spraying onto the cobbled street beneath him. He could feel the life draining from him, his energy ebbing away with each passing moment. But still, he struggled to hold on, to cling to the hope that he might make it through.

"Did you save Birel?" Jacob gasped, his voice barely audible above the sound of his laboured breathing. Robin looked over to Gregor, hoping against hope that the answer would be yes. But when the big tavern owner shook his head, Robin felt his heart sink like a stone in his chest.

Jacob's eyes flicked up to meet his brother's, their once-bright colour now dulled by the smoke that had filled the air. "You saved me," he whispered, his voice barely more than a whisper. "I can't believe it."

Robin could feel the tears streaming down his cheeks, unstoppable, and hot against his skin. He reached out to take Jacob's hand, feeling the warmth of his brother's skin against his own.

"I had to," he said, his voice choked with emotion. "You're my brother. I couldn't just let you die."

"They are running for their boats." Gregor got to his feet. "They still have Birel," he snarled angrily.

"The box?" Jacob asked weakly.

Gregor looked around; in the fighting, he had lost it. The courtyard was strewn with fallen bodies, some dead, some injured. "I don't know, lad, is it important?"

Jacob hesitated for a moment. He supposed not. He would prefer to have kept something that valuable away from the clutches of Talos, but... Talos. Jacob sat up, wincing slightly as he pushed himself.

"Talos, where is he?"

Robin groaned; the large man was burned, but he wouldn't let that keep him down. "I think he ran towards the docks." Robin retrieved his father's long old bow and Jacobs staff from where they had fallen.

"Give me Maahes," Jacob demanded, his delicate bruised hands reaching out towards the ancient staff. Robin handed him the double lion headed rod. Jacob could feel the power returning to him as his frail fingers wrapped around the shaft of Maahes. A shiver of energy surged through his veins. His lungs still burned, and his feet and thighs were blistered and bloody, but he felt power again. Jacob's pain was replaced by a feeling of pure icy cold rage.

Jacob muttered the words to himself, his voice hoarse and ragged. He could still feel the intense heat from the fire that had engulfed him. His body was battered and bruised, his clothes torn, singed, and stained with blood. But he refused to be beaten.

Jacob, with support from his brother got to his feet and began to walk. He leaned heavily on his staff, the double-lion heads seeming to come alive with each step. Flames flickered and danced around the brass figures, casting an otherworldly glow around him. The air seemed to sizzle with heat as he approached the docks.

Jacob surveyed the scene before him with a sense of grim determination. The galleons were preparing to launch more longboats, loaded with soldiers. The rebellion in Havendale would soon be crushed.

"Never be afraid of the rage that is fire," he whispered to himself, his eyes blazing with a fierce determination. "For when the fire burns hot, it dies fast. But should you ever find my rage cold, be afraid. Be prepared to be scolded by the ice."

He limped forward, his staff tapping rhythmically on the cobbles. The lions on his staff seemed to roar with each step, a warning to anyone who would dare stand in his way. He would not rest until justice was served, until the inquisition were defeated, and driven from his home. "Robin, get up high and spot Birel," he ordered, not even checking, just knowing his brother was behind him. The mob of villagers had followed Jacob to the docks. Most were armed, holding the maces and halberds of the enforcers they had beaten. Some of the hunters had their bows ready.

The docks were a flurry of activity, with people rushing about and shouting as word spread that the Inquisition had been pushed out of Havendale. However, the jubilation was short lived. The five huge galleons slowly lowered landing craft into the water, each bristling with weapons wielded by black-clad enforcers. The villagers, once hopeful in their victory, now felt a creeping sense of unease as they watched the approaching ships.

Each galleon was a massive vessel, capable of carrying between one and two hundred soldiers. The bay was soon filled with landing craft, their hulls slicing through the choppy water as they approached the shore. The enforcers bristled on each rowboat, their pikes, spears, and halberds gleaming in the sun. The villagers couldn't help but feel small and insignificant in the face of such an overwhelming force.

Suddenly, a bolt from a crossbow sailed through the air, clattering against the cobblestones of the dock. The sound echoed, a warning shot from the lead boat. The villagers fell silent, watching as the boats drew ever closer. It was clear that this act of defiance would not go unpunished.

Gregor mounted a box of crates. "Anyone with a bow, fire back!" he yelled.

The hunters of Havendale weren't a trained army. They didn't fire like an army. Instead, they fired like hunters who had spent many years living on land where a missed shot meant life or starvation. About a dozen hunters fired; most found their mark, leaving cries of agony or death from the oncoming boats. They were about two hundred yards out. The hunters were unleashing their arrows quickly and effectively.

Meanwhile, the Inquisitors' crossbows had yet to hit anyone. However, the boats were getting closer and closer. Gregor seemed to have taken charge of the defence of the village. He was yelling orders around the docks marching up and down. The ragtag band of citizens had armed themselves with a collection of fishing hooks and spikes and whaling spears. They were no army. There was no discipline, unlike the approaching enforcers, who rowed in perfect time with each other, inexorably closer. They were now the ones who were outnumbered. The hunters could fire a good few aimed shots in a minute, but there were only a dozen hunters with arrows, and only a few minutes before the troops would be here. Jacob looked out over the dark sea; the boats was closer now. There was the occasional scream as a villager was struck by a lucky shot from the approaching Inquisitors. Inside Jacob mind it raged with fury. He watched the oncoming storm. Soon, they would be swarmed by the troops, and they would all die.

Jacob called over the yells of the docks towards his brother, who had climbed a warehouse. "Where is she!" he cried to his brother.

Robin unleashed his arrows in quick succession. The reservation of hurting or killing another person was now a distant thought. This mechanical action was echoed repeatedly: draw, aim, fire, draw, aim, fire. He saw man after man fall into the icy cold waters drowning or killed outright by his arrows, but they were just numbers. His burned arms flared with pain with each shot, and the raw red skin was bleeding freely, but he didn't pay any heed. His mind worked past the pain, only focusing on the goal of repelling those who would attack his home.

Jacob's voice echoed clearly over the ruckus of the docks. "Where is she?"

"I cannot see her," Robin shouted back between shots. He checked his quiver; only a couple of arrows remained. *Better make them count,* he thought. Robin aimed at a captain with a crossbow in the lead boat. He drew, aimed, fired. His arrow sailed silently across the water before arching down, neatly embedding itself into the black helmet of the captain, who toppled forward slowly, his limp hands dropping his crossbow into the sea, his body following, sinking to the cold depth of the bay.

"She isn't in the boats," he finished; he had one arrow left. He looked at his solitary shot. Should he save it? He thought to himself. Or take out one more before the enforcers reached them.

As the army of the Inquisition grew closer, their crossbows were hitting with increasing accuracy. Gregor was calling for everyone to take cover, his loud voice booming above the commotion. Jacob shook his head. His dark eyes burned with a flame. In his mind, his light was a blazing supernova. His magic soared higher than he had ever felt it. In his mind, he could hear the words of Thoth warning him, but he ignored it, the pain that wracked his body, the hell he had endured, the torture of his friends, this false god trying to dominate his village through fear. No more. He looked across the sea.

"Are you sure she isn't in the boats?" he called up to the roof as Robin unleashed his final deadly shot.

Robin confirmed as he leapt down from the warehouse. He ran across the docks to his brother, he was out of breath, and his burned arms were gushing blood, but the agile hunter seemed unfazed. Seeing Robin like this fuelled Jacob's rage. The only family member he had left had almost been killed by the actions of these Inquisitors. Jacob spoke in a strangely grave tone, his words seeming to echo.

"Everyone, hide!" he called out, and he turned to his brother.

Jacob's words flowed like a river, coursing with emotion and vivid imagery. "Anger is easy to come by," he began, his voice low and intense. "But it takes skill and finesse to wield it effectively. To channel it towards the right target, at the right time, in the right amount, and for the right reason. Let your anger flow, like water in a river. There's nothing wrong with that. But hatred... hatred is like a stagnant pond, festering with rot and disease. A poison that seeps into your soul. Forgiveness is the little paper boat that can sail on the current of anger. Let the river of your wrath carry those boats to a place of understanding and humanity. I have dammed my rage for too long. But now, I will let it flow." As he spoke, Jacob's eyes glinted with a fierce light, his magic pulsing through him with newfound strength.

The tempest of emotions that had been raging within Jacob slowly ebbed away, leaving behind a sense of tranquillity that seemed almost otherworldly. His eyes, once wild with fury, now shone with a fierce determination that seemed to burn brighter than any flame. He turned his gaze towards the approaching fleet, and with a soft whisper, he unleashed the full force of his magic.

""Etarenicni,"" he intoned, his voice carrying on the winds that whipped around him. A blinding light suffused his entire being, and as the glow intensified, his skin seemed to peel away, revealing a core of pure, unadulterated rage that burned with the intensity of a thousand suns. The flames that wreathed his body grew in size and ferocity, forming a mantle of blazing inferno that encircled him in a searing embrace.

Jacob visualized the scene in his mind's eye, the water molecules began to vibrate, breaking down the ties between them. Hydrogen and oxygen split, heat causing steam to envelop the rowboats on the water. With a swift motion, he extended his hands towards the boats, and flames erupted into the ocean between the galleons and the dock.

"Now you will know the pain of being burned alive! You will suffer the sorrow of everyone you condemned to death," he bellowed. He wept, his rage driving him beyond all restraint. As he unleashed his raw power across the bay, the inferno around him licked at his flesh, causing blisters, and melting his skin. The water exploded like a volcano of fire. The soldiers' screams of agony were gut-wrenching as the sea around them boiled. Jacob remained focused, drawing strength from the light in his mind, and could feel each life being extinguished before him. He couldn't help but revel in their downfall. '""The voice in Jacob's head grew urgent and desperate. "Slow down," it pleaded. "Too much." Thoth's voice echoed with terror and panic, before ending with a cry of agony.

But Jacob was consumed by his rage, his passion fuelling his power. He continued to draw upon it, ignoring the burning pain that wracked his body. Thoth's voice called out again, begging him to stop, but he refused to listen.

As he directed his power towards the attacking boats, flames erupted across the water, turning everything in their path to ash. The heat was intense, scorching Jacob's skin and causing it to bubble and blister. But still he persisted, his rage unquenched.

The boats disintegrated into flakes of ash, their passengers baking alive in their armour before sinking to the bottom of the bay. The flames consumed everything in their path, leaving nothing but destruction and death in their wake. Finally, as the inferno died down, all that remained were the cold, lifeless depths of the bay.

Robin watched in horror as he saw his brother was still engulfed in a blazing inferno, his body writhing in agony, but he did not fall. Jacob's eyes burned with an intense light as he lifted his hands towards the nearest galleon, He sought out the thoughts of a single young, frightened girl. When he found none, he clenched his, and with a fierce concentration, he commanded the sea to swallow the ship whole. The flames erupted with a deafening roar, consuming the vessel and its crew in a wall of fire. The screams of terror and the crackle of burning timber echoed across the bay, piercing the cacophony.

As the fire around him raged on, patches of Jacob's skin continued to smoke and peel. He gritted his teeth, ignoring the searing pain as he turned his arm towards the next ship. His fingers trembled with exertion, his body failing under the strain of the relentless flames. But his will was unbreakable, his hatred unquenchable. He would not rest until every last enemy lay vanquished at his feet.

Robin's voice was lost amidst the sounds of the crackling flames and the screams of the doomed soldiers, as he called for his brother to stop. Jacob's flesh had already started to peel off his bones, and his eyes had taken on a terrifying glint. The heat radiating from his body was almost unbearable, yet Jacob remained focused on his destructive mission. The air around him was thick with the acrid smell of burning flesh and hair.

Robin, desperate to save his brother, lunged towards him, and Jacob was knocked off his feet. He fell backward, his body hitting the ground. For a moment, Jacob lay still, his eyes closed, his body wracked with pain.

As the seconds passed, Jacob's fiery aura began to dim, and the light slowly faded from his eyes. The rage that had consumed him for so long was finally spent. In its place, he felt only emptiness and the searing pain of his burned and mutilated body.

Jacob had exacted his revenge. Most of the ships were destroyed, and the soldiers were dead, but Jacob was left with nothing but the ashes of his own rage. As Jacob stared up at his brother's big, brown eyes, he saw the love and concern etched on Robin's face. He began to sob, his body wracked with exhaustion and pain.. Time seemed to stretch on endlessly, each moment feeling like an eternity as Jacob's consciousness slowly slipped away. His thoughts, which were once sharp and precise, began to blur like the embers of a dying fire.

Jacob's eyes grew heavy, and his will and power were spent. He wanted to hold on, wanting to save Birel who remained onboard one of the surviving ships. But his pain and exhaustion were overwhelming, and his grip on consciousness faltered. The young mage slipped into a deep slumber, his actions having saved Havendale from destruction. But the cost to his soul was high, as several hundred Inquisition soldiers now rested at the bottom of Havendale bay.

Robin stood on the shore; his eyes locked on the horizon where the fleeing galleons disappeared into the misty distance. His heart sank as he realized that his dear friend Birel was still onboard, at the mercy of her captors. The town of Havendale was in ruins, the aftermath of the brutal battle that had just taken place. Bodies littered the streets, the smell of smoke and blood thick in the air. With Jacob unconscious and Maganwyth having long since left there were no healers to tend to the wounded. The priests tried to offer comfort, but their words felt hollow in the face of so much devastation. The injured cried out for Maganwyth and Jacob, but they wouldn't be coming.

As Robin looked around at the destruction and chaos, he felt a deep sense of despair wash over him. The only comfort he could take was in the fact that they had repelled the Inquisition soldiers and saved their town from total destruction. The toll on their people had been immense, and Birel was still lost to them.

Robin closed his eyes and took a deep breath, trying to steady his emotions. He knew that they would rebuild and heal from this tragedy. But for now, he could only stand on the shore, watching the disappearing ships.

Chapter 30

The Flight

Robin stood tall, his broad shoulders squared against the wind, as he kept watch over his little brother, Jacob. They were surrounded by a crowd of onlookers, their faces twisted in a mixture of awe, fear, and resentment. The villagers had seen what Jacob was capable of during the battle, and they couldn't shake the notion that he was a demon in human form.

They whispered and murmured amongst themselves, Robin could feel their animosity growing. They were afraid of Jacob, afraid of what he could do.

Robin knew that he needed to get out of there, to leave before things turned violent. The people of Havendale were afraid, and they were looking for someone to blame for all the destruction that had occurred.

Robin's muscles strained as he carried his brother's frail body through the ruined streets. Jacob was a black charred mess, with patches of raw flesh peeking through the blackened crust. Robin's heart raced as he imagined the excruciating pain his brother must be enduring.

As he carried his brother body towards their small hut, Jacob's grip on the staff of Maahes remained like a vice. The brass lions' heads atop the staff seemed even more menacing now, their eyes seemed to glow as they entered the dimly lit hut. Robin set his brother down gently on his straw-stuffed bed and immediately began to apply aloe to the burns. Jacob's flesh sizzled and steamed as the aloe worked its magic, Robin remembered his brother explaining how it was necessary to prevent infection and to promote healing.

For several days and nights, Robin remained by Jacob's side, tending to his wounds, feeding him water and thin broth, and praying for his recovery. The stench of burnt flesh and the sound of Jacob's ragged breathing were his constant companions. The town had returned to some semblance of normalcy, but Robin was in his own world of worry and despair.

Then, one day, a timid knock interrupted Robin's vigil. He rose to answer the door, his heart heavy with dread. When he opened the door, he saw Gregor and Eyia standing before him, their faces etched with concern.

"Hello." Robin rubbed his weary eyes.

Eyia stepped forward, her face still a mash of bruises. She held forward a pot of beautiful-smelling stew. She spoke, lisping through broken lips and teeth. "For you."

Robin took the pot in one hand but continued to gaze down at Gregor and Eyia. "How many years have we known each other?" he asked Gregor.

The fat man stammered. "Since you were born, lad."

"And you have never been here to my house before," Robin continued.

Gregor shook his head. "No, but I had to."

"It's about Birel?" Robin asked.

Eyia stepped forward, again speaking with her broken face, "I'm sorry, my husband can't speak his mind. My grandmother was an Aldari, and I know the stories of the old magic." She paused briefly, "I know it isn't always evil. It is about the user." She tried to look around Robin to catch a glimpse of Jacob, "Your brother saved my life, but I need him to save my daughter." Robin looked over the frail woman at Gregor, then back to the woman again.

"Jacob hasn't woken since the attack," he explained. "He lives, but I cannot bring him around."

"Probably for the best," Gregor grumbled.

Robin shot him an angry glance. "What do you mean," he demanded.

Gregor raised his hands apologetically, "He saved my wife. I have no quarrel with you or your brother." The large barman paused. "But…"

"There is always a but…" Robin repeated a line he had heard from Jacob.

Gregor continued to pause. He rubbed his heavy sausage hand across his ruddy chin. "But not everyone feels the same as we do. So be warned, the village is very on edge," he cautioned, his eyes pleading urgently.

"They will try to hurt Jacob?" Robin asked.

"He killed several hundred Inquisition soldiers, and he is a sorcerer!" Gregor implored with the huge hunter. "I have been told." He cast a glance at his wife. "That not all witches are the same, and some are good, but few of the village would believe this." This as subtle warning was as much as Gregor could give, and he hoped the simple hunter would understand. He gave the man another urgent look. Robin watched him through narrowed eyes. If he got the warning, he gave away no hint. He remained with his barrel-like arms resting against the door frames gazing down at the two innkeepers.

"You finished?" Robin asked.

"They are coming for you!" Eyia iterated in no uncertain terms. "They want to hand you over to the Inquisition to prevent any reprisal."

Robin nodded, "My brother is resting. We will speak when he awakes. Thank you for the food, and good evening." He gave them a pointed stare. A thought crossed his mind, and he handed back the pot of food. "Pass this to Wanda." He thrust the crock to Gregor. "She will need it more," he insisted.

Giving up food went against everything that Robin knew or believed. You ate what you killed was the motto he lived by. "I bid you good evening." He closed the door.

"That was kind of you, brother," A haggard voice came from behind him.

Robin froze, a mix of horror and relief washing over him at the sight of his brother. He had feared the worst, and yet here was Jacob, alive, albeit horrifically disfigured. He tried to speak, but the words caught in his throat, and he could only stare at his brother in disbelief.

Jacob's rasping voice broke the silence, and Robin turned to face him fully. The sight of Jacob's twisted and melted face made Robin's stomach turn. His brother's features were barely recognizable, and yet there was still a fierce determination in Jacob's eyes that shone through the mangled flesh.

The staff of Maahes, with its double lion head, seemed to pulse with an otherworldly light, Jacob clutched it tightly in his left hand. Robin could feel the magic emanating from it, a tangible force that seemed to fill the small hut.

"You're alive," he whispered, his eyes filling with tears. "I thought I had lost you."

Jacob's gaze softened, and he gave his brother a weak smile. "Not yet," he said, his voice barely above a whisper. "But I fear that I am forever changed."

Jacob continued with regret. "I was a fool, brother. I revealed myself." The frail young man limped across the hut towards his usual chair. "Please bring me some water."

Robin tended to his brother with great care, providing anything he asked. Jacob ate heartily, devouring his meal with a ferocity that surprised Robin. He had never seen his brother consume so much food. When Jacob finished his first portion, he even asked for a second, devouring it just as quickly.

288

After finishing his meal, Jacob remained seated by the fire, staring at the dancing flames for what seemed like hours. Robin watched him, unsure of what to say or do. Jacob was still so weak and fragile, and the burns on his body were a reminder of the horrors they had faced. Jacob sat there with a steel gaze staring at the flames, his staff standing tall beside him.

Jacob finally spoke after many hours; the fire having burned glowing embers. "Brother,

"I have changed," Jacob said with a sense of despair in his voice.

"You will heal," Robin said reassuringly, hoping to comfort his brother.

"I don't mean just physically," Jacob snapped back, his irritation palpable. He waved his hand over his face, and with a flare of magic, his features returned to their former state, free of scars.

"Noisulli," Jacob muttered under his breath, Robin looked at his brother, who was now miraculously healed, his once-melted skin looking as good as new. But Robin knew the truth: the healing was nothing but an illusion, and underneath it all, his brother still suffered.

"I mean, the god I used to communicate with has vanished," Jacob continued, his voice heavy with sorrow. "I no longer perceive him in my head."

Robin didn't know how to respond. He knew how much the god had meant to Jacob, how it had guided him through all of his trials and tribulations. To lose that connection must have been a devastating blow.

"Maybe he's just hiding," Robin offered tentatively.

Jacob shook his head. "No, he's gone. I can feel it."

There was a heavy silence between them, the crackling of the fire was the only sound in the small hut. Robin didn't know what to say, how to help his brother through this loss.

"The magic?" Robin asked tentatively.

"No, that is mine now." Jacob smirked. "Do you remember this brother?" he asked. "*steppup wodahs,*" he whispered to the flames with an echoing voice. The fire flickered and erupted in sparks that danced around the room, and the lights played with each other, casting shadows on the walls of dragons and knights fighting.

Robin looked around startled. The shadows showed the story of a brave knight destroying a dragon. It was a story Jacob had shown him before, but to see the shadows dancing around the walls playing out the melodrama was still amazing. Jacob dispelled the illusions. His face melted back into its horrific visage and the shadows faded.

"Let me rest brother." Jacob spoke finally.

***

Robin continued to tend to his brother, carefully dressing his wounds and providing him with nourishing meals. Despite his care, Jacob's scars were severe and would never fully heal. Each day brought new visitors to their door, offering thanks and praise for Jacob's bravery in saving Havendale. Wanda, the young woman who had once been so afraid of Jacob, came to express her gratitude, followed by Celina, who thanked him on behalf of her sister. Herod and other villagers came to offer thanks as well, but they also brought warnings.

"The priests are rallying the people against you," They told Robin, "they say that your brother is a warlock, that he has made a pact with demons. They're calling for his head."

Robin felt chills run down his spine with each warning. He had always known that the people of Havendale were superstitious and fearful, but he had never imagined that they would turn on his brother like this. He knew that he had to do something to protect Jacob, but he wasn't sure what.

For three weeks, Jacob had been physically healing, but his mental state remained tormented. The visions of the battle continued to haunt him, and the absence of Thoth's voice made him feel lost and alone. His thoughts were consumed by the faces of the men he had killed.

Despite all of this, he could feel a newfound strength within him. His magic seemed to have become a part of him, always present and ready to be summoned. He no longer had to struggle to find the light within himself. As he waved his fingers in front of the fire, it responded to his touch, flickering and dancing at his command.

But with this newfound power came a sense of isolation. The villagers who once respected him as a healer, him now feared him, and the priests continued to spread rumours and warnings about his dangerous abilities.

One evening with a heavy heart, Robin walked into the hut, his broad shoulders slumped, and his head hung low. He slammed shut the door behind him, sending a tremor through the rickety old cottage. Frustration was etched on his face, he cursed under his breath, striking the wall with a heavy fist. Turning to face Jacob, he growled, "No one will speak to me. I don't like this."

Jacob looked up from the fire, his scarred and twisted face bearing a solemn expression. "They fear me, brother," he replied. "Their fear will turn to anger, and from that anger, they will do what they will later regret."

Sighing heavily, Robin slumped into a nearby chair, kicking up a cloud of dust that swirled around the room. "Will this blow over?" he asked Jacob, his voice laced with worry.

"Unlikely," Jacob muttered, his gaze fixed on his misshapen hands. "The anger will grow; the fear will grow. Even if we make no provocation, the mob will form. Every time they see me, they'll be reminded, and every ailment I treat, they'll suspect magic. The inquisition will return."

"But you saved them," Robin protested. "How can they not see that?"

"Some do," Jacob conceded. "But the mob's collective psyche is manipulated by a relentless barrage of provocative and fear-mongering messages. They're being programmed to react with suspicion and hostility."

The weight of the situation hung heavily in the air as the brothers sat in silence, each lost in their thoughts.

***

It had taken another week for the murmurs of discontent to escalated into an angry mob. The priests' hateful words had fuelled their rage, drowning out any rational thought. The stark beauty of winter had given way to a softer season, with the sky now a delicate blend of greys and the trees resplendent in their leafless elegance. As the chill of early spring gave way to longer days, the town began to stir with new energy. Flowers of every colour bloomed, painting the streets with an effervescence that promised warmer days ahead. Robin sat on his porch, watching the world come alive. His gaze drifted from tree to tree, taking in the new greenery and the light breeze that carried the sweet scent of spring flowers. But on this serene evening, the rage had boiled over. As he sipped his cool drink and admired the view of the bay, he noticed a swarm of people making their way towards him from the village.

The throng of people swarmed like a hive of angry bees, their eyes wild with fear and hatred. They were a boiling cauldron of primal instincts, fuelled by a toxic brew of rhetoric and misinformation. The air was thick with the stench of anger, and the cacophony of their furious shouts and jeers filled Robin's ears.

As he watched the mob approach from the village, he couldn't help but feel a sense of disappointment creeping over him. These people, who he had known his whole life, were now unrecognizable. They had become mindless puppets, blindly following the hateful propaganda fed to them by the priests.

The horde was devoid of reason and empathy, their minds consumed by an insatiable lust for violence. They were whores for rage, willing to support nonsensical acts of violence over any rational course of action. And they blamed Jacob for their woes.

As Robin rose from his chair, he could feel the weight of the moment bearing down on him. The fate of his brother hung in the balance.

The large figure of the hunter loomed over his porch, his eyes locked onto the approaching mob. He stood tall, his broad shoulders squared, and his grip tight on the large metal mace he had kept from the Inquisition's attack. The weapon gleamed menacingly in the dim light of the approaching dusk, and he had no intention of hesitating to use it against the hate-filled crowd if necessary.

The sound of the approaching mob grew louder, the angry shouts and footsteps creating an ominous rhythm that reverberated across the bay. Robin remained steadfast; his weapon held tightly in his hands. As the crowd drew closer, Robin's palms grew slick with sweat, but he remained motionless, ready to defend his brother against their former friends and neighbours.

They were a ragtag bunch, wielding homemade weapons ranging from pitchforks to torches. But Robin was unfazed, his gaze unyielding as he stared down the angry crowd. The mob hesitated for a moment as they neared his cottage, their eyes drawn to the massive figure blocking their path.

As the priests at the front of the mob hesitated, Robin flexed his muscles, causing his arms to bulge against his leather jerkin. His formidable appearance gave him an almost godlike aura, and the mob spread out in front of his hut, their anger tempered by fear of being the first to face this giant.

Robin didn't speak. He remained an immovable statue, his clear-blue eyes scanning the crowd, seeing the faces of his former friends and countrymen barely recognisable. They were twisted into visages of anger and abjuration. A little of the innocence inside Robin died. His view of a fair and just world where good would always triumph and evil always lost shattered in front of him.

"Give us the warlock!" demanded Herod's voice from the frenzied crowd. Robin recognised the man immediately, and his heart sank at the sight of his friend's twisted expression. Herod held a wicked fishhook in one hand and a flaming torch in the other. Only a few days previously Herod had come as a friend to warn them that this would happen, now he was a member of the baying mob. The flickering flames of the torches cast an eerie glow across them, making their eyes gleam with malice.

Robin stood his ground, blocking their path. He tightened his grip on the mace, ready to defend himself and his brother. "No," he stated firmly.

"He's possessed by the warlock!" cried one of the priests, his face contorted in rage. "We must treat him like he's the spawn of the demons!" The priest brandished his torch as he spoke. Suddenly, a rock flew out of the crowd and hit Robin on the side of the head. The force of the impact made him wince and left a deep, jagged cut on his skin.

The mob began to shout and jeer, demanding blood. More rocks were hurled at Robin, but he refused to back down. His steely resolve kept him standing, unmoving and unyielding, and none of the mob wanted to face him directly.

The door to the hut creaked open, and Jacob appeared, draped in a long grey cloak that trailed behind him. His body was frail, and he leaned heavily on his staff. He raised a hand, and as he spoke the strange word, "Reirrab," the stones hurled at the hut froze mid-flight, as if hitting an invisible wall. Jacob drew himself up straight, using his staff for support, as the villagers continued to hurl rocks and other objects that harmlessly impacted against his magical shield.

"Let me speak," Jacob's voice boomed across the bay amplified by magic. "You have come here to burn me alive or drive me from my home," he continued. "You fear me, and perhaps rightly so. I have seen the destruction my power can cause." He sighed deeply. "I have no wish to harm any of you. I want to cause you no more strife or worry. So, I will take my leave." Jacob lowered his hands, "I ask only that you give me until the morning."

The crowd of villagers seethed with anger, their eyes gleaming with a fever of bloodlust. They wanted to see Jacob suffer. One of the members of the mob hurled their torch, and it soared high through the evening sky, landing on the roof of the hut. Robin watched in horror as the thatch quickly caught alight. "No!" he shouted.

"Quickly, get our packs," Jacob commanded, urgency in his voice. Robin darted inside. They had prepared for this moment. The flames of their burning home gave off an eerie light on the chaotic scene unfolding before them, the villagers hurling torches and rocks at them, only to be reflected by the invisible magical shield.

Jacob gritted his teeth, feeling a surge of anger and frustration at the senseless destruction. But he knew better than to retaliate against innocent people who were only fuelled by fear and ignorance. "The blame is not on them," he muttered to himself. "Let's go before it's too late."

The fire grew more intense, as if it were alive and determined to consume everything in its path. Their childhood home, the place where they had grown up and created countless memories, was now being reduced to ash and rubble. The pain of watching it all burn was almost unbearable.

Robin emerged from the hut with the packs on his shoulders, and Jacob gave him a reassuring pat on the back. "We're ready to leave," he said firmly. He snapped his fingers and whispered a word of magic, "'Redliweb.'" The crowd in front of them fell silent, their eyes glazed over as they stood frozen in place.

Jacob wasted no time, pulling his brother by the shoulder and pushing them through the stunned crowd. They stumbled past the villagers, who were too shocked to react, and headed towards the woods. Behind them, the roof of their home collapsed with a deafening roar, sending a plume of fiery ash into the night sky. The embers danced and flickered in the wind, like a swarm of glowing fireflies before slowly fading away and drifting to the ground.

As the effects of Jacob's spell wore off, the villagers of Havendale slowly came back to their senses. They stood there, staring in disbelief at the sight before them. The smouldering inferno of the twin's home illuminated the night sky, casting flickering shadows over the faces of the bewildered crowd. The heat from the flames reached into their very souls, warming their bodies but shaming their hearts. They looked around, but their memories were lost to them, replaced only by a sense of emptiness and loss.

As the hours dragged on, the fire began to die down, and the darkness gave way to the pale light of dawn. The stars faded into the sky, replaced by a dull grey hue. The once-thriving village of Havendale was now eerily silent, save for the crackling of the still-smouldering embers of the twins' home.

As the first light of dawn began to paint the sky with shades of pink and orange, Jacob and Robin continued their trek along the mountain path. The chorus of trees echoed around them, as if singing in harmony with the natural world. The pebbled path beneath their feet was a work of art, etched by the rain and the melting snow of winter, with the occasional imprint of soles that had passed through. This route was the long route to the hamlet of Solum. It was rarely used, even during the warmer months, and had become somewhat of a forgotten path.

The Spine Mountains were a natural wonder, towering above the landscape, with greenery that snaked its way around the mountainside. The path Jacob had chosen wound its way deeper into the mountains, with each step offering new vistas and perspectives. The journey was a respite for their minds, an escape from the troubles that had plagued them.

As they walked, Jacob limped and leaned heavily on his staff, his body exhausted from a long night. When he finally called for a rest, Robin quickly set about preparing their food. The stillness of the forest provided a natural beauty that elevated the simple flavours of their meal. They ate in silence, taking in the tranquillity of their surroundings.

The quietness of the country picnic was interrupted only by the occasional bird song or rustle of leaves. As they ate, they gazed out at the breath-taking views around them, a world of natural wonder and beauty.

Jacob and Robin sat in silence. Jacob savoured the moment, feeling a sense of peace that had been absent for far too long. He turned to his brother, who sat hunched over his breakfast, lost in his own thoughts.

"Cheer up, brother," Jacob spoke, breaking the silence.

Robin looked up, his eyes heavy with grief. "How can I, Jacob?" he replied, his voice barely above a whisper. "Our home is gone. We have nothing."

Jacob sat with his back against a tree, basking in the warm rays of the sun that filtered through the leaves. Robin sat opposite him, watching his brother's smile grow wider with each passing moment. The air was fresh, and the scent of pine needles and wildflowers drifted on the breeze. It was a perfect day, and Jacob felt alive.

"I am happy, brother," Jacob explained, his eyes closed as he let the warmth of the sun seep into his bones. "We are free now. Free to go where we want, do what we want."

Robin nodded slowly, a small smile crept to his own lips. He couldn't remember the last time he had seen Jacob so carefree. "Where do you want to go?" he asked.

Jacob's smile grew even wider. "Anywhere. Everywhere. We could explore the world, see new places, meet new people learn new things."

Robin laughed, the sound echoing through the forest. "I've always wanted to be a knight," he shrugged, his eyes shining with excitement. "Or we could save Birel?"

Jacob paused, "Let us find a way to save her,"

"Are you serious?" Robin asked.

"Why not?" Jacob shrugged,

The two brothers sat in silence for a moment, savouring the freedom that lay before them. The world was theirs, and they could do anything they wanted, yet they were determined to try to find their friend.

"Did I ever express my gratitude for saving my life?" Jacob asked, breaking the silence.

"No need," Robin replied with a grin. "I wasn't going to let anyone kill my little brother."

Jacob laughed, the sound pure and joyous. "If anyone is going to kill me, it'll be you," Jacob joked, throwing a handful of grass at Robin.

Glossary

Abrias: A skilled and loyal Arbay scout who serves as the bodyguard of Heir Prince William. Known for his sharp eyes and quick reflexes, Abrias is fiercely loyal and dedicated to protecting the prince.

Adamantine: A rare, valuable metal with exceptional strength, durability, and resistance to magic. Often used for creating weapons, armour, and other items requiring maximum protection.

Aibois: A crew member on the Lorelai ship from Arbay. Known for his adaptability, strong work ethic and loyalty to the crew.

Ailwhyn Evensong: A young Aldari woman who is the host to the goddess Gyia, granting her powerful magical healing abilities. She is also an indentured servant to Heir Prince William Nadrog and must navigate the politics of the royal court while fulfilling her duties as a healer.

Albian: A prosperous Princedom located near the capital of the Empire, known for its fertile lands and strong economy. The people of Albian are renowned for their industriousness, love of the arts, and strong sense of community.

Aldari: A humanoid species of Haulfin with a youthful appearance, long pointed ears, and glowing eyes. They were once leaders of what is now the Empire and favoured hosts by the gods due to their long lives. However, they are now indentured servants of humans, primarily kept for their valuable skills. Despite their servitude, many Aldari maintain pride in their heritage and culture.

Altran: The capital region of the Empire, located in the centre of the Empire, and the name of its capital city. It is the seat of power for the Empire, home to the Imperial Palace, and the centre of the Church and Inquisition. The city is divided into several districts, each with its own unique character and purpose.

Andresila and Jerisavlja: Two Veela, magical humanoid creatures known for their striking beauty and enchanting singing voices. They are often associated with love, passion, and desire and can become fiercely competitive and aggressive when provoked. The Veela's singing voices are so powerful that they can entrance anyone who hears them.

Arbay: A Princedom of the Empire, situated in the southern region of the continent. It is a vast and arid desert land, known for its nomadic tribes and unique architecture. Despite its harsh environment, Arbay is a source of valuable exotic materials such as spices and rare herbs. The people of Arbay are proud and independent, and their warriors are renowned for their skill with the scimitar.

Aurialla: The goddess of Winter Night, a deity associated with the winter season, snow, and icy winds. Worshipped in various old religions, Aurialla is believed to bless her followers with good fortune during the winter months. Often depicted as a beautiful woman with long white hair and a frosty aura, she was once widely honoured through festivals and rituals.

Balis Gestalt: An Aldari crime lord who controls the criminal underworld in the slums of Trindon. He is known for his ruthlessness, cunning, and extensive network of informants and enforcers. Gestalt is feared by many in Trindon and is considered a significant threat to the safety and security of the city.

Baron Harkeeve: The ruling noble of Taros, a princedom that often rivals with Gont. He is known for his cunning political strategies, luxurious living, and his desire to extend his power and control over the surrounding lands.

Baron Von Rikton: An enigmatic figure from the mysterious land of Rwelvencrest, known for his great magical powers and hypnotic charm. Little is known about his origins, but his name strikes fear into the hearts of many, including the witch Maganwyth. His intentions remain shrouded in mystery, but his influence is felt throughout the land.

Birel: A young woman who resides in Havendale with her parents who own an inn in the town. She is a childhood friend of Jacob and Robin and is known for getting into mischief with Robin. She has a secret crush on Robin, but her feelings are not reciprocated.

Captain Bob: A fat wharf rat who makes his home in the hat of Lotheran, the captain of the Lorelai.

Carlos: A scribe in service to Talos Tarus, the Inquisitor General of Gont. Carlos is known for his extreme religious devotion and unwavering loyalty to the Inquisitor. He is a devout believer in "The One True God" and is willing to do anything to further the cause of the Inquisition.

Catrin Queen: The youngest daughter of the ruler of Vantoth, a skilled warrior woman who has fought on the border between Vantoth and Rwelvencrest. Her bravery, independence, and compassion make her a respected leader among her people.

Celina: A young woman, who is the eldest daughter of the Blacksmith of Havendale. She is known for her exquisite beauty and kind personality.

Darla Queen: The powerful matriarch and ruler of Vantoth. Known for her skill in battle and strategy, she is respected and admired by her subjects. Her youngest daughter, Catrin Queen, follows in her footsteps as a skilled warrior and protector.

Dewar: A species of Haulfin, known for their short stature, muscular build, and thick, hairy faces and bodies. They are a proud and stubborn race, with a strong work ethic, and can live for several hundred years. However, since the rise of the Empire, they have been enslaved and forced to work in mines and metalworks across the empire.

Emperor Leopold of the fifth House of Ulis: The current Emperor of the Empire, known for his tactical genius and military prowess. His reign has seen significant territorial expansion, but he is criticized for his ruthless tactics and lack of concern for his soldiers' lives. He is the father of Karl, the heir apparent to the throne.

Emperor Sigmund Von Ulis: The first Emperor to rule over the Empire, reigning over 2000 years ago. He is widely regarded as a legendary figure and his reign is known as the Sigmundian era, which marked the beginning of the Empire's expansion and the establishment of its political and social structures.

Erin: The wife of Raoulf and mother of Jacob and Robin. She resides with her family in the village of Havendale. She is a beloved member of the community and often volunteers her time to help those in need.

Eyia: The wife of Gregor, who runs The Travelers Rest inn in Gont. She is rumoured to have some Haulfin ancestry.

Falia: The younger sister of Celina and daughter of the Blacksmith of Havendale. She is known for her beauty and catches the attention of Jacob but is responsible for breaking his heart.

Father Yusef: An old priest who found and adopted Erin, Jacob, and Robin's Mother. He raised her as his own in the small village of Gont.

Felix: A large man who has a grudge against Lotheran, the captain of the Lorelai.

Fester Hill: A fortified city in eastern Gont known for its strong defences, strategic importance, and large military presence. It is home to several noble families and serves as a centre of trade and commerce.

Gneth: A Gnomus who serves as a lieutenant to Balis Gestalt, the Aldari crime lord in the slums of Trindon.

Gnoumus: A species of Haulfin known for their small size and foul-mouthed nature. They resemble withered old men and are often used as slaves for menial tasks such as cleaning latrines.

Prince Godwin Nadrog: The electoral Prince of Gont and the father of Heir Prince William Nadrog.

Goodmead: A small town located on the northern shore of the Everlong Sea. The town is known for its production of mead, a popular alcoholic beverage made from fermented honey.

Gregor: Innkeeper and father to Birel, and husband to Eyia. Runs the Travellers Rest in Havendale

Haulfin: A derogatory term used to describe non-human beings in the Empire.

Havendale: A coastal town on the northern shore of the Everlong Sea, renowned for its fishing and whaling industries. It is the hometown of Jacob and Robin.

Hebon: A Princedom known for its rigid caste system and abundance of spices, located to the far east of the Empire.

Heineroth: An old soldier and bodyguard who has served Sir William Nadrog, the Heir Prince of Gont, for many years. He is not only a skilled warrior but also a mentor and friend to the young prince.

Heir Prince Sir William Nadrog: The firstborn son of Godwin Nadrog, the Prince of Gont. William is a skilled fighter and commander, as well as a charismatic leader. He is also known for his strong sense of duty and honour.

Herod: A dock hand who works at the Havendale harbour.

Hobby: A race of Haulfin commonly used as household slaves by humans in the empire due to their fastidious nature. They are gluttonous and typically about half the height and weight of a human.

Hurk: A race of Haulfin characterized by their large size, muscular builds, and leathery skin. They are native to Taros and are known for their limited intellect and powerful physiques. Hurks are often used as slave labour and are exported by Taros to other parts of the empire.

Inquisition: A powerful religious organisation that is dedicated to rooting out heresy and enforcing the doctrines of the dominant faith. They operate with the authority of the empire and have the power to investigate, arrest, and punish those deemed to be deviating from the accepted beliefs. The Inquisition is known for their harsh methods, including torture and execution, and their influence is felt throughout the empire.

Inquisition Enforcers: Agents of the Inquisition, a powerful religious organization that enforces the teachings of the church in the Empire. They are feared and respected in equal measure, as their authority is absolute, and their methods are often brutal.

Irra: An ancient god of pestilence and disease, often depicted as a shadowy figure wielding a staff. Irra is associated with dark magic and sacrificial rituals.

Ivan: A hunchbacked servant of Baron von Rikton, known for his medical knowledge and skill as a physician. He played a key role in delivering Jacob and Robin.

Jacob: A young man who possesses a keen mind and discovers he has the ability to harness the power of the gods. Despite his physical frailty, Jacob becomes a powerful force in the world and goes on a journey of self-discovery and growth. He is the son of Erin and Raoulf, the adoptive grandson of Father Yusef, and has a close bond with his twin brother, Robin.

Karl of the fifth House of Ulis: Heir to the Empire, son of Emperor Leopold.

Kazun: A female Dewar and member of the crew of the Lorelai under the command of Lotheran.

Konrad Tarus: The son of Talos Tarus, the Inquisitor General of Gont. He is a young boy who idolizes his father.

Kubra: A large, fearsome creature resembling a snow yeti that inhabits the frozen mountain ranges of the north. Known for their size and aggression, Kubra's are covered in thick white fur and have razor-sharp claws and teeth.

Laban: A skilled hunter who mentors Robin and teaches him how to hunt in the forest.

Lord Richard Lightfoot: A renowned mercenary commander known for his tactical skills and leadership abilities. He was the former commander of Heineroth.

Lorelai: A small cutter captained by Lotheran, known for his daring exploits and piracy along the Everlong Sea. The ship is swift and nimble, perfect for evading larger vessels and navigating through rough waters. The crew includes Kazun, Trigger, and Abois.

Lotheran: A notorious pirate and captain of the ship Lorelai. He has gained a reputation as an unpredictable but cunning leader.

Mable: The owner of The Comely Wench, a seedy tavern in the pirate town of Holum.

Maganwyth Puzzlecrow: An enigmatic and ancient witch who resides in Havendale. She is known for her skill and power in healing, and a deep understanding of the old ways and ancient traditions. Little is known about her past or origins, but many believe that she has been around for centuries, if not longer.

Malek: An Aldari man who served as the host of Aurialla, the goddess of winter. He sought to rid the North of human influence and brought an eternal winter to the region.

Margaret Nadrog: The wife of Renwalt Nadrog and a skilled manipulator and politician. Known for her beauty and grace, she often assists her husband in his quest for influence.

Nergal: An ancient god of plague and pestilence, often depicted as a skeletal figure with a crown of thorns. He is said to wield the power to bring epidemics and other forms of sickness upon those who have angered him.

Olivia Tarus: The wife of Talos Tarus, the Inquisitor General of Gont. She is a supportive and devoted wife and mother, who loves her husband deeply despite the nature of his work.

Penthos: A minor goddess of sorrow and grief, daughter of Nyx, the goddess of night. She is associated with the expression of sorrow.

Quorth: A small Princedom in the eastern part of the Empire, mismanagement and corruption have led to economic decline, causing many citizens to resort to criminal activities. The ruling House of Quorth's lavish lifestyle has worsened the situation.

Raoulf: The father of Jacob and Robin, and husband to Erin. He is a skilled hunter and woodsman in the village of Havendale, where he has lived all of his life. Raoulf is known for his strong will and protective nature towards his family. Raoulf has a kind heart and is well-respected by the villagers. He is a loyal friend to many.

Renwalt Nadrog: A member of the royal family of Gont and uncle of Sir William Nadrog. He is ambitious and cunning, willing to manipulate those around him to gain power. Despite being second in line to the throne, he has no loyalty to his nephew and has been known to plot against him in secret.

Rhinland: A central Princedom of the empire known for its half-timbered houses, castles, and skilled blacksmiths who produce high-quality armour and weapons. The region is ruled by a prince who resides in Rhinefort castle and is proud of its heritage and prosperity.

Robin: Twin brother of Jacob, known for his physical strength and hunting skills. He is often relied upon for protection and support by his brother, but also possesses a kind heart and strong sense of justice.

Rwelvencrest: A foreboding and cursed land located northeast of Gont, perpetually covered in thick fog and inhabited by foul creatures. It is not part of the empire, and most people avoid the area altogether. Gont and Vantoth maintain a vigilant guard on their shared borders with Rwelvencrest.

Samuel Hagemeister: Son of the Havendale dockmaster, known for his manipulative and dishonest behaviour. Often avoids punishment due to his father's position.

Saurii: A humanoid species with a reptilian appearance that is a rare species of Haulfin. Most of them have either fled or been wiped out, although some are still kept as slaves within the empire.

Snow Wolves: A species of large, powerful wolves native to the Spine Mountains. They are known for their thick white fur and tough, padded paws that help them move easily over snow and ice. While not typically aggressive towards humans, they are highly territorial and will defend their territory fiercely if threatened.

Solum: A remote hamlet located on the Long Road around the Everlong Sea, with only a few dozen families living there. It is self-sufficient and surrounded by thick woods, making it difficult for outsiders to find.

Staff of Maahes: A powerful magical artifact with a long wooden staff and two lion heads carved at the top. It was originally wielded by Nergal, the god of plague and pestilence, and is a feared weapon in the hands of those who can wield it. Its exact powers and limitations are not fully known.

Steinhardt: Court Vizier to Gont and scholastic tutor to Heir Prince William Nadrog.

Talos Tarus: The Inquisitor General of Gont, responsible for maintaining the purity of the faith and eradicating heresy. He is a stern and imposing figure, known for his unwavering devotion to his cause and his willingness to use any means necessary to achieve his goals. Despite his intimidating demeanour, he is devoted to his family.

Taros: A wealthy Princedom located to the south of Gont. It is ruled by the powerful and cunning Baron Harkeev, who has amassed vast wealth and influence through the slave trade. Taros is often at odds with Gont, and the two Princedoms have a long history of rivalry and conflict.

Telegos: The largest town located on the north shore of the Everlong sea. It is an important hub for trade and commerce, with its port being responsible for most of the shipping to the mainland of Gont.

The One True God: The monotheistic religion that is the only accepted faith in the Empire. It was established 2000 years ago with the rise of the empire, and its doctrines are enforced by the Inquisition. The religion teaches that the One True God is the creator of all things, and that the emperor is his chosen representative on earth. The Inquisition is responsible for rooting out heresy and enforcing the doctrines of the faith, often using extreme measures to maintain the purity of the religion.

The Triumvirate: The three gods who lead the pantheon of the old religion, representing the light, darkness, and balance. They are revered by the Haulfin.

Thoth: A deity of the old religion who shares Jacob's mind, and provides him with extraordinary abilities. Thoth is known as the god of knowledge and is also referred to as Djehuty.

Trigger: A hobby, and crew of the Lorelai under Lotheran.

Tryrial: Son of Heineroth and a close friend of William Nadrog. He is known for his good looks and sense of humour and is well-liked by many in the court.

Urn of Nergal: A magical Urn that kept the god of plagues trapped for centuries.

Veela/Vila: Mythical creatures with the ability to enchant men with their beauty and allure. They are often depicted as female humanoids with bird-like features and the ability to transform into swans.

Wanda: A prostitute who lives in Havendale.

Weasley Weston: Young Lord of Wayrest, the second-largest city in Gont. He is a close friend of William Nadrog.

Woodvale: A village located near Havendale and known for its large dock that serves as a major hub for shipping wood to the mainland city of Wayrest.